CROWN AND CHAIN

CROWN AND CHAIN

*STRANGER MAGICS,
BOOK FOURTEEN*

ASH FITZSIMMONS

Print Edition ISBN: 978-1-949861-35-8

Cover design by BespokeBookCovers.com

www.ashfitzsimmons.com

JULY 25: FRANK

Few aspects of parenthood come with clear instructions. Oh, you learn quickly enough how to keep your offspring alive—regular feeding and watering, plus a watchful eye, go a long way in that regard—but no one prepares you for the quirks of living with a tiny being for whom common sense is still a project in the works.

That night, I was treated once again to my daughter's paradoxical reaction to exhaustion, in which instead of crashing, she turned into a wide-eyed chatterbox bouncing off the walls of our flat. I had only myself to blame for her condition—it was Aurie's first birthday, and I'd commemorated the occasion by allowing her to gorge herself on hamburgers and fries for breakfast, serving up more of the same after she returned from her tutors, and capping off the evening with a family party of sorts. It being a Tuesday night, we couldn't exactly have a blowout event, but the entire Away Team—my artifact-hunting Arcanum colleagues—as well as the spouses and the Team-adjacent cadre, had come by after dinner with presents and cake. Personally, I'd never cared for cake—I'd derive the same pleasure from dumping a bag of sugar into my mouth, which is to say none at all—but it was tradition, the confection came topped with pink icing roses, and since Aurie got to light *and* extinguish her candle, she was a fan.

She'd grown rapidly, my little girl, and if not for magical wardrobe assistance from the wizards and faeries in our lives, I'd have struggled to keep her clothed. Bee

Powell, the castle's GP, estimated that she was roughly nine or ten from a physical standpoint, judging by the human growth charts. Mentally, however, Aurie proved much tougher to classify. In some respects, she was more advanced than her appearance would suggest. Her tutors, a pair of wizards who'd retired from teaching and could be trusted to keep their mouths shut about their unusual pupil, sent home glowing reports about her inquisitiveness and eagerness to learn. On the other hand, she remained a seemingly endless source of energy, particularly at bedtime, and she slept with a small army of stuffed animals, burying herself in a rainbow of plush.

I fretted, of course. I'd spent the last year trying to keep Aurie alive, then trying to be certain that I was doing right by her. But when I'd brought Aurie in at six weeks, concerned because she was walking and speaking in full sentences but had yet to curb her biting reflex, Bee had tossed out the milestone chart and sat me down for a long talk. "There is no manual for raising a dragonet," she'd said as Aurie read a picture book and gnawed on her finger. "She's healthy and growing. Relax, Dad."

Bee hadn't been entirely correct on that count. There was, in fact, a manual—or rather, a collection of notes concerning the care and feeding of the species—but it was back in Faerie, and since the author had penned it on *dragonhide*, it gave me the creeps. More importantly, those notes had been made about dragons growing up more or less as nature intended: with their clutchmates, raised by their mother, learning to fight and fly and hunt for themselves. No addendum to that old scroll covered our case: a lone hatchling raised by her father in a spellcraft-forged body she was never built to inhabit, wingless but able to work out her algebra lessons on her own.

So yes, I fretted. I worried that I was going to damage her beyond all repair, that I'd already caused her untold harm. *Nothing* about our family was normal, least of all me. But as the alternative had been letting her limp around the barn in Faerie on three and a half legs until one of my siblings "mercy-killed" her, I'd done the best I could in Glastonbury.

One year down. We weren't out of the woods yet—dragonets didn't fully mature until five or so—but I'd have allowed myself a tiny sigh of relief had Aurie just been willing to go to bed.

"I'm not sleepy," she protested as I tucked her stuffed menagerie around her. She always hugged one of her toys as she went to sleep, the well-worn blue dragon that Ted Girard had given her as a homecoming gift, but she insisted on having a dozen others within reach. "Can't I stay up? It's my birthday," she wheedled.

"And you have school in the morning," I reminded her. "Do you want to be miserable tomorrow?"

She glared up at me, twin curls of smoke rising from her nostrils.

"None of that, young lady." I picked up the newest addition to Aurie's plushie haul, a sparkly pink pony with cartoonish proportions. The thing looked weird, but she'd squealed on opening it and run to hug Ted, so I supposed it was a hit. "Do you want to sleep with the one Uncle Ted gave you?"

Her eyes lit up. *Mine.*

I chuckled at the thought and squished it in beside her shoulder.

If I'd squinted, Aurie might have passed for any other young girl in the castle, just a face in the middle of a pile of much-loved toys. True, she was unusually pale, but that was a side effect of the transformation bind. The spell that Toula Pavli had constructed took its cues from what was available, and since most draconic pigmentation goes into the scales instead of being wasted on the hidden skin beneath, the bind translated scales into hair and otherwise left us looking washed out. For my mother and me, this part of the spell presented something of an inconvenience—I ended up with white-blond hair and looked like I'd spent decades hiding from sunlight, while she had apparently borne a resemblance to a dark-haired horror movie waif. As Aurie had inherited her mother's beautiful blue-green coloration, however, Toula had further tweaked the spell on her so that her hair matched mine. But even that wasn't enough to make her perfectly blend. Red-eyed like me, Aurie had taken to wearing dark glasses around the installation to ward off questions. Adults stared—they'd pretend otherwise, but I could always feel their minds when they puzzled over me, trying to process my size, my unusual features, or both. Children, however, did nothing to disguise their naked curiosity, and I didn't want Aurie fielding unnecessary questions. The castle we lived in was an insular community, and a strange child attracted attention simply by not being in class with the others—there was no need to add fuel to the fire.

Aurie had no friends her age, but given the dearth of dragons in the mortal realm, there was little I could do to rectify the situation. She grew and matured so much faster than human children did that I'd have struggled to identify her peers—were they the infants her age, just learning to walk and babbling syllables, or the girls a decade her senior? She loved the nights when she stayed with the Copelands and their fifteen-year-old daughter, Allie, but in another year's time, she'd physically surpass the teenager. Unfortunately, in terms of socialization, our options were limited.

But the Team had been there for us from the beginning. My work family of misfits and oddities had embraced Aurie from her egg days, and I was touched that they'd come out in force that night for a child's birthday party.

Try to sleep, I told her, covering her eyes with my palm. *Fifteen minutes, okay?*

When I pulled my hand away, she was still gazing up at me, but I thought I detected the first sputtering of her racing internal engine. "Can I get up then if I can't sleep?"

"Sure." Smoothing her hair from her face, I rose from the edge of the bed and turned to go. "But you must try to sleep first."

She huffed but made no other protest, and I'd almost slipped out of the room when she called, "Dad?"

"Mm?"

Aurie picked up her new pink horse and ran her fingers through its glittery mane. "Is Uncle Ted really my uncle?"

I hesitated, thrown by the unexpected query, but there was no point in lying to her. "No. Uncle Ted is my friend, and he loves you like an uncle would, so that's close enough."

"I thought he looked too old to be your brother," she replied, and put the toy aside. "Do I have any real uncles?"

In the moment, I was grateful that my mental blocking abilities put Aurie's to shame. The innocent question twisted like a hot knife in my gut, but I tried not to let on.

To that point, I hadn't discussed my family with Aurie. She knew that her mother had died before she hatched, but she'd never shown much interest in hypothetical relatives. Then again, Aurie was growing up, and she wasn't stupid—she had to know she'd come from *somewhere*, and I'd rather her approach me for answers than go snooping in unprotected minds.

"I have three sisters and two brothers," I said, keeping my voice as neutral as possible. I couldn't have conveyed that information telepathically without revealing far too much emotional baggage to a little girl who just wanted to delay her bedtime. "We're not close."

"Oh." Her brow scrunched as she considered that information. "Why not?"

"Disagreements. Nothing for you to worry about tonight," I said, and tried again to leave.

But Aurie was quick on the draw. "Do *you* have any real uncles and aunts, then?"

"Probably," I replied, leaning against the doorframe with my arms folded. "My mother never knew her siblings—she was a late hatch. I'm sure they're in Faerie somewhere."

"What about your dad? Did he have siblings?"

"Couldn't tell you. I've never met him."

That was exactly the wrong answer, as Aurie sat up in bed, scattering stuffed animals in all directions. "You've *never* met your dad? Not ever?"

"No, but—"

"Did he die?"

The news genuinely distressed her, I noted, but I tried to put her at ease. "Most dragons don't know who their father is. Their mothers raise them alone."

"Why?" she demanded.

I could only shrug. "Instinct. A female wants to mate, a male mates with her, and they go their separate ways."

"But *you* didn't leave my mom," she pointed out.

"Because I'm weird like that," I told her, and bent down to retrieve her lost stuffed lamb. "No more stalling, hatchling. *Sleep.*"

Aurie lay back down and let me tuck her in again. "Dad?"

"Yes?"

She reached for my hand, and I clasped hers. "I'm glad you didn't leave," she murmured.

"Me, too," I said, giving her little hand a squeeze. "I love you, Aurie. Happy birthday."

As I started to close the door, she asked, *Can I have a drink of water?*

What did I say about fifteen minutes?

She snorted as the latch clicked shut.

Leaving my daughter to wind down, I flopped onto the couch and closed my eyes.

Too soon. It was too damn soon to be having the family talk with her.

No, she wasn't a hatchling any longer, but she was my baby all the same, a little girl who sneaked uncooked sausages from the fridge and drew pictures for my office and smiled far more naturally than I ever would. She still thought the world was a friendly place. I didn't want to take that from her, but if she pressed me for answers...

One year. I hadn't been back to Faerie since the night Aurie hatched, and with the way things were looking, I might never return. I hadn't expected any of my siblings to reach out—we'd seldom understood each other, and they'd probably chalked my anger up to "Runt being Runt again"—but the fact that I hadn't received so much as a request to talk from my mother stung.

Why should it, though? Mom never had time for me. I was the late hatch, the one she couldn't wait for. The first face I'd seen had been Ros's, not hers. As much as I loved Ros, and as grateful as I was for everything she'd done on my behalf, part of me still wished my mother could have been bothered to raise me. Yes, the hatchling bond was strong, and I'd bonded to Ros, but Mom could have tried to win me over. Instead, she'd more or less surrendered custody of me to a teenage girl, who'd done her best with a clingy, awkward dragonet. Given our history, Mom's silence shouldn't have hurt as much as it did.

Maybe my mother didn't understand what she'd done. She and my siblings had been right about everything: it was almost incomprehensible that Ione had allowed me to stay while she nested, beyond belief that I'd finished the job for her, and insane that I'd protected Aurie, who'd hatched wingless, with a hole in her heart, and missing half her front-left leg. They'd tried to set things right once Ione died, encouraging me to give up on her tiny clutch—with their mother gone, the eggs should have died, too. They hadn't seemed to understand that Ione's sudden death had sent me plummeting into a depression the like of which I'd never known, and leaving our children to die wouldn't have helped my mental state.

Dragons don't pair-bond, but somehow, against all reason and instinct, I had.

I'd loved Ione. Looking back, I couldn't be certain if

she'd felt the same about me, but regardless, there had been *something* between us. Maybe it was because Ione was a runt, too, and I wasn't as intimidating as my brothers. Maybe she thought my eccentricities were intriguing. I knew she found me physically appealing—she'd made that much plain. And when her season had come, she'd waited until I fought off my brothers and took to the sky with me, my first and only mating.

I'd allowed myself to imagine a future with Ione, who'd consented to let me be part of our children's lives. Even if I'd divided my time between Faerie and Glastonbury, I'd have had her and a family of my own, and I'd dared to hope that *someone* in that damn barn might understand me.

But I'd lost Ione, who'd barely had time to register her surprise when the aneurysm burst in her brain. I'd guarded her nest, clinging to the idea that I could save her eggs, but as usual, I'd come up short. As grateful as I was for my daughter, I couldn't forget her two brothers, who'd died before they could draw breath. And as for Aurie, though Ros had done everything in her substantial power to save her, she'd still hatched with deformities.

I'd begged my mother to understand, to protect Aurie, to allow her to grow up with her cousins. Instead, Mom had told me to take her and go.

Maybe Mom didn't understand how deeply she'd wounded me, but it would be a cold day in hell before I made any overture toward reconciliation.

Still, what was I going to tell my daughter? She knew that she was wanted, that her mother had loved her and had been excited to meet her, that I would protect her with my dying breath. She knew that Ros frequently asked about her—often through Ros's longtime boyfriend, Sam Rockwell, as Ros fried any phone she touched. She knew that the Team loved her and looked after her when I couldn't be around.

She didn't need to know that my family had tried to kill her. Not yet.

As I lay there, hoping Aurie would drift off instead of coming to me with a terminal case of dehydration—a favorite stalling tactic—I thought about the part of my family I didn't know.

My father was a cipher. I'd wondered about him for years, the mental version of playing with a loose tooth. Given my clutch's variety of scale pigmentation and what little was known of draconic genetics, I couldn't have made a solid guess at his coloration. I was sure he was closer to my brothers' size than to mine, but other than that, I had little to go on. Mom never spoke of him, and the impression she gave me was that questions on the subject would go unanswered.

Ros, of course, would know who he was. Mom had mated in Faerie, and as Ros had the realm's long memory at her disposal, she could have given me the play-by-play. She would know where my father roamed, whether he'd sired other children—whether he was still alive.

I'd toyed with the notion of seeking him out, but sense had counseled against it. How could that possibly end well? If I found him and introduced myself—assuming he didn't attack me first as another male in his territory—how would he react? With bemusement? Antipathy? Disappointment?

I'd never followed through with the urge to find him. The notion of disappointing yet another parent was more than I wanted to confront. But over the last months, as I'd struggled to be a good father for Aurie, my thoughts had circled back to my unknown progenitor. *Someone* had to be responsible for making me as strange as I was—the blame couldn't be placed solely on Ros.

Maybe I'd ask her. Not tonight, maybe not anytime soon, but...

Perhaps.

I had almost drifted off on the couch when I heard Aurie's door creak open. *Dad?* she called. *Has it been fifteen minutes yet? I still can't sleep.*

Sighing, I sat up and patted the cushion beside me. *Come on, birthday girl. Let's find something boring on television.*

Her footsteps rapidly padded over the rug, and Aurie jumped onto the couch and snuggled up to me, stuffed dragon firmly tucked under her arm. I found a soothing documentary about whales, the sort of thing I'd watched during the dark days when I'd nested and starved and hoped that any of my children would live, and I rubbed my daughter's head until her breathing slowed toward sleep.

JULY 26: TOULA PAVLI

"Thank God the Games are over," said Arnold Lowe as he sank into one of my office chairs. "I'm too old to be dealing with drunk students, I really am."

He had a point. Drunk teenagers were annoying, but drunk teenage *wizards* had a far larger arsenal of destructive amusements at their fingertips. This year's Games had been particularly raucous outside of the competition hall, and after a few accidental fires, I'd been forced to send fourteen participants home. It was difficult to assign full blame: Arc 7's kids always brought the party with them from the Outback, Arc 2's had the home field advantage and knew every decent watering hole in Somerset, while the Arc 1 crew, temporarily liberated from the tyranny of American alcohol laws, rushed to make idiots of themselves. At least the inter-installation fighting had been minimal—the most obnoxious of the Arc 1 bunch had stayed home in protest of my continued presence in the Arcanum, which suited me *just* fine. Still, as teenagers aren't known for being the most responsible creatures at the best of times, the alcohol had led to a few "hold my beer and watch this" moments, and the castle courtyard still bore blackened patches as proof.

Bert Wold, who'd awoken one night during the Games to find the Arc 3 kids hosting a rave on the roof of his residential tower, nodded beside me on the couch as he doctored his tea. "They're getting more creative, I think. Should we fear for the future yet?"

"You're too young to be crotchety," I chided between

bites of croissant.

Bert was the baby in the room, still a bit shy of fifty, while Arnold and I had quietly noted the passing of our eighty-fourth birthdays that year and tried to put the unpleasant business behind us. Then again, part of me wondered if Bert had bypassed childhood entirely and sprung from his father's head like Athena, kitted out with a sweater vest and thick half-moon spectacles. On his stuffier days, he could have passed for my father, while Arnold looked every bit of his years. As for me...well, fae blood did have its perks. I hadn't aged since my mid-twenties, a fun fact that did nothing to improve my standing in the Arcanum.

The truth of the matter was that my days as grand magus were numbered. I'd taken office almost twenty-five years before, not because I had the Council's enthusiastic support, but rather because they'd had no stronger candidate available. My promise from the get-go had been that I would step aside when a more qualified wizard appeared—someone with the talent to run the Arcanum but without my oft-disparaged "attachments" to Faerie.

I couldn't help who my parents were or the freakish talent they'd bestowed on me. My big brother, Val, was a king in Faerie, but he didn't put so much as a toe out of line around Arc 2 or the wider Glastonbury area without my say-so, and precious few people within the castle's walls knew of my romantic relationship with that realm's *other* king, Coileán. But I'd been damaged goods from the start, the flashpoint for the Conclave debacle, and we'd suffered an invasion from the Gray Lands on my watch. I wasn't going to keep my ceremonial chain forever. And so, with an eye to the future of wizardry and the stability of the magical community, I met with my predecessors in office twice a year to consider potential replacements rising in the ranks.

Unfortunately, the pickings had been slim for some time. Bert's brief, disastrous tenure as grand magus, like

Helen Carver's two decades before his, had demonstrated the danger of putting a talented, naïve twenty-something at the helm, but the established magi were largely problematic. The few on the Council with sufficient talent to take up the position were either poor leaders or quietly supportive of the Conclave's brand of old-blooded bullshit—and since I'd been forced to quash the separatists when they almost killed one of my own, I wanted to avoid putting a wizard with Conclave sympathies in power. Left with no one among the ranks to whom I could confidently pass the baton, Arnold, Bert, and I studied the best of the installations' rising stars and bided our time.

As Bert deemed his tea satisfactory with a little smile, Arnold crossed his legs and sighed. "What have we got, Toula?"

I opened the manila folder on the top of the short stack beside the breakfast spread. "My favorite, hands down, is still Amita Bhattacharya. Twenty-four, excellent marks in her magic classes, never placed lower than fifth in combat *or* technical craft in her year—"

"Her wards are beautiful," Arnold murmured.

"I know, right? Her work evaluations are glowing," I continued, riffling through the papers I'd assembled, "and I think that if we slotted her in as a Council aide now and put her on the grand magus track, she'd be ready by her early thirties. I mean, guys, she's *brilliant*. Speaks five languages, and she learned them all the hard way. Plus," I said, leaning into my pitch, "I could use her selection to push for an eighth installation on the subcontinent. If we finally built one and all of southeast Asia didn't need to make the trip to Mongolia, don't you think that would be a boon? I could train Amita here for a few years, set her up as the installation head at the new facility, and then give her the big chair, assuming she doesn't burn anything down." Leaning back on the couch, I smiled at the men and sipped my tea. "Thoughts?"

Arnold steepled his fingers. "Perhaps on a trial

basis…"

"No."

We turned to Bert, who shook his head. "Amita is a scholar through and through. She's angling for a spot as an archivist."

"Again, she's intelligent," I protested.

"And far too much like me. Perhaps a better socialized version of me," he allowed, "but she'd be miserable as grand magus. I've spoken with her enough to say this with confidence. Brilliant, yes. Talented, certainly. But the Council will run over her."

"She bears observation," said Arnold, jumping in before Bert and I could argue. "Let's check back in six months, yes?"

"Fine," I muttered, closing Amita's folder. "Who else is up?"

Arnold took the next folder from the stack and skimmed the top sheet. "Kibwe Jumbe. I refereed his last bout, and that young man can *cast*. Excellent marks, too," he mused, flipping through the folder. "If we tracked him as an aide—"

"In four years, perhaps. He's *sixteen*," said Bert. "I'm impressed as well, but he's far too young for us to be making judgment calls."

"Kibwe's a no-go," I replied, and shrugged as Arnold regarded me quizzically. "Kid wants to go to university and be a doctor. He's been picking Bee's brain for months, and she's shepherding him through the process. Wouldn't hurt to have another true MD in the Arcanum, right? Bee can't practice forever."

"You think he'd work with her here?" Bert asked.

"Maybe as a residency. He seems set on coming home to Arc 5 eventually."

"Well, then, good for Giza," Arnold muttered, and put Kibwe's folder aside.

The three of us considered the last folder, though no one moved to touch it.

"Which leaves Leander, I suppose," said Bert, eyeing the folder as if it might sprout fangs.

"Yeah." I picked it up and paged through it until I found the most recent evaluation from Kathleen Fuchs. More effusive praise about her favorite aide, as expected. The installation head had selected him personally, and she had a right to be proud. Leander Kirby had been first in his class at Arc 1, a talented twenty-nine-year-old wizard with an old-blood pedigree and a boyish *aw, shucks* smile that could charm the habit off a nun. Tall, blond, blue-eyed, and well built, he was Captain America with a pine wand. On paper, he was a shoo-in for magushood and a solid contender for my office.

But I didn't trust the little cleft-chinned weasel.

Perhaps it was nothing more than paranoia. Like Bert, Leander had mastered the art of the mental block at a tender age, and so I couldn't casually snoop when he accompanied Kathleen to full Council meetings. He was handsome, dutiful, and superficially pleasant, but I couldn't get a read on him, which set my warning bells jangling. Adding to the strikes against him was his home installation: I didn't trust anything that came out of Arc 1 without proper vetting. It wasn't just that the Arc 1 magi had never cared for me as a group. Whether through ignorance, stupidity, or sympathy for the cause, they'd allowed Eva Stanhope, then their second in command, to feed information to the renegade Conclave for years. I'd had no use for the separatists, who'd made it their goal to return the Arcanum to a "purer" state, free of the influence of new-blooded wizards or, worse still, fae-blooded mongrels like me. Still, I'd tolerated their exodus to a compound in the Alaskan wilderness until Eva and a magus-turned-Conclave-defector, Francine Leighton, broke into Arc 2, left my brother's adopted daughter for dead, and tried to pin her murder on Bert. Though I'd done what I could to clean house in the wake of the Conclave's forced reintegration into the Arcanum fold, I suspected that a significant number of their former member still thought that James Mulligan, who'd casually murdered a good chunk of the witches and lesser fae of the Fringe during his coup and imprisoned hundreds of others in darkness for a decade, might just have been misunderstood.

So yes, maybe it was my paranoia talking, but the fact that neither Bert nor Arnold was jumping up and down over the prospect of Grand Magus Kirby suggested that my instincts weren't entirely wrong.

"Anything new from Kathleen?" Bert asked.

"More of the usual. He probably walks on water, to hear her tell it."

Arnold sat in silence for a moment, drinking his tea, then put the cup down and met my gaze. "There are stirrings in the silo. A suggestion that Leander might be just the trick to get the Pavli out of Glastonbury."

"Do tell," I muttered.

"Nothing formal as of yet, no petition circulating, but…" He hesitated, then said, "If Arc 1 made a push for him, you know Arc 7 would fall in line."

"Probably."

"He's got the charisma," said Arnold. "Send the boy on a visitation tour, and I wouldn't be surprised if he converted more than half of the magi."

"Even here," Bert murmured.

"*Especially* here," I said, and sipped my tea.

Ideologically, the Arcanum's magi and membership tended to fall into two camps. First were the traditionalists, the old-blooded families with pedigrees back to Simon Magus and their hangers-on, the well-bred wizards who considered me an abomination, even if they were savvy enough not to call me such to my face those days. They were the ones with family members who'd done well for themselves under the Mulligan regime—which had retained power by holding innocent hostages in unimaginably cruel conditions—or run away to join the

Conclave, only to end up bound or executed. The wizards in that group might not publicly express their support for Mulligan's policies, but neither were they particularly bothered by the number of Fringers he'd killed or tortured in order to keep faeries out of the mortal realm.

Then there was the other camp, a mix of old- and new-blooded wizards who'd decided that even though I was far from ideal, I wasn't the worst thing to happen to the Arcanum since its founding. Those of them who'd been alive for the Mulligan trial had paid heed to the regime's atrocities and disavowed them. While I couldn't say that any of them were thrilled to have me in office, a witch-blood of wizard and fae lines—a high lady, Mab's mongrel brat, the spawn of a mass murderer, the Arcanum's charity case who'd come home with a vengeance—they knew that I was working for peace among the realms.

I'd done my best. Faerie was no problem—I was a friend to the queen, Eleanor, a sister to one king, and a lover to the other—and the Three had proven willing to come to our defense. In the mortal realm, I'd reached an unofficial truce with the Minor Arcanum, leaving them to manage their own affairs unmolested. I had Fringe coordinators in Faerie and the mortal realm on speed-dial. The Dark Company, the mortal realm's organization of shifter spies, had given us no problems in years.

We'd even established ties to the Gray Lands—or Conota, as the natives called it—after rebuffing their late queen's attempted invasion. My Arcanum detractors still held the Hope Lozano affair against me, claiming that Nath would never have bothered us had I not protected the girl. *That*, as anyone familiar with the inter-realm political landscape knew, was a crock of shit. Nath would have invaded eventually—all I did was give her a pretext to do so. But we'd succeeded in ending her reign, and the new king, Arik, who'd married Hope, was nothing but courteous. For the first time, the powers of all three realms were in a position to come together and discuss their issues instead of simply shooting on sight, which I considered no small feat. With our relations practically stable, I even volunteered my services as a relay for Faerie and Conota, as making phone calls directly between those realms was next to impossible.

I'd earned the supporters I had by showing that I wasn't a megalomaniacal sadist eager to rip the Arcanum apart and let Faerie squabble over the pieces. I'd proven myself competent. But for my detractors, nothing I ever accomplished would be enough. Toula Pavli, witch-blooded traitor, had to step aside eventually—and I feared that Leander might develop his own following before much longer.

"You know," joked Arnold as I put Leander's folder back on the stack, "we could always say to hell with it and give the bloody chain back to Simon Magus."

"Don't tempt me," I replied, and topped up my tea.

When I took over the millennium-old Arcanum, I'd never expected to meet its conquering founder—well, the magically rewound version of him, a teenage boy who still answered to Eadwig and detested his former self for Simon's atrocities. Burdened by Simon's memories but gifted with his lifetime accumulation of magical knowledge and formidable ability, Eadwig was a prodigy by any metric, an unparalleled talent. He'd spent the last year trying to break a curse on a newly discovered wizard, Quinn Dellucci—and not just any wizard, but good old Mulligan's grandniece. While she'd saved the life of Frank's infant daughter, Quinn now existed in a sort of living death, working in the Archives at night, hiding from the sun, and drinking blood to survive.

We tried not to use the "V-word" around her.

Those of us who knew the truth protected the identities of Quinn and her grandfather, Mulligan's brother, a dud abandoned by his birth family, just as we kept Eadwig's history tightly under wraps. I didn't want to explain to the Council that their illustrious founder was living among them once again…only this time, he thought himself a monster and had sworn to the Minor Arcanum that he'd never hold power.

I'd wondered whether I would have stepped aside if Eadwig wanted the position. He had talent in spades, and while his current persona was young, he carried with him the wisdom of his previous conquest and rule. Eadwig *could* have done the job, no question. But his first stint as grand magus had ended in genocide, and while Eadwig seemed like a different person from Simon in many ways, I wasn't sure whether a second term in office was in anyone's best interest, least of all Eadwig's.

Which left us with our prospects: a would-be archivist, a future medical student, and Leander.

Grateful that I didn't need to make an immediate choice, I leaned back on the couch and cradled my teacup. "Plenty to think about, guys. But there *is* some good news today."

One of Bert's bushy eyebrows arched. "Oh?"

"The Games are over for another year."

"And thank God for that," said Arnold, raising his cup to us in salute.

JULY 27: EADWIG

The problem with a subterranean office, quiet and insulated though it may be, is the lack of natural light. When one lives in the glow of electric lamps, marvelous things though they are, every hour is identical to the one before and after, an eternal parade of time cast in a soft yellow hue. I suppose this isn't a true hardship for most, those who instinctively look at clocks for cues and listen to their stomachs, but when I throw myself into a matter, be it a new book or a promising lead on an answer to a question, I find myself ignoring my body's signals until I pass out over my work.

Perhaps this pattern improves my productivity. I can't truly say, though it's embarrassing to be awakened by a concerned colleague first thing in the morning when you have no recollection of where the night went.

By then, after tolerating my eccentricities for a year, the Away Team had ceased to be alarmed when I spent the night in my office. They had assigned to me a modest space in a quiet corner of their suite, equipped it with a desk and chair and ample bookshelves, and left me largely to my own devices. At first, the computer they'd given me sat untouched much of the time—in full honesty, I didn't trust myself not to break it—but within a few weeks, I grew accustomed to its functions: the search portals for the library and the Archives, the books and documents digitized to protect them from unnecessary handling, and finally, the Internet, source of rough translations and answers to the questions I was too embarrassed to ask.

They were kind, my new colleagues—well, I say "my colleagues," though our work had little in common. They scoured the world for missing magical artifacts, while I hid in my office and limited my focus to a single, possibly impossible, problem: break the curse that had rendered Quinn Dellucci an ambulatory corpse without killing her in the process. But as my existence was a delicate issue—explaining the sudden appearance of an unaccompanied youth with a strange accent in a castle full of wizards was a job best avoided—I'd been passed to the Team's quarters and told to blend in. Fortunately, the transition had been peaceful. If they resented my presence among them, they gave me no indication. Indeed, they encouraged me to request assistance as needed.

It helped that two of their number were similarly time-displaced. While I had slept for nearly a millennium, Marcus had missed twenty-two centuries and Artur fifteen, and they understood much of my predicament. "There are no stupid questions," Marcus had assured me early in my subbasement tenure, when the two had stepped into my office for a quiet word and locked the door behind them. "Everything feels wrong, and it will *continue* to feel wrong, but you'll adjust. The best advice I can offer you is to not dwell on what you've lost. Mourn it, but don't let yourself despair. There is no going back, so we make do with what's before us now."

"Stay busy," Artur had counseled, then paused to take in the stacks of books I'd already requisitioned from the floors above. "Though I suppose you're doing so. But you needn't live down here—the city's an interesting place, and if you want to go into the field with us, I'm sure Ted would make allowances."

Curious though I was to explore the world beyond the castle's walls, I had yet to see the benefit of disrupting the Team's scheduled work or pausing mine. Unfortunately, I found little scholarship relevant to Quinn's curse, meaning that I was forced to return to first principles and try to forge a path forward from there, a frustratingly slow process.

Everything came back to the grail, a trap created by the original Three of Faerie to punish an Egyptian wizard who'd earned their ire. Drinking from the grail conferred immortality of a sort: it left the drinker in a unique stasis bind that preserved him but, medically speaking, left on him the cusp of death. If the bind broke, the drinker would die instantly. The only way to maintain the bind was with regular consumption of blood—only human blood sufficed—and to further the misery, the bind rendered the drinker nocturnal by necessity, as sunlight would incinerate him.

Simon, my previous self, heard whispers of the grail for decades. He'd pursued it during his blood-soaked campaign of conquest. But not until he was captured and tortured in Faerie did he learn of the grail's true nature—and oh, how his captors had laughed at his folly. When they returned him to the mortal realm, he was far too broken to continue his pursuit of the grail, but he decided that destroying it might constitute a small good deed against what he finally recognized as the evils of his life. And so he'd locked himself in rejuvenating sleep, intending to reverse only a few years of aging. Instead, he'd been left ensorcelled far too long, and I was the result.

The blood on Simon's hands stained mine, too. Breaking Quinn's curse wouldn't absolve me of his sins. It wouldn't make me clean, wouldn't undo the damage he had wrought. But it was *something*, a small step in the right direction. The sooner I restored Quinn, the sooner the accursed grail could be destroyed. And since the intended purpose of my existence was to see that grail returned to dust, every day that passed without a solution was another indictment against me.

My flatmates, the nominal adults tasked with keeping me out of trouble, never pressed me for progress updates. Marcus reminded me about once a week to come up for air, especially when I'd neglected to bathe for a few days in a row. Kitty, his wife and the de facto head of our flat, reminded me that I would be of no use to anyone if I drove myself mad and that eating and sleeping on a regular basis were not acts of indolence. Artur, less mothering than her sister, simply grabbed my arm every so often and ordered me into the courtyard to see daylight. Rounding out their company was Quinn, who slept in the room adjoining mine and never complained when our paths crossed. Seeing her smile and hearing her thank me for trying only served to remind me of all my failures in the endeavor.

And then there was Beth, my undeserved consolation.

So engrossed was I in my work that evening that I didn't hear Beth's footsteps in the carpeted hallway of the Team's suite, nor did I register her quick double-rap knock on my office door. Only once she entered the room and touched my shoulder did I realize I was no longer alone, and it's quite probable that I shrieked, as I know I jumped in my chair.

"Just me," she said, grinning as I clutched my chest. "Hi, Ed."

"Hello," I managed as my heartbeat slowed from a gallop.

"It's eight-thirty. Have you eaten yet?"

Quickly, I worked the mental computation necessary to match the label with the expected daylight topside. The days were shortening from midsummer, but I supposed it was still a bit before sunset. "No," I admitted, patting the book on the desk in front of me. Fourteenth-century French wasn't my strongest language, but the magus's theories on stasis binds held promise—untested theories, but a foundation I could build upon. "Lost track of time."

"As usual." She moved a notepad to the side and perched on the edge of my desk. "Well, seeing as I haven't eaten, either, and seeing as my internship duties for Ted are *long* over for the day...want to go to town and get pizza?"

"What about your lesson with Artur?"

"Over and done with, and I've already dried my hair," she replied, flipping the end of her blonde ponytail over her shoulder as proof. "Take a break. You'll think better with a full stomach."

"I'll *sleep* better with a full stomach," I countered, but I marked my place and pulled the cord on the brass desk lamp. "Do you mind if I, uh..." I gestured to the wrinkled clothing I'd been wearing for the last two days, which had begun to acquire a distinctive funk.

"Oh, sure. My wallet's upstairs, anyway," she said, and pulled me from the chair. "Come on, before we both die of hunger down here."

In that brief moment as I followed her out of my office and into the corridor, another woman flickered in my mind's eye—a brunette in her thirties, perhaps, wearing a long burgundy dress and coaxing me away from my work to the dining table. She had a kind smile, that woman, and soft green eyes...

Béatrix.

No.

I shook my head to dispel the vision and the feelings it stirred. That was *Simon's* memory, not mine—his wife, a stranger to me. But just as Simon haunted me, so too did his memories live on in my mind. Though I'd never seen the woman in the flesh, I knew her voice, her dimples, the way she laughed at herself whenever she tried to tease the sounds of my language from her Norman tongue...her scent, the curve of her neck, her firm breasts, the way she arched her back and gasped at the moment of—

No.

As a young man, I admittedly possessed a keen interest in sex, but watching through Simon's eyes as he pleasured his wife made my skin crawl.

I wanted nothing to do with him. Had I known of a priest who could exorcise his ghost from my thoughts, I'd have begged for relief. But Simon was my past and future, inextricably entwined with my soul like a choking vine around a sapling. I had no choice but to live with him…and to suppress, whenever possible, those memories of the intimate moments that had spawned seemingly a quarter of the Arcanum. Simon had fathered twelve children, after all, and their bloodlines had been lovingly charted and preserved by their distant grandchildren, who pointed back to him like a trophy.

Few of them, I imagined, thought of their progenitor as anything but a conquering hero who had subjugated the world's wizards in order to bring them peace. They didn't know his paranoia, his madness, his self-loathing. They didn't know that Béatrix had wept for the first year of their marriage every time Simon took her to bed, mourning the convent life she had lost. They didn't know about the many lovers their hallowed ancestors had taken, or how Simon brought others into the marital bed with Béatrix's blessing, women and men who could satisfy his appetites while she attended to her own.

Not just humans, either. For God's sake, Simon and Grivam had carried on for years. The king of the *merrow*. The man wasn't even content to keep his urges limited to his own species.

The man. Me. A version of myself, a past I couldn't allow myself to repeat, but…

Once, while wasting a moment in idle online browsing, I came across the phrase "brain bleach." How dearly I wished such an elixir existed. I wasn't prudish, but experiencing Simon's escapades secondhand was miserable. Then again, since I was Simon in some respects, perhaps it was only fitting that I spend the occasional moment in my private hell.

Desperate to clear my thoughts, I concentrated instead on Beth as we climbed the spiral stone staircase out of the subbasement. She was beautiful in the way of girls on the cusp of full womanhood, all legs and gentle curves, slightly taller than me flat-footed. Whereas Béatrix had been quietly dutiful, Beth had fire in her veins and lightning in her eyes when angered. Béatrix had been a good mother. Beth had tackled me before I could kill myself. And the part of me that I thought of as *me*—Eadwig, seventeen, the boy who'd fallen asleep at the turn of the eleventh century and awakened a thousand years later—was hopelessly smitten with her.

The boy wanted her. The man who had been Simon wasn't opposed to the notion, either.

I tried to rationalize my desire by pointing to our flatmates. Kitty, sister to both Beth and Artur on different sides, had married Marcus the previous spring. The bride had been twenty-seven at their union; the groom...well, technically, he was eighty-odd times her age, though he'd spent most of his life in a deep stasis bind and emerged with the mind of the young man he'd been before losing consciousness. Marcus and Kitty suited each other in nearly every respect. But as for me, frankly, I didn't know *what* I was: ancient but youthful, mentally caught between my two selves. The boy wanted to hold Beth's hand and taste her strawberry lip gloss and see how much further he might be permitted to go. The man could have offered lectures on the subject, had I not done my utmost to shut him up whenever he surfaced outside the confines of my office.

As much as I despised Simon, I couldn't deny that he had been a first-order scholar of magic. A voracious reader and lifelong hoarder of books, he was a giant in his day—a legacy that continued, I realized, as I encountered later scholarship built upon his work. As I progressed in my research, I was shocked by the *familiarity* of so much of what I read, which brought with it a disturbing sense of déjà vu. I should have known nothing—I was an untrained novice in the ways of spellcraft—but now, with Simon's memories crowding in on my own, I recognized theorems and passages on which I'd never laid eyes. This led to awkward moments, like the time I requested a ninth-century manuscript from the Archives, impatiently waited a week for delivery, then skimmed three lines and remembered that I—or Simon, rather—had read it years ago *and* written the marginal notes. The handwriting all over the damned thing was, in fact, my own, the ink faded with age but the concepts as fresh as ever in my thoughts.

The more I studied, the stronger grew my recall of Simon's useful knowledge. I learned to trust my instincts as I worked, selecting and rejecting books for review before I could quite articulate my reasons. At least Simon was helpful in that regard. True, I would have relinquished his knowledge in an instant if it meant removing the rest of him from my soul, but while I was stuck with him, I took advantage of the little good he provided.

Unfortunately, Simon wasn't content to emerge like a summoned tutor only when asked, and more of the invasive memories flitted behind my eyes as I followed Beth out of the Archives. Reluctant to dwell on Béatrix all night, I said, "Talk to me, please."

Beth turned, but whatever she saw in my expression must have convinced her that I was having one of my episodes again—the moments in which the memories I tried to push into their hole bubbled forth like a spring of bitter water. The heightened focus I employed in my research held them at bay, but once I let down my guard, they burst through my defenses. I'd explained this to Beth when she'd stepped from her room for a midnight snack and found me curled into a ball beneath the window, rocking and muttering to myself in a tongue whose last native speaker—besides me—had died centuries before she drew breath. She'd shaken me back to the present and asked me what I needed. *Talk to me*, I'd begged. *Everything inside is too loud.*

"Artur's back to being merciless," said Beth, taking my hand as if the warmth and pressure could tether me to that moment. "She gave me the weekend to recoup, but she tossed me around tonight."

"She wasn't impressed by your performance?" I replied, dragging my internal focus to the Games the week before. Compared to Simon, Beth was no great talent— she freely admitted that she'd never merit a spot on the Council—but three years of extracurricular training with Artur had toned her limbs and improved her speed and stamina. Squaring off against a fae opponent who considered magic to be but one weapon in her arsenal had made Beth quick on her feet and more secure in her casting, and she had won her year in solo combat. While she hadn't advanced beyond that, she'd performed respectably against the class above hers, and Kitty had given her trophy pride of place on the kitchen table ever since the Saturday awards brunch. Beth seemed unusually content, as if she'd summited the longed-for mountain and finally seen the world laid out beneath her feet, and I was proud of her. Of course, considering how she'd been attacked at her moment of victory and left unconscious in the infirmary the previous year, I was also relieved to get through the event without having thrown anyone into a wall on Beth's behalf.

"Oh, no, Artur thought I did well," she said, tightening her grip on my hand as we traversed the long castle corridors. "Which is the problem. If she thinks she sees potential, she amps up the pressure. Don't get me wrong," she hastily added, "her lessons are great, and I wouldn't trade them for anything. It's just, you know, in the moment…"

"Bolts hurt?"

"Yeah, but it's the sword you've got to look out for. That woman is a *beast.*"

I'd have expected nothing less. Artur had been a king

once, just as Simon had ruled as a monarch of a different sort. Though I didn't see it often, on occasion, I caught a look in her eyes that seemed to suggest we had a tacit understanding. The difference between us was that she had struggled to repel invaders from her lands—a just cause, if ultimately futile—whereas Simon had attempted to conquer the world and the realms beyond it. Artur's earlier life had become too distorted in mythology to be recognizable...and in a way, so had Simon's. There was little of the glory about his reign that the current Arcanum seemed to imagine.

"She'd work with you, too, if you wanted," Beth offered. "It'd get you out of the basement for a bit."

"Appreciated, but I'm not fond of broken bones." And burdened as I was with Simon's memories of what had happened to his body at faeries' hands, I was in no hurry to give Artur an excuse to take aim. She had already threatened to kill me if I hurt Beth, and I had no doubt that she could carry out the threat.

That I had feelings for Beth—and, to my surprise, that Beth appeared to reciprocate—was no great secret in the flat, but no one *discussed* it. Beth was the baby of our sextet, and the incarceration of her mother had left her brittle and broken at a tender age. Kitty had begun the rebuilding process with the love her sister craved, while Artur had fortified her with confidence. The angry child who had been shipped off to Glastonbury had matured into a capable young woman, and I had nothing but respect for her. But in her sister's and her quasi-sister's eyes, Beth remained something of a child, meaning that any time she spent alone in my company was to be viewed with great caution.

Still, she and I made that time. As much as duty shackled me to my office and the regulations of Arcanum life forced Beth into her classes, we found excuses to see each other—a quick meal, an evening boardgame, a drink of pilfered liquor on the roof of our residential tower.

Though I'd known her barely more than a year, the youth in me could envision myself making a life with her, and nothing in Simon's memories cautioned against it. Simply put, I was happiest in her company, and true happiness was an emotion I'd seldom felt since waking in a foreign world. Beth made me feel like *Eadwig*—like I was supposed to feel, not like the haunted creature I'd become.

Her voice soothed my internal storm as we made our way through the maze of passages and up to our flat, and I clung to its rhythms as if they were setting the pace of my own heart. At the door, as she scanned us inside, she said, "Put on something you don't mind walking in. I want to go the long way to town—it's a nice night."

"Noted," I replied with an exaggerated bow.

She giggled as she brushed past me, heading for her room on the far side of the kitchen. "Hey, Quinn," I heard her say. "Running late?"

Poking my head around the corner, I found Quinn standing by the sink, drinking from a steel tumbler. She had several such cups, all kept in a special cabinet; the three of our flatmates with fae blood couldn't touch the metal without burning themselves, while Beth and I had no desire to accidentally grab Quinn's things. She swore that there would be no harm, that the dishwasher did a fine job of sterilizing whatever went into it, but since Quinn's tumblers exclusively held blood, no one seemed interested in poaching.

"Taking it slow," Quinn replied. The tumbler's straw, also made of steel, hid the evidence of her breakfast. "I was due a few hours off, so I slept in."

I wasn't entirely certain what sleep consisted of for Quinn. According to her grandfather, who had administered every medical test in his repertoire, her body was dead. Her heart had stilled, her digestion ceased, and she bothered to breathe only when she needed the air to speak. Her flesh barely deviated from room temperature. The only thing keeping her moving and thinking was a complex stasis bind. The cursed grail from which she had drunk had almost killed her, with the bind preserving her at the moment of her death. Her body repaired itself, and she still possessed the modicum of magical ability she'd exhibited as a young wizard, but without a constant supply of magic sustaining her, she would fall dead.

Not that her current form of life was anything spectacular. Oh, Quinn seemed happy enough in her work. Having been trained in the mundane methods of preservation of aged books and artwork, she had easily secured a position in the Archives, where she could serve as both student and teacher to the wizards who specialized in magical preservation techniques. But the curse had bestowed on her a deadly sensitivity to sunlight—an experimental exposure to dawn had made her skin *smoke*—and so Quinn passed many of her working hours alone, toiling through the night while the rest of the Archives' staff slept. She had procured a wardrobe of hooded sweatshirts in case she accidentally worked too long and was caught by the sun, a real challenge during the long British summer.

And then there was the matter of her strict diet. The curse, designed as it was to render the drinker a monster, forced her to consume nothing but human blood. Without it, her body would fail. While she slept, the enchantment on her made use of her food, repairing her injuries and producing fluids like saliva and tears. No other sort of blood could be employed for this purpose, and anything else she ingested beyond the odd sip of water was promptly vomited up. Fortunately, Bee Powell could replicate blood bags in the infirmary's supply, and the magically produced substitute seemed to do Quinn no ill. Overall, however, her fate was ghastly, and she had done nothing to deserve it.

Quinn had sacrificed herself to save Frank's infant daughter, drinking from the cup that Simon had been unable to find and destroy. The least I could do was find a way to break the curse without killing her. And yet, there I was, traipsing off to town to enjoy myself with Beth while Quinn passed another night alone.

"We're going to grab pizza," Beth informed her, cocking her thumb toward me as I slunk in the direction of the staircase. "I got busy with Artur and missed dinner, and you know what *he's* like."

She chuckled. "Enjoy. I'd blow off work and chaperone—"

"*Quinn*," Beth groaned.

"—but lucky for you, I really like the painting I'm working on right now." Giving Beth's ponytail a friendly yank, she picked up her cup and slung her bag over her shoulder. "If you're not back when I come home, I'm telling Kitty. Have fun, kids," she said, and headed out.

Five minutes later, I'd made myself closer to presentable, but guilt continued to dog me as Beth and I slipped out of the castle complex, through the camouflaging ward, and onto the road toward the center of Glastonbury. Had Simon been clever enough to work his rejuvenation spell properly, I mused, none of this would have happened. He would have found the grail and destroyed it centuries before Quinn's birth, and she wouldn't be condemned to the darkness.

If Simon's spell had gone according to plan, I would never have existed.

I certainly wouldn't have had Beth in my life, but why did I deserve her? Simon had created order on a tide of bloodshed and misery. He hadn't deserved happiness. *I* didn't deserve it, either.

Perhaps she divined the direction of my thoughts from my silence, or perhaps her intuition was accurate again, but Beth snaked an arm around my waist and pulled me closer. "You're trying," she murmured. "That's all you can do. Quinn knows, and she appreciates it."

"Trying isn't good enough."

With a little sigh, she guided me into the grass, gripped

my shoulders, and held my stare. "I have faith in you, Ed. Maybe you'll figure it out tomorrow, or maybe it'll take another year…ten years…whatever. But if this thing can be cracked, then I think you're our best hope of solving it."

"Tell that to Quinn tonight," I muttered, cutting my gaze to the ground.

Beth tightened her hold until I looked at her again. "*You're doing your best,*" she replied, emphasizing each word. "Did Quinn seem upset to you?"

"No…"

"Because she's not. Because there's nothing wrong with you and me saying to hell with it all for a few hours and going out for dinner. Yeah?"

I maintained my silence.

"*Yes?*"

When I hesitated again, Beth leaned in until our foreheads touched. "You don't have to make amends for every shitty thing Simon ever did," she whispered. "Especially not all at once. At least let's eat dinner first."

Laughter escaped me before I was quite aware that it was bubbling up, brief but genuine, and Beth smiled in the twilight as she locked her arm around mine. "Forget about him for tonight," she said as we pushed onward again. "Tell me about Jórvík."

"What would you know?" I asked, surprised at the enquiry.

"Let's start with everything. Put Simon's memories aside and tell me something you know to be true."

Her body was warm against mine that summer evening, and for an instant, I found myself lost in the heady sensations of the moment, perfectly myself, unburdened by the faces and voices of someone else's past as I relished the sweetness of the present.

"It was the only city I knew," I said, my steps falling in tempo with Beth's, "and honestly, I think this one's nicer."

JULY 31: FRANK

I couldn't get the question out of my mind.

In the past, my ruminations about my missing parent had been brief, just fleeting musings regarding an absent progenitor I was unlikely to ever meet. But in the six days since Aurie's birthday, I hadn't been able to push my father from my thoughts. Maybe it was Aurie's shock at the revelation that I knew nothing about him, or perhaps it was a product of my own first year of fatherhood that sent my imagination circling in that direction, but I finally resolved to ask Ros what she knew. I wasn't anticipating a warm, tearful meeting—for one thing, dragons don't cry—but knowing *something* about my father would at least put my mind at rest.

That morning, after I saw Aurie off to her tutors, I sent Ted a message to let him know I'd be working from home. I read and made notes until lunchtime—we were heading to Siberia in two days, and I wanted to be prepared—then spent the afternoon packing until I could put off the moment no longer.

Settling back on the couch, I contemplated my scuffed phone. Like most human-designed objects, it seemed too small in my grip. I might have been a runt, but by local standards, my bound form was oversized, slightly more than two meters tall and sufficiently muscular to make even angry drunks think twice. Still, as I steeled myself to contact Faerie, I couldn't help but notice how the phone seemed to shake with the tremor in my hands.

You're being ridiculous, I chided myself, then quickly

scrolled through my favorites until I found Sam.

The phone rang twice on his end, and having remembered that I didn't know what time it might be in the other realm, I was about to hang up and send him a message when the line clicked open. "Hey, Frank," he said, his Texan twang still as pronounced as ever after twenty-five years in Faerie. "Afternoon?"

"About three here. Are we synchronized?"

"Close enough. What's up? Want me to get Ros?"

Manners told me to at least enquire after Sam's health and well-being, but he and I both knew that I seldom called to chat with him. Oh, I liked him well enough, and he made Ros happy as her mate, which was all that mattered to me. But Sam had long ago resigned himself to the position of phone intermediary without a fuss, first as the operator when I needed to speak to Ros, and later as the scribe whenever Ione had wanted to contact me. He was a good sport about the awkward situation, and if I tended to get to the point with him, he never seemed offended.

"If she's not busy," I replied.

Sam laughed at that. "She could have an invading army on the border and still find time to talk to you, bud. Hang on…"

Sudden static on the line told me that Ros had manifested nearby. Though virtually omnipotent in Faerie, she couldn't touch a phone without reducing it to a hunk of useless plastic.

"She wants to know where you are," said Sam.

"At home. Do I need to send a reference picture?"

I heard him mumble away from the mouthpiece, then said, "No, she's got it. Take care," he added, and rang off.

Seconds later, an inter-realm gate blazed open in the middle of my den, a roughly circular lightning-rimmed hole between the realms that widened until I saw Ros sitting in an overstuffed easy chair, her blonde hair falling loose over her shoulders. Sam's house, I realized—well,

Sam and Ros's house, though as corporeality was no longer her default state, Ros had no need of a proper dwelling. As Faerie's consciousness, she was everywhere in the realm, all-seeing and immensely powerful. Her predecessor had seldom deigned to appear in physical form, and when Ros did so, she glowed.

"Hey, stranger," she said, tucking her legs onto the chair as she smiled at me. "How was the party last week?"

I felt her mind probing for mine at the edge of the gate. Ros couldn't leave Faerie, and though she could extend part of herself into the mortal realm, her power was drastically reduced beyond her border. I reached for her and felt the familiar contours of her thoughts, the voice I'd known since my earliest days.

"Aurie had a blast," I replied. "She loved the cat, by the way."

Sam had dropped off their gift a few hours before the party, a stuffed housecat with blue eyes and soft gray fur that purred when petted and hugged. That it was the product of enchantment was undeniable, especially considering the way the thing's tail would spontaneously twitch and its eyes blink. Personally, I thought it looked a bit like a haunted doll, but Aurie had named it Whiskers and carried it draped over her shoulder, chattering to it as it rumbled.

Ros grinned at the news. "Aw, great. I'd hoped she'd like it." She paused then, considering my expression and the limited access I'd granted her to my thoughts. "You're troubled. What's going on?"

This was the moment, now or never, and I took a deep breath as I frantically assembled my words. "I, uh…I was putting Aurie to bed the other night, and she asked about my family, and…"

Ros waited, her forehead furrowing.

"I want to know about my father," I blurted before I could lose my nerve. "Please."

Her face froze.

"I don't need to meet him or anything," I said, rushing to reassure her. "I just…I want to know what he's like. Is he even alive?"

After a long, silent moment, Ros said, "He…is alive. Yes. But…"

"But?" I prompted.

Again came the hesitation, which did nothing for my nerves. "Are you sure you want to know?" she asked.

"I'm not expecting someone overly paternal, if that's what you're worried about."

Her teeth raked over her bottom lip. "I can answer your questions, and I'll do it, if that's what you really want. But you need to remember that some opened boxes can't be closed again."

I frowned at her very un-Ros-like reluctance to speak as a worm of doubt twisted in my gut. "What's wrong with him? Did he kill someone I like?"

"No…"

When nothing further appeared to be forthcoming, I sat forward on the couch and held her stare. "For me. Please, Ros. I need to know."

She nodded once and murmured, "Okay. Here's the truth."

Ros didn't need to sigh before she began. Her body was a construction of her own power, after all, and she was beyond such mundane necessities as drawing air into her temporary lungs. But before she was the realm, she'd been Ros Bolin, and the habits she'd built in her previous life hadn't entirely faded. Though she'd improved her poker face in the last decades, I knew her eyes and her mind too well to miss the anxiety lurking there—and the sigh only increased my certainty that I wouldn't like what followed.

"Your mom went off to mate for the first—and so far, only—time when she was seventeen," Ros began. "It wasn't a great experience."

Considering what I'd gone through with my brothers in fighting for Ione, I could well imagine. Males had the worst of it, but from what I'd gathered, females sometimes became victims of their suitors' combat.

"She found a guy she liked on her first day in season," Ros continued. "Big male, experienced. He's sired about a dozen clutches to date. Looks a lot like Horus."

My eldest brother, the first of us to hatch and the largest of our clutch, had scales almost the same shade of red as his eyes. Even as his brother, I had to admit that he was a handsome specimen. I'd assumed that Ione would favor him of us all, or maybe Rego, who was jet black like Mom and only slightly smaller than Horus—another solid pick. It was no surprise to any of us that both of my brothers successfully mated long before I did.

"So, uh…Georgie and her new pal had their fun, and he flew off once they'd finished," said Ros. "But there were four smaller males nearby, part of a young clutch. They were only about seven or eight years old…" She squinted into space as she reviewed the realm's memories. "Eight, yes. The biggest of them was green, the white and the purple were about the same size, and there was a smaller red, but he had spunk. Anyway, they figured out that there was a female in season ready for the taking."

As hurt and angry as Mom had made me, the thought of her being hunted in that fashion left me sick. Mom was no runt—she was at least a third again as large as Ione had been—but males grew larger than females. Hell, even I had outgrown her. "They attacked?" I asked.

"They started jockeying with each other, and when she tried to lose them, they chased her. Bit and clawed her pretty badly as they fought to get into position. But Georgie was faster, and while they were squabbling, she managed to get a little distance."

"Good for Mom," I muttered.

"Yeah, but she was flying hurt, she was hungry, and she was weakening. So Kura stepped in."

That took me by surprise—I'd seen Kura from time to time when she manifested around Ros, but I'd never known the former realm to show interest in something as banal as dragon mating. "How so?"

"She told Georgie to land, and once your mom was down, Kura transformed her."

"She did *what?*"

"Transformed her," Ros repeated. "Since Georgie went through the process with Toula as a kid, Kura figured that she wouldn't freak out. Plus, it's much easier to hide someone human-sized than it is a full-grown dragon."

"True," I allowed, but the news disturbed me. When Mom was about Aurie's age, she'd spent a couple months hiding in the mortal realm in human guise. I knew she hadn't enjoyed the experience—she'd warned me about how unpleasant she'd found it before I asked Toula to cast the same sort of transformation bind on me. "Why didn't she just make a gate to let Mom escape?"

Ros shrugged. "I know what my predecessors did, but I don't always know the *why*. But Georgie hid in some bushes until the males flew off, and she might have stayed there overnight had the storm not come up."

"Kura's idea as well?"

"She was concerned by the state of Georgie's injuries." After worrying her lip a moment longer, Ros said, "Those bushes where your mom was hiding were part of the formal grounds of the estate of a guy called Owain."

"Fae?"

"Half, fortunately. He stepped outside at the sound of thunder and saw one of Georgie's legs sticking out of the shrubbery, and he investigated. Found a naked young woman battered to hell and back, so he tried to ask her who she was and what had happened. She didn't say anything, and he assumed that whatever had befallen her was so traumatic that she'd gone temporarily mute. So, being a decent sort of fellow, he bundled her up, helped her inside, dressed her, washed off the blood, and put her to bed with a healing enchantment."

"Decent," I concurred.

"Next day, Georgie woke up ravenous, and Owain fed her and put her back to bed. She still wouldn't talk to him, and he thought it best to give her time to recover before trying to figure out where she'd come from." Ros paused and drew her legs up more tightly. "Georgie woke in the night feeling *much* better, and, uh…well…she was still in season."

Suddenly, and with a sickening lurch in my stomach, I could envision where Ros's story was heading. "Don't tell me they—"

"She'd seen enough of my parents by then, I guess," said Ros, who appeared to be feeling just as uncomfortable as I was. "Hormones plus curiosity. Owain woke to find Georgie in his bed. He started to protest that she didn't need to repay him like that, but she shushed him, and he didn't put up much of a fight. Didn't put up a fight at all, I should say." She pointedly cleared her throat and skipped the details. "Once they finished and Owain fell asleep again, Georgie slipped out of the house, Kura transformed her back and broke the healing enchantment, and Georgie went home. She laid your clutch a week later."

When Ros fell silent, I pressed, "There were no other males who mated with her, then? Just the big red one?"

"He was the only dragon who succeeded."

"So he's my father?"

"He…is your *siblings'* father," she said slowly.

"I don't understand," I began, frowning. "If there was no one else—"

"I said there was no other dragon."

The truth around which she was dancing hit me like a sledgehammer between the eyes, and when the ringing in my ears subsided and I returned to my senses, I realized I was slumped slack-jawed on the couch. Ros had risen from her chair and stood at the edge of the gate, wringing her hands. "Frank?" she asked as I blinked through the stupor. "Sweetie? Answer me. Are you okay?"

I licked my lips—my mouth felt desiccated—and sat up

straighter. "You're joking," I mumbled.

She shook her head.

"*How?*"

"Kura experimented on you, just as she did on me. Just like Conota did when he fused humans and horses into the kadalin, you know? She was curious to see what the outcome would be, so she worked on you to give you a chance at hatching. But that's why you were a week behind the others—"

I shook my head and held up my hands to stop her. "Just…answer me plainly. Is Owain my father?"

"Yeah," she murmured.

"And…I am…"

"There's no set term," she replied, grimacing. "Draconid lesser fae, maybe, but that's a mouthful."

"Moon and stars," I muttered, resting my head in my palms. "I…I don't know…" Suddenly, a terrible thought made my head shoot up again, and I stared at Ros in horror. "My sons."

She hugged herself.

"Is that why they died?" I whispered. "Because I'm—"

"Ione had *many* problems," she said, "and all of your children inherited some of her genetic issues. But…"

"I killed them."

"Frank, honey…"

Barely hearing her, I shook my head as my eyes began pricking. "*I* killed them. Not Ione. Oh, no…no, I…"

"Frank—"

"*Why didn't you tell me?*" I shouted through the gate, seeing once again those silent eggs, the dragonets too deformed to ever hatch. "I should have known, *Ione* should have known…Aurie would be whole if not for me…"

"Aurie would be *dead*," Ros snapped, yanking me out of the pit into which I'd been plummeting. "Your brothers would never have nested for Ione, and you know it. Her clutch would have died with her if they'd had *any* other father. So yes, building a viable fetus out of the genetic assortment you and Ione gave me was beyond challenging, but if you weren't wired the way you are, all of my meddling would have been for naught."

By then, the tears had begun falling, and I swiped them away. "Why didn't you tell me?" I asked again as my chest tightened. "You've known for twenty-five years, Ros! *Why?*"

"Because I didn't want to hurt you," she said. "I *never* wanted to hurt you. And considering how messed up everything is with you and your family, I didn't want to make things worse." She watched me as I struggled to process that bombshell, then quietly said, "If I screwed up, Frank, I'm sorry. I'm not infallible. But I kept this quiet because I love you, and I wanted you to find happiness, and...*shit*," she muttered as I silently wept. "You found Ione, and you loved her so much, and I didn't want to ruin that."

"She had a right to know. Before she chose me, she should have known."

"I'm sorry."

It took me a moment, but I finally asked, "Does Owain know about me?"

"No," said Ros. "Kura didn't tell him, and Georgie never suspected that she had a mixed clutch."

"He should know," I muttered. "Principle of the thing."

"Do you want me to tell him?" When I nodded, she said, "All right, then. Will you be okay if I go for a little while?"

"I'm not going to do anything stupid, if that's what you're worried about."

"Promise me."

"I promise," I replied, and watched as the gate sealed.

I don't know how long I sat on that couch, staring into space, simultaneously seeing nothing and feeling far too much to handle. I made no move to stop the tears, but the flashes of rage had subsided. Ros had meant what she'd said—I sensed no duplicity in her thoughts—and I couldn't find it in myself to be angry with her for trying to save me from pain. Grown and changed though we both were, I supposed I would always be her little abandoned hatchling on some level. Honestly, I didn't mind. It was nice to know that someone worried about me, as my mother certainly didn't seem to give a damn those days.

But at some point that afternoon, as I scrambled to make sense of the secret Ros had just revealed, a thought burst forth, bright as a flashbulb: *This makes sense.*

My longer incubation and smaller size. My restlessness around the barn, where my siblings contentedly lived much of their comfortable lives. The fact that I'd spent most of my years under a transformation bind that Mom had been overjoyed to cast off after a mere two months. My love of books and fascination with the Arcanum's lost treasures, which my siblings could never understand. And my little stunt with Ione's clutch, which flew in the face of every draconic instinct.

Of course I was weird. It wasn't because I'd bonded to Ros or because I'd spent so long in Glastonbury—I'd lacked some of those instincts from the beginning. Not all, but enough to set me apart from the others.

That's Runt being Runt again.

Just as the pieces began falling into place, I winced at the light as a fresh gate sliced open where the last one had been. This time, Ros wasn't in her house, but rather standing beside an ornamental fir tree. A gray stone wall rose behind her, presumably the side of a building, though I couldn't see well enough from my position to pinpoint her location. "So," she said without preamble, "question. Owain is *dying* to meet you. Can he come over?"

Having imagined my information session with Ros ending somewhere along the lines of *He's alive, he's out there, and you really shouldn't go looking for him*, the news that my presumptive father wanted to speak to me came out of the blue, and I stammered for a moment before managing,

"Uh…sure. Just let me tidy up…"

"Back in a sec," she replied, and closed the gate.

My flat was completely unprepared for company—the breakfast dishes remained in the sink, I hadn't cleaned properly in a week, and my computer and several stacks of books and papers remained on the table where I'd been working. This wasn't what I'd envisioned, I wasn't prepared, I was still wearing my ratty working-from-home rugby shirt with the holes in the elbows, and my glasses…

My glasses. Where the hell were my *glasses*?

Too late, I remembered that I'd left them on the bathroom counter. I never met new people without them on, not with eyes like mine—no matter what I did or how I disguised myself, I seemed to trigger in humans a deep, subconscious warning against large reptiles, though the glasses helped. But the third gate was already opening, and I barely had time to jump up and move away from the couch before the rift widened.

The little I could see of the world beyond the gate continued the gray stone theme—perhaps the inside of the building I'd noted a moment before—and an arched window to the left admitted the sunlight onto what looked like a thick oriental rug. But all of that was background information captured by my peripheral vision and stored away for later analysis. My focus was reserved for the youthful-looking man on the other side.

Even by human or fae standards, he was small, perhaps a hair shorter than Ted and a good two heads below me. He'd tied back his light blond hair into a low ponytail, much as I had that day, but his complexion held more color than mine, which too closely resembled the underside of a dead fish. His attire was unremarkable, a button-down in a gray check over dark-wash denim, but I stared at his face, briefly wondering why it looked so familiar before I recalled seeing a version of some of his features in the mirror that morning. True, his eyes were different, gray to my red, but they crinkled around the edges as he looked up at me.

He was, I realized, beaming.

"Frank?" he asked.

I nodded.

"Moon and stars," he breathed in Fae, "you're so *tall!*"

I wasn't at all sure of how to respond to that, and he jumped in again before I could attempt to do so. "Sorry, Lady Roslyn warned me, but…my goodness. *Oh*, my goodness. May I…"

"Uh…please," I said, beckoning him through.

He wasted no time, and his smile didn't waver. "I can't believe you exist," he said, throwing his arms around me in a surprisingly tight hug, and thumped my back hard enough to dislodge food.

By nature, I was not a hugger, but two and a half decades with Ted had prepared me for almost any embrace. I returned Owain's gesture as well as I could— like smiling, it didn't come naturally to me—and finally, he stepped back and let me catch my breath.

"I'm sorry," I said, "I know this must be a shock, but when Ros told me, I thought you should at least know—"

"Don't be *sorry*," he insisted. "This is incredible!"

"It is?"

Impossible though it seemed, his smile widened. "I have a son," he said, and hugged me again before I could deflect.

At least he wasn't throwing bolts, I reasoned, waiting for him to break away again. "Ros *did* tell you about, uh…my mother—"

He switched his hold, instead gripping my arms and looking me square in the face. "She did, and I remember your mother well. Nice to finally know her name and what she was doing at my house—I've wondered for years what happened to her. But Frank, I don't give a damn where you came from—you're my son. My firstborn."

"I…am?"

He nodded emphatically. "And I'm so sorry. Had I

known you existed, I would have reached out before now—please believe me, I would have."

Cautiously, I stretched my mind toward his, looking for the truth. Owain had left himself open, and he seemed unbothered as I tentatively slipped into his thoughts.

The man was *ecstatic*. Overjoyed. Surprised that my voice was at least an octave lower than his and trying to pinpoint my admittedly trans-Atlantic accent. Momentarily thrown by my lack of pigmentation—nothing unusual there—but seeing the same familiarity in my face that I registered in his.

"I'm so pleased to meet you," he said, and released me once more. "And I do apologize for the lack of notice…"

"I'm sorry, I would have cleaned," I began, but he waved it off.

"Don't go to any trouble on my account. Is this your home?" he asked, finally glancing around the room. "I was told you lived in Glastonbury."

"Arc 2," I confirmed, mentally cataloguing the scuffs and dust on the furniture. "The flats here aren't large, but it's comfortable. Would, uh…" I paused, rubbing the back of my neck as I felt my way through the unfamiliar terrain. "Would you like the tour? I assure you, it's brief."

Owain, perhaps flailing as badly as I was in his own way, perked at the offer. "Certainly! Lead on."

"Um…well, this is the den," I said, sweeping one hand toward the couch and the television on the wall. "Kitchen's over there, dining table is currently buried beneath my work…"

He peeked around the wall into the kitchen, and for the first time, I was grateful that my appliances weren't made of brushed steel. "A little cozy, isn't it?"

"I don't do much in the way of cooking if I can help it. The castle's dining hall serves three meals a day."

"*Ah*. Is the food any good?"

"Can't complain. Want to see the rest?"

He followed me down the hallway toward the

bedrooms. While the official floorplan showed only two in my flat, I had enough faeries in my life to work around the laws of physics when I'd needed to expand.

"Master bedroom," I said, cracking open the door and wincing at the state of my unmade bed. "Bath is unremarkable," I added as I pointed to the door, then escorted Owain along. "And this is Aurie's domain," I continued, stepping aside to show him her room. "There's no telling what state she left it in this morning, but—"

"Aurie?" he asked, slipping past me to look at the plushie wonderland.

"Aurora. My daughter."

Owain stiffened, then wheeled around, joy in his eyes once more. "You're a father? Lady Roslyn didn't say anything about that!"

"I suppose she thought one child at a time was sufficient," I offered. "But, uh…yeah, my little girl sleeps in here with roughly a ton of polyester fluff. Are you all right?" I asked, concerned that I might have overdone it.

Fortunately, he didn't invent a pressing need to be elsewhere. "Never better! I'm suddenly a father *and* a grandfather…do you have any pictures of her? I'd love to meet her," he hastily explained, "but not until you're comfortable with that."

"Thank you," I said, and tried my best to smile properly. "I might have several scrapbooks in the den…"

Whatever expression I managed seemed to convey my intended response—a real issue for me, as my first smiles had seemed either pained or like precursors to an attack, to hear Ros tell it. Owain followed me to the other room and took a seat on the couch while I pulled three thick albums from their shelf and dropped them on the coffee table. "She just had her first birthday last week," I explained, flipping to the most recent set of pictures, which I'd glued in along with pieces of the colorful crepe bunting and gift tags. "Here, these are from the party."

He scanned the page, his brow furrowing. "Where is

she?"

"There," I said, tapping Aurie's face in three of the first four pictures. "She was a big fan of that pink crown for some reason."

"I thought you said she was *one*."

"She is. We, uh…" I paused, unsure of how Owain would react, then said, "We mature quickly. She'll be grown by the time she's five—hence all the albums."

"Wow," he murmured, and flipped the page. "Well, then, I'm certainly glad to have found you now while Aurie's still young enough to spoil."

Relieved, I walked Owain through the rest of the party photos, identifying my colleagues and swelling with pride every time he commented about how adorable my daughter was—I couldn't argue with him. When he asked to see more, I showed him the middle album, which covered the last snows and the wet British spring. Aurie seemed to shoot up in height with every layer of clothing lost, as if her heavy winter gear had been restraining her. Owain made a constant stream of appreciative noises, lingering especially on the photos of Aurie and me together. As I put that album aside, he reached for the final book—her first few months—and I realized my mistake too late to stop him from opening the cover.

Kitty, bless her, had stepped in when I was too exhausted and strung-out to think clearly in the moments following Aurie's hatching, and she'd captured a set of baby pictures while Aurie napped after her first meal. Because she was a conscientious friend, she'd even cleaned the traces of sheep's blood and viscera off Aurie's snout before documenting the moment. I'd put a copy of each of her snapshots in the album, and I kept my favorite of the set on my desk in the subbasement, a reminder of my daughter in her unbound, blue-scaled glory.

God, she'd been *tiny*. Relatively speaking, of course.

But while I loved the results of her newborn photoshoot, I hadn't planned to thrust the pictures before

Owain, who'd already had a major shock that day. "Sorry," I said, reaching for the album. "Let me just put that with the others—"

"No, wait." He pointed to a picture of my sleeping hatchling and asked, "Is that…"

"We're both under transformation binds," I said slowly, and held my breath as I waited for his reaction.

Owain stared down at the pictures again, then said, "Little darling just collapsed in the grass, didn't she?"

"She sleeps *anywhere*. I caught her napping in the empty bathtub once. If you turn the page, the bound pictures begin…"

He stayed my hand as I tried to flip to the shots of Aurie's impromptu homecoming party, when the Team had come over in force to prepare my flat for a baby while I struggled to hold myself together. "Lady Roslyn told me about your bind," he murmured. "You needn't hide that, son."

Son.

Fighting tears for the second time that afternoon, I nodded and stayed with Owain on the couch as he looked through the pictures. When he finished, he said, "Was I imagining things, or was there another room by Aurie's?"

"I'm not hiding any other children," I assured him. "It's just my home office, but if you want to see…"

"Sure, show me."

I rose and led him to the windowless room, which I'd lined with bookshelves. A secondhand desk occupied one of the short walls, but every other bit of available space ringing the room was filled with overladen cabinetry in a mishmash of colors and styles, the detritus of Arc 2's surplus furniture that I'd repurposed as needed.

"Bit of a book collection," I explained. "A hoard, you might say."

Owain seemed unruffled by my packed library. "Any particular theme?"

"Magical texts, by and large. It's amazing what you can

find at estate sales."

"Is that so? May I?"

I thought he was just being polite—after all, faeries have no need for treatises on spellcraft—but Owain peered at the spines with pleasure. "Ooh, is that...oh, *lovely*," he said, pulling a slim, dusty volume from its space. "Pietro Pesaro. First printing?"

"Second. How do you know Pesaro?"

"His theories on unified thaumaturgical principles were extraordinary—extraordinarily *wrong*, mind you, but a masterpiece of logical deduction built off of a few key fallacies. And then you have the magi who followed him, trying to correct the flaws in his work—"

"One bookcase to your left, up two shelves. Augustin Duodo, first printing."

"Brilliant fool," said Owain, sliding the later book free to inspect it. "I think the Pesaroites gave up in the nineteenth century, did they not?"

"From what I've seen," I replied. "But bear in mind that I don't have a full Arcanum education. Everything I've learned has been piecemeal—a lot of on-the-job training and far too many hours in the Archives here. It's possible that there's later Pesaroite scholarship, but I don't know of any."

Had it been suggested that I'd not only be meeting my father that day, but also discussing texts by obscure magi, I'd have laughed at the absurdity. But there we were, all the same, and I kept waiting for the hammer to fall.

"You've got an impressive collection here, regardless," he told me. "Lady Roslyn mentioned something about travel and research?"

"The Away Team. We hunt for misplaced books and magical objects before they can be misused, more or less. Some archaeology, a lot of hiking and camping, and a fair number of dead ends, but we've had our successes."

"I want to hear all about it," he replied, then glanced toward my desk and cocked his head. I didn't know what had piqued his curiosity—I'd decorated the empty space above the desk with a framed canvas of a wooden warship, but that was the only item of note.

"What's this?" he asked, approaching the painting. "The ship…"

"HMS *Terror*," I said, stepping closer to study the fine details of the rigging. "Early nineteenth century. Built as a warship, then used for polar expeditions."

I couldn't quite read Owain's expression as he contemplated the painting. "Why the *Terror*?"

"She and the *Erebus* were locked in ice and went down during an attempt to find the Northwest Passage. Everyone aboard died because they chose a poor route and weren't prepared. Considering my line of work, I look at the *Terror* as a warning," I explained. "Play stupid games, win stupid prizes."

Owain nodded, then casually opened a gate in the middle of my office. "Wait there. I'd like to show you something," he said, and slipped through.

The room on the other side was, without question, a *substantial* library. Stone walls lined with uniform wooden bookshelves rose perhaps ten meters to a vaulted ceiling pocked with skylights. The space between the walls, at least as wide as my entire flat, held tables and comfortable-looking chairs, and a smattering of books and papers covered nearly every horizontal surface.

"What is this place?" I called through the gate, careful not to come too close. Spells and enchantments on living things broke as their subjects entered Faerie, and I didn't want to accidentally end up full-sized in my flat and thereby take out the whole tower.

"My study," said Owain, stopping before a section of wall. He'd left gaps between the bookcases, most of which he'd decorated with framed paintings and other hanging artwork. Selecting a painting, he pulled it off its hook and carried it back with him into my office, which by then looked shabby and cluttered by comparison. With an odd smile on his face, he turned the painting around and held it up for my inspection.

The *Erebus*. Obviously painted by the same artist, perhaps as a matched set.

"You're joking," I said.

"Not at all. I found that in a gallery in London years ago—must have been the nineties—and reframed it." Glancing from his painting to mine, he said, "I think it should remain here. If you'd like it, that is," he quickly added. "The two would look nice together."

"I can't take your painting," I protested. "And if you bought it in London, you probably paid far too much for it."

He arched an eyebrow, and a pile of banknotes appeared on my desk. "Fae, you know? And you're right about overpaying, I'm sure, but I'd be happy to part with that painting if you have room for it."

Maybe he'd missed the first thirty-one years of my life, but my father was trying. "Thank you," I said. "I'm sure I could rehang the *Terror* to make space."

He smiled and carefully leaned it against a bookcase, ensuring that it wasn't touching any of the volumes. "So, now, will tell me about your work?"

"I'd be happy to," I replied, catching sight of my desk clock, "but Aurie will be home any minute, and she'll want a snack before dinner—"

"And I shouldn't be here when she arrives," Owain finished.

"You could stay…"

He patted my arm and shook his head. "Let's get acquainted properly before we add Aurie to the mix. I don't want to rush you, Frank. But, um…if you'd ever like to come over, you're welcome to use my study…"

"Kind of you, but there's the bind to consider."

"*Right*," he muttered, making a face. "Yes, that. Slight complication, but we'll work around it. When can I see you again?"

As much as I wanted to invite him back the next day, I'd been on enough work trips to know that it would be packed with last-minute preparations. "This week is bad for me—I'm off to Siberia on Wednesday, and we could be there through the weekend. What about next Monday? Noon?"

"Works for me," said Owain. "In case something arises, how should I contact you? I don't want to cause a scene..."

I pulled my phone from my pocket. "Any chance you've got a number?"

He frowned at the device, and then his eyes widened in comprehension. "Moon and stars, is that a *mobile*? The last time I was in this realm was, oh, about 2005..."

"They've come a long way," I replied, chuckling as I started to put my phone up. "Guess that was a stupid question—"

"No, wait. Power yours on."

I obliged, and after Owain considered it for a moment, a duplicate appeared in his hand. "I think I put an address book on this..." he muttered, and poked at the screen until a decidedly retro input menu appeared.

We traded contact information—Owain picked a random string of digits, a typical feature of the faerie-made phones I knew—and then, with a parting grin, he stepped back into Faerie. "Be careful out there. I'll see you soon," he said, and closed the gate.

I stood alone in my office for a long moment, glancing at the painting and the pile of cash on the desk to convince myself that I hadn't hallucinated the whole affair, and I might have remained there for the rest of the evening had the outer door not slammed open. "Dad!" Aurie called. "I'm home! Do we have bacon? I'm *starving*."

Coming, hatchling, I told her, then shoved the money into my desk and hurried out to supervise before Aurie could accidentally microwave a metal tray again.

AUGUST 2: MARCUS

Having experienced both winter and summer outings in Siberia, thanks to Ted's scheduling hiccups, I could say with utter confidence that I preferred the warmer months. The remote taiga through which we hiked that afternoon, following a partially overgrown footpath, spread around us in an uninterrupted sea of larches and evergreen undergrowth, all making the best of the waning summer before the deep freeze set in. Our destination for the night was a meadow near a well-established stream, which sounded pleasant enough until one read the cautionary notes left around the margins of the hand-drawn map: *Avoid bears. Listen for wolves. Moose are larger than you think.*

The map had come from the hand of Sarangerel, an elderly Mongolian wizard who spent just enough time within the confines of Arc 4 to replenish her supplies and assure her friends that she was still alive before she returned to the wilder parts of Asia. She used only the single name in the old style, Antony Copeland's contact at Arc 4 had explained, reserving her clan name and patronymic for the most formal of occasions. There being no other Sarangerel within the installation, no one seemed to mind.

As I, too, had largely switched to using a single name by then, I had no room to critique her choice. In my former life, I'd have never considered relying solely upon my praenomen, but single names were commonly used in Faerie. On those rare occasions when I needed more, I'd taken to borrowing my wife's surname, as "Marcus

Connolly" raised far fewer questions than did "Marcus Valerius Maximus."

Sarangerel was something of a legend around Arc 4, a ghost who appeared in her quarters for an hour or a day before vanishing into the outside world once more. Though a talented wizard, she had shown no desire to pursue magushood or any other position within the Arcanum's bureaucracy, instead avoiding it—and, to a lesser extent, people in general—as much as possible. Had she been aware of its existence as a younger woman, I suspected she might have abandoned the organization for the far less structured Minor Arcanum, but Sarangerel was in her eighties, and she probably couldn't have been bothered to formally renounce the Arcanum after a lifetime of barely paying it any mind.

Eccentric though she may have been, Sarangerel was a prolific writer, and she'd chronicled her decades of wandering in extensive detail. Curious, clever, and quick with an invisibility spell, she'd trekked through lands few outsiders had seen, and Arc 4 was the richer for her notes, photographs, and sketches. Indeed, though she seldom wrote about magic, the Archives had digitized and translated her work, recognizing its value in more mundane areas of study.

It was Mal Stowe who'd discovered Sarangerel's writings while perusing the offerings at Arc 2 for travelogues. Some of the Team's better finds had come from the jottings of wandering wizards, and when he learned of her massive collection, he threw himself into her journals, going so far as to track her treks with a wall map, thumbtacks, and colored string. I suspect that his initial interest was due to the fact that so many of her trips took her through lonely areas—the sort of places that, say, a lupine shifter might shed his clothes and go for a run without being shot. Though Mal had inherited his shifter mother's ability to block mental snooping, the man could be so *transparent*.

But as he dove deeper into Sarangerel's work, he read her account of a curious object she'd seen as a young woman in a small Siberian village: a massive silver-colored ball that seemed to thrum with magic. She'd described the item as spherical, taller than she was, and covered over with an inscription in a language unknown to her. Sarangerel hadn't bothered to copy the characters, however, and although she wrote in both Mongolian and Chinese, she gave no indication as to what other languages she might speak, making identification of the ball's origin next to impossible.

The opportunity was too good to pass up. Mal brought the matter to Ted's attention, and Ted gave the expedition his blessing...though he suggested reaching out to Arc 4 first instead of wandering Siberia and hoping to stumble across Sarangerel's find.

Antony, a near-witch who'd been an Arc 2 librarian in his youth before joining the Team, had maintained contact with Akino Haruki, who had begun his career in the Arc 4 library at the same time. When Antony requested his assistance in arranging a meeting with Sarangerel, Haruki had laughed aloud, then sobered when he realized Antony was serious. Sarangerel, he explained, didn't *do* meetings. She came and went on her own schedule—even the installation head had difficulty tracking her down. But Haruki had agreed to keep an eye out for her as a favor to a friend, though he'd warned us that if he managed to catch her, we might need to drop everything and head to Mongolia.

Two months later, the call came at one in the morning. Antony jumped out of bed, apologized profusely to his wife, Madison, then grabbed Mal and rang our flat to see if anyone was awake. The odds were decent—Quinn might come home at any hour of the night, and as Artur and I were fae and technically ancient, we needed little sleep. He managed to catch Artur, who put aside her book and pulled me out of bed without a second thought.

My sister-in-law possessed many virtues, but gentility wasn't high on that list.

The four of us hurried to Arc 4 by gate, arriving outside their dining hall, a concrete room with small windows that had apparently changed little since its Soviet days. "The Bloc" was just that: gray, institutionally bland buildings picked up and dumped together in a sparsely populated corner of Mongolia, camouflaged with spells and connected with tunnels against the weather. Of all the Arcanum installations, only Arc 7, in the heart of the Outback, was less popular as a residence. Much of the animosity toward Arc 4 was due to the location. Though the austere beauty of the mountainous terrain provided a scenic backdrop, the installation was isolated, hours from Ulaanbaatar. Winters, I could well imagine, would be miserable.

Haruki met us before we could wander the halls and hurried us into his office within the library, apologizing for the early wakeup. Well, I *believe* that was what he said; his English was heavily accented, and my untrained ear struggled to keep up with his rapid conversation. Antony, however, managed it flawlessly—a perk of being a native speaker—and I soon gleaned the gist of the matter. Sarangerel had returned overnight and delivered a fresh journal to the library for safekeeping, and Haruki, who'd just so happened to be working late, had convinced her to stay through breakfast and talk to us.

"Will we need a translator?" Antony asked as we entered the utilitarian library. "My Chinese is next to nil, and I can't even ask for the bathroom in Mongolian."

Haruki chuckled and shook his head. "Her English is good. Sarangerel is a natural…uh…what is the word?"

"Polyglot?"

"Yes, *that*. And I told her about your group. She is prepared."

Mal and I traded glances. "Wasn't planning to go full wolf on her," he quipped. "This is a friendly visit."

"I mean no disrespect," said Haruki over his shoulder. "The lady prefers to be prepared. It has kept her alive, you see."

"Wise," Artur murmured beside me.

Haruki showed us into his office, half of which was filled with an old steel table and matching chairs. At the far end, sipping from a white porcelain mug, sat a wizened woman with a deeply lined and tanned face, a pair of thick white braids falling over her hunched shoulders, and cunning dark eyes that appraised us as we filed in. Antony took the lead, nodding almost as far as a formal bow, and pulled a notepad from his satchel. "Good morning, ma'am," he began, and gestured to a chair. "May we join you?"

Sarangerel indicated her assent with a dip of her chin, and Antony and Mal pulled out their seats. Mal, who had barely a trace of his half-fae father's talent, had managed to entirely dodge the fae metal allergy. Artur and I were not so lucky in that regard, and we took up positions against the wall.

If the old woman was concerned by our presence, she remained outwardly serene. "What is it you want to know?" she asked, her voice gravelly but still strong.

Mal produced his notes about her work and explained our interest in the silver sphere. She nodded as he described it—time, at least, had not dulled her memory— then beckoned for Antony's notepad. "I can give you the map," she said, taking his pen from him as well. "You make gates?"

"We can," I replied.

She glanced my way and grunted acknowledgement. "Good. You have my pictures?" she asked Mal.

He dug through his backpack until he found printouts of her photographs. "These?"

Flipping through them, Sarangerel nodded again, then began to sketch a map. "The one with the cleft boulder— use that as your focal point. Do not appear by gate in the village. Nothing I photographed offers good cover. You will walk north from the boulder for a full day, and the following morning, you will reach the village, if it still stands. It was small when I visited, but that was fifty years ago and more. Farmers, fur trappers. Nothing to bring tourism."

"Where's the ball hidden?"

She laughed softly as she drank her tea. "As I said, boy, it has been fifty years. If the thing remains, you will feel it." She paused, then asked, "Do you know why I did not photograph it? I tried, but the leakage from the ball was so strong that my camera was broken beyond repair. I forced myself to find civilization and a camera shop, but that was no use—the man opened it and said it looked as if the machinery had melted. So if the thing is still in the village, you will know."

"And how should we gain access to the village?" Artur asked, folding her arms. "If it's as remote as you recall, then the people will surely be wary of foreigners."

"Oh, without question," said Sarangerel. "Which is why you will want Mikhail."

"Who is Mikhail?"

She smiled to herself. "There are wizards in this world who care nothing at all for the Arcanum."

"He's Minor Arcanum, then?" Artur pressed.

"Yes," she said as Haruki stiffened with unease. "You have a contact among them?"

"That depends on who's asking and what's required."

Her sly smile widened. "I think I might like you, girl."

"Pretend that we knew a sleepwalker," Artur continued, mirroring Sarangerel's expression. "For whom should we ask?"

"*If* you knew of such a person, then I would advise you to ask for Mikhail Yezhov. He trades among the smaller settlements of Krasnoyarsk Krai. Something of a healer. If he will introduce you, the villagers will speak."

The audience ended quickly thereafter—we could sense

that Sarangerel was eager to be on her way—and we returned to the dead of night in Glastonbury. As our days were then close to synchronized with Faerie's, there was little we could do within the bounds of common courtesy beyond send a message and wait for morning.

Artur had spoken the truth: we knew sleepwalkers, wizards with the rare ability to access a liminal space through a form of deep trance. Somehow, within this state, they could communicate with each other and contact others who lacked the ability. I couldn't speak to the specifics—I knew just enough about my own power to not be an immediate danger to society, and the nuances of spellcraft and other wizardly domains were far beyond my expertise. But I did have personal knowledge of two sleepwalkers. Since one of them was Eadwig, who'd sworn off the practice—Simon had committed atrocities in his sleep—that left Badger Parsons, my cousin Seamus's wife. I hadn't spent much time with them, but I assumed that a request to call me would be returned.

And it was, just as I was dragging myself into the kitchen to make coffee the next morning. Seamus listened to the problem, then explained that Badger would be unable to assist us. Sleepwalking was impossible from Faerie, and as his all-too-mortal wife was ninety-three, she wouldn't leave that realm and suffer the weight of the nearly twenty-five years she'd spent in Faerie crashing upon her at once. Glamoured though Badger was to match Seamus's eternally youthful appearance, even Ros couldn't restore true youth to her, and the physical shock of returning to the mortal realm, however briefly, could be fatal. But he offered to reach out to the wizard who'd trained Badger, Carey Jones, and make the request on our behalf.

While I'd met Carey, one of the senior members of the Minor Arcanum, ours was barely an acquaintance. Seamus, however, was on sufficiently friendly terms with her to call New Mexico in the middle of the night, as I soon received a call from the groggy wizard. She brushed off my apologies, but she swore she'd be buying Seamus a clock and stapling it to him.

Four days later, Carey called again with a phone number. "He'll talk to you people," she said, "but he won't make the introductions without some guarantees."

"Such as?" I asked.

"No harm to him, no harm to the villagers, and if the owner of that damn ball wants to keep it, you won't take it by force."

"Done. But the ball *is* still there?"

"Apparently," she replied. "He didn't take me out to show me around, but that was the impression I got. And I'm serious, now—don't screw around out there," she continued, her tone sharpening. "You know how much convincing it takes to get my people to do anything for the Arcanum?"

Considering the organizations' long animosity, I had little doubt that this Mikhail had required substantial persuasion. "Don't suppose it would help if we left the wizards at home, would it?" I joked.

Carey snorted. "*Fuck*, no. And you weren't thinking of bringing *him* along, were you?"

"Who, Eadwig? Of course not."

"Good. See that you don't." Warming again, she said, "Have fun, now. Try not to start an inter-realm war."

After a month of conversations and assurances, Mikhail decided to lead us in. Antony, who had taught himself a little Russian, took the lead in the negotiations and was relieved to find that Mikhail's English fluency far surpassed his stumbling attempts in the opposite direction. Mikhail agreed to serve as guide and translator, and he gave us a date for the rendezvous that worked with his preplanned summer travels through the region.

"Is there any sort of hotel nearby?" Antony had asked

him, just in case civilization had encroached upon the distant village in the years since Sarangerel had visited.

The only answer he'd received was hearty laughter, and so we'd packed for camping.

If nothing else, Sarangerel's map was accurate. We reached the meadow around five that evening, though as we were all still on Glastonbury time, no one quite knew when it was supposed to be, only that we were hungry and footsore. The mosquitoes had plagued us all day, held off through a combination of weak personal shields, deep-woods insect repellant, and a steady stream of smoke from Frank's nostrils, and no one objected to the idea of hiding in tents for a few hours. As the sun began to decline, a cool breeze picked up, and we set about arranging our campsite.

For the first time in a while, our expedition was a boys' trip. We usually traveled in mixed groups—not by edict, but rather because most excursions called for members of the Team with particular skills or areas of expertise. But the date that Mikhail chose for our meeting happened to fall in the middle of the girls' getaway to London, where they'd arranged to visit museums, see a show or two, and enjoy massages. Lakshmi Gupta had declined the outing, as she and her husband were taking time off to play with their granddaughter, but Kitty and Daphne Hopkins had planned a week's worth of bonding time. Maria—Kitty's best friend, my distant granddaughter, and the Team's supervisory magus—had signed up for the festivities, as had Beth, who was making the best of her brief summer break. They'd even coaxed Artur into joining them, though something within me refused to entertain the notion of her enduring a pedicure.

With the women away, we were down to five in the field—Ted, Frank, Antony, Mal, and me—while elderly Bob Norge remained in the office in case of emergency. As August was relatively warm, no one needed to bunk with Frank to survive the Siberian night, and we quickly pitched a semicircle of one-man tents around the campfire. Dinner was pouches of rehydrated stew—I could produce coffee from the ether, but not fine cuisine—but anything tastes decent after a day of hiking. Satiated, we secured the rest of our foodstuffs and set the watch. There would be no true darkness so far north, merely a period of twilight, but still, we decided that keeping an eye on the forest would be prudent.

Ted and Antony retired to their tents, and I thought Mal had joined them until I caught his head poking out of his zippered door. "You guys going to be okay for a while?" he asked.

Frank and I shrugged. "Going for a run?" Frank asked.

"Not like I get the chance back in England," he replied, and vanished into his tent once more. Seconds later, a monstrously oversized brown wolf slid out from between the flaps and shook himself.

"Have a good time," said Frank, settling into one of the camping chairs we'd put aside for the trip. As isolated as we were, there was no harm in opening a quick gate into the Team's storage closet to grab furniture instead of hauling it all day. In truth, we could have slept in our own beds—a few photographs of the site would have been sufficient to allow me to make a gate back the next morning—but if the girls were having a spa day, then at least we could manage a campout.

Mal's tail wagged, and after sniffing the air, he took off at a lope toward the trees and vanished into the underbrush.

I dragged a chair close to Frank's and refilled our coffee mugs. He'd been strangely quiet that day, almost preoccupied, but prudence counseled against attempting to poke through his thoughts without an express invitation. Guessing at the cause of his concern, I said, "Aurie will be fine. She likes Madison, doesn't she?"

"Sure. I hate to impose, especially with Antony out here—"

"You *have* met Madison, yes? If she were opposed, she'd say something. Besides," I added, "you know Allie will play with Aurie until she drops. She seems good with children."

"This is payback for all the years that we entertained her at work," said Frank. "But...you know, that's my girl, and part of me expects the worst when I'm away..."

I couldn't fault him for that. How many times had I awakened in the darkness and jumped out of bed, sure that my son was asleep nearby, only to remember where I was and how very long ago he had died? My therapist couldn't tell me when or whether those episodes would cease, but Kitty never complained when I slid beneath the blankets again on those nights and pulled her closer to me.

While Frank and I sat in contemplative silence, drinking our coffee and resting our feet, a chorus of howling began to echo through the forest. I sat up straighter, pricked by the primal warning that raised the hair on the back of my neck, but Frank seemed unconcerned by the distant wolves.

"Do you think Mal will be all right?" I asked.

He took a long sip and crossed his legs. "Eh, safe enough. He's a big guy. Might even try to run with them, I don't know."

We listened as the howling seemed to move toward the north and fade.

"Just curious," I said, "but do you suppose Mal has ever tried to...you know?"

Frank eyed me over the top of his dark glasses. "Mate with one of them?"

"Yeah."

"No, and I think he'd be insulted if you asked him that."

"Which is why I'm not," I replied, and broke a green branch off of a tree several meters away. It flew into my hand, shedding its needles, and I prodded at the fire to energize the flame. "I mean, it's his business what he does out there, but…"

Frank said nothing for a moment, then murmured, "Shifters consider themselves human before anything else. I would be surprised if he's ever experimented in that fashion, and he would probably be appalled at the idea."

"Understood. And is there any way that we might forget to mention this conversation to Mal?"

The corner of his mouth ticked in a flicker of amusement. "Just keep the coffee coming."

Mikhail Yezhov was a stout, sun-wrinkled man with a bushy gray beard and a hairline that had receded almost to the back of his skull. As promised, he met us by a rust-eaten truck abandoned to the forest, a landmark about half an hour's walk from the village. Antony, who'd spearheaded the negotiations to that point, was polite and thanked Mikhail for meeting us, but our boss, in true Ted fashion, pumped the poor man's hand and grinned like a child who's discovered that the room full of toys is all for him.

I'd worried—Ted's general ebullience could be a little much to the unaccustomed—but Mikhail warmed to him within minutes. The two were probably of an age, somewhere around seventy, and as Ted seldom met a stranger, he had Mikhail laughing at his terrible jokes long before we reached the village. But as the path grew more distinct and the smell of smoke wafted our way, our guide sobered and motioned us into a tight huddle.

"Do you feel it?" he murmured.

I didn't need to *feel* it—I could see how the colorful swirls of untapped magic around us had intensified. There was a source nearby, no question about it, but unless the villagers had stumbled upon a gate into Faerie, I couldn't imagine what would produce such an uptick against the realm's background levels.

"It's still here," Ted whispered.

Mikhail nodded. "Protected. I know where it is kept, but let me secure permission from the owner before we do anything else."

Having agreed to follow his lead, we trailed after Mikhail until we reached the edge of the village, a collection of small houses, snowmobiles, and an old Jeep scattered around a muddy central square. The alleged village barely qualified as a settlement, such a difference from the wealth of cosmopolitan Moscow. It seemed less a planned community than a haphazard campsite fortified with wooden walls against the winter. Judging by the cautiously appraising look being given us by the nearest of its inhabitants, an elderly woman with a pipe stuck in her sunken, toothless mouth, tourism had yet to reach this corner of Siberia, and it would probably never be welcome.

Mikhail spoke first to the old woman, and while I couldn't make sense of his words, his tone conveyed familiarity and friendship. Her expression softened, and as they conversed, she pointed to her knee. Mikhail reached into his bag and produced a wand, and I saw the magic around the woman's leg flare as he wove a quick healing spell.

"And *that*," muttered Antony, "is the Minor Arcanum for you. The Council would shit themselves if they witnessed this. Blatant use of magic in front of mundanes…"

"Yeah," said Mal, "but who are they going to tell? The wolves aren't big talkers."

As Mikhail finished, the woman patted his arm and smiled at him, and he motioned us closer. "This is Dina Lobanova. Came up here as a trapper with her husband years ago. He died young, she remained. Now, she looks after the three men left here," he said, pointing to the houses around us. "Youngest and strongest of them. The rest of the village has moved on."

If Mikhail's assessment was accurate, I could hardly envision the settlement lasting another five years. But the spell Mikhail had placed on Dina's knee was sufficient to allow her to push herself from her chair and walk with him toward the house on the far end of the square. Like its fellows, it was, to be polite, modest, though the adjacent barn appeared to be in decent repair.

Dina strode to the front door, rapped three times, and let herself in without waiting for an invitation. I heard the mumbling of a male voice answer her greeting, but we didn't follow her to investigate. A few minutes later, a stooped man shuffled out, leaning heavily on a metal cane. He wore a thick jacket even in the warmth of August, but as his clothing seemed to hang from his thin frame like scraps of cloth on a skeletonizing corpse, I suspected that he was always cold. His milky eyes squinted at us, and when Mikhail spoke, he turned in the direction of the wizard's voice and smiled.

"Cataracts," Ted whispered. "Poor guy's probably half blind or worse. What the hell is he doing up here? Where's his family?"

Before we had time to hypothesize, Mikhail again beckoned us closer and spoke rapidly to the old man, who punctuated his speech with nods and the occasional grunt. When the man replied, his voice carried a tremor of age, and Mikhail leaned closer to hear him.

Finally, our guide turned to us. "This is Igor Sokolov. He owns the ball, and he has agreed to show it to you."

Our procession—by then having picked up Dina as well—made the slow journey to the barn with Mikhail at Igor's elbow in case the older man should stumble. Igor lifted the wooden latch and allowed Mikhail to pull the door open, then limped inside and stopped before a massive object covered by a mildewed tarp.

"What the hell *is* that?" Antony demanded.

I couldn't answer him, but standing as close to it as we were, I could imagine why Sarangerel's camera had malfunctioned. Whatever lay beneath those dirty wrappings was *hemorrhaging* magic.

Igor mumbled for a moment, and Mikhail offered a translation. "His great-grandfather found it in a swamp while trapping and brought it home, thinking it might be valuable. Two days later came the Tunguska event. The blast damaged the forest and the homes of some men he knew, but his home and family were spared. He considered the ball lucky and decided to keep it." Mikhail paused to let Igor continue, then said, "It's remained in the family ever since. Some of Igor's cousins left for city life long ago, and he is the last living out on the land. He would like to move south, somewhere with plumbing and electricity, but he fears that if he tried to sell the ball, it would be confiscated from him."

"May we see?" Ted asked.

With Igor's permission, Ted and Frank pulled off the tarp, and I was suddenly glad not to have volunteered for the task.

The ball was silver, brighter than steel and strong enough to make my skin tingle in warning. I took a preemptive step back, then tried to calculate the size of the thing. Sarangerel had described it as taller than she was, but that didn't do it justice; the elderly explorer was shorter than average, while the silver ball rose above Frank's head. Even if it were hollow, it had to be worth a fortune.

The fact that magic was leaking from within it was another matter entirely.

Frank moved closer to peer at the characters carved all over the ball. "Runes," he announced after a brief inspection. "Scandinavian or Anglo-Saxon, I think."

Ted joined him with a penlight and soon nodded. "Think you're right. Looks like futhorc to me, but don't ask me to translate."

"Likewise," Frank muttered. "So what the hell is it doing in the middle of Siberia?"

Safely lurking in the doorway of the barn, I pulled out my phone. "We could guess, or we could call the one person we know who easily reads futhorc."

The five of us from the Team traded glances, then looked at Mikhail, who regarded us bemusedly. "So," said Ted, sidling closer to him, "we know a fellow who can translate what's on the ball."

"That would be useful," the old wizard replied.

"Yeah…except it's Eadwig."

Mikhail stiffened. "You mean—"

"The kid who's not quite Simon Magus. We won't bring him out here if it would make you uncomfortable, but having spent the last year with the guy, I'm pretty confident that he won't go on a killing spree."

He folded his arms as he considered Ted's reassurances. "You have him on a leash?"

"I've got a twenty-two-hundred-year-old faerie standing over there who could wipe the floor with him," he replied, cocking his thumb toward me, "so yeah, more or less."

Mikhail's dark eyes widened.

I waved.

"Bring the boy," he mumbled, and slid closer to the ball.

The hour in Glastonbury had to be nearly midnight, I reasoned, but the matter wouldn't wait. As it so happened, Eadwig was working late once again, and he hurried through the gate I opened into his office as the villagers goggled. "In the barn," I told him. "Can you read—"

The boy stopped in his tracks and stared, struck silent until he managed to whisper something that sounded very much like *fuck*.

"What is it?" Ted asked. "Have you seen something like this before?"

Eadwig stepped close enough to run his fingertips over the runes, then appeared to snap out of his daze and scowled. "It's leaking."

"We'd noticed," said Ted.

The boy moved back, then motioned in the air until a bright lattice of spellcraft floated up from beneath the ball's surface. "There," he said, pointing to two holes in the netting. "Probably casualties of the closure fifty years ago. It's a strong spell, but those are seam points…" With a few flicks of his fingers and a whispered word, the holes repaired themselves, the outflow ceased, and the spell sank back within the ball.

Antony cleared his throat. "Did, uh…did Simon—"

"Fashioned that spell as a protective barrier," said Eadwig, who returned his attention to the inscription. "Cuthbert's work was brilliant, but once the ball was filled, they realized that it needed reinforcement against leakage."

Ted's brow furrowed. "Cuthbert…"

"My crafter," the boy murmured as if in a stupor. "This was his greatest achievement. Large enough to power an army for a week. I only brought it into the field once. Lost it in the mountains. We'd been surrounded for two days, and the snow wouldn't abate…" He stopped suddenly and shook himself like a wet dog, then put a bit of distance between himself and the ball. "Sorry. Memory."

"You're fine," Ted soothed, but the telltale sparkle flickered in his eyes. "This Cuthbert…he made some gold balls, too, didn't he? Handheld ones? Kind of like magical batteries?"

"He did. This one held exponentially more raw magic, but the others were much simpler to transport."

Ted turned to us, grinning. "Those balls kept Arc 1's wards running during the '13 closure, and they got Faerie open again. If the softball-sized ones could hold that much power, what sort of a punch do you think Big Boy here could pack?"

"It wasn't intended to punch," said Eadwig. "It was intended to *annihilate*."

"And it really shouldn't be left in a shed in the middle of nowhere," said Antony. "Mikhail, could you ask Igor what he wants for the ball, please?"

Mikhail passed the message, then grunted at Igor's reply. "He wants enough to take Dina and the other two and leave this place. Winter is difficult at their age, and he'd like to go south. He saw Novosibirsk once as a young man and would like to move there."

"Where is that?" I asked.

"Southwest of here. Largest city in Siberia." Rubbing his chin, he said, "I keep a flat in the city, but I seldom use it for more than storage. It would be enough for the four of them."

"Are you willing to sell?" Ted asked.

At that, Mikhail flashed a calculating smile. "I have a figure in mind. What are you offering?"

I made him a *very* wealthy man that morning.

Using banknotes as models, I quickly produced the equivalent of several million pounds from the ether—enchantment is useful in that respect—which we split two ways: half for Mikhail as consideration for the property, and half to the villagers, enough to buy them a comfortable existence for the rest of their days. With the money bagged and distributed, the villagers packed the few possessions they wished to bring with them, and then Frank dug through Mikhail's memories for an image of the flat, which he passed to me for gate-making purposes.

With Mikhail having assured us that he would see them settled, I gave him my number to call for a gate back to his waiting vehicle outside the village, then turned to the matter of the ball. That time, Eadwig took the lead, opening a gate into our conference room, temporarily shrinking the long table to the size of a toy, and then floating the ball into the cleared space. It was far too wide to fit through the door, but structural limitations never seemed to present true problems around the installation.

We trooped back into the subbasement behind him and sloughed off our camping gear. Unencumbered, Mal squeezed into the conference room to take a better look at our find beneath the fluorescent lights, and Ted hastened after him. Frank and Antony shared a look of understanding before filing into the room after our boss, leaving Eadwig and me in the corridor.

"I've stabilized it," he murmured, "but obviously, we can't leave it in there forever. Thoughts? A storage room in the Archives? I'd say destroy it and be done with it, but in case of emergency, I'm sure it has no equal. Cuthbert was a genius."

By then, I had my phone to my ear and heard my aunt's groggy greeting on the other end. "My apologies, Toula. Please come down to the office. You need to see this."

AUGUST 4: EADWIG

"Do you remember our grounding technique?"

"I tried," I protested, but Dr. Fitzgibbon—Wanda to her patients—wasn't accepting excuses that morning.

"Try again," she ordered. "Right now."

Sprawled supine on her comfortable office couch, I stared up at the colorful blobs she'd painted on the ceiling and attempted to ground myself in the present.

Sight: the abstract painting above me, placed there for patients who spoke more freely when they didn't stare at the doctor.

Sound: my own breathing, faster than it should have been. The rhythmic pounding of blood in my ears. The muted cries of children playing in the Fringe settlement's expansive park.

Smell: myself, unfortunately. I hadn't bathed in two days, so busy had I been with Toula and her few trusted magi. More pleasingly, Wanda's biscuits, hints of vanilla and chocolate.

Touch: the smooth cloth of the red couch cushion beneath my hand. The warmth of morning sunlight falling on my face through the window in the side wall.

Taste: biscuits again, a far better sensation than the previous night's intermittent bouts of vomiting.

"That's it," Wanda soothed. "Your muscles are relaxing, sweetie. Deep breaths, try to be present here with me."

After a few minutes, I no longer felt quite so much like a clenched fist and eased myself upright. "Better," I said, turning to face her. "That's better."

I could feel the weight of her blue eyes on me, assessing my body language. Wanda was a true Fringer, lesser fae and barely gifted, physically frozen in her mid-sixties although she had seen her first century. She reminded me of a sparrow, tiny and delicate, but she possessed a quiet strength that might go unnoticed until long after a therapy session had ended. Wanda got what she wanted out of her patients, and if one avenue failed, she had another three ready as backups.

While the Arcanum had counselors of its own, Toula had insisted that I schedule regular sessions with Wanda instead. I saw the wisdom in her plan: Wanda had, by then, counseled Maria, Kitty, Marcus, and Artur, and she could be trusted to keep my confidence—or as much of it as one *could* keep in Faerie. I was never thrilled to return to the realm, burdened as I was with Simon's horrible memories of the place, but Wanda's office was a biscuit-filled oasis, a place where I could say anything without fear of condemnation.

Perhaps it was the decades she'd spent in Faerie, or maybe it was the result of her long career as a therapist—including her work with the Fringers freed from Mulligan's torture—but Wanda was unflappable. She knew the horrible things my other self had done, yet she continued to work with me when Simon's memories crowded my thoughts and commandeered my dreams, pushing me to the brink of a breakdown. She'd never seen a case like mine—no one had—but she recognized distress and the signs of mental trauma. Those memories of a life I'd never lived were frequently unpleasant, but even the best ones left me feeling like an untethered passenger in my own mind. For that reason, she had taught me the grounding exercise, a practice to help me focus on the present and regain control.

But grounding wasn't always sufficient, as the night's fits had made clear.

"What set it off this time?" asked Wanda, crossing her thin legs. "Any ideas?"

"I know exactly what did it," I muttered. "The Team found something from Simon's past, and when I saw it…" I struggled for the words, then said, "Many feelings, all tied to it. I know Arnold meant well, and taking notes of what I remember about it was in the service of scholarship, but…"

"He kept dredging the memories up?"

"I swear, by the end of the day, I didn't even feel like myself anymore. I was Simon looking out through Eadwig's eyes, and…" I ran one hand over my opposite arm as if warding off a chill that only I could sense. "The longer I stayed in his memories, the more I lost control."

She cocked her head and tapped her pen against the armrest of her couch. "Are they just bad memories, or do they frighten you?"

"Both."

"Why are you afraid?"

"Because I know what he's capable of doing," I replied. "Maybe it's irrational, but I'm afraid that if I spend too long in his memories…"

When I didn't finish, she did it for me. "You're afraid of becoming Simon."

I nodded.

Wanda uncrossed her legs and shifted forward on the couch, the better to hold my gaze. "I want you to understand something, Ed. We are not merely the product of our genetics."

Having heard this speech before, I didn't ask her to explain the term.

"If I were to take identical twins and raise them in different countries with different families and friends, they would share some similarities, but they wouldn't be copies in every respect. Now, you and Simon both experienced trauma, but at different ages, and trauma of different natures. Your world now is vastly unlike his was. You're not going to rise up and start a war, honey."

"I suppose not."

"So putting that aside, do you two share traits? I'm sure of it. You're bright, you're tenacious, and he must have been as well. But think of Simon as you having been pushed to an extreme you'll never reach. Do you know what a funhouse mirror is?"

"No…"

She pulled out a tablet computer and called up an image of the distorting glass. "Simon is that reflection," she told me. "Some good parts, maybe some terrible parts, but that's *Simon*, not Ed." Settling back, she said, "I think it would be beneficial for you to grapple with some of his memories. I'm not saying to dwell on them," she hastened to explain before I could argue, "but acknowledging them, spending a little time understanding them and thereby understanding Simon, could help you assimilate him."

"But I don't *want* to assimilate him!" I protested. "I want him out of my head!"

"I know, dear, but I don't think that's possible." As I struggled with her suggestion, she continued, "I'm not saying that you should try to become him or make apologies for him—I want you to make your peace with him. For good or ill, he's part of you now. Once you're able to come to terms with that, I believe your attacks will subside." After a brief pause—I suppose she waited to see whether I would fight her—Wanda said, "You're not alone in this. Talk to me, let's see if we can work through some of these memories together. Okay?"

"Okay," I mumbled, and produced a glass of water from the ether. I'd have preferred something stronger, but Wanda frowned upon getting drunk during therapy.

"Let's start with whatever the Team found. Tell me about it."

I drained half my drink before answering her. "Cuthbert's greatest creation," I murmured, staring into space as it rose again in the darkness behind my eyes. "A storage device for raw magic. The small ones he'd made for Simon were wonderful things, useful, *practical*—you could hold one in your hand—but they drained quickly when called upon by an army of wizards. *This* one was a great sphere taller than a man, and you can imagine how much magic it could hold. Took weeks to fill."

"Sounds impressive."

"A masterpiece of crafting," I agreed. "We had to pull it in a cart. But we thought it might be necessary, you see—there was a holdout arcanum in…well, I suppose it would be Russia," I mused, trying to overlay Simon's maps with the ones I'd seen more recently, "in the mountains. The Caucasus range. Eastward progression was slow because of the terrain, and they were a gifted band of wizards—I don't think there was a witch among them. Even using gates, it was difficult to navigate, and I…"

With a shudder, I dragged myself back to the present, to *myself*.

"Long story short," I told Wanda, "it's a bad idea to attempt an invasion of Russia in the winter. The army was caught by an early blizzard. Whiteout conditions. The other arcanum attacked while Simon's forces were disoriented, and in the chaos, the horses with the cart bolted. I think they fell into a ravine. Simon didn't go after them—his army was thoroughly routed, and he called a retreat. Returned in the spring and slaughtered every one of those wizards," I muttered, "but that's another matter. Simon never found the sphere, and from what Ted said, it was recovered in a Siberian swamp a century or two ago. I've no idea how it got so far east or why no one melted it down for the silver in all that time, but such are the mysteries of the universe."

"Seeing it upset you?"

"It…*surprised* me. And it brought up all the memories of that campaign, and, uh…"

"Of Cuthbert?" she asked gently.

In the course of our sessions, though it had been

terribly awkward for me, I'd told Wanda about Simon's many lovers, some of his favorite faces among the multitude residing in my head. She'd assured me that my feelings were valid and unsurprising. My last true memories before waking in Glastonbury had been those of a sixteen-year-old boy who, though interested in all things carnal, had yet to experience the delights of the flesh with another person. I wasn't a prude—I'd cast a lustful eye on a few of the girls of my village, and though the realization had been confusing at the time, I'd found one of the young men strangely charming. But when I awakened, I'd suddenly been in possession of a *detailed* record of Simon's sexual escapades. If the man had spent a few years in a life of celibacy to maintain his cover, he'd more than made up for it.

Wanda and I had unpacked quite a bit, beginning with my attraction to men. She'd insisted that I could have equally valid feelings for men and women and that certain attitudes had shifted since my childhood. I had no reason to doubt her: on the Team, Bob had been married to his husband for more than forty years, while Bee made no secret of her wife. Even Toula had casually referenced former girlfriends in our occasional conversations. "We're all wired a little differently," my therapist had explained. "If the dating pool is a buffet, some people eat nothing but salad, others go only for the crab legs, and still others like a little of everything."

Simon had certainly sampled that buffet's length, and he had *many* pleasant memories of his partners, but he had loved only two of them: his wife and Cuthbert. His marriage to Béatrix had been a matter of politics and duty, and their relationship had grown from tolerance to a love built on familiarity and mutual understanding. But Cuthbert had captured his heart from their first meeting, and to Simon's relief, his affection had been reciprocated. The two could never have been together in any public sense—aside from the obvious impediments of his marriage and their gender, Cuthbert had come into Simon's camp as a witch-blooded servant to one of his magi—but Simon had taken the younger man into his household as his personal aide, pleased to be in the company of his fair-haired, blue-eyed lover. Once he realized that Cuthbert could craft, however, Simon set him exclusively to that task. Cuthbert's wands were peerless, and his spheres only highlighted his brilliance.

But Cuthbert had never possessed a strong constitution. Two years after the disastrous Russia invasion, he'd died of a fever as Simon nursed him in his own tent. Simon had been heartbroken, but he'd done the proper thing and sent Cuthbert's body back to his homeland for burial. Béatrix, who was a kind soul, had taken him into her bed that night so that he would not grieve alone. Her favorite paramour had died only the previous autumn, and she still mourned him.

Simon never truly got over Cuthbert's death. And because I'd inherited Simon's past, I felt the loss of a man I would never meet.

"It's okay to be sad," said Wanda. "If you want to talk about Cuthbert again—"

"It's not Cuthbert who's making me ill," I replied, cutting her offer short. "Not this time."

"Mm. What's on your mind, then?"

I held my tongue for a moment as I collected my thoughts, and then I met her eyes. "The sphere that Cuthbert built was designed to provide power enough for an army in an environment depleted of magic. Have you any idea how much magic that thing can hold?"

She grimaced. "Quite a bit, I gather."

"More than merely 'a bit.' Even with the last fifty years of leakage, it still felt *very* full to me. And now it's locked in a secure room in the Archives."

"And that worries you?" she asked.

I nodded slowly. "No one should be able to tap that much raw power. Certainly not anyone in the Arcanum. I know the horrors of which we're all too capable."

Wanda did her best after that to reassure me—Toula was responsible and had shown no indication that she wanted to transition to a warlord—but the feeling of dread that the sphere had conjured within me refused to dissipate.

I had touched it, after all. Reinforced it. Imagined the faces of my enemies as I tapped the reserve power to call down fire and lightning upon them.

I'd commissioned the beautiful, damnable thing, God help me.

And should it fall into the wrong hands, then God help us all.

AUGUST 7: FRANK

Don't get your hopes up. That was my internal mantra all weekend as I counted down the days until my second meeting with Owain. I told myself to temper my expectations—maybe something more important would arise for him, or perhaps he'd think better of pursuing any sort of relationship with me. It wasn't fair for me to expect a storybook parent, and anyway, as I was almost thirty-one, I didn't exactly *need* a father in my life. Still, my hopes kept climbing like persistent vines each time I knocked them back.

On Monday morning, after I sent Aurie to her tutors, I told Ted I was taking a personal day and cleaned the flat, even sweeping beneath the beds and wiping the fingerprints off the microwave buttons. I dressed carefully, making sure to choose clothing that time that I hadn't worn through in the weak spots, and added my glasses, just in case. By eleven, I'd hung Owain's painting of the *Erebus* in my office—it fit perfectly beneath its mate—and I plopped down before the silent television, too anxious to read and certain that I was overlooking something crucial.

When my phone rang, I almost jumped out of my seat, and I hastily dug the device out of my pocket. *Owain*, the ID told me, and I struggled to keep calm. This was it—he was canceling, he'd double-booked his calendar, maybe another time. Not the end of the world, I told myself. At least no one was trying to kill Aurie.

I took a deep breath, cleared my throat, and answered the call. "Hello?"

"Frank? Hi!"

He sounded chipper enough. "Hi," I replied. "Uh...is everything all right? If you need to reschedule, I—"

"What? No, of course not. I'll be there in an hour," said Owain. "I was just thinking that we set this close to lunchtime, and I didn't know if you'd eaten."

So he wasn't canceling on me. A small weight seemed to fall from my shoulders as my tension drained. "No, not yet. Do you want me to pick up something from the dining hall?"

"Well, uh, actually," he said, suddenly sheepish, "I put in a pork loin this morning, and I thought I'd bring it, but then I remembered that I have absolutely no idea what you like, so..."

"You *cooked?*"

"Tastes better than eating everything raw," he joked. "But if you don't care for pork, that won't hurt my feelings—"

"No, no, that's great," I interrupted. "Thank you. To be honest, I'm not really picky when it comes to meat."

I could hear the relief in his voice. "Wonderful. I'm partial to this rub, so here's hoping it's palatable. Now, what about sides? Any allergies? I should have asked yesterday..."

At that, I tried to tread carefully. "I'm not allergic to anything, as far as I've seen, but, uh...I'm partial to fried potatoes in just about any form, rice if sufficiently sauced, and that's about it."

"I see," he mumbled. "Not one for a nice summer salad?"

"Obligate carnivore. My palate's skewed—"

"Oh!" He huffed a frustrated sigh. "I should have thought of that, I'm so sorry—"

"You *did* just mention surprise pork loin," I replied. "I'll try almost anything, but know that I'm not the best judge."

He let me go soon thereafter, claiming he needed to

make preparations, and I hastily set the table. Five minutes after twelve, a gate opened in my den, and in came Owain with half a dozen covered dishes and a couple bottles of wine floating behind him. "Red or white?" he asked as lunch arranged itself on the kitchen table.

I winced apologetically. "Bloody Mary?"

"Can do." The red vanished, the white poured itself into a stem that appeared from midair, and Owain cocked an eyebrow. "I make mine strong," he cautioned.

"Challenge accepted."

Chuckling, he gestured my drink into existence, a deep red concoction filling a glass the size of a beer mug. As I peered at the unexpected garnish, he explained, "Bacon with maple syrup and peppercorns. I came across that at a bar in the States…sixty years ago, perhaps? Better than a skewered gherkin, I think."

The syrup gave me pause, but the overall effect was brilliant, a perfect bite of crisp fat, cracked pepper, and glorious *bacon* flavor. Owain watched expectantly as I sampled it, then grinned when I groaned in happiness. "I have no complaint with traditional bacon," he said, settling in at the table, "but the crunch of its American cousin does work well on occasion. Hope you're hungry," he added, and uncovered the spread.

The pork was a thing of beauty, expertly cooked and flavored with a spice blend leaning heavily toward rosemary. To that, Owain had added a warm potato salad, a cold salad of beans and greens, a basket of rolls, and two huge bowls of tender, thick-cut chips fried in duck fat, one with a parmesan-garlic seasoning and one merely salted. "Didn't know which you would prefer," he said, "but I can certainly fry a potato when called upon to do so."

My contribution to the meal was ketchup of questionable freshness from the refrigerator door, but Owain didn't care. "Tell me all about Siberia," he said as we tucked in. "How was it? Where were you? I've been along the eastern coast, but I've never seen the interior."

"Beautiful scenery, odd find," I replied, and attacked my pork with relish. *Five of us went out, we camped Wednesday night, and had it not been for the wolves nearby, I'd wholeheartedly recommend it.*

I glanced up from my plate to find Owain regarding me with wide eyes, then mentally kicked myself. The Team had long grown accustomed to my mealtime eccentricities—my appetite was comparably huge, and rather than waste time at the table, I worked steadily at my food and joined the conversation without resorting to vocal communication. Of course, I hadn't bothered to prepare Owain, and I was sure I'd startled him...

"You're a telepath," he said, his smile blossoming.

I put down my fork and nodded. "Sorry. Force of habit."

"Moon and stars, don't *apologize*." He paused, then thought, *If this is easier, I don't mind.*

To a natural telepath, the fae version of mind speech is odd, and the rare human who can manage it feels even more awkward. Pure draconic telepathy is wordless, the simultaneous transmission of thoughts, feelings, and even sensory information—and it's overwhelming to anyone unequipped to process it. My mother, my siblings, and I had worked out a simplified form more akin to what faeries did when they spoke mind to mind, transmitting only words without most of the emotional coloration. But even those faeries who had the knack seldom chose to employ telepathy unless they required privacy, whereas it was my default mode. I hadn't learned to speak until I was almost six, and mastery had come only with practice, a scaffolding spell, and coaching from Daisy Hornby, who at the time was a speech pathologist in training.

"Don't put yourself to any trouble," I told Owain. "I do it so that I don't keep everyone at the table for an extra hour while I finish eating. Does it, uh...I mean, I'll stop if it bothers you—"

"It doesn't bother me," he insisted. "And you don't

need to be embarrassed, Frank."

Sure, Owain wasn't a natural mind reader, but my hunching must have made a deep mental investigation unnecessary to divine my mood. "If you're certain…"

"I am." He took a bite of his roll and motioned me on. "So you were camping?"

I sent him a quick view of our riverside campsite, complete with cool breeze and whining mosquitoes, and he beamed like I'd presented him with something rare and precious.

By the time the pork loin and most of the chips had disappeared, I'd told Owain about months of excursions and most of my colleagues, and my Bloody Mary was running low.

"Craziest place you've ever been," he said, gesturing my glass back to full and adding more bacon garnish. "Work or otherwise."

I didn't have to think long. "Conota."

"Where?"

"The Gray Lands."

Owain almost dropped his wine stem, but he fumbled and caught it before it could spill over his plate. "What on earth were you doing *there*?"

"Kitty wanted to find her sister over there three years ago, Nath gave her almost no time to search, so I volunteered as transport. Worked out well until I was shot, but you know, we all have bad days," I said, biting my bacon strip in half.

That didn't seem to reassure him. "Who *shot* you?"

"Band of raiders. I took care of them. And really, it was for the best," I continued. "We met Hope that night, she patched me up, we got her out of there, then Nath launched an invasion—"

"I remember that well. Camped outside the castle here for a few days when the king called for volunteers."

"Yeah, I got around during that mess," I said, trying not to think of finding Ione alone and terrified in the Outback. "Anyway, the next summer, I ended up driving Hope and Arik, her childhood sweetheart, halfway across the States in a RV before a predatory swarm could eat the poor guy's brother—"

"I'm sorry, *what?*"

"The cynaeli call them 'Hidden Ones,' and considering how many teeth they had among them, I didn't stop to ask them what they call themselves. Arik's father wanted to get rid of the son who'd moved to this realm—ugly family politics," I explained. "But to wrap this up, Arik's their king now, he and Hope married about a year and a half ago, and I went back to Conota for the wedding. *Strange* place, not somewhere I'd want to explore on my own, but I think that's the craziest trip I've ever taken with a colleague. Well," I amended after a sip of my drink, "as far as pure work trips go, now, there was one time in Colombia when we stumbled onto some heavily armed guards with a cocaine operation, and I ended up eating…"

"Frank?" Owain asked as my voice faded. "Are you ill?"

Slowly, trying not to spill it, I put my drink back on the table as a horrifying certainty fell upon me. "*Fuck,*" I whispered.

"What's wrong?" he demanded.

"I ate one of the guards."

Owain hesitated. "You…"

"In self-defense. The others ran once they saw me, but…"

There's nothing quite like realizing you've engaged in a bit of mild cannibalism to put you off your meal. While the practice was accepted among dragons, the idea hadn't sat well with me, and I'd never gone that far…or I hadn't *thought* I'd gone that far.

My father seemed to know the path down which my mind was racing. "To be fair," he said, "we didn't know about each other until last week, so you couldn't have known that you're somewhat human when you, um…"

"He didn't suffer."

"Did he shoot you, too?"

I shrugged. "He tried, but his aim was shit."

"Then I hope the whoreson was delicious," said Owain, and drained his wine.

Desperate to change the subject before I ruined everything, I said, "Would you tell me about your family?"

I'm sure that he knew exactly what I was doing, but he put the empty glass aside and smiled. "Yours, too, you know. Coffee?"

The brew he produced from the ether was comparable to the best I'd ever had, rich and unburned, and I drank it black while he doctored his. After a moment, and with his coffee now the color of caramel, Owain took a test sip and nodded. "So, the family. Suppose I should start with myself and work back…"

"Please."

"Poor place to begin. I'm not exactly *interesting*," he replied, but humored me. "My mother was fae, my father was an Englishman born of a Welsh mother. I was their only child together, and that was 1547."

I tried not to show my surprise. To an outsider, discerning a faerie's age was little more than a guessing game, as they all stopped aging in their twenties. Owain's eyes gave him away—once they reach their centennial or so, faeries' eyes look subtly wrong for their faces, too old to match the rest of their features. Mundanes don't know what they're seeing, but anyone who's spent time in the magical community can pick out a faerie with a few years on him. I knew Owain had to be older than his seeming age—had he worn sunglasses, he and I could have passed for contemporaries—but I hadn't expected someone with half a millennium under his belt.

"Are they still alive?" I asked.

He shook his head. "Mother died in a stupid fight with

one of her sisters when I was your age. We were never close—she hadn't intended to get pregnant, but she decided to have me anyway, and then she gave me to Father almost immediately."

"In England?"

"Heh. *No*," he said, and sipped his coffee. "Father was Mother's plaything. A prisoner."

"Changeling," I murmured.

"Precisely. He met her a tavern one night, she liked what she saw, and so she knocked him out and took him home with her. Must have been a rough awakening," he added, making a face. "But he made the best of it. Mother wanted a good-looking man in her bed, and Father played his part. The problem—well, *one* of the problems of their arrangement, beyond the whole 'kidnapping changelings' thing—is that Father was restless."

"Not surprising that he wanted to go home," I said.

"More than that. You see, his father was a shipbuilder, and he'd been trained as one as well, but he desperately wanted to be a sailor and go exploring, see the world." Owain paused and regarded me with a knowing expression. "Sound familiar?"

"Perhaps," I replied, pleased at the connection. I *had* come from somewhere. "What was his name?"

He smiled and lifted his cup. "Hugh White, just like his father and grandfather before him. He bucked the trend and named me for his mother's father—"

"Wait, stop," I interrupted. "*White?*"

"Fairly common surname, though I've seldom had cause to use it," he said, his brows knitting. "Something wrong?"

In response, I rose, retrieved my wallet from the counter, and pulled out the identification card that granted me all-hours access to the Archives. Passing it to Owain, I said, "Ros came up with that on the spur of the moment my first day here. I've used it ever since."

He glanced at my card, then laughed aloud as he looked

up at me again. "Frank White. I'll be damned. Of course, she would have known the truth—"

"Not then. That was before she took over from Kura."

"Hmm. Prescient. Well, it was your grandfather's name, and you're entitled to it. I dare say he wouldn't object." Sipping his coffee, Owain continued. "So there Father was, trapped in Faerie at Mother's mercy, but he was clever enough to keep her mildly entertained—he saw how changelings could be punished and gave her no reason to abuse him. She grew bored of him around the time that I was born, and when he offered to take me off her hands, she decided that would be an excellent arrangement. Mother even gave him leave to build a ship, which he did piecemeal and finished when I was seven. We used to spend months together exploring the western sea, mapping the islands and such. I've still got my charts and journals," he added with a wistful smile. "When I was twenty, I moved out of Mother's house and erected my own, and she allowed me to do with Father as I liked—she had no need of him."

"Nice."

"Faeries aren't known for their sentimentality, dear boy. Not the full-blooded sort, at least. Anyway, as I said, Mother was killed about ten years later, and Father and I continued to split our time between my house and his ship."

Owain paused then, and I detected the sudden jolt of sadness that he tried to repress.

"I would have been perfectly happy keeping matters as they were," he said quietly, "but I knew that wasn't what Father wanted. He'd barely seen his homeland, let alone the far shores he'd imagined as a boy. And so, when I was fifty-seven and he was about eighty-five, I secured the queen's permission and brought him home."

That took me aback. "Did you know—"

"That he would age all at once? Absolutely. He was old and gray before I closed the gate. But that's what he wanted, and I had no right to deny him."

"You didn't leave him on his own, did you?" I asked, imagining the sort of fate that would have befallen a penniless old man in early seventeenth-century England.

But Owain smiled sadly. "Of course not. I glamoured myself to make us look more like father and son, then passed myself off as a wealthy merchant, purchased a ship, and hired a crew. My captain was a fortuitous find—he was a lesser blood who suspected me when I paid my tavern bill with unmarked gold coins, but once I explained that I was trying to fulfill my father's wishes, he agreed to retain the services of the right people. Good man, he was. About a month after our arrival in this realm, we set off with a loaded ship, and I told the crew that we were going wherever Father wished. They thought I was mad—I'd spent a fortune on what amounted to a glorified pleasure cruise—but I paid well, and they had no reason to complain."

I laughed to myself. "Must be nice to pull money from thin air."

"Oh, not just money. Useless when you're in the middle of the ocean. No, through some *remarkable* chance, the food stores never ran out, the water barrels never ran dry, fresh fruit and vegetables would turn up in odd places, and we kept finding wine and beer in the hold. Whenever the ship needed minor repairs, it just seemed to fix itself. The captain said the men weren't sure whether I was an angel or a demon, though a few suspected my true nature but kept it quiet."

"Good idea."

"They weren't well-schooled, my crew, but they weren't stupid," said Owain, refilling his coffee. "And that was probably the easiest voyage they ever made. I think we only hit two bad storms the whole time, and we were out for almost three years."

"*Really?*"

"Thirty-five months to circumnavigate, London and

back. Father had the time of his life. He and the captain got on famously, and they taught me to navigate by the stars—you can't do that in Faerie, you know, the sky's too variable."

"Been there, done that," I muttered. "Got lost at sea with Ros when I was Aurie's age."

My father's brow furrowed. "Not for too long, I hope."

"No, no, we found the coast that night. But, uh…do you know someone named Carille?"

He chuckled. "Unfortunately. Why do you…" He stopped, regarded me quizzically, and then laughed aloud when he put the pieces together. "*You?* That was you? The garden party from hell?"

My transformed body insisted that furious blushing was the only appropriate action. "You try flying into fireworks and see what happens."

"I'm not criticizing," he hastily replied. "No, that was the best party I've ever attended at Carille's. *Thank you* for cutting that damn concert short. Every year, I swear—the woman refuses to accept that her songs are atrocious."

"Ros said she wanted my head."

"Well, that *was* an impressive aerial bombardment of shit. I mean, did you see the result? *Everywhere.* I wasn't in the splash zone, but I saw it happen."

My face burned. "Sorry. But, uh…yeah, I know astral navigation isn't possible over there."

"Took me a while to master it, but we certainly had time," he said, following my lead *far* from Carille. "And maps—our captain was a far better mapmaker than I was, but he was kind enough to teach me. We saw so much. Sailed to the Caribbean and turned south, rounded the continent in Tierra del Fuego, and passed into the Pacific. Stumbled onto the Galapagos," he said with a grin. "And I'm almost positive that we saw New Zealand, though I can't prove it, and the captain knew that he couldn't publicize anything we found on our voyage—it would have raised too many questions. But we sailed around the

South Pacific for a time because by then, Father was fading. His body was failing him, and the climate suited, so we remained there until he died in his sleep."

"I'm sorry," I murmured.

"Don't be. He died happy and content, and that's the best any of us can hope for." He drank his coffee and stared into space for a moment, and I didn't have to be a mind reader to know where his thoughts strayed. "We buried him on an uninhabited island, and I decided that I'd seen enough by then, so we struck out for home. We had to go the long way—there was no Suez Canal back then—so we rounded Africa and came up the eastern Atlantic. When we reached port, I gave our crew enough gold to keep them comfortable for a decade, and to the captain's pay, I added the ship itself. With that settled, I took my journals and drawings and returned to Faerie—to a very quiet house," he said, looking at his plate, "but it was home. I've been back to this realm since, on occasion, but that was my only long residence here."

"I suppose all of your family is in Faerie these days, anyway," I replied.

He shrugged. "What's left of them. I have a few half siblings through my mother, but they're full-blooded, and we're not close."

"Cousins?"

"Fewer than you might think. By the time you were born, only two of my mother's siblings remained, and Oberon murdered many of my cousins."

"Ober—" I began, then froze. The former king's final invasion of Faerie had predated me by a couple decades, but even I knew which faeries he'd targeted for execution.

Owain glanced up, saw my expression, and faintly smiled. "I was at sea the whole time. Took Father's ship out a few days before Oberon arrived, and by the time I returned to shore, my little uncle was regent. Poor Aiden."

"*You're...*"

"One of Titania's grandsons," he offered. "Certainly

not the most infamous of the lot."

I realized I was gawking but couldn't help myself. "You're a *lord*."

"Not a high one. Sorry," he said, laughing weakly.

I barely heard him as my mind whirled. Owain was one of Coileán's nephews, which meant...

I was of the blood? Descended from one of the original Three? *Me*?

So was Ros, albeit distantly—she was Titania and Oberon's fourth great-granddaughter, if I had the generations straight. In that case...

"Ros is my *cousin*," I mumbled, trying to envision the family tree.

"Not directly," said Owain, "but yes, we're kin."

"Second cousins, three times removed. I think. Holy *shit*," I whispered, then quickly pushed back from the table and grabbed my phone.

"Going somewhere?" Owain asked, putting his cup aside.

"Just a minute," I replied, and called Sam. As soon as he answered, I said, "I need to see her. Is she around?"

Sam had barely answered in the affirmative when a fresh gate opened by the couch, revealing Ros on the border with a nervous little smile on her face. Hurrying across the flat to meet her, I said, "You knew!"

Ros wasn't omniscient in the mortal realm, but I was broadcasting by that point. "I thought one shock at a time would be easier," she said as her face relaxed. "Yeah, bud, we're cousins. If you had any talent whatsoever, you'd have decent claim to a title—"

"Come again?"

"Look at Dad—he's only one-sixteenth fae. You're a full quarter."

I didn't recognize the stone-walled room in which Ros was standing—nothing unusual there, as I'd barely been inside of any buildings in Faerie—but I immediately knew Coileán's voice when he asked, "Would someone like to tell me what the hell is going on?" He appeared beside Ros a few seconds later, and I reasoned that she'd manifested in his office. The king seemed surprised to find me standing on the other side of the gate, and even more so when he noticed Owain behind me. "Okay, I'll bite," he said, turning to Ros. "Explain."

"Georgie had a mixed clutch," she replied. "Owain is Frank's father."

Several expressions crossed Coileán's face in rapid succession—confusion, disbelief, unease, pensiveness—and I hastened to reassure him before he could decide this was an untenable situation. "I won't breathe a word about this. No one else will know, I won't do anything to embarrass—"

"*Frank*," he interrupted, and crossed through the gate. I tried to backpedal, but he reached me before I could navigate around the couch and gripped my arm. "Most of my relatives are assholes on a good day. You're at least a few steps up from that. Welcome to the family."

All I could do for a moment was blink stupidly at him, but I managed, "Seriously? You're not upset?"

"I've known you since you were, like, this big," he said, holding his hand at his waist. "No, I'm not upset. Surprised, maybe a little disturbed—"

"Kura transformed Georgie," Ros offered. "Owain had no clue who she was. And remind me, how many times have you hooked up with a merrow?"

Coileán turned back to the gate, huffing in frustration. I couldn't see his face, but Ros's smirk spoke volumes.

"Enough said," he muttered, looking up at me again. "Relax, Frank, no one's going to blast you. But do remember that Toula prefers to be kept apprised of random faerie visits to this secure installation, eh?" he added, and pointedly cut his eyes to Owain.

"I swear, Uncle," said Owain, "I haven't left this flat—"

"And see that you don't without her permission,"

Coileán replied. "Speaking of permission, I don't recall you clearing this visit with me."

"I approved," said Ros as Owain stuttered. "Frank wants to spend time with his dad. You going to fight me on this?"

"No," he said testily, "but we limit trips out of the realm for a reason."

"Granted, but we're talking about *Owain*. What's he going to do, buy a few more books? Shop for a new garlic press? Owain's not the problem."

"I understand that, but if we make too many exceptions—"

"You didn't. I did. End of discussion."

Coileán sighed. "This would all be so much simpler if Frank could come over—"

"Right," I interjected, chuckling, "because Toula would *love* getting a call every time I visited. The woman has better things to do than put my bind back together."

Owain lifted a finger. "I could probably do *something* close—"

"Not as well as Toula does," said Ros. "She's got Frank's down to a science."

Coileán folded his arms, considering me, then glanced at Ros. "I don't suppose there's anything you could do for him that would let him make his own."

To my surprise, Ros hesitated.

"*Is* there?" Coileán pressed. "Could you sufficiently amplify?"

"I…" She winced. "Maybe?"

Love her though I did, I couldn't hide my frustration. "You couldn't have mentioned this years ago?" I demanded. "I've been tiptoeing around magical fields all this time to prevent accidental breakage, and—"

"I don't know what I can do," she said, cutting me short. "What Kura did with Dad and Aiden, and what I've done with Maria, Kitty, Marcus, and Artur…I mean, Faerie has had time to figure out the mechanics. You present a whole different set of variables, and Kura meddled so much just to get you *born*, and I can't say exactly what the outcome would be if I poked around in turn. I do know that it would be excruciating for you, whatever I did," she continued, "and the last thing I want to do is hurt you…"

While she made no effort to disguise her concern, the potential was too great for me to let it go. "Most likely outcome?"

Ros's mouth tightened. "*If* it worked the way I think it would—and keep in mind that this is hypothetical—I think I could get you to the point of autonomous shifting. Set that body as a second default for you and give you the ability to flip between them."

"Like Mal?"

"More or less. Maybe even a touch of talent, but you're not going to come out of this as the greatest enchanter the world has ever known."

"I'm not worried about that," I told her. "But being able to shift at will would come in handy."

"Sure," she muttered, "*if* it works. There's always the possibility of something going wrong."

"How so?" asked Owain.

Ros kept her eyes on me. "I did my best to save all three of your children, and you saw how that turned out. You are…unique, Frank, for better or worse. If you want this, I'll try, but just know that it scares me to death."

She looked like she needed a hug, but stuck as we were on opposite sides of the gate, I couldn't help her.

"If you're willing," I said, "then yes, I want to try, but I need to talk to Aurie first. Late this week?"

"Whenever you're ready, bud." Turning to Coileán, she said, "We're interrupting. Why don't you make this easy and give Owain a blanket pass to visit Frank, hmm? *You* certainly spend enough time over there."

She didn't specify that he regularly sneaked off to be with Toula, but the threat in the omission was clear to anyone with sense. Coileán and Toula didn't need word of their scandalous relationship spreading further than it already had, and Ros damn well knew it.

Faced with an argument he wasn't going to win, Coileán conceded with a roll of his eyes. "Fine. Owain...don't make me regret this, eh?" he said, and marched back into his office.

"Thanks," I whispered once Coileán was out of earshot.

Ros nodded, but she didn't smile. "Call Sam when you want me," she said, and sealed the hole between us.

Owain repeatedly offered to go home after lunch, insisting that he didn't want to butt in where Aurie was concerned until I thought the time was right. "You're her father, and I'm the interloper," he said after cleaning up the scant leavings. "I want to meet her, Frank, but this is your decision. You can tell her what you're planning to do without me here."

"I don't want to dangle that in front of her," I replied, putting on more coffee. His was spectacular, but my nervous energy demanded an outlet. "Promise me something."

"What's that?"

I pried open the cannister and began measuring out grounds, trusting that he could weaken my extra-strong brew if he so desired. "You won't try to kill her."

"Of course I won't try to kill her!" he protested—and to my relief, he sounded aghast at the notion. "Moon and stars, she's my granddaughter. Look, I know that faeries can be terrible parents, but most of the time, it's the full-blooded ones you've got to watch."

Owain stood silently in the kitchen, waiting for me to respond, but I said nothing until I'd started the coffeemaker. "What did Ros tell you about why we're living here?" I asked, avoiding his gaze.

"Not much, just that you enjoyed your work. She didn't

mention Aurie at all, remember?"

I held on to the lip of the counter, grateful for the anchor. "Aurie's mother died halfway through incubation. I took over, and my siblings wondered why I wouldn't let them get rid of the eggs. Then two of the eggs died. Our sons. Given my particular makeup and Ione's genetic issues, Ros could only save Aurie, and she was born with multiple problems."

"I'm so sorry," Owain murmured.

"She's doing better now. Cardiac issues have resolved, and her bind fixed her left arm—it's missing from the elbow down. And in this form, it doesn't matter that her wings are entirely absent. Nothing to be done about that. But…"—I paused, pushing down my anger at the memory of that night—"when she came out without two and a half limbs, it was strongly suggested that we kill her and be done with it. I begged Mom to intervene, and she told me to take Aurie away. That was a year ago, and I haven't spoken to any of them since." To my frustration, my throat was tightening almost to the point of uselessness. *It would be nice for her to have family who didn't want her dead.*

Tense as I was, I almost jumped when Owain's hand landed on my back. "Please believe me," he said softly. "I won't hurt her. You have my word, son."

And so, worried though I was, I found myself sitting in the den with Owain and my long-cold coffee when Aurie let herself in. "Dad?" she began, scanning the flat for me, then saw my companion and paused. "Uh…hi?"

"Go put your things down," I told her, and Aurie hurried off to her room. *She's a little shy around new people,* I warned Owain. *It's probably a phase.*

"It's fine," he whispered. "She's adorable."

Before I could remind him that he was seeing a transformation bind, Aurie returned, glasses off and blue dragon in her arms. The toy was the closest thing she'd ever had to a security blanket, and the stuffing leaking from the rip in one leg served as a testament to how often she sought it out. She skulked on the edge of the room, looking to me for a cue, and scuffed the toe of one pink tennis shoe against the floor.

I coughed, hoped I wasn't about to make a terrible mistake, and said, "Aurie, remember last week when you asked me about my dad?"

She nodded, hugging her toy.

"Well, uh…this is your grandfather."

Her eyes lit up. "*Really?*"

"Hello, sweetheart," said Owain, and I glanced back in time to catch him smiling at her.

Aurie took a tentative step closer, examining him. "You've got a bind, too?"

"Not exactly," I said. "Owain is one of Coileán's nephews."

Her eyebrows furrowed as she contemplated that. "Hang on. So…"

"You and I are a little different, and I'll explain everything after dinner, but Owain couldn't wait to meet you…"

I felt her confusion and concern, but overriding both was her curiosity about the stranger in our midst. As she inched closer, Owain said, "Who's your friend, there?"

She tightened her grip on her dragon. "This is Blue."

"Well, that's certainly an appropriate name," he replied. "May I see?"

As I silently reassured her, she took a seat on the coffee table and handed Owain the toy. "Very nice," he said, turning it over in his hands. "But it looks like he's hurt, doesn't it? May I fix him?" When Aurie nodded, he flicked one finger over the rip, which neatly sewed itself up. Passing the patient back to Aurie, he said, "There, that's better. Give him a try."

She squeezed her dragon, and a genuine smile crossed her face. "Want to see the rest of my toys?"

"I'd be delighted," he replied, and followed her back to her room.

AUGUST 8: FRANK

Having only had one boss in the course of my career, I had no one against whom to compare Ted, but something told me that he was one of the good ones. Ted loved our work, but more than that, he had never shown anything less than love for his people. Short, chubby, just north of seventy, and a wizard of merely middling ability, he would nonetheless fight anyone who threatened the Team—sort of like an overly friendly pug who channeled his inner rottweiler whenever the times demanded it. If you were on the Team, or even associated with it, then as far as Ted was concerned, you were his responsibility.

When I sent him a message asking for a private breakfast meeting a few hours after Owain finally coaxed Aurie into bed, he agreed without hesitation, and he grinned as I met him in his office. Seldom one to miss meals, Ted had dashed through the dining hall while I saw Aurie off to school, and his desk was covered with takeaway boxes: doughnuts, a few hard-boiled eggs, and a thick pile of bacon that he knew better than to touch once I started on it.

"What's up?" he said as I closed the door and sank into one of his guest chairs. "No one's pregnant, are they?"

A fair question. The last time I'd asked Ted for such a meeting, I'd broken the news about Ione's clutch.

"No," I replied, "but I do have a family issue."

His brow creased. "Is Aurie—"

"Perfectly healthy," I assured him before he could worry. "Uncle Ted" took his role seriously. "But, uh…I'm going to need a little time off."

"Sure, whatever you like. Can I be nosy, or do I need to butt out?"

"Will you keep this quiet for now?"

Ted spread his hands and picked up a doughnut. "Mum's the word. Hit me."

Five minutes later, once I'd finished filling him in on the unexpected side of my family tree and my plans with Ros, the pastry remained untouched in his fingers. "Holy hell," he murmured, then put the doughnut atop a notepad. "Are you okay, Frank?"

"Surprisingly…yes," I replied, reaching for the bacon box. "It's nice to have an answer as to why I'm so screwed up."

He snorted at that. "You're not screwed up—"

"I am, objectively speaking, a *terrible* dragon."

"Then we'll claim you, and gladly." He popped open his breakfast Coke and swigged. "Allow me to extend a formal welcome to the human race, even if it's only a quarter of you we're talking about."

"Definitely not the quarter that gave me my looks," I joked.

"Looks are overrated," he replied, slapping his belly. The palm trees on his shirt, one of his dozens of Hawaiian-inspired numbers, jiggled with the impact. "And I don't give a damn *what* you are, Frank. You're one of the best guys I know, it's an honor to call you a friend and a colleague, and you take whatever time you need."

"Thank you," I murmured, touched by the sentiment. Ted was seldom one to bottle up his feelings. "I should only need a day or two, assuming everything goes according to plan."

"And if it doesn't, we'll make arrangements, eh? Now," he said, remembering his abandoned doughnut, "who's watching Aurie while you're away?"

Though Ted was always willing and had kept an eye on Aurie a few times while I took a night off, my daughter's go-to home away from home was the Copelands' flat...which meant that I needed to tell Antony what was going on, too.

In truth, I didn't mind filling him in. Antony was Ros's age—they and Bee had been classmates once, back in Montana—and he and I had been the first two recruited to the Team. I was there for his wedding to Madison, and I'd watched their daughter, Allie, grow from a rambunctious little hellion with a Nerf gun into an almost responsible teenager. When I brought Aurie home, the Copelands had jumped in with tips, techniques, an assortment of tiny outfits that she quickly outgrew, and an open offer of babysitting. I tried not to abuse their kindness, but they never complained about watching my daughter when I was in the field—Allie found little children fascinating, and as Aurie quickly matured, Allie came up with new games for them to play.

But more importantly, I knew that if something happened to me, my daughter would have a home.

That morning, after I left Ted, I found Madison in her library office and asked if I could speak to her and Antony—who, unlike his wife, had a tendency to stroll into the subbasement long after the morning rush subsided. She insisted on calling home and ordering him to meet her at work, and because crossing Madison seldom turned out in Antony's favor, he soon joined us. Quietly, I gave them a pared-down version of what I'd told Ted and asked if they wouldn't mind watching Aurie for a night or two. "I know it's on short notice," I concluded, "and if you're busy, I'll certainly make other arrangements—"

"Of course we'll keep her," Antony interrupted, "but let's not overlook the bigger issue: are you okay?"

"I think so," I told him, and though I meant it, I was grateful that he and Ted had asked. "Excited, maybe a little nervous—"

"I'd have your head examined if you *weren't* nervous," said Madison, tapping her pencil against her leather blotter. "Ros is powerful, I'll grant her that"—Antony vehemently nodded—"but this must be uncharted territory for her, too."

"She kept Maria alive," I countered.

"Maria's heart stopped half a dozen times. She gave me the details one night when we had everyone over to watch football. Said it hurt like hell when she wasn't on the wrong side of death." When I hesitated, she pressed her point. "I'm not saying this is a terrible idea, Frank, and I'm sure you would prefer to have control over your own body—I really can't imagine living like you have," she admitted. "But are you rushing into this to…what, to impress someone you've just met?"

Madison meant well, and what she was saying made sense, but I shook my head. "This isn't about Owain, it's about me. And yeah, it would be nice to have power over myself instead of depending upon Toula to sneak me back in the building."

"Whatever makes you happy," said Antony. "You know we're here for you, right?"

"And honestly," Madison added, "you needn't bother asking us to take Aurie. Pack the little dear's bag and drop her on the mat, and we'll handle it from there."

Her husband rolled his eyes. "You just want liver and onions."

"The *only* time anyone eats it with me is when she sleeps over!"

"That's a sad ulterior motive, Madison," I replied. "But thank you." Pausing, I looked them both in the eye. "For everything."

Neither of us slept well that night. I tossed and turned, thinking through all the ways that Ros's attempt could end in catastrophe, while Aurie grunted and flopped around in her sleep, sending toys cascading to the floor. Around two the next morning, I gave up and rose to make coffee, intending to be marginally productive before my absence. The brew cycle was popping to its conclusion when the floor creaked, and I looked around the kitchen wall to find my daughter in her nightgown, clutching Blue and watching me with wide, worried eyes.

Some moments don't require words. I lifted her and held her against my shoulder as always, and she wrapped her little arms around my neck. I silently spoke to her of safety and love, telling her more without the confines of speech than I could ever verbalize, but she whimpered as she clung to me.

I knew her fear too well. The hatchling bond was virtually unbreakable, and I remembered my distress at that age whenever Ros left me. But Aurie had handled separation well to that point—this was something new and deeper. Uncle Ted would never hurt me, but she didn't trust Ros on this count.

Trying not to accidentally convey to her my own trepidation with an errant thought, I murmured, "Ros has the strongest talent I've ever seen. She won't mess this up."

What if she does? What if you don't come home?

"I will come home," I promised, unwilling to consider the alternative.

Dawn found me on the couch, stroking Aurie's head as she slept in my lap. She'd grown too large to fit well, but she did her best. Though my legs had fallen asleep, I didn't want to wake her, but before long, it was time for her to dress for school. I pried her off the couch, sent her to the shower, and fried up several packs of bacon to tempt her appetite, but she picked at her food and kept her eyes locked on me as I moved between the stove and the table.

"Can I go with you?" she blurted as I sat beside her.

"Not this time, hatchling," I said, rubbing her back. "And you're going to have so much fun with Allie tonight..."

But Aurie's eyes filled as I spoke, and her lip began to tremble. The thought I received from her was a blast of panic, the fear that she would never see me again, and it took all of my practice-honed skill to keep my similar concerns hidden from her.

As neither of us had any appetite, breakfast went to waste, and it pained me to see the dark circles under my daughter's eyes before she put her glasses on to leave. But before she could collect her books, a knock drew me to the door, and I opened it to find Antony on the other side. "Is something wrong?" I asked, fearing the worst—after all, several of the wizards on the Team were far from young.

"Not at all," said Antony with a smile, then leaned past me to wave at Aurie. "Hiya, kiddo. Would you be interested in blowing off school today and going to the movies with me?"

Aurie perked at the offer, but she looked to me for permission.

"I think that would be a great idea," I said, mentally conveying my thanks to Antony, who acknowledged the thought with a quick nod. "Is anything good playing?"

"Oh, definitely. Your pick," he told Aurie. "And maybe pizza for lunch afterward—would that be okay?"

My daughter wasn't stupid, and she knew as well as I did that Antony was trying to distract her, but she was young enough to go along with the program. While she was still excited about the free day, I gathered her overnight bag and slipped it onto her shoulders. Her distress returned when I knelt to hug her, but Antony came in with the assist. "You listen to me, baby," he said, raising Aurie's chin with his finger. "Your dad's tough, and he's going to be just fine. Don't you worry."

As Antony led her out, I said, "I'll phone her tutors—"

"Already taken care of it," he said, and reached up to squeeze my shoulder. "You worry about you today, big guy. We've got her."

Antony was no mind reader, but I could see in his thoughts the message he was trying to convey without letting Aurie know: *If this goes wrong, we'll take care of her.*

"Thank you," I whispered, and closed the door before I could reconsider.

With an hour until the appointed time, I made my final preparations: seeing that the appliances were turned off, packing a small bag, and changing into a bathrobe. Though I'd never been as prudish as my colleagues, the necessity of disrobing before transformation left me feeling awkward and quite literally exposed. Clothing, as annoying as it could be, had become a normal part of my life, and it was never pleasant to be the only naked one in the room—until, of course, I was unbound, at which point drawing comparisons seemed silly.

I'd almost reached the point of nervous pacing when my phone rang. "Ready when you are," said Sam. "But I was told to tell you there's no rush, and if you want to think about this—"

"I'm ready."

Seconds later, a gate opened—not onto the familiar meadow around the family barn, as I'd feared, but rather onto an expansive, manicured lawn before a stately, turreted stone manor house. I leaned from side to side, trying to take in the ornamental gardens and mature trees beyond the edge of the gate without crossing.

"I thought you might be more comfortable somewhere away from the barn," said Ros as she manifested. She seemed tense, her shoulders a little too tight. "No need to drag Georgie and the others into this right now."

"You haven't told Mom?" I asked.

"I won't until you want me to."

"Not yet. Is Sam—"

"Back at our house." Glancing over her shoulder at the figure hurrying toward us across the lawn, she explained, "I brought you to Owain's place. You're going to need somewhere to recuperate, and he's more than willing to have you."

I considered once again the mansion on the other side of the grass. "Huge for one person."

"This is Faerie, bud. You know we don't do things by halves around here."

She stepped aside as Owain jogged the last stretch, and he panted as he greeted us. "Sorry…bread was burning…"

"Believe me, I'm in no hurry," said Ros, but when I didn't suggest putting this off, she sighed and nodded curtly. "Okay. Come on through, and I'll do my best. Bag?"

I tossed my gear through the gate, and she caught it and put it aside. Ros moved beyond the edge of the gate, giving me a touch of privacy, but Owain remained standing in front of me, an eager smile on his face. "Want a hand?" he asked, reaching toward the rift between realms.

"Appreciated, but that's not a good idea," I replied, unknotting my bathrobe belt.

His brow furrowed. "Why are you, uh…"

"Undressing? Because as soon as this bind breaks, anything I'm wearing will become confetti." I ran through my checklist once more—my phone and glasses were in the bag, I'd brought a toothbrush, the coffeemaker was unplugged—then held the robe closed and cleared my throat. "You'll want to stand back."

"*Way* back," Ros cautioned. "Get behind the gate for protection. There's about to be a lot more of Frank, and I don't need casualties today."

Once Owain had slid out of my sight, I tossed the robe onto the couch and steeled my nerve. Crossing didn't hurt—on the contrary, the moment of unbinding felt glorious, like being cut free of a full-body corset—but what followed wouldn't be pleasant, to say the least. I could back out, Ros wouldn't mind…

No.

All my life, I'd been a misfit. While I'd found a home as one of Ted's square pegs, I'd always been haunted by the *why*s. Why wasn't I like my brothers? Why couldn't I be happy with my family? Why did none of them ever quite seem to understand me?

Now I knew. Taking this next step—embracing the potential I'd never expected to find—was a much-needed move toward self-actualization. I wasn't just a runt playing dress-up in semi-human guise—this *was* me. My interests, my thoughts, my *feelings* were explainable.

And I'd take whatever Ros could offer.

"Incoming," I called, then took a running leap at the gate.

The bind fell apart in a rippling wave as I dove like a baseball player stealing home. I braced for impact as my arms—now my front legs—hit the grass and skidded, my claws digging in to stop me from plowing longer divots in Owain's lovely lawn. My neglected wings unfurled like twin drag chutes, and as I came to a halt, I stretched my neck and tail, reveling in the sensations of being in my own skin. When I looked back toward the gate, Ros suddenly seemed tiny—a familiar perspective, as I'd outgrown her long before my first birthday. Hell, I'd been large and strong enough to carry her at a month old. She didn't bat an eye at my transformation.

But Owain...

Shit.

As Ros closed the gate, he stood stock-still and stared up at me, mouth agape and eyes huge in his face. Kicking myself for letting my bind break around him—seeing all of me had to be too much, *far* too soon—I moved deliberately, trying not to spook him, and stretched out in the grass. Sure, my head was taller than he was, but as long as I kept my mouth closed and my teeth hidden...well, maybe he wouldn't run.

I'm sorry, I began, *I know it's a lot*—

That was as far as I made it before his paralysis broke.

His slack-jawed expression shifted toward a disturbingly Ted-like grin, excited and perhaps more than a touch on the manic side. "Oh," he said, taking me in, "you're *beautiful*."

Could have been worse, I decided, and lay still as he edged closer.

Ever so slowly, he reached up and touched the side of my face, the light pressure of his fingertips barely noticeable as he slid them along my scales—in the *correct* direction, thank goodness. *I'm not going to bite*, I joked. *And I had breakfast this morning, so you're safe for at least an hour or two.*

"Incredible," Owain whispered.

You've never seen a dragon up close, have you? I'm not impressive.

"Could have fooled me. Moon and stars, you were tall before, but—"

"Guys," Ros interrupted, "I hate to break this up, but unless someone was planning on hunting down a flock of sheep for lunch, I need to get to work."

I could feel Owain's reluctance as he moved away. He was curious, yes, but his strong undercurrent of trepidation surprised me.

It was a nice change of pace, I decided, to have a parent who gave a damn.

With Owain out of range, Ros approached and folded her arms. "We don't have to do this, bud. There's no shame in waiting."

I know.

"Once I start, that's it. We're in it for the duration."

Understood, I replied, trying to ignore the anxiety radiating from her.

"And I can make no guarantees. I have theories and probabilities in mind, but I won't know exactly what I can do until I dig in."

That's fine.

She hugged herself more tightly. "I love you, Frank. I don't want to hurt you."

Mere words proved insufficient in that moment. I spoke to her without the encumbrance—desire, acknowledgement of risk, forgiveness, love.

Finally, unhappy but resigned, she took a step back, dropped her arms to her sides, and closed her eyes. Unnecessary, I thought, given that Ros's physical form was only a temporary construct, but I supposed that old habits endured even after the flesh had become optional.

"Last chance," she murmured.

I'm ready.

"Okay, then. Brace yourself."

I was expecting pain—everyone I knew who'd undergone work at the realm's hands reported that it was a miserable experience, the sort not to be wished upon one's worst enemy—but I had no clear frame of reference. The closest I'd come to witnessing it had been when Kitty grabbed Artur's enchanted sword and accidentally started the process the slow way. She'd screamed and collapsed, but I'd seen nothing further once Marcus hustled her into Faerie. Surely Kitty had been in the middle of the pack for complicated work, a witch-blood in need of suppression and amplification, a case slightly more complex than Aiden years before. Artur and Marcus must have been easier—as quarter-bloods, they required only amplification to bring them fully into their power. Even Joey, who'd started with a much lower percentage of fae blood, had been back on his feet within minutes. Kitty had needed recovery time because of the damage the sword inflicted, and Maria...well, she was hardly a fair comparison, a wizard but for the teensiest strand of fae genes, suppressed and amplified beyond reason while covered in burns and sporting a hole in her chest. But if Maria could pull through under those conditions, then I reasoned that I could endure whatever Ros threw at me.

All of my careful rationalization went out the window as soon as Ros's power hit. Pain the likes of which I'd never known flared from deep within me, converting every cell into a tiny, brilliant point of light in a galaxy of agony. Somewhere in the distance, I heard a roar, but I could only focus on it long enough to recognize it as my own before the pain pulled me back into my personal hell. This was a mistake, a *stupid* mistake, I was on fire, combusting, exploding...

My last thought before the welcome blackness took me was of Aurie. If I didn't make it home to her...

Stupid Runt. Always stupid Runt.

The next sensation I felt was thirst—hike-twelve-hours-in-the-desert thirst, a thirst strong enough to rouse me from sleep. I couldn't force my eyes open, but that didn't particularly bother me; the warmth on my face suggested sunlight in the room, and something told me that it would *hurt* when it reached my eyes.

Where the hell was I? And in what form?

Slowly, I worked the tip of my tongue out of my mouth, though even that little movement pained me. The air smelled like Faerie—a strong scent of magic, coupled with the absence of dark magic—but more than that, the nerves around my mouth suggested that my tongue was relatively broad. Retracting it, I carefully ran it along the edge of my top teeth.

Flat. Human form again, then. Okay, I could work with this body.

If I wasn't mistaken, I was curled up on my right side. Wiggling my head ever so slightly, I thought I detected the give of a pillow, but I couldn't bear to press down harder and be sure. My front-right limb—arm, leg, whatever it currently was—lay atop the presumed mattress, and I rubbed my index finger against it, detecting the texture of a smooth sheet. Yes, a bed.

Just to be certain, I bent that finger until it made contact with the adjacent digit. Apparently, I had thumbs again. They came standard with the transformation bind, but I had no idea what Ros had worked out...nor did I want to investigate, as even shifting my hand against the sheet sent flares of pain up my arm. Breathing felt like being stabbed, and I began to wonder if something had gone horribly wrong.

But I was still so thirsty, and as I saw it, I had two choices: either remain motionless in the fetal position until I died of dehydration or rip off the metaphorical band-aid and get out of bed. Surely I could manage to stand, I told myself. I was a decently strong guy unless my brothers ganged up on me. And no matter how bad I felt at the moment, the hurt was less than it had been before I lost consciousness.

I could do this.

Counting down from five, I started to reach for the edge of the sheet, then stopped short with a yelp of pain. Trying not to cry out, I moved more slowly, edging my hand along, but I gave up the exercise when my arm worsened to feeling like it was on fire.

As I lay there whimpering, I heard footsteps, then smelled Owain's woodsy cologne. A shadow descended between my eyes and the sunlight, and when my mind reached into the void, it bumped against his. Scared and aching, I forgot caution and the prudent voice that warned me to go slowly with him.

Dad?

"I'm here," he said, relief coloring his thoughts. "Thank heavens. I didn't know how long you were going to be out."

I wish I were still unconscious. Everything hurts.

A moment later, the fire in my arm began to cool, then died. The rise and fall of my chest was no longer quite so horrible, and when I groaned and pried my gummy eyes open with two fingers, I found my father watching with concern.

"Is that better?" he asked. "I can add another layer to the enchantment..."

No, I thought, grateful for the relief of the numbing construction. *That's good.* I hesitated, then asked, *Am I...okay?*

"You will be. Any interest in dinner? Lady Roslyn said you should eat."

Dinner?

"You slept all day—it's nearly sunset. Come on, let me help you."

He pulled me up until I could sit on the edge of the bed, then guided my arm around his neck and took my weight as I wobbled to my feet. "Easy, there," he soothed as I tried to find my balance with the world spinning. "Little steps. We'll take the shortcut," he added, and opened a gate into a massive dining room.

Soon, I was slumped in a chair, staring out the wide windows at an ornamental pond behind the house. I thought I saw a pale deer drinking on the far side in the twilight until it raised its head and bounded away.

Unicorn. Sure.

Around that time, I noticed that I was wearing navy silk pajamas. They weren't mine, and I had no idea where they'd come from, how they'd appeared on me, or why I was back in condensed form. I still hurt, even with the numbing enchantment, but the goblet of water I'd drained upon sitting had helped my overall situation...whatever it was.

Before I could risk rising to find more to drink, my father returned with a meal best described as "carnivore's delight": a roast pig, apple and all, a pair of golden-brown chickens, a rack of lamb, a beef tenderloin topped with a horseradish sauce, and even a whole fish, gutted and ready to be devoured. He positioned the platters within my reach, refilled my glass, and took a seat across the table. "Hope something there tempts your appetite," he said, waiting for me to serve myself.

If I weren't so thirsty, I'd be salivating, I replied, and sampled a hearty portion of everything.

While I ate, my goblet continued to refill, and the aches in my empty stomach and dry throat faded. As I turned my attention to a bowl of meatballs I'd overlooked on the first pass, I asked, *What happened out there?*

"I…honestly, I'm not certain," he replied, lowering his fish-laden fork. "You were fine one minute, and then you started convulsing…it sounded like you were in terrible pain."

Agony.

He met my stare and held it. "Poor boy. I didn't know what to do, and Lady Roslyn kept telling me to stay away…"

Probably for the best.

"You say that, but you weren't the one listening to your child scream."

I'm sure I wasn't screaming—

"Close enough. Shortly after you passed out, she switched you back into that form and clothed you"—one mystery solved, I noted—"and said we needed to put you to bed. You were shaking—chilling, I think. I kept piling blankets on until the sweating began, and…well." He shrugged. "She left me, and I did the best I could, but if she'd *mentioned* the fact that you'd need numbing, I'd have worked that up before you awoke."

She may not have known, I replied, and considered the fingers of my empty left hand. *So…is this a bind?*

"Nope."

We turned at the sound of Ros's voice and found her standing near the door. "Hey, bud," she said with a weak smile. "I'm sorry, you're still pretty miserable right now, aren't you?"

Given Ros's quasi-omniscience within the realm, we both knew the question was rhetorical. *Feeling better.*

"The pain should be manageable by morning. You slept through the worst of it." She moved closer and pulled out the chair beside me, then plopped down with a sigh. "Not as bad as Maria—I don't think *any* augmentation will ever be that gnarly—but you were a challenge, and I did some serious tampering. Let Owain feed you, then get back to bed. There's no point in sitting up just to be miserable."

What did you do?

"First, do me a favor and verbalize, will you? Let me check."

I took a sip of water and obliged, though my throat protested. "Telepathy has fewer moving parts, you realize."

"I do, and you sound normal to me, so...yay." She mimed wiping her brow and sat back in her seat. "I was correct about the limitations of what I could do, but I think I've got you functional. The good news is that you're shifter-adjacent now—I flipped you to get you in the house, but it's under your control. No more binds."

"If you want to test that," my father interjected, "I'll help you outside—"

"Yeah, don't ruin the plaster," said Ros, glancing at the chandeliers above us. "But you can test it without going all the way."

How so?

She grinned. "A true shifter has two forms, you know, and they're either one or the other at all times. *You*, however, now have a continuum to play with. Just think about what you want to happen."

Hesitantly, I considered my empty hand, hoping I wouldn't overdo it and accidentally break the house. As I watched, opalescent scales began to form up each finger and down my wrist, and my filed-down nails sharpened into claws. The thumb didn't move out of position, and Ros chuckled at my surprise. "Like I said, a continuum," she explained as I marveled at the result. "You want to go into a swordfight with a backup bare-handed disemboweling option, that's your call."

A moment's concentration made my claws retract and scales vanish. "You're *good*."

"Thank you, but you haven't played with the best part

yet. Take off your shirt."

I cocked an eyebrow. "Why?"

"Humor me, Frank."

Though still a little wobbly, I stood, unbuttoned the nightshirt, and gave myself a quick inspection. "Looks normal."

"Been hitting the gym, I see."

"*Ros.*"

"What, I can't appreciate a nice set of abs? Well done. Those would make a grown man weep."

I cut my eyes across the table, but my father's only response with a sheepish nod.

"Anyway," said Ros, "here's the fun bit: that continuum I mentioned does include wings."

"While I'm like *this*?"

"Your body will adjust. Give it a shot."

Having discovered the trick to flight at a month old, I'd sorely missed my wings—flying dreams had peppered my sleep for years. Focusing on the memory of my absent limbs, I suddenly felt my shoulders make a painless shift, and a weight both familiar and foreign settled along my back. I glanced to the side, saw a scaled-down version of one wing stretch toward the buffet table, and did absolutely nothing to hide my surprise and pleasure.

"He doesn't always smile when he's truly happy," I heard Ros murmur to my father. "That's a learned gesture. You'll hear the thought instead."

"Can I actually fly with these?" I asked her.

"No reason why you shouldn't be able to—*ah*! Sit!" she snapped as I started for the door. "Damn it, bud, you're convalescing!"

The door slammed, but that didn't deter me. Ignoring my continual ache, I crouched, then leapt for the ceiling. Muscle memory broke my fall before I could descend, and with a few rapid flaps, I was airborne and making steady loops around the room.

"You're going to make it hurt worse," Ros protested,

glaring up at me with her arms akimbo.

I beat my wings furiously to hover, pleased to find the exercise easier than it was in my original form—my wing-to-body ratio had increased. *As if you wouldn't do the same.*

But she continued to watch with disapproval, and I made a two-point landing that almost became a four-pointer when my weak knees buckled. "Play all you want tomorrow," she chided as she caught me. "You need to rest tonight. And you haven't let me finish."

I grunted as she helped me back into my chair. *There's more?*

"The metal allergy?" my father asked.

"Nah," said Ros. "Iron and silver shouldn't be a problem because I couldn't give you enough power. You were patched together to begin with, and there's only so much I can do to work with those components—"

Wait. Power?

She shrugged. "Just a touch, unfortunately. That's the bad news. You'll never be able to manage much in the way of enchantment, but—

You're telling me I can enchant? I interrupted, gobsmacked.

For Ros, who had grown up with exceptional talent and acquired power beyond imagining, it must have seemed a little pathetic that I was excited about the bare rudiments, but she laughed at my shock. "Many lesser bloods can manage a bit, and whatever else you are, you're a quarter fae." She stole a meatball and popped it in her mouth, then offered the cook a thumbs-up. "Finish eating and go back to bed," she told me, but she paused as she started to leave. "Oh, and Frank?"

Yes?

"I hope you don't mind being stuck looking about twenty-five for a long, *long* time to come." She grinned as I caught her meaning. "I couldn't do much for you regarding talent, but immortality was surprisingly easy to manage. Just try not to get your head lopped off out there," she added, and vanished.

I wasn't tired—my mind whirled with the potential ramifications of what Ros had wrought—but my body ache worsened until I slid into the guest bed again. My father fussed over the numbing enchantment as I made myself relatively comfortable, then nodded, satisfied with his handiwork. "Get some rest," he said. "Call me if you need anything. I'm a light sleeper, and, uh…" He considered the bedding. "Do you need more blankets? Fewer?"

I'm fine, thanks.

"If you're certain." He gestured to the nightstand, and a pitcher of water appeared. "Seriously, don't hesitate. I'll probably be reading for a while."

As he turned to go, I thought, *Thank you for letting me crash at your place.*

He smiled. "It's yours, too. Not to say that there's anything wrong with your flat," he hastily continued, "and I'm certainly not pressuring you, but if you ever want to come over, use the study…anything…"

His mind was open to me, and I sneaked a peek, trying to judge how much of the offer was nothing more than manners. What I found there stunned me.

Hope.

He'd been alone since his father's death, a solitary figure in an oversized mansion, unable to forge many true connections with the rest of the court, much less his kin. And then, from nowhere…a son. A granddaughter.

His apparent fondness for us was genuine. He wasn't being politely kind—he wanted a family, and he saw so much of himself and his father in me. He worried that I would find him odd or annoying, as so many others had, that I wouldn't want anything to do with him…but he held on to hope, all the same.

"Thanks, Dad," I said.

I felt his pleasure even once he waved the lights out and retreated deeper into the house, leaving me in peace to sleep.

Still, I wasn't quite ready to succumb without one last experiment. Pushing back the blankets, I eased myself upright and held out my hand, palm up. I'd been around enough faeries to know how this was meant to work, and if I *did* have a smidgeon of talent, then maybe...

I felt something click within me, like flipping a switch I'd never known existed, and a small white flame blossomed in my hand. It was barely the size of a tennis ball—tiny beside the fireballs I'd theretofore seen lobbed—but it was real, and it was mine.

I extinguished it with a thought, then flopped to the mattress and surrendered.

Aurie shrieked with happiness when Madison escorted her home the next evening after dinner. While my daughter clung to my waist, I rubbed her back and gave her sitter a weary grin. "As always, I'm not sure what I'd do without you..."

"My pleasure," said Madison. "Allie's so grown up these days, and it's nice to have someone around who still thinks I can do a decent pedicure."

Aurie hastily shucked off her shoes to show me her new purple toenails, which I complimented before sending her to her room to prepare for bed. When I joined her a few minutes later for tuck-in, she was already buried in her mound of stuffed toys, and I repositioned a few to prevent suffocation. "Did you have fun with the Copelands?" I asked.

"Uh-huh. Missed you."

"Missed you, too, hatchling." I picked up a plush zebra and added it to the pile. "Want to see something?"

"Yeah."

She peered out from the hole in her toys and blankets as I called up my little fireball again—slightly larger now, though still more of an annoyance than a true weapon. "Just a touch of talent," I explained as her eyes widened.

"Not anything like your grandfather's, but—"

"Teach me?"

"I can't," I said, snuffing the flame in my fist. "That's a side effect of Ros's work."

"Will she do it to me, too, then?" Aurie pressed. "I'm big enough."

No, I wanted to say, picturing her as an unconscious, dehydrated infant in my arms, *no, you absolutely are not big enough.* Molding Aurie into a form capable of living had taken all that Ros could give, and the thought of asking her to make heavy tweaks left me nauseated even before I factored in the notion of standing by helplessly while my child screamed in pain.

"We'll talk about it when you're older," I told her, and smoothed her hair from her borrowed face.

AUGUST 11: ROS BOLIN

Ellie's depression was a curious thing, a feral cat that slunk close to her on occasion, only to bite and scratch until it disappeared. I could predict some of its appearances—it returned almost like clockwork around her husband Walt's birthday in April, their anniversary in September, or his death date in December—but sometimes, the depression came upon her without identifiable cause, a shadow that plagued the queen until her mood lifted of its own accord.

I recommended therapy. Ellie had never properly grappled with her part in Walt's death, and forty-odd years on, she still grieved his loss terribly. But she was a private person with a *starched* upper lip, and she refused to seek counseling. Though I insisted that Wanda had a long track record of keeping her patients' disclosures confidential, Ellie decided that therapy would be too risky. She couldn't afford to show weakness to her court, especially considering the number of her siblings who jostled with each other for favor. As Ellie had no children, one of her brothers or sisters stood to inherit the court in case of her demise, and anyone within a few dozen bodies of the throne knew his or her place in line and exactly who needed to be removed in order to advance. With so many sharks in the water, Ellie kept up a solid front with aplomb. Not even Coileán and Val, who had been there when Ellie received Walt's head in a box, knew of the frequency or severity of her dark days. She hid them masterfully from almost everyone...but she couldn't hide from me.

Omniscience has its highs and lows.

My suggestion that Ellie make an appointment with Wanda was rebuffed for several reasons, among them the risk of detection. None of the Three made regular appearances in the Fringe settlement, as they scared most of the locals, a community of witches, lesser bloods, and others with little to no magical ability. If Ellie were to suddenly come to town on a weekly schedule, people would notice, and they'd ask questions. I pointed out that she could go to Wanda's office by gate, but Ellie's paranoia insisted that *someone* would spot her and spread the word. Fine, I countered, bring Wanda to the mansion instead—those of Ellie's staff who'd withstood her period of madness (and...*creative* punishments) during the Mulligan years could be trusted to keep quiet. But no, that wouldn't do. She refused to take the risk, and so she suffered in silence, putting on a cheerful mask as duty required.

I did what I could to distract her during the roughest times, showing myself in to chat when she started to sink and relaying anything I'd seen that was even mildly entertaining. Sometimes, I could make her laugh or coax her outside for a few minutes of fresh air and sunshine, and she'd brighten for a bit. Other times, she wanted nothing more than to be left alone to cry in peace, and I tried to respect her privacy. I might have been the realm, but contrary to what the Three believed, I didn't always set out to be an obnoxious busybody.

But August had come on her like a noxious fog—too early to be her anniversary sadness, one of the rogue bouts that struck hardest because they arrived without warning. Focused though I was on Frank, I *had* tried to help Ellie, but none of my usual tricks had broken her funk that time—and as her mood showed no sign of lifting, I was running out of good ideas.

I paid attention that morning when Ellie called Toula. The two women had never been bosom buddies, but they were friendly, and Toula had pulled Ellie back from the edge when I was just a kid. Val and Coileán might have been Ellie's colleagues, but court politics were always a tricky subject. Far safer, perhaps, to reach out to the grand magus, who could be trusted not to spill the dirt to her brother or her boyfriend unless Ellie was about to do something catastrophically stupid.

As I couldn't hear Toula's side of the conversation—phones and I did *not* mix—I listened to Ellie's end and flicked through her thoughts for context.

"I apologize for calling so early," Ellie began from the security of her office desk, phone in one hand and steaming cup of Earl Grey in the other. "I've a favor to ask of you, if you'd be so kind." She paused long enough for a brief sip, then said, "Is there any way I might prevail upon you to arrange a meeting with Hope?"

Damn it. *Oh*, damn it.

I liked Hope Lozano—Lady Imaranta of High Vale, now queen consort of Conota. Anyone who took care of Frank in his hour of need was okay in my book, never mind that time Hope raised an army of dead Britons to stop Nath's invasion of the mortal realm. What could I say? She was spunky.

But if Ellie wanted to meet with Hope, I didn't have to look at her thoughts to know what she was planning. Cynaeli on her father's side, Hope had inherited that people's gift for communication with the dead, albeit on steroids. A well-trained cynaeli could sufficiently energize a spirit to make him visible and audible to mundanes, the sort of full-body apparition that would make a paranormal investigator dance for joy. Hope could energize *throngs* at once, though it sapped her strength. Still, I knew darn well that Ellie didn't want a crowd. If she was asking for a chat with Hope, then there could be only one man on her mind.

Toula called back a short time later. Hope was willing to come, and Artur had agreed to loan them Afallon, the closest thing the mortal realm had to a protected neutral territory, for the occasion. Technically, the island was Artur's, the single piece of ground over which she still exercised sovereignty, but she seldom turned away visitors. Its primary purpose those days was as the Team's offsite retreat, a way to get everyone out of the subbasement and down to the sea on occasion.

Toula and Hope had compared their clocks, and Hope was available the following afternoon around five Glastonbury time. Ellie quickly flipped through her mental calendar and found a conflict: a meeting with her sister Irem, which had been on the books for a fortnight. But Ellie and I both knew that Irem would do little beyond complain, and so Ellie decided to reschedule that unpleasant visit. The meeting was set.

Ellie barely slept that night, unable to quiet her mind, and passed the wee hours with a recent monograph by one of her former postgrads, now a senior historian in her own right. She thought of the young woman she'd mentored, who'd worn her hair in a neon pink mohawk and bought her own piercing gun. Judging by the author photo, the pink was still there, though in a more conservative cut, and the woman's earring count had fallen to six. Ellie felt the passage of time most keenly in moments like this, looking at the face of a grandmother whom she recalled as a bright student on the cusp of twenty-four, which did nothing to ameliorate her depression. Her thoughts returned to the many other young women in her long life—those she'd taught, those she'd loved, and the few she'd married, either to preserve her cover as a wealthy man or to save them from more conventional marriages. It was never difficult for her to tell which of the available daughters in her social circles was repulsed by the idea of sleeping with a man, and while she never revealed her true nature to them, she offered them an escape. As long as her wives exercised discretion in carrying on their liaisons, Ellie didn't care who they brought into their beds…and if she was invited to join on occasion, that suited her well enough.

Walt Drummond had been her only husband, the first partner to whom she'd confessed about being fae, and they had adored each other. While I wasn't sure if I bought into the notion of soulmates, those two presented a strong case. But they knew from the beginning that their time would be limited, as Walt was an all-too-mortal witch. They made the best of it for decades, but when Ellie finally had the chance to save him—to bring him to safety in Faerie, which would preserve his life as long as he remained in the realm—she blew it. Walt had gone to one last conference, Coileán's vengeful daughter had attacked him, and shortly after his body washed ashore, Ellie had received his head—kept alive through an enchantment, which had broken at the border, killing him as she'd hurried him into Faerie. Ellie *couldn't* have saved Walt, but still, she blamed herself for his death.

Naturally, this bothered Walt to no end.

What lies beyond death is a mystery, even to me, and the dead share few secrets. Those who connect with the living long enough for a brief conversation are often frank about the prohibition against disclosure on them—there are some questions that they simply are not permitted to answer. I'd seen precious few of the dead in Faerie, hints of consciousness that flickered in and out of the realm, but their minds were closed to me. Far more of them wandered the mortal realm, and while they couldn't cross into Faerie, they could linger close enough to the border to reach me.

It was Kura, my predecessor, who'd first met Walt. Presenting himself as he had last been in life, a gray-haired man in thick glasses and a tweed jacket, Walt was never pushy, but he asked for news of his wife. He had reason to worry: Ellie had inherited a throne and an unruly court, lost her husband, and faced the Mulligan crisis within a matter of months. Walt had watched helplessly while

Ellie's fight to regain control of her life devolved into near-madness, her deterioration marked by the tenor of her letters. Perhaps as a form of therapy, perhaps out of loneliness, Ellie had regularly written letters to Walt. She'd never expected an answer to her one-sided correspondence, nor did she know that Kura and I had been sharing them with Walt for years. We'd repeatedly offered to pass along a message for him, especially when Ellie sank into one of her emotional troughs, but Walt always declined. "She has a long life ahead of her," he'd explained when I, young and frustrated, had demanded to know why he wouldn't give her so much as a word. "I'm an anchor. She needs to free herself, and it won't help if she clings to me."

But that had been twenty-five years ago, and Ellie had yet to move past her great loss. She hadn't taken a lover, though she could have had her pick of the court—aside from her power, Ellie was a redheaded stunner, and in her good moods, she practically glowed. None of that mattered. Ellie wanted her Walt. She still wore her wedding ring. And though I itched to tell her that he was still there, fretting over her, I respected his wishes.

Now, as Ellie stepped through the gate from her office onto Afallon's manicured meadow, the ball was in Walt's court.

She'd placed the gate near a vine-covered pavilion with a lovely sea view, and she perched on the edge of one of the wooden patio chairs, outwardly serene but for the bouncing of her knee. Bound as I was to Faerie, I couldn't join her, but I could see enough to appreciate what Artur had done with the place. The massive lodge—the only building on the island—could have slept at least a couple dozen people, while the flowers and fruit trees scattered around it flourished in that climate only through magic. A salty breeze blew in from the Bristol Channel, a pleasant accompaniment to the late-afternoon sun and scattered clouds. Had I not been so worried about Ellie, I'd have been happy that she was taking a break in such a scenic location.

A few minutes after Ellie arrived, another gate opened near the pavilion, and out stepped Hope and her husband, Arik. He closed their gate behind them, perhaps out of consideration for the intricate wards that hid the island from mundane eyes—an outward flow of dark magic from Conota would do the protective enchantments no favors. Safe on the island, neither of them had bothered to glamour themselves. Hope, who resembled her father's family, was a slight woman—several inches shorter than me, though she was tall by cynaeli standards—with a deep purple complexion, blue eyes, and long black hair, which she wore in a simple braid over her shoulder. Arik, though somewhat paler in the way of the subterranean cynaeli, was similarly built. Both had their human mothers to thank for their height, but whereas Hope had come by her appearance naturally, Arik wasn't what he seemed. His father, my counterpart in that realm, looked nothing like either of its magically gifted peoples, and he had a nasty habit of impregnating women who piqued his interest.

That Conota did so was repugnant to me—the notion of acquiring his partner's consent never seemed to have crossed his mind—but I had an idea of how he managed the trick, especially as he wasn't the one actually carrying a child. I couldn't quite work out how *I* could procreate, however. I never stayed in corporeal form for long, and while I had no doubt that my Sam would make a wonderful father, he understood my physical limitations. Still, I would have loved to have a child of my own, and it disgusted me that Conota took advantage of whomever he liked and never deigned to reveal himself to his children unless he decided to crown them.

Ordinarily, Conota's dalliances presented no problem: the women were generally unaware that he had come to them, while the children of their unions inevitably favored their mothers and were raised by their unsuspecting presumptive fathers. But Arik's mother had been human, a young woman stolen as a concubine and murdered when her captor tired of her. Conota had a history of meddling far worse than mine or any of my predecessors', however, and he had given his son features that would fool his supposed cynaeli father. Beyond their looks, Arik and Hope seemed well suited for each other, judging by what I'd gleaned when they spent time within my realm…and considering the tension in Arik's shoulders and the way he protectively wrapped his arm around Hope's waist, he knew *exactly* why her presence had been requested.

Hope, however, smiled at Ellie and extricated herself from Arik's grip with a little pat on his wrist. "Howdy," she said, her accent still odd but closer to an American variant after having reconnected with her Oklahoman mother. "It's nice to see you again, Lady Eleanor."

The honorific was unnecessary, of course, but as she'd spent a couple years navigating the complex Conotan social hierarchies, I expected that Hope had learned the value of the occasional deferential gesture.

Ellie smiled back at her, though her face was strained, and she clasped her hands tightly in front of her. "Lady Imaranta. You're looking well."

Hope traded a glance with Arik, who nodded, then beamed at Ellie. "Thank you. It's not *quite* public information yet, but I'm expecting."

"So let's not tax her, hmm?" Arik cut in.

"Oh, no, of course not," Ellie hastily replied, "and…congratulations, dear, that's wonderful news. You've not been too ill, I trust?"

"No worse than most," said Hope, "and with Mama and so many of the former concubines still living with us, I've got more expertise around me than I know what to do with." Sobering slightly, she moved closer and searched Ellie's face. "What can I do for you? Toula didn't know why you wanted to see me…"

Ellie hesitated, and from my position at the edge of the

gate, I saw her face redden as she began to tear up. "I'm sorry," she croaked, "I—"

"Take your time," Hope soothed. "I'm in no hurry."

While Ellie furiously blinked and glared into the distance as she willed herself back under control, Hope and Arik shot glances over her shoulder, where Walt stood with his hands in his pockets. Putting the pieces together, Hope cut her eyes to me in query, and with the limited distance between us, I was able to convey a message: *She's depressed. That's her husband. He hasn't wanted to make contact before now because he's hoping she gets over him.*

How long ago did he die? Hope asked.

Forty-six years and change. Before either of us.

Her face moved in a flickering grimace. *Yeah, that's not working.*

By that time, Ellie had taken a few deep breaths, and she sounded somewhat more like her usual self when she told Hope, "I know what you were able to do for Val with his wife and grandson, and I've heard there were others, and I...I was just wondering..." She swallowed hard. "Has there ever been anyone for...me?"

Hope looked toward Walt again. While I wasn't privy to her end of their conversation, Walt replied, "I'm really not sure that this is a good idea." Her eyes narrowed, and he said, "Yes, I know, I'm not *blind*, but—"

"There is someone here," Hope interrupted, addressing Ellie again. "A man."

Ellie's breath quickened. "Who?"

"He hasn't given me his name, but...human, I suspect. Maybe a head taller than you are. Wrinkles, obviously aged, but don't ask me for specifics—I'm no good at judging. Uh...gray hair, receding in the front. Glasses with gold frames. Brown eyes, I think, and if he'd step a little closer, I wouldn't need to squint."

A curious series of emotions, hope and trepidation, flashed across Ellie's face. "Walt?" she whispered, and wheeled around.

I don't know what finally broke Walt's resolve. Maybe all it took was seeing his wife like that, simultaneously desperate to find him and afraid of what she'd discover.

"Do it. Please," he murmured.

Sensitive as I was to magical currents, I felt the air thrum as Hope sat in the grass and called upon the ambient dark magic, transmuting it into pure energy. Her power shot toward Walt like a lightning bolt. Though he didn't seem to feel the impact, he changed as he rode that current, strengthening until Ellie, who couldn't otherwise see spirits, cried out with joy and ran for him.

"He's not solid!" Arik barked before she could plow through Walt.

Ellie skidded to a halt in the grass, her tears falling freely and unnoticed. "Darling?" she asked, reaching toward her husband with trembling fingers.

Walt moved into her open arms and cupped his hand against her cheek, not quite touching her but close enough that she must have sensed him. "Hello, love. Don't cry on my account…"

She looked up into his eyes. "It's really you?"

"It's me," he whispered, nodding.

"I've missed you so much," she said in a barely audible murmur.

"I miss you, too, dear girl," he replied. "Terribly. But Ellie, I want you to be happy. You shouldn't be alone. I'd so hoped that you'd find someone new by now—"

"I don't *want* anyone new! I love you, Walter!"

He smiled wistfully. "And I love you. I will always love you. But you've got such a long life ahead—don't waste it mourning for me."

Forgetting their limitations for an instant, Ellie tried to grip his arm and went straight through it. "Oh! Sorry," she mumbled, withdrawing. "I, ehm…I'm sorry, I didn't mean—"

"You can't hurt me," Walt reassured her, chuckling until she laughed at herself. "I'm all right, dearest. You needn't worry."

"Good. *Good,*" she said, and rubbed the back of her neck. "There's so much I want to tell you, I barely know where to begin—"

"If it helps, I got your letters."

She jerked in shock. "My…how…"

He cut his eyes to me, and Ellie's jaw dropped as she made the connection. "Ros, and Kura before her," he explained. "They've read every one of them to me—and before you become cross with her," he added, pointing toward the gate, "she's been asking me to reply for years."

Ellie sounded hurt instead of angry when she spoke. "Why haven't you?"

"Because I thought it would do more harm than good. If you didn't know I was there, maybe you would move on, find someone…"

"*Walt.*"

"I'm so sorry, love. Silly old fool like always, eh?"

"You've never been a fool," she said, carefully trying to rest her palm against his face in turn. "And thank you for loving me enough to let me go, but…I can't do it. If I'm holding you here, if I'm harming you, let me know, and I'll try, but—"

"I'm here because I want to be here," he reassured her. "Because no matter how much I pretend, I can't let you go, either."

"Stay with me. Come to Faerie, I'll find a way—"

"It's not possible, Ellie. I'd have followed you decades ago if I could cross. But I'll be here," he insisted. "Ros knows I skulk about. And should you want answers to your letters, my darling, then you'll have them."

Arik cleared his throat and moved closer to them. "Sorry to cut this short, but Hope—"

"Of course," said Walt, casting a guilty glance her way. "Let's not tire her. I can't thank you enough," he said to Hope. "Truly, young lady, I'm in your debt—"

But Ellie wasn't ready to say goodbye again. "Just a

little longer, please," she begged, frantically looking between Arik and Hope. "*Please*. Hope, if you were in my place and it were Arik…"

Hope's face tightened—whether with pity or with the strain of empowering Walt, I couldn't tell—but Walt intervened before Arik could. "I love you, Eleanor," he said, facing her once more. "And I promise you, I'll be here. Be happy, my darling." Looking to Hope once more, he said, "Thank you."

"*No!*" Ellie cried, but Walt had time only to smile at her before he faded from her view. Screaming her frustration, she sank to her knees, pressed one hand to her mouth as if trying to hold back the rising sob, then burst into tears.

"Oh, I hope I haven't made matters worse," said Walt, kneeling beside his weeping widow. "Ellie, love, I'm sorry."

"Another time," Hope offered as Arik helped her to her feet. "Once the baby is born and I've regained my strength, I'd be happy to come back."

She and Arik waited while Ellie pulled herself together, and after a moment, Ellie turned her face up to them. "Thank you," she managed. "I…I appreciate it more than you know…"

"It's my pleasure," Hope said gently. "Really, we can do this again."

"You're very kind, and I don't mean to seem like an ingrate, it's just…that's the most I've had of him in years…" Her voice faded, and she looked sadly at the place where she'd last seen him. "Thank you."

"You know," said Arik, opening a fresh gate home before Hope could get any dangerously altruistic ideas, "he's still there. He can hear you."

Ellie's green eyes opened wide. "*Where?*"

"Right in front of you," he explained as Walt took a seat in the grass. "And he doesn't appear to be in any hurry to leave, so say whatever you need to say—he's listening."

"I can see and hear him, too," I interrupted from my gate. "I can't do what Hope does," I hastily told Ellie before she could get too excited, "but I wouldn't mind passing messages for a while. Frank and I certainly ask it often enough of Sam…"

"That would be appreciated," Walt replied as Ellie wiped her face dry. "Playing Chinese whispers is better than nothing, eh?"

"I'll try not to garble it," I told him, and lifted a hand in farewell to Hope and Arik. "You two take care. Good to see you again."

"Do keep us posted on the baby," Ellie added, and Hope grinned as Arik escorted her home.

Once the three of us were alone, I said, "I'll do my best to repeat Walt verbatim, but go easy—it's much harder to anticipate what you two are going to say with you sitting outside the realm. And yeah," I muttered as Walt arched an eyebrow, "I know how creepy that sounds."

Ellie took a deep breath, then looked almost precisely in Walt's direction, and he scooted to the right to complete the illusion. "I want you to know that I'm terribly sorry," she began. "For everything. I didn't know that the gate would kill you, and—"

"Hold it," I cut in as Walt began to talk over her.

"Ellie, listen to me," he insisted, staring into her eyes even if she couldn't see him. "It's not your fault. My God, woman, you tried to save me! I've *never* blamed you, so please stop blaming yourself."

She listened while I relayed the message. "Had I done the responsible thing and come clean with you earlier about, you know, inheriting a fucking throne…"

"I do *not* blame you. Let that be the furthest thought from your mind." He started to reach for her, then remembered and dropped his hand. "You have so much on your shoulders already, love, and no one to help you. Don't let me make it worse."

Ellie hesitated, nibbling at her lip. "You're not just

saying that to make me feel better?"

"Heavens, no," said Walt. "I have nothing but love for you."

And though she sniffled, she smiled.

The half hour they spent together, sitting in the grass on that remote island, was the happiest I'd seen Ellie in months, maybe years. Even with the awkwardness inherent in conversing with an unseen partner who was using me as a mouthpiece on a lag, she spoke with animation, laughing at old jokes and bringing Walt up to date on anything she'd left out of her many letters. The talk had turned to Rufus Stowe, whom they'd known as an historian before either Rufus or Ellie realized the other was fae, when I heard the door to Ellie's office open behind me.

As the consciousness of the realm, I no longer had a one-track mind—I was simultaneously aware of every thought and action within Faerie's borders. But just because I was aware of what was happening didn't always mean that I was paying it much attention, particularly when I manifested and focused on the people around me. I was working overtime that day as well, as I was preoccupied with my somewhat complicated role in the conversation beyond the gate. Thus, when Irem let herself in, I was almost taken by surprise.

"Sister?" she called, her hands on the hips of her elaborate green gown. "I've been *waiting*. Where are you?"

Caught off guard, Ellie jumped and looked back toward the gate as Irem swished closer. "Oh, *damn* it," she said, smacking herself in the forehead. "I apologize, Irem, I meant to reschedule with you yesterday, and it slipped my mind."

Her sister—another redhead like their father, but blue-eyed and more pinched in the face—huffed at Ellie's apology. "You forgot me? Am I not worth so much as a note?"

"Back off," I ordered. "It was an honest mistake, and she's had a lot to deal with. I'll make sure she resets your meeting within the week."

Irem smirked at me, but she didn't offer any direct backtalk. She might have been my senior by centuries, but she couldn't take me in a fight, and we both knew it.

"What are you doing, anyway?" Irem asked, sweeping past me onto Afallon. "Sunbathing?"

Bristling, Ellie pushed herself to her feet and smoothed her long blouse. "First, your presence is not required here, and second, how the hell did you get past the guards?"

Irem chuckled at Ellie's indignation. "I'm still on your schedule, dear sister. Your aide admitted me to the waiting room, and when you continued to ignore me, I let myself in. Really, you should find better help."

"I don't recall giving you permission to leave Faerie. Return at once."

That had to rankle—the Three had closed the borders to most of their courts, and the only people they allowed to leave were those among the half fae who had business in the mortal realm and could be trusted not to pick fights. A bored faerie within the realm was danger enough; a bored faerie with a world full of defenseless mortals with which to play was a disaster in the making. And so the Three had done the wise thing, keeping their people close in order to avoid such problems as the taking of changelings and the creation of more half fae, which, historically, was done by subterfuge or force most of the time.

"You didn't," Irem reluctantly allowed. "But seeing as I'm here now and you're not busy—"

"I am, actually," Ellie snapped.

"With *what?*"

"Not that I owe you any explanation, but Lady Imaranta was kind enough to meet me here and allow me to speak with my husband. I found that *marginally* more important than listening to you whinge about whatever's bothering you today."

Her sister laughed in disbelief. "You ignored me for *that*? How are you still upset about a dead mortal?"

Unable to understand Fae, Walt glanced at me and asked, "What's so funny?"

You don't want to know.

"And you—you met with a creature out of the Gray Lands here? *Alone*? Without any guards? What sort of imbecile are you, Eleanor?"

"The kind who doesn't make a show of force unless it's necessary," Ellie retorted, cheeks flaring, "and especially not when asking for a favor."

"So you put yourself at her mercy, did you? Idiot."

"Oh, of *course*," she shot back, "and with Ros standing right there. Had I needed to retreat, the way is clear. For your information, she's a lovely young woman, and her husband has never been anything but gracious toward us—something you could stand to learn from. Now, if you'll excuse me, you're interrupting. Return to Faerie at once, see yourself out of my house, and don't come back until I send for you."

With that, Ellie resumed her seat in the grass and smiled in the general vicinity of Walt. "Sorry, love," she said, segueing back to English. "Where were we?"

I should have been more observant.

I should have paid attention when Irem stepped to the side, watching Ellie chat with thin air instead of returning to Faerie. I should have noticed the calculating gleam in her eyes.

But she was outside the realm at that moment, her mind shielded from my constant probing, and I was preoccupied with my role in Ellie and Walt's conversation.

I should have anticipated the retaliation.

Instead, it was Walt who saw the bolt building in Irem's hand, Walt who yelled, "Shield! *Shield!*" But Ellie was deaf to Walt's warning, and just as I realized what was happening, Irem's bolt was striking true.

Ellie didn't suffer. She sat motionless for the space of an exhalation, her body not yet comprehending the significance of the two-inch-wide tunnel left in her head by the bolt's passing, and then she toppled onto her side without a word.

Connected as we were, I knew the moment Ellie died. The channel between us, the conduit of my power to her as a queen, was cleaved at her passing, and a new one formed in the same instant. I upheld Kura's arrangement with the Three, after all, and the rules were clear. When one of them died, the throne went to their eldest surviving child. If no child were available, then the heir would be the eldest living sibling.

Oberon sired thousands of children in his long lifetime, many of them half-fae castoffs who'd been killed as demon spawn in the mortal realm. Ellie had been one of his half-fae children, forced onto her unwilling mother, but she'd been clever enough to make a life for herself before my uncle nearly beheaded Oberon, leaving the court to her. And in turn, childless Ellie's heir was another of Oberon's daughters.

Irem.

I could have struck her dead. I could have stopped the transfer of power that sent her, howling in agony, to her knees. Indeed, I wanted nothing more at that moment, but the group mind cautioned me against it. Kura had withheld Val's rightful power for almost a quarter of a century, and I knew too well how much it had pained her to do so. Instead, as I tried to cope with the shock of losing Ellie, I took what little satisfaction I could from watching Irem suffer through her boost...and I made no effort to speed up the process.

Motion from the corner of my eye made me turn in time to see Ellie sit up—well, a version of her, at least, one far less substantial but without a hole through her skull.

"What..." she began, blinking in confusion, then noticed Walt kneeling in front of her, watching with horror. "*Walt*" she cried. "How...what just..."

Her voice faded as she glanced down and saw that she was tangled in her own corpse.

"I'm so sorry," he said in a rush, "I tried to warn you, but she was too quick, and...oh, Ellie, no," he murmured. "This wasn't meant to happen..."

Walt reached for her, once again cupping his hand against her cheek, but I could tell that Ellie felt it that time. She leaned into his touch and closed her eyes, then covered his hand with her own.

"I'm sorry, love," he said as she clung to him. "I should have been faster—"

"I'm free." Opening her eyes, she began to smile as she studied his stricken face. "I'm finally free of that court. And you..." She froze, terror flashing in her expression. "Are you going to leave me?"

"No, *no*," he soothed, and smiled reassurance. "Never again."

As I watched, his form shifted, rapidly rewinding the years until he seemed a match for her apparent youth, a dark-haired man with a smooth face...though yes, still sporting glasses. Ellie cried out and threw herself toward him, and he scooped her up and kissed her deeply. She wrapped her arms around his neck like a bride being carried across the threshold and drank him in with her gaze.

"What happens now?" she whispered.

Walt's smile veered toward impish. "Is it possible that for once, *I* know something you don't?"

"It wouldn't be the first time," she chided.

"A rare occurrence, then, my dear Richard."

"Oh, *you*." Chuckling, she snuggled closer to his chest, then turned to look at Irem, who was shaking like she'd grabbed a high-voltage wire. "That little bitch just murdered me," she said, but in the tones of one discussing a moderate inconvenience.

"And she gets the court, I'm afraid," I told Ellie. "I don't have much say in the matter."

"If she wants it so badly, let her suffer with it," she replied. "The boys will ruin her fun soon enough...*oh*," she mumbled, her face falling. "The boys. Damn it, I can't even say goodbye. Can't very well return to Faerie, can I?" she mused, considering the gate. "And even if I could, they'd never hear me."

"I'll give them your regards," I promised as my temporarily physical throat tightened and my eyes pricked. "Anyone else?"

She nodded. "Nico, if you would, and Lucian. They've been so good to me. Toula and Aiden, please. Your mum and dad. Amy...Sam..."

"They'll know," I assured her.

"And Rufus," she concluded. "Please, *please* send him my best—*our* best," she amended as Walt vehemently nodded. "Tell him I'm sorry I couldn't say goodbye properly."

"I will." Fighting the lump that threatened to choke me, I said, "Goodbye, Aunt Ellie. If I don't see you two around, have fun out there, okay?"

Her face softened as she watched me try not to cry. "I'll miss you, Ros. Take care of yourself, and, ehm..." She shot Irem a pointed glance. "Give her hell for me, won't you?"

I managed to smile as they faded from view, finally in each other's arms.

By the time that Irem, now glowing with the white corona of the Three, was able to push herself to her shaky feet, I had willed my sorrow down beneath my anger. As she wobbled back toward the gate, I blocked her path and glared. "By the terms of the old agreement, I acknowledge you as the queen of your sister's court and your father's before her," I said. "But you just killed my friend, and I will *never* forgive you for that. Clear?"

She snorted and rolled her eyes. "I have power, little girl. I don't need *forgiveness*, especially not from a mongrel like you."

Though I wanted to slam the gate in her face, I decided to be the bigger person and slid a step to my right. "Nice to see that we're off to such a great start," I told her as she returned to the realm...and as she stopped in her tracks and put her hand to her temple, I laughed to myself. "Oh, did no one mention that you and I are linked now? As long as you're in my realm, I'll be that little voice in the back of your head." A quick burst of will was all it took to make her yelp with the shock of a headache. "Try to learn some manners, why don't you?"

Wincing, Irem stalked off, threw open Ellie's office door—well, hers now—and slammed it behind her.

I gave myself a moment to breathe, metaphorically speaking, then manifested in Rufus's office in the Fringe settlement. School might have been out for the summer holiday, but he was so engrossed with a new book about the Vietnam War that he screamed and almost tumbled out of his chair when my radiance fell upon him.

"Hi, Dr. Stowe," I said, once again the teenager in the principal's office, as he clutched at his chest. "I need your help."

He regarded me warily. "I don't have to be a regent again, do I?"

"Not this time," I replied, then stood behind his guest chair and told him everything.

When I fell silent, he looked by turns aghast and heartbroken, and he tossed his book aside and rose. "What do you require from me, my lady?"

"Hands." Opening a fresh gate to Afallon, I explained, "I'm going to need my strength. Could you please take care of Ellie?"

Rufus slipped into the mortal realm, saw his old friend's body, and gritted his teeth as he struggled to keep his composure. "Did she say what she wanted done?" he asked, his voice cracking.

"I don't think she really cares, but I'd rather not leave that here to rot."

He crouched beside the corpse and closed her eyes for the last time, then took her cold hand and squeezed it. "Be well, my queen," he murmured. "Wherever you two are, be well."

As he released her, the body turned to dust, which the eternal breeze caught and blew away over the sea. He stood in silence for a time, watching the summer sun make its slow descent, and with his back to me, I allowed myself to cry in peace.

AUGUST 12: COILEÁN

Under ordinary circumstances, I wasn't partial to tuna. Perhaps I spent too many years assuming that the gray flakes from the can were the best parts of the fish, and the thought of mixing it with mayonnaise, eggs, and vegetables left me queasy. But that was before Toula starting inviting me to dinner. Whatever else could be said for the woman, she knew her way around a kitchen and put my skills to shame. Pot roast? Perfection. Delicate quail? I ate every bite and could have downed the bones. And then, one night, she presented me with a tuna steak topped with a coarsely chopped sort of salsa and waited for my reaction.

All reservations aside, I took a bite. One would be a fool of the highest order to push aside dinner made by the person with whom one is sleeping, after all. And because, by then, I knew I was in love with Toula, I steeled myself to eat the whole thing—I didn't want to hurt her feelings.

It was amazing.

Years later, I still didn't know her secret, but when she suggested tuna for our next date night, I readily agreed to procure the fish in advance.

We coveted those few hours we stole together, especially when our realms' clocks were more or less synchronized. Toula had her hands full with the Arcanum, receiving phone calls at all hours of the day and night from installation heads who couldn't be bothered to calculate the time in Glastonbury, while I spent most of my energy keeping my court from self-destructing. The pettiest of disagreements between two faeries can spiral into a deadly feud if allowed to fester, and so I filled the role of enthroned referee, doing my best to keep the chaos to an acceptable level.

It was never *simple*. Aside from the long-established grudges that flared with new slights and the novel reasons my people found to snipe at each other, I also had to resolve the disputes that arose along our borders. With Val's people to the north of us and Ellie's to the south, squabbles along the boundary lines were a fact of life—and they would have been so much worse had my colleagues and I not agreed that ninety-nine percent of them were stupid nonsense. While Ellie and I had a rocky start, we'd come to a working arrangement. Val was easy to negotiate with and far too old to put up with bullshit from his court, and that suited me well.

But regardless of the expected in-fighting, the three of us had made it work. There was, within reason, peace in Faerie, three courts cohabiting in the realm in a way they hadn't for a thousand years. Better still, we had an open line of communication with the Arcanum, a more than friendly relationship with the Fringers living within our borders, a permanent envoy from the piq, contacts with the Minor Arcanum and the Dark Company, and even decent relations with our counterpart in Conota—a far cry from the days when Faerie's only potential help came from the fickle merrow. Maybe the situation would never be perfect, but it was functional, a web of alliances stronger than the sum of its parts.

Still, I could see room for improvement, most personally where Toula's and my relationship was concerned. We'd been an item for nearly forty years by then, but only a select few in Faerie knew our secret, and fewer still in the mortal realm. Had the Council known that their grand magus was slumming with me, Toula would have been out of a job, and my court certainly would have looked askance at a witch-blood in my bed. Yes, we knew that political stability had to take precedence over our libidos, but I wearied of the subterfuge. I wanted to spend a proper date night with Toula at a restaurant without worrying that someone would see us. I wanted us to move freely around each other's homes instead of sneaking about with hoodies and well-timed gates. Hell, I wanted to do something as small as hold Toula's hand in public without fear of an inter-realm scandal. But my talent was for magic, not miracles, and I remained grateful for what we had. Toula was brilliant and brave but playful in private, a kind woman with a competitive streak a mile wide, and she had no reservations about calling me out as she saw fit.

I didn't deserve her, but *damn* did I love her.

As usual, dinner that Saturday night was delicious, Toula's perfect tuna steaks served with polenta and a grilled medley of summer squashes. We ate on the balcony of her apartment within my palace—she'd set it up during the Mulligan years and never dismantled it—while the sun sank. A warm breeze blew over my garden, carrying the scent of the ever-blooming roses up to our table, and Toula smiled as I topped up our wine. "You know," she said, "I have nothing scheduled for tomorrow morning, and if your calendar could be cleared …"

I grinned. "Ahead of you, Glinda."

"Oh, *good.*" Her blue eyes twinkled as she sipped. "It's been a long week, and I don't know about you, but I could use a little time between—"

Whatever she said after that was lost beneath the wave of horror, fury, and sorrow that swept across my mind. Not my thought—I knew that had originated with Ros, but she wasn't showing me the cause.

I heard Toula say my name and realized that I'd pressed my hands to my ears and was rocking in my chair. Fighting against the alien consciousness that resided within my own, I told her, "Something's wrong. Ros is upset."

"Over what?"

"I don't know."

Frowning, she called, "Ros? What's going on, hon? Talk to us."

Under ordinary circumstances, that would be enough to summon her—unlike her predecessor, Ros frequently manifested to make her wishes known. But that evening, she failed to materialize, and her anguish only grew sharper.

"God, I hope nothing's happened to Sam," Toula murmured.

Somehow, I didn't think she'd have been so coy had harm befallen her boyfriend. I rose enough to pull my phone from my pocket and called Val, hoping for insight.

Unfortunately, he had nothing to offer. "You hear it, too?" he said in lieu of a greeting.

"What's wrong with her?"

"I have no idea. Have you asked Ellie?"

Scowling at the device in my hand, I tapped at the screen until I initiated a three-way call, then waited for her to pick up. But her phone continued to ring, and after a moment, I hung up on her and put Val on speaker. "Think she went for a walk or something?"

"If she did," he replied, "she didn't ask *my* permission."

"Actually," Toula interrupted, leaning closer to the phone, "I think she's on Afallon."

"Afallon?" her brother repeated, bemused. "For what purpose? Something with the Team?"

She made a face, then sighed. "Ellie asked me to arrange a meeting with Hope. Three guesses as to why, and the first two don't count."

No further explanation was necessary. Val, Toula, and I had been present when Ellie unwrapped her late husband's head like the Christmas gift from hell. If she'd left the realm for a few hours to try to see him again, I wouldn't hold it against her. The idea that Hope could tell a person which spirits were haunting him was intriguing, but I'd never had the guts to ask her if anyone wished a word with me from beyond the veil. Given the gallons of blood on my hands—including Val and Toula's mother's—I wasn't sure whether I wanted to know.

(In fairness, Toula had killed my mother first, and both of the old queens had wanted us dead. Still, while neither of us lamented our mutual lack of mothers-in-law, reciprocal matricide *was* an odd facet of our relationship.)

As the three of us hypothesized about the cause of Ros's distress, her emotional tide withdrew, leaving Val and me with the knowledge that she was displeased even if she was no longer shouting about it. Her silence troubled me, but I knew well enough not to press for answers until she was prepared to provide them. In my experience, it's best not to antagonize someone who can give you a migraine on a whim.

Eventually, Val hung up, and Toula and I turned to the business of dessert: crème brûlée, one of the few dishes for which she got to play with her tiny blowtorch. I made coffee as she finished the ramekins, and we settled in. My only complaint was that with the long summer evenings, there was no need for candlelight on the balcony—not a mood killer, though I liked the touch of ambiance during our rare meals together. While Toula and I were on the same wavelength as to our after-dinner plans, we lingered at the table, neither of us rushing off to the business of the bedroom. Appearances aside, we weren't a pair of desperate twenty-somethings, and I relished the easy freedom of dinner alone with her—no worries about protocol or inadvertent offense, no questions as to which of my guests were scheming against the others, just the two of us and a second helping of crispy, sugary pudding.

We were in the midst of negotiations over which movie we'd watch on our next date night when I caught the lightning flash of a gate opening in her den. Both of us jumped up from the table, only to find Val striding through and closing the gate with an offhanded wave. Noticing us, he opened the balcony door and beckoned us inside. "Better come in. Ros told me to meet her here, so I didn't bother with your guards."

In truth, my guards were mine in name alone. Val had trained most of them, and part of me suspected that even if he'd held a gun to my head, some of the guards would have thought long and hard about tackling their former captain. They'd hardly bat an eye if they learned he'd sneaked in. But their opinion on that score didn't matter. I counted Val as a friend, and there *was* the tiny fact that I was sleeping with his sister to consider.

"Did she say why?" Toula asked.

He shook his head. "She's not happy, but that's all I could glean from her. Is there any more coffee?"

"Kitchen," I began, but before Val could help himself, Ros appeared behind him.

She looked haggard and miserable, a far cry from her usual self-assurance, and she waited in silence while Toula and I hurried in from the balcony. "Might want to sit down," she said, nodding toward the couches in the den, and claimed one for herself while we took our uneasy seats.

"What's going on?" I asked. "Is Ellie coming over, too?"

"No." She gripped the edge of the couch cushion and slowly exhaled. "Ellie's dead."

"*What?*"

Ros waited as the three of us spoke over each other, then wearily lifted a hand to get a word in. "Impromptu sneak attack from her sister. The good news is that Ellie's with Walt now—I watched their reunion."

Good for Ellie, perhaps, but cold comfort for the rest of us. Though I'd long since moved past my brief, ill-advised infatuation with her, I'd respected the woman.

"And the bad?" asked Val.

"The sister who killed her is now the queen. Irem. She's fully fae and a handful on her best day, so…" Ros shook her head and stared into space. "I expect her to call the court tonight. Didn't want it to come as a surprise to you."

"Moon and stars," I whispered. "She killed Ellie—how is she the queen?"

"Because that's the deal we inherited," she said bitterly. "And by the terms of that deal, as long as she doesn't attack the two of you," she continued, pointing to Val and me, "I can't touch her."

"You could empower someone within that court to do so," Val murmured. "Worked for Aiden, did it not?"

"Yeah, but Kura only worked on him after Oberon strolled in and declared war. Don't think I haven't been mulling this over," she insisted. "If I asked Rufus, he'd do it in a heartbeat. But now's not the time."

"So she gets away with it?" Toula snapped. "Murders Ellie, gets a court, no repercussions?"

Ros's mouth tightened. "At the moment, yes."

"That's bullshit."

"Before you decide to challenge her to a duel or something else incredibly stupid, remember that she's a queen now," Ros reminded her. "A fully functional queen. You're good, Toula, but you don't want a fair fight with that. And should you think of dragging those two into this," she added, holding Toula's furious stare, "be aware that they would be breaking the old agreement if they tried to kill her. Under the terms, I would have no choice but to back Irem."

"But this is *Ellie* we're talking about!" she cried.

"You think I like this? If she gives me an opening, I will *gladly* strike her dead. But until that time, we're stuck with her, so put on your diplomacy hats and make the best of it." She sighed and glowered at the corner of the room. "I'm sorry, I'm not exactly a ray of fucking sunshine right now. Ellie asked me to tell you all goodbye. I think she felt bad about not being able to do so in person. If it's any consolation, she didn't suffer."

Suddenly, I heard the clarion call of Irem's summons echo across the realm: *Come. Your queen commands it.*

Val and I traded looks, and he pushed himself to his feet with a muttered, "I suppose we should pay our respects, shouldn't we? She must be in such a state of mourning."

"Bitch," Toula swore. "Can't I just kill her a little, guys?"

Her brother offered her a hand as she stood. "Personally, you have my blessing, but looking at the bigger picture…"

"Do you really want a war between the Arcanum and the largest of the courts, Grand Magus?" I interjected.

"No," said Ros before Toula could respond. "The answer to that is an emphatic *no*."

Toula grunted as she straightened her shirt, then locked eyes with Ros and said, "Find a loophole, kid. Any loophole. You know I'm good for it if you need backup."

I could have made my way to Eleanor's house in my sleep. The marble and limestone mansion she'd designed for herself was a touch on the gaudy side for my taste—of course, given that I'd redesigned my mother's palace, I didn't have much room to critique—but she'd chosen a beautiful setting on a bluff overlooking the western sea and landscaped the area with an ornamental lake, mature trees, and a lawn smooth as a putting green. The place suited her, and over the years, even if only due to familiarity, it had grown on me.

But when I opened a gate at the end of the avenue of oaks leading to the front door, the mansion was gone.

Irem had left the trees—perhaps she had yet to turn her eye to the grounds, particularly with night approaching—but where Ellie's stately home had stood now arose a castle that put mine to shame. It was easily twice the size of mine and seemed to be built of rose quartz, a fantasy confection of towers and turrets that jabbed toward the heavens without regard for a logical floorplan or basic physics.

"Shit," Toula muttered as we gawked at the new construction. "That thing's one rainbow and prancing unicorn away from 'fairy princess' territory."

"What do you mean?" asked Val.

She patted his arm. "You were never a seven-year-old girl, and it shows."

"She means it's gaudy as hell," I offered, crossing my arms. "If there's glitter, I swear…"

"My lord? Uh…my *lords*," said a voice behind us.

I turned to find what appeared on a casual headcount to be most of the Stowe clan approaching the avenue. Martin and Rohese, both of them half fae, had been a couple since the early fifteenth century and raised thirteen children, most of whom lived in the Fringe settlement. Vivi, the only girl and the baby of the bunch, was also the only Stowe child born with almost no talent, but she'd found a place for herself as the settlement's de facto mayor. Her brothers built the settlement, provided security, kept the pantries stocked, and ran the school—all but Lucian, a gifted chef who oversaw Eleanor's kitchen. He was not among the family pack that night, nor was Vivi…nor, I noted with relief, was their brother Rufus's son, who lived in Arc 2. A shifter on his mother's side, young Mal had found a home on the Away Team, but something told me that the new queen wouldn't appreciate his presence among the luminaries of her court.

The speaker was Rufus, who'd thrown on a navy blazer and dark green necktie for the occasion, and if the light wasn't playing tricks on me, his eyes were unusually puffy. "You heard, I take it?" he said as his family gathered in.

"Ros gave us the news," I replied as diplomatically as possible. "My condolences, Rufus. I know you two were close."

He nodded, jaw clenching. "Thank you. She's at peace. But, uh…"

"But what are we going to do with *that*?" Toula

finished, cocking her head toward the new castle.

"Essentially." He shoved his hands into his pockets and stared past us at the architectural monstrosity. "I must admit that I have somewhat mixed feelings about my new queen. Were you planning to stop by, or are you here to admire that shit pile from a distance?"

The rest of the Stowes seemed to tense at Rufus's frankness, but as far as I was concerned, he could say what he wanted. Rufus, like my brother Aiden, had spent a year as regent, and he'd done a fine job of holding Eleanor's court together while she recuperated. He wasn't a lord, but I respected him.

"Ros hinted that we should do the diplomatic thing," said Val, "but…" He grimaced as he took in the sight of the palace. "That's an unfortunate choice of domicile, isn't it?"

"I might choose a stronger word"—Rufus cut his eyes to his worried mother—"or I might just keep my big mouth shut. Want to sneak in with us?"

We accepted the offer—better to enter unnoticed than to make a scene—but parted company with the Stowes as soon as we were past the gate. Val and I didn't want Irem to get any dangerous ideas about where that family's loyalties lay, though to be honest, I suspected that they were more loyal to the Fringe settlement than to any of the courts.

Slipping through the throng of confused faeries, we made our way across the courtyard toward what appeared to be the primary entrance, judging by the presence of four guards at the double doors. None of them looked pleased with their assignment, and I was shocked to find Nico, Eleanor's captain, among their ranks.

Nico and Val locked eyes as we neared, and Val addressed him with a thought, including Toula and me in the conversation: *What do we need to know?*

The captain's face remained a careful blank, but I heard the distress in his reply. *Lady Ros told me everything. I can't defend her, Val, I can't.*

You can. Why does she have you on the door?

Doesn't trust me, does she?

Val snorted. *Does she trust any of you?*

Not that I've yet seen. You've come to meet her, I assume. Please don't tell me you were planning an assassination—I don't have the heart to fight you tonight.

Rest easy, thought Val, flashing a slight smile. *Where is she, anyway?*

Go straight inside until you reach the staircase, then you'll want to go up three floors for her throne room. Watch yourselves on the stairs, he added. *The stone is too polished.*

We nodded our thanks, and Val clasped Nico's hand as we passed into the tower. King or not, Val had spent most of his life as a guard, and the two of them had looked out for Ellie and me more often than I cared to admit.

Following Nico's directions, we carefully mounted the stairs, joining the flow of Eleanor's people—now Irem's people, I reminded myself. Ellie's face appeared in my mind, and I pushed it down into my memory. There would be time for mourning later, and if we were lucky, a time for reckoning. For now, we played the game.

Irem's throne room, made of more rose quartz, could have comfortably fit two football fields down its length and soared like a cathedral to a peaked roof. The rounded windows set at regular intervals were covered in what appeared to be moonstone, semi-opaque and opalescent. She hadn't bothered with chairs or any sort of refreshments, and she was already seated atop a golden throne when we showed ourselves in.

One of the guards at the door did a double-take on noticing us and leaned close to my ear. "Shall we announce you, my lords?" she whispered.

"Let's not interrupt her show," I replied. "This is Irem's night, after all."

But our presence didn't go undetected for long. Not ten minutes after our arrival, one of the guards approached the throne to murmur a message to the queen, who amplified her voice and called across the room, "Coileán, Valerius." She paused. "Mongrel."

"Bitch," Toula muttered under her breath.

"Irem," Val replied, amplifying his voice in kind as the court whispered and turned to locate us in the crowd. "We heard your summons."

"Funny," she said, crossing her legs, "I don't recall inviting you."

Sharing a look with Val, I took my turn. "We've come to meet you and, uh...to offer our condolences for the loss of your sister. She will be dearly missed."

Irem scoffed. "Had I wanted to speak with you, I'd have summoned you directly. As it is, I'm far too busy ruling a court to waste time eulogizing my idiot sister with you."

At that, Toula could stay silent no longer. "Ellie wasn't an *idiot*. She helped create the peace among the realms, so whatever else you think of her, give her the credit she's due. And maybe this is just me as the magus in the room," she said with a sarcastic chuckle, "but last I checked, there were *three* courts to consider, and that's just in this realm, babe. Before you go blowing shit up, maybe you should have a little chat with the people who actually know how this place is run."

I squeezed Toula's shoulder before she could ramp up any further. "You know, on Eleanor's first day, she met with me, with the incoming grand magus, and with a representative of the Fringe. You've joined an exclusive club, Irem—at least get to know the other members and where we stand."

But the new queen merely shrugged. "And why should I care about any of that? My sister's alliances are not *my* alliances—and in case there was any doubt that I am not my sister, allow me to demonstrate."

With that Irem stood and addressed the gathered court. "My people, rejoice. Your liberation is at hand. From this moment on, you are prisoners here no longer."

"Oh, no," Toula whispered. "No, *no*, don't do this…"

Irem paused for effect, smiling down on the crowd. "The mortal realm is once again open to you. To *all* of you. Go forth and do as you please."

As the full-blooded faeries began to cheer and their half-fae neighbors looked on in horror, Irem pointed to the three of us and smirked. "Let the games begin. Your move."

AUGUST 13: BERT WOLD

Sunday morning was my favorite time of the week. With much of the castle sleeping off whatever amusements they'd managed on Saturday night and even the rest of the Council seldom embarking upon anything close to business before noon, I had our wing to myself. Free of distractions and the expected interruptions of working in an office, I could close myself off with a pot or two of tea and devote the quiet hours to my thaumaturgical research, the side projects beyond the scope of my official duties.

In truth, I should have been shunted onto a research track as a child, not groomed for politics. People frustrated me in ways that books seldom did, and all the magical ability in the world can't transform one into a competent leader. My two and a half months as grand magus were the greatest blot upon my record, and while I appreciated being permitted to keep my magus's chain and the access to the Archives that it bestowed, I would have preferred a modest space elsewhere in the building where I could be left in peace to read and write. Sunday morning was the closest approximation of that ideal that I was going to manage, however, and so I looked forward to my half day of uninterrupted work.

But as I headed down the corridor toward my office that morning, I heard the sound of glass shattering against one of the castle's stone walls—and to my surprise, the destruction seemed to be coming from the grand magus's office. Hoping I wasn't running into a fight, I pulled out my wand—for effect, really, I seldom had use for it—and threw open her door with a shield at the ready against the vandal.

There was no vandal. Rather, Toula sat slumped on one of her couches with a bottle of amber liquid on the table before her, and judging by the pile of broken glass on the far side of the room, she'd been drinking for a while.

I hastily shut and locked the door, then approached with caution as she created another tumbler from the ether and poured herself a generous two fingers. "Toula?" I murmured. "What's wrong? Are you...drunk?"

Her eyes, though red-rimmed and swollen, focused on mine. "Comfortably numb," she replied, and took a sip. "I've been sobering up whenever it works too well, so...cheers." She tilted the glass in my direction, then gestured to the other couch. "Help yourself. This goes down easy."

At close range, I could make out the distinctive aroma of whisky. "What are you drinking?"

"Dunno, but it's good. Filched it from the boy."

The boy would be Lord Coileán, whose name she only spoke around the executive wing when there was no possibility of anyone surmising that the two were romantically entangled. The king being a known connoisseur of spirits, I imagined that whatever Toula had swiped from his collection was probably top-shelf, but I tried not to drink straight whisky before the afternoon.

"Not that it's any of my business," I said, taking a seat opposite her, "but have you two quarreled?"

"I wish that's all it was." She sipped again, then wrapped her hands around the tumbler and stared at me. "Can I trust you to keep your mouth shut for now?"

"Certainly." Unlike some magi, I'd mastered mental blocks at a young age, and as long as I stayed out of Faerie—and away from Frank, who could get through my walls with a bit of persistence—her secrets were safe with me.

"Eleanor's dead," she mumbled.

Of all the news I'd anticipated, that threw me for a loop. "*How?*"

"Her goddamned sister. Shot Ellie in the head, inherited the court, and now Ros has ordained that we can't do jack shit about it."

"You're joking."

"Not in the least. So to sum up, my friend was murdered, my hands are tied, and the new queen is a full-blooded idiot who just released her court to have fun in *this* realm."

"Oh, my God," I said. Half faeries could be reasonable—Toula was proof of that—but full-blooded faeries were basically psychopaths. "Surely Ros can—"

"Ros won't step in unless Irem violates their little agreement, so no, she's not doing anything. 'Stay out of the mortal realm' wasn't part of the pact back in the day, so we're screwed now." She drained her glass and tossed it across the room to join its predecessors in shards on the floor. "The guys are strategizing, but there's not much they can do at the moment. I went ahead and called Conota to give them a heads-up—Arik and Hope saw Ellie shortly before she was killed, so they're shocked, to say the least."

"And the others?"

Another glass manifested in her hand, and she poured as she spoke. "Fringe knows. The Stowes are members of that court, so Vivi's in the loop. I haven't reached out to the Company, but they'll know before long—they always do."

"What about the Minors?" I asked. "They need forewarning—"

"Agreed, but I can't very well tell them before I make it public here, can I? And when I drop this bomb, the Council will have a fucking *cow*. This is the closest thing to a declaration of war that we've seen from Faerie since…shit, since the Mulligan takedown," she muttered, and sipped. "I don't want a war with the courts, Bert. Not even with *a* court. It's not something we can win on our own. I mean, I beat Ellie once, but only because she'd so weakened herself with bonds that she barely knew what planet she was on. Irem's at full strength."

Forgetting my alcohol policy, I made my own tumbler and helped myself to Coileán's brew…and yes, it was possibly the smoothest whisky I'd ever quaffed. Whatever else could be said for the man, he had a distiller's nose. "You can't keep this a secret, Toula," I said. "Not for long. There's too much at stake from a rogue court."

"Think I don't know that, bub?" A little wrinkle of concentration formed between her eyebrows, and she put two fingers to her temple until her face relaxed. "Sorry, just making sure my head doesn't get too cloudy. I've been at this for a *long* time tonight."

"Today, actually."

She grunted and drank. "Yeah, I know I can't keep this under wraps indefinitely, but I don't want to start a panic unless I have to. My plan is to watch for faerie attacks, wait and see whether we're going to have an immediate crisis. Maybe the inmates will be so enraptured by the outside world that they behave themselves."

"And maybe I'm the second coming of Christ," I replied.

"Hallelujah."

As we drank in silence for a moment, I was struck by how much older and wearier Toula appeared that morning. Physically, she was unchanged, an eternally youthful woman in a ratty purple tunic and wash-worn leggings who'd taken to wearing her black hair in a pixie cut and dying the tips blue. Perhaps it was grief, or maybe the weight of the clash that we both knew was impending, but her shoulders seemed bowed, and as I met her eyes, I noticed the beginning of the fae look within them—eyes that had seen too much of the world to match the rest of the face.

"Bert," she murmured as she finished her latest drink, "I need you to promise me something."

"What's that, then?"

"If this goes nuclear and I'm pushed out of office—"

"Oh, come, now—"

"I'm serious," she interrupted, cutting my protest short. "You and I both know that there's a significant chunk of the Council unsure about where my loyalties lie. If we start seeing faerie attacks, they may remove me as a liability. Let's not kid ourselves."

"If we're attacked, you're the best link we have to the other two courts," I countered. "The Council would be foolish to kick you out now."

"Yeah...but this is the *Council* we're talking about," she muttered. "With that in mind, if I'm shown the door, I want you to promise me that you'll stay on the Council. They're going to need voices of reason and restraint, and I count on you and Arnold."

"I have no plans to resign," I assured her, "but really, let's be reasonable. Who would we choose to replace you? There's not yet a solid contender for grand magus."

Toula stared at me briefly, then poured again. "You don't think so? Arc 1 might disagree."

"Who, *Leander*? He's not ready in any sense of the word."

"Do you think that would stop his fan club?"

I pondered the question, saw too clearly the answer to which neither of us wished to give voice, and helped myself again to the whisky. "You have my word," I told her. "Whatever I can do to hold the Arcanum together."

AUGUST 26: VALERIUS

To no one's surprise, it is difficult to establish diplomatic relations with a party who refuses to accept one's invitation to the table.

Infuriated though I was by Eleanor's murder, I couldn't afford to allow my personal feelings to worsen the uncertainty that Irem had brought to the realm. The Three needed to parley in order to make clear our positions on such matters as inter-court relations, not to mention inter-realm security. Though Coileán and I had theretofore seen eye to eye on most issues, I strongly suspected that Irem would prove a challenge. Our best hope, as I saw it, lay in putting before her the facts that she might have missed while passing her time flitting between extravagant parties. Unlike some of Oberon's children, Irem had nothing to do with her sister's regime, and I was hard pressed to think of a less suitable candidate for the throne. Rules were rules, however, and so we were cursed with the obnoxious child.

But my attempts to extend a hand of peace, if not friendship, were rebuffed. As Irem had dismissed most of Eleanor's staff, my own aides struggled to get word to the queen through the usual conduits. I sent Kiet, the captain of my guards, to ask Nico for assistance, but Nico had been stripped of his command and relegated to sentry duty on the outskirts of Irem's estate, and the new captain, one of Irem's sometime-lovers, refused to see his counterpart. In the end, it was my chief of staff, Bonnie, who came through for us—hardly a shock, as Bonnie was nothing if not eminently capable. Adopting a siege tactic, she simply made camp outside of the castle's main doors and asked for a meeting. The guards on the doors were some of Eleanor's half-fae hires, so no one bothered to chase her away, and Irem agreed to a meeting three days later to make the annoyance disappear.

Coileán and I opted not to go to Irem with our retinues or security, deciding that showing up without assistants would make a better, quieter show of strength. Full-blooded as she was, Irem was primed to take offense at the smallest perceived slight, and I saw nothing to gain by antagonizing her in her own home...no matter how much I wanted to blast a hole through her. Eleanor was never my dearest friend, but I'd come to respect her, which was far more than I could say for her sibling.

A quartet of Irem's guards met us at the outer gate, none looking particularly pleased by the assignment. I scanned their faces and recognized the lot of them—some of Nico's best, the sort that a prudent queen would keep close to her person. That she'd relegated them to gate duty gave me little confidence in the state of her guards and wounded my professional sensibilities.

"Good afternoon," I said, showing them my empty hands. The gesture was a mere formality—I could do terrible things without a weapon—but the four seemed oddly nervous, and I tried not to make their task difficult. "Will you escort us to your lady?"

Three of the guards looked toward the fourth, a dark-haired woman—Nico's third, as I recalled—who cleared her throat but kept her voice low when she spoke. "Yes, my lords, we'll show you in." She hesitated, then held my gaze. "Times are different, are they not?"

"So it would seem," I replied, conscious of the weight of her eyes. That she wanted to say more, I had no doubt, but I suspected the queen had established a connection with the guard's mind. Coileán had never seen the purpose of keeping a line open to his staff at all times, but his mother had thus availed herself on many occasions over my centuries of service. What better way to protect oneself against treachery than by monitoring the thoughts of one's staff? The practice had been tiring to her, but she was sufficiently paranoid to employ it, and those of us who served her had learned to discipline our minds for fear of angering a woman who'd preferred to strike before asking questions.

Carefully, I worked my way below the guard's superficially placid thoughts to the turmoil beneath. It was difficult to make sense of the ideas to which she didn't dare give the form of words, but I caught enough of her meaning before I quickly withdrew.

"Let's be on our way," I said. "I'd hate to keep your lady waiting."

As we followed the guards, Coileán cut his eyes to me and frowned. *What was that all about?*

Something's wrong in the castle, I replied. *The guard finds it distasteful, but I didn't get the details—Irem's listening in.*

Oh, great. His face remained neutral, betraying nothing of our conversation. *If it's bad enough, can we blast her and get it over with?*

No, Ros interrupted, *not yet, and would you please stop making this worse than it already is?*

I'd not seen her in days, though I'd felt her growing agitation since Irem's self-coronation. Ros sounded frustrated—curious, given her enormous power—and if I wasn't mistaken, somewhat worried. *What should we expect?* I asked her.

She's got a changeling in there.

Beside me, Coileán stiffened, and I gripped his arm before he could do something rash. *Already?*

Snatched a few days ago. The kid's alive, but she's scared to death, and Irem gets physical every time she cries.

Remind me again why I can't kill that bitch, Coileán thought, clenching his teeth.

Because we're successors in interest to a bargain none of us brokered. Take it up with Kura, said Ros. *I'm warning you now so that you don't force me to fight on her side, so keep it together, okay? Please?*

You just told us there's a kid in there. I'm not supposed to be upset? he retorted.

Speaking as someone who grew up in an abusive situation, I'm at least as upset as you are, she shot back, *but for the good of the realm, I'm trying to give Irem time to come around on her own. She needs to decide for herself that the rules you've worked out are to her benefit. So hold your fire and try not to start a war, eh? For me?*

Coileán's mental grumbling didn't need words to make his feelings on the matter clear.

Our audience, the lead guard quietly informed us on the way through the castle, would be in the queen's throne room.

An *audience*. Not a meeting of equals, but rather a privilege bestowed upon inferiors. My temper flared as I caught the meaning of our escort's careful choice of words, and from the look on his face, Coileán was likewise peeved—pissed, as my sister might say. But I was old enough to know the game, to stand back and watch Irem's offensive so as to learn how best to counter it. As for Coileán…well, I did worry about the boy, but for the moment, he seemed to be biding his time. I hoped he could suffer whatever petty insults Irem threw without escalation, as I had no desire to mediate that afternoon.

Soon enough, the guards opened the doors to the throne room and escorted us inside. The room was unchanged from the last time I'd seen it, still cavernous and pink, but the crowd had been thinned to six: four additional guards flanking the throne, Irem, who perched atop her seat and watched us as we neared, and a small figure crouched at her feet. As I neared the dais, I began to make out the changeling's details. Young, maybe eight or nine, still baby-faced. Pale blonde hair, ice-blue eyes. Fair skin marked with black and greenish bruises on the cheek and arms. A sleeveless gray dress, too large for her small frame. Bare feet. And most notably, a golden collar locked tight around her little throat and attached to a leather leash, which Irem held looped around her wrist. The child trembled as we approached, shrinking against the throne, and Irem gave the leash a sharp tug to still her.

Though she looked nothing like my granddaughter once had, I could only see Maria in the changeling's face, and it took all of my self-control to clamp down on the swelling tide of horror and fury within me. I didn't need to look at Coileán to know how he felt about the tableau; his anger radiated from him like heat from a bonfire. Again, I grabbed his arm before he could react, and though he yanked free of my grip, he fumed in silence.

"Well?" said Irem as we drew closer. "What do you want?"

In light of Coileán's mood, I took the lead. "We've found it mutually beneficial if the Three meet on occasion," I replied, forcing myself not to stare at the pitiful child. "An opportunity for us to clear the air and work out any grievances without resorting to formal measures. Perhaps we could take this to your office?"

"No." She leaned against an armrest and smirked. "If you have something to say, then say it and stop wasting my time."

"We mean no offense," I soothed, hoping Coileán could play along, and then, as casually as I could, I asked, "Who's the girl?"

Irem patted the child's greasy hair, and the girl whimpered. "My new pet. Do you like her?"

"Your…pet?"

"A gift. One of my old bedfellows found her three days ago and gave her to me. She's not particularly obedient, but with enough practice, I'm sure she will learn."

"Hm," I said, swallowing the curses I wanted to hurl at her. "Have you given the child Fae?"

Irem shrugged. "Not yet."

"Is she mundane, then?" I continued. "Surely not a wizard…"

At that, the new queen laughed. "What difference does it make? They're all mortals, and they're ours for the taking."

Let me do the talking, I thought as Coileán began to open his mouth. He glared at me but held his tongue, and I pressed my luck. To Irem, I said, "I see that you've had to use force with your changeling. You know, she might be more obedient if she could understand you."

"Perhaps," she allowed.

"May I? I'm familiar with the process."

Irem glanced at the girl again, then tossed her head dismissively. "If it pleases you. I don't care."

"Thank you," I said, and approached the dais. The child shrank from me, seemingly trying to curl into a ball against the throne, and though I hated the fear in her eyes, I kept myself guarded. She stifled another whimper as I crouched beside her and swiftly built a numbing and healing construction, but when the enchantment began to take effect, her look of terror shifted toward confusion, and then hope.

"So," said Coileán, taking up a position on the other side of the throne, "tell me about your new place. Quite different than Ellie's style. What was your inspiration?"

A distraction, I realized—and Irem played right into his hands, angling away from the girl and me while she boasted about her castle. *Thank you,* I told him, then turned my attention to the child. I didn't want to hit her with the linguistic enchantment before warning her of what was to come, but as my familiarity with modern human languages was admittedly limited, I tried English and hoped for the best. "Do you understand me?" I murmured.

Her eyes lit up, and she nodded.

"English?"

"Svenska," she whispered, then tried again when I frowned. "Swedish," she said, her voice high and halting.

"I learn at school. I am nine, so not perfect yet, but…" She offered a weak shrug. "It's good."

"What's your name?"

"Johanna."

"I'm Val. Are you a wizard, Johanna?" She seemed unfamiliar with the term, and I tried a different approach. "Your family, what do they do?"

"We make potatoes," she said. "You take me home?"

"How did you come here?"

"I walk home from school, and a man come and take my arm, and I kick him, but he bring me here. Please, *please* take me home."

Her eyes filled, and I thought of Haleigh Lozano, Hope's poor mother, snatched after school to serve as a cynaeli lord's concubine. At least Johanna was too young for such use…or so I hoped. But as much as I wanted to grab the child and run, I couldn't risk a war with Irem. Not yet.

"Listen to me," I said as I finished the healing enchantment. "I'm going to give you the local tongue. This will not hurt. You *must* obey Lady Irem. She is very powerful, and if you continue to disobey her, she will beat you again."

I placed my fingertips on her temples and concentrated, and Johanna's eyes flew open wide with the shock of the experience. After a few seconds, I whispered in Fae, "Can you understand me now?"

She hesitated, then nodded. I hoped the tears falling down her cheeks were the result of surprise instead of pain.

Don't say anything, I thought to her. *Not a word. Try not to look so shocked.* Once she'd stilled herself, I continued, *We'll do what we can to see you safely home.* I cut my eyes to the other side of the throne, where Irem was still blathering on about the size of her ballroom. *We can't free you today*—her face fell at the news—*but we're not abandoning you here. I'm so sorry for what they've done to you, child. We'll make this right.*

"Now," I said aloud, "be good and do as Lady Irem tells you. Is that understood?"

The best reassurance I could offer her in the moment was a wink, but a smile flickered across her face. "Yes."

Task accomplished, I stood and retreated from the throne, and Coileán cast a glance at the bruised child. "I'm sure the girl is entertaining," he said to Irem, "but her family must be frantic. My mother took my daughter as a changeling, did you know that? *Your* sister's daughter, actually. Losing her child did horrible things to Meggy."

One of Irem's perfect brows rose. "Your point? If you're trying to appeal to my better nature—"

"Nothing of the sort—I expect there's not an altruistic bone in your body. But you should know that Meggy was Toula's dear friend," he said, folding his arms. "Toula saw how Meggy turned out. She takes the stealing of changelings *personally*. So even if that kid's mundane, the Arcanum's not going to stand for this."

If Coileán had hoped to give her pause, the effort appeared to have failed. "The *Arcanum?*" she said, chuckling. "You honestly believe that those weaklings are strong enough to kill me here? With the largest court at my disposal?"

"Perhaps not," I said quietly, "but I'll remind you that Toula is my sister, and I will not stand for aggression against the Arcanum."

"Yeah," Coileán interjected, nodding. "I mean, Toula probably couldn't beat you on her own. *Probably*. She did knock out Ellie that once. But I've seen what the Arcanum's finest can do, and if you add them in…plus two other courts…surely that would tip the balance against you."

"A threat?" said Irem. "Cute."

"Just providing you with some facts," he replied.

"Then allow me to return the favor," she said with a cold smile. "You don't want another inter-court war. You have no stomach for it. And once word circulates that my people are coming and going from the realm as they please, how long do you suppose your people will allow themselves to remain imprisoned here?"

Before Coileán or I could counter that, she sat back on her throne and crossed her legs. "And while we're exchanging *facts*, boys, the fact of the matter is that I see no purpose in allowing the dregs to squat in this realm any longer."

Coileán frowned. "What dregs—"

"She means the Fringe settlement," I said, cutting him short and fighting the urge to throttle the smirking queen. To her, I said, "The Fringe came here as refugees. They've been useful allies, they keep to themselves, and they don't cause trouble. We've protected them by mutual consent for decades."

"You realize that most of the people in town are mortal, yes?" said Coileán. "Some of them have been here close to fifty years. Forcing them out now would be a death sentence for many."

"I fail to see how that's my problem," Irem replied. "And I hereby revoke my consent."

"Then we'll continue to protect them," I said.

"You'll need to do more than that. It's come to my attention that the ones doing the most for your little refugee pets are of my court—you know the Stowe boys, don't you? I think I'll order them to cease rendering aid and forbid them from entering the place."

By then, Coileán's overtaxed patience had nearly frayed. "One of them is married to a shifter. How do you see *that* going down?"

"An order is an order. Now, if you two like the Fringe so much, you can protect and feed them. But remember, I've given my people liberty—and if they want to explore your little town, I won't keep them out."

As Coileán began to sputter his protest, I spoke over him. "Let's step back and be rational. Irem, we understand that you are not Eleanor and will approach these matters from, uh…a different perspective," I said, trying to be diplomatic, "but surely you can see what's at stake. We've had peace among the courts for years. We're at peace with the Fringe, the Arcanum, the Minor Arcanum, the Company, Conota. If you refuse to put boundaries on your court, if you attack the Fringe settlement and steal changelings, you risk a dissolution of that peace. And for what? That child at your feet isn't worth a multi-realm war. Help us maintain the status quo," I urged, stepping closer to the dais. "The current arrangement benefits us all. Don't you see that?"

"Certainly," she replied, resting her chin in her hand. "But I've been so *bored* of late, and I'm ready to have a little fun."

Though I yearned to put a bolt through Irem's head, I grabbed Coileán and opened a gate before he could start a fight. *Be strong*, I told Johanna, then dragged Coileán back to my office and slammed the gate shut to the sound of Irem's laughter.

"Moon and stars," he shouted, finally free to explode, "what the *fuck* are we going to do?"

I motioned my door closed before my aides could investigate the sudden disturbance, then pulled my phone from my pocket. "The sensible thing," I muttered, and tapped at the screen. A moment later, as my sister greeted me, I said, "Come over when you can. We have a *problem*."

AUGUST 28: TOULA PAVLI

Knowing damn well that Irem wouldn't give me the time of day if I asked, much less a private meeting, I went with plan B and called Vivi in the settlement. She couldn't tell me when Irem would next hold court, but her brother Lucian remained in the queen's employ and had access to the schedule—and with the Fringe on high alert and word of Irem's little changeling making the rounds, he was only too happy to share information with his baby sister.

So it was that I strolled up to the castle in my best red ceremonial robe and chain of office that morning, holding my back straight and trying to project a take-no-prisoners attitude. In truth, when I'd heard the news from the boys two days prior, I'd been ready to go in with guns blazing, but they'd talked me down, and then Ros had popped by to stress what a bad idea that would be. Pound for pound, I wasn't Irem's equal in pure strength, but I *was* a talented wizard with a strong current of enchantment reinforcing my casting, and my ability was literally off the Arcanum's chart. I was *spoiling* for a fight with the murderous queen. Still, I grudgingly allowed cooler heads to prevail and agreed to try a less bloody approach.

That didn't mean I had to be diplomatic about it.

"What's up?" I said to Nico, who was once again on door duty.

He gave me a once-over, from my black eyeliner to my steel-toed boots—a custom job with the steel on the outside for maximum efficacy, should I need to kick a faerie—but maintained his poker face. "Grand Magus."

"Going to give me a hard time if I tell you I'm here for a word with your boss?"

"Am I to assume that your brother did not send you?"

I pointed to my heavy necklace with both thumbs. "Does this say 'errand girl' to you, Captain?"

The corner of his mouth twitched. "Not in the slightest, but I wanted to be certain. Do you need an escort?"

"I've got it, bub," I replied, and patted his shoulder as I slipped into Irem's pink fortress.

The few people I passed on my way upstairs gave me a wide berth, and the guards posted at the entrance to the throne room just stepped aside when I marched toward them. I strode down the middle of the room—I swear, the tasteless cretin hadn't bothered to install so much as a runner to interrupt the Pepto ambiance—and suddenly found myself the focal point of the several dozen fantastically attired petitioners who'd come that morning to ask favors of their queen. That they were fully fae, I had no doubt; the half fae I'd known tended not to dress like period drama extras in the throes of couturial madness. Sure, I was strutting around in a hooded robe like I was en route to a university graduation, but at least I'd dressed for my job—I wasn't the idiot choosing to wear, say, a flouncy lime-green high-low dress and four-inch heels on a smooth stone floor.

As I neared the throne, I sized up the people around me, deciding which I could knock out without much effort and which might give me a headache. Fortunately, no one seemed to be in a fighting mood, though I knew too well how quickly that could change.

And then I saw the kid at the foot of the throne. Johanna, Val had called her, and the description he'd given me was spot-on. The poor thing was still collared and leashed, still wearing a gray sack of a dress like an old-timey street urchin, and her uncombed hair had begun to mat in places.

Eyes on the prize, I told myself, then held my chin a little higher, planted my feet, and bellowed, "Irem! We need to talk."

The room's chatter stilled as the petitioners looked from me to the queen, waiting to see how she would take my interruption.

If Irem lacked decency, she made up for it with confidence in spades. Crossing her long legs beneath her ridiculous purple tulle skirt, she regarded me in silence for a few seconds, then said, "What do you want, little girl?"

A few of the faeries around me tittered, but I resisted the impulse to throw them against the walls.

"It's 'Grand Magus,' thanks," I replied. "'Lady Fotoula' if you're feeling fancy. But we can talk diplomacy later. I'm here for the changeling."

Irem's eyebrows rose in mock surprise. "*My* changeling?"

"You have no right to keep her. *None* of you have that right," I said, glaring at the assembled. "The Arcanum considers the kidnapping of changelings to be a threat to our sovereignty and to the security of the mortal realm. Now, maybe this is news to you," I replied with a faux smile, "and if so, I'd hate to leave on bad terms. What do you want for her release?"

She smiled, then reached over the armrest to pat the cringing child's head. "I'm not in a bargaining mood, little girl."

Moving a few steps closer to the throne, I saw the fresh bruises on the kid's arm, but I could make out no hint of the healing enchantment Val had supposedly built on her. Irem must have broken it once the guys left. My temper, all too fae at moments like that, began to spike. "You think this is a joke?" I asked Irem. "Notice that I'm not holding a wand. That's not an oversight—I don't *need* one. Freak of nature, some say—I'm much stronger than I should be. And since I'm not leaving without Johanna there, either you can do the smart thing and release her to my custody, or I can kick your ass here and now while all these nice people watch."

Irem laughed, but I knew I wasn't imagining the flicker of uncertainty on her face.

"I beat Ellie unconscious once," I said, praying the bluff would work. "I'd really rather not resort to violence here, but if you leave me no choice—"

The first bolt from the throne came flying at me like a missile, but my shield was faster and strong, absorbing some of the blow and sending the rest ricocheting into the walls. Chunks of rose quartz fell to the floor, and I threw more power into the shield while Irem considered the result of her deflected shot. She had a good game face, I'd grant her that, but I saw the uncertainty in her eyes. I wasn't going to be an easy kill. Maybe she'd take my threat seriously...

Maybe not. Two more bolts flew my way in rapid succession, each stronger than its predecessor. My arm shook with the strain of holding the shield together, but as more pieces of the throne room fell from the impact sites, I glared at Irem and yelled, "That all you got? Ellie could do better than that!"

Suddenly, Ros manifested between the dais and me, holding out a hand to each of us like a referee keeping two prizefighters at bay. "Enough," she barked. "Toula, stand down."

Faced with a threat I knew I couldn't overpower, I backed up a few paces but continued to hold my shield.

"Thank you," she said, and turned to Irem. "Release the girl. *Now.*"

Irem tightened her grip on the leash and smirked at the glowing figure on the floor. "And if I don't, mongrel?"

The leash snapped a millisecond before Irem's golden throne disintegrated into atoms, sending the queen to the hard dais in an undignified heap. Before Irem could begin to pick herself up, she flew toward the high ceiling, only to plummet helplessly toward the unforgiving floor. She screamed as she fell...but just before she made contact, she came to an abrupt halt in midair, then was tossed like a ragdoll onto the stone below the dais.

Irem groaned and fluttered her eyes, but when she looked up, she must have seen little more than Ros, who planted a foot atop her chest and leaned close to the dazed queen. "*I* am the true power in this realm," Ros murmured, though as the crowd had fallen silent, her voice carried like a shout. "I give you power, and I can withdraw it. There will be no more changelings taken, is that *absolutely* clear?"

The queen, who had to be in considerable pain from her rough handling, mumbled something vaguely in the affirmative.

"I gave you a chance to see reason on your own," Ros continued. "I've tried to stand back and let you feel your way through this for more than a week. But since you're too much of an idiot to listen to hints, I'll be plain." Johanna's collar split in four pieces and fell to the ground, and as the child hugged herself, Ros looked at her and spoke gently. "I'm so sorry, sweetheart. Go with Toula— she'll take you home."

Hesitantly, Johanna stood, and when Ros nodded encouragement, she leapt from the dais and ran toward me. I dropped my shield and caught her, lifting the trembling girl into my arms as she buried her face against my neck.

But by then, whatever momentary fog the head blows had given Irem had begun to clear. "You can't do that!" she protested. "She's *mine*—"

The thought ended in an ear-splitting screech of pain, and Ros's foot bore down harder on Irem's sternum. "You're nothing but a spoiled child," she said, "and if you try my patience, I'll show you *exactly* what I can do." Looking up from Irem, she gave the retreating faeries a long, hard stare, then leaned closer to their sobbing queen. "Call me 'mongrel' again, little girl, and I *will* kill you. It'll hurt me, but I'll enjoy every minute of it." Finally, she stepped off of Irem and sneered as the queen continued to cry—whatever pain Ros had inflicted, she'd meant it. "You're a disgrace. Clean yourself up. And if there's anything more than hot air between your ears, you'll go find Coileán and Val, *beg* their forgiveness for your rudeness, and try to learn something about how this realm is run. Is that clear, or should I use smaller words?"

As Irem sniffled and rubbed her head, Ros joined me. Johanna gasped and tightened her grip on me—and really, given Ros's mood, I didn't blame her—but Ros didn't lay so much as a finger on the child. "Again," she murmured, "I'm so very sorry for your ordeal. Toula will take you home—just tell her where you live, and she'll bring you there."

"Absolutely," I agreed, rubbing Johanna's back. "We'll get you cleaned up first, okay?"

"Okay," she mumbled.

"Is there anything I can do to make this up to you?" Ros asked.

Johanna thought for a moment, then whispered in my ear.

"Sure, hon, that's easy," I told her, and nodded to Ros as I opened a gate to my brother's house. "I've got it from here. Anything you want me to pass on to the boys?"

Ros flashed an almost predatory smile. "Oh, don't worry about that. They're *well* aware of what's happened here today…and there's a ton of shampoo and such in Maria's suite," she added. "Bonnie's on standby if you need anything."

Johanna was still trembling when I filled the deep bathtub and left her with fresh towels and a toothbrush. By the time she poked her head out of the bathroom, Bonnie had swept in to oversee the affair, and as Bonnie had successfully wrangled Maria and Kitty for years, I didn't put up a fuss.

She tutted over the state of Johanna's bruises, then sat her down at the table in Maria's bedroom and asked what she'd like for lunch. Her first request, which we finally worked out to be a sandwich involving shrimp, was beyond Bonnie's culinary repertoire, but Johanna happily accepted shrimp on a pizza. As soon as the pie manifested before her, she dug in ravenously, and Bonnie set about detangling and drying her hair. "Did Irem even feed you?" Bonnie asked as Johanna took a massive bite.

"A little," she said once she came up for air. "It wasn't very nice."

With the girl clean, Bonnie turned to the task of dressing her, as we couldn't send her home in the filthy rag she'd been wearing. Bonnie asked me to find some pictures of children's clothing, then scrolled through the offerings on my phone, pursed her lips in thought, and waved half a dozen ensembles into existence atop the bed. Johanna stared, pizza momentarily forgotten, and Bonnie assured her, "Anything you like. We'll make it fit."

Soon enough, Johanna was admiring her new dress, leggings, and purple tennis shoes in the mirror, her other favorites had been packed into a bag, and Bonnie had given her face one last inspection for stray crumbs. "Imagine your home in your mind," I told Johanna. "As hard as you can."

She closed her eyes and scrunched up her face with concentration, and I easily found the scene in the front of her thoughts: a modest farmhouse surrounded by fields with a dark green swath of forest in the distance. Picturesque, certainly, and under better circumstances, I'd have enjoyed stopping for the bucolic view. As it was, I had an awkward job to do, and Scandinavian sightseeing would be relegated to another day.

I opened a gate and told Johanna to take a look, and she beamed. "My house!" she cried.

"You're good at this," I said, then took her hand,

silently thanked Bonnie, and escorted the child back into the mortal realm.

The house sat at the end of a long gravel driveway, a small but neat building with bright blue shutters. A few other structures dotted the property—barns and storage sheds, I assumed—but before I could question Johanna about them, I heard a shout from the house and saw a man and a woman racing for us. Johanna called to them, and I released her to run into her parents' arms.

By the time I reached them, Johanna's mother was holding her, sobbing, while her father met me with tears in his eyes. "She said you rescued her from a bad woman," he began, his English accented but otherwise perfect. "What happened to our daughter? Who are *you*?"

It was a fair question, not least because I was still wearing my robe and chain. "A friend, and that's all you need to know," I replied. "Incidentally, Johanna said you're having trouble with your car."

He frowned. "The engine is nearly dead, yes, but what does that—"

"Why don't you show me?"

As his wife hustled their daughter into the house, he bemusedly led me to the nearest barn, where I found a black Volvo parked beside a tractor. The car was at least twenty years old and flecked with rust around the undercarriage, and the tires, if not bald, were dangerously close to the line. "It's been a slow death," he told me, flopping one hand in the direction of the car. "But the tractor needed repairs in the spring, and that was more important than the car."

"Johanna asked if I could fix it for you," I said. "If that's all right..."

Though he still seemed deeply perplexed by the situation—I certainly couldn't blame him—he popped the hood and gave me a peek inside. In truth, I couldn't have diagnosed the problem on sight, but a whispered spell was sufficient to replace the guts of the car with a new engine.

I heard the man gasp and retreat a few steps, but I continued my restoration work, fixing the paint, retreading the tires, and defogging the headlights. Sliding behind the wheel, I started the car and grinned as the engine rumbled. With a quick check of the fluid levels, I closed the hood and folded my arms. "I once had a girlfriend who was *deeply* into cars," I said. "We didn't last long, but she taught me a few things about vehicle maintenance."

His mouth opened and closed like a landed fish's for a few seconds before he managed to whisper, "How…"

"Magic, pure and simple. Now, if I were you, I'd keep a close watch on your daughter for a while, just in case. And, uh…if you'd be so kind as to be quiet about the rest of this, I'd greatly appreciate it."

Stunned, he nodded, but as I was turning to open a gate home, he recovered his voice. "What should we tell the police? The town? Our friends have been looking for Johanna for days."

I thought quickly. "Tell everyone that she fell into a cellar while exploring an abandoned house and only just found her way out. That should cover it."

Briefly, I flirted with the idea of giving the three of them false memories, removing myself from the picture and making Johanna believe the story about being trapped in a cellar. But memory changes were accomplished only through dynamic binds, and the practice left a foul taste in my mouth—not to mention that I'd be magically tethered to the objects of those binds, slightly weakened by the effort it would take to maintain them. I'd brought Johanna home and done the family a favor—surely, I reasoned, that would be sufficient to buy their silence.

I hoped.

"But who *are* you?" the father demanded, then yelped as a lightning-rimmed gate appeared before me.

"Someone who doesn't have a problem punching up," I muttered. "Tell Johanna goodbye for me, won't you?" I added, and sealed the hole behind me.

AUGUST 30: COILEÁN

A knock at the door broke my concentration, but I was grateful for the excuse to put aside the petition I was reading. Three of my few remaining nephews, all fully fae, had been tormenting each other over fishing rights to a pond for two months. Never mind that the realm was pocked with many such ponds or that the subject of the dispute was utterly ordinary, a lake perhaps five acres in size with nothing in particular to recommend it. But each of the little idiots had laid claim to it, and since sharing is a concept alien to the fae psyche, I'd been forced to arbitrate when they came whining to me.

The source of my relief turned out to be the captain of my guards, Mina—one of my nieces, though infinitely more reasonable than her obnoxious cousins. "What's up?" I asked, turning over the petition and sliding it to the far side of my desk.

She slipped into my office and closed the door, then approached so as to keep her voice low. "You have visitors requesting an audience."

"*Today*? I just held court yesterday…"

"I know, but it's the Stowes."

That cut my griping short. "Which ones? Rohese and Martin? Rufus and Poppy?"

Mina grimaced. "All of them, I think. Well," she amended, "not Vivi, and I didn't see the grandson, but he's in Glastonbury these days, isn't he?"

"Yeah, the kid's with Ted's group," I said, and frowned at my bookcase. I had no complaint with the Stowes—on the whole, they looked after the Fringe, and I'd never heard Ellie even suggest that one of them was causing trouble. But they belonged to Irem's court, and the fact that they'd shown up at my door en masse and unscheduled suggested that I wouldn't like whatever they had to say.

Still, I couldn't leave them standing in the corridor all morning. "Show them in, please," I told Mina.

She nodded and went out to fetch them, and I stood and came around my desk as they filed into the room, all twelve brothers and their anxious parents. "I'm sorry about the insufficient seating," I said, gesturing to the pair of couches before the fireplace. "What can I do for you?"

I'd directed the question toward the eldest Stowes, but they hesitated and glanced down the pack toward Rufus. When none of his brothers jumped in, he sighed and took the lead. "Not to put too fine a point on it, my lord," he said, pushing back his blazer to shove his hands into his pockets, "but I don't trust Irem as far as I can throw her. That stunt with the changeling was appalling—"

"You didn't see the child," Lucian muttered.

"*I* did," I told him.

"Yeah, well, that was only the beginning, it seems," Rufus continued, "because about half an hour ago, she ordered the court out of the settlement. Announced that it was off-limits until further notice. Maybe I'm just paranoid, but I worry about what might happen if we're not there."

"Trust me, you're not paranoid," I replied, and leaned against my desk. "She doesn't see the point of allowing the Fringe to remain here."

The brothers grumbled at that, and their mother's face grew more drawn.

"Lovely," Rufus muttered, "And to top it off, she fired Luce yesterday."

"Why?" I turned to Lucian, who'd served as Eleanor's chef for nearly all of her reign. "What did you do, put arsenic in her coffee?"

"I did nothing, my lord," he replied, shrugging. "Seems my brother's not the only one with a touch of paranoia."

"And so she dismissed the only person in this realm with a Michelin star. Sheer brilliance." I shook my head and folded my arms. "What are you asking me to do, go to her and argue for an exception for you in the settlement? I'll try, if you want, but I don't see that succeeding. Ros publicly humiliated her two days ago, and I think we can all imagine what sort of mood she must be in right now."

"Actually," said Rufus, "we wanted to know if you'd have us."

That gave me pause. Switching courts was a rare occurrence—it required the consent of the king or queen into whose court one wished to transfer, and it left one without a social network. By our design, the courts seldom interacted—indeed, it was an ill-kept secret that the best place in the realm for an inter-court meetup was at The Tavern, the settlement bar—so shifting allegiance meant starting over. Then again, the Stowe clan had kept largely to themselves for centuries, favoring human society to the company of their court. They weren't highborn, so there were no titles on the line. Nor were there marital complications to consider, as the only Stowe children to have married had chosen a shifter and a perfectly mundane human.

"I realize we're no great prize," Rufus continued, "but we don't need much space—most of us live in the settlement these days, anyway. If you'll let us, we'll do there what we've been doing all along. Might even find a job for Luce."

"*Someone* competent needs to man the deep fryer," quipped Adam, a longtime bartender in town.

Lucian winced at the suggestion, and I tried not to laugh at his distress. "If you're serious about this," I told the Stowes, "then I'll accept you. Ros, any complaint?"

She appeared beside my crowd of visitors and shook

her head. "Nah, I've got no problem with them. Your call."

"We're absolutely serious," said Rufus, and his brothers and parents nodded their agreement.

"Then I accept your fealty," I replied. As a few of the Stowes sagged with relief, I said, "If you'd be so kind, return to the settlement and keep up the good work. And…" I frowned, comparing their faces with my memory, then remembered which was the eldest son. "Ned, you're still handling security, are you not?"

He offered a curt nod. "Yes, my lord, with Matthew and Harry," he explained, picking them out of the pack. "Seamus and Badger maintain order internally, or at least what little of that needs doing, but we watch the border."

"Good to know. Val and I are taking seriously Irem's threats concerning the settlement, and we're planning to send reinforcements…" I hesitated as his face fell. "Something wrong?"

Ned cleared his throat and held himself up straighter. "With all due respect, if possible, could we be sent *trained* guards this time? Your nieces and nephews were kind to assist when Lady Eleanor lost her senses, but, ehm…"

I couldn't help snickering—he was trying so hard to be diplomatic. "You'll have proper guards, I swear it. Mina and Kiet are making their selections. Now," I said, turning to Lucian as Ned mimed wiping his brow, "as for you, Chef…much as this pains me, if I tried to bring you into my kitchen, Astrid would murder me in my sleep."

"She's an excellent cook," said Lucian.

"Yeah, but I attended enough dinners at Ellie's to know what I'm missing."

He smiled. "Please tell her that should she ever need a hand, I'm willing to assist. Better than the fryer," he muttered, cutting his eyes to grinning Adam.

"Never fear, we'll find a kitchen for you, lad," said Ned, elbowing Lucian hard enough to make him double over. "You make a lousy soldier."

"Gee, thanks," he wheezed. "Remind me to spit in your dinner—"

Another rap at the door pulled me from the fraternal ribbing, and I looked over to see Mina return. "Pardon the interruption, but you have another visitor waiting."

"Who?"

"Nico," she replied with a little smirk.

"*Nico*?" I echoed, then considered how much of my office was currently occupied by Stowes. "Eh, I suppose we have room. Show him in."

Mina did as I asked, then closed the door behind her, leaving Nico to consider his unexpected audience. "I apologize for coming unasked, my lord," he began, absently rubbing one elbow.

I waved the apology aside. "Be welcome, Captain. What brings you here?"

His mouth moved into a brief, mirthless smile. "Not a captain anymore, I'm afraid. Lady Irem has seen fit to dismiss me, and…well—"

"Have you come to swear fealty?" I interrupted.

He paused, considering my expression, then nodded. "If I may."

"Oh, *please* let him," Ned interjected. "He's a competent soldier. I'll take him now, as he stands, unarmed…"

"Seems you have a fan," I told Nico as Rohese furiously tried to shush her son. "And yes, I'm happy to have you. I also have a job for you, because as you can see, Ned will be distraught if send you anywhere other than the settlement."

Nico glanced over and returned Ned's smile. "Defense, I trust."

"Exactly. But I want you and Ned to work out the details with Mina and Kiet. Help them assemble a team to bolster the town's forces. I realize this is your area," I added to Ned, "but they know Nico, and the guards will be more comfortable if he's involved."

Ned lifted his palms in surrender. "I take no offense, my lord. He's been at this quite a bit longer than I have."

"You've done well, boy," said Nico, clapping him on the shoulder, then turned his attention back to me. "If it suits you, my lord, we'll find Mina now before her shift ends."

"Be my guest," I replied, and looked at the waiting Stowes. "There's plenty of empty land along my northern border. Perhaps it would be better for you to build closer to Val's people than to Irem's. There's a large parlor at the end of the hall—make yourselves comfortable, and I'll ask Aiden to bring you the maps so that you can choose homesteads, if you want them."

My visitors filed out with their thanks, but I caught Rufus before he could follow his brothers. "A word?"

"Certainly," he said, and loitered near the bookcase while the last of the Stowes took their leave.

When we were alone, I headed for my bar. "What's your poison, Rufus?"

"Will you think me weak if I stick with beer before lunch?"

"Nah." I cracked open a bottle of lager, poured myself a generous scotch, and waited while he took a test sip. "Decent?"

"Indeed. What's the occasion?"

I lifted my tumbler. "To Ellie."

"Hear, hear," he murmured, and clinked his bottle against my glass before drinking deeply.

"I wanted to express my condolences properly," I said once he came up for air. "The last days have been somewhat chaotic, you understand—"

"Absolutely."

"But be that as it may, I know how fond she was of you. Respected you greatly. And I, uh…well, I'm very sorry for your loss."

Rufus waited while I drank, then said, "She didn't suffer—Ros assured me."

"You handled her, um—"

"Arrangements? Yeah." He downed another gulp of his beer. "And I've had to fight the urge to take a shot at Irem every time I've seen her. But wherever Ellie is now, she and Walt are together again, and I'm happy for them. Those two always were so in love." He paused, considered his unlabeled brown bottle, then said, "She held herself together well after his death, all things considered. Except for those few years—"

"Even then, she could have been worse."

"Please don't threaten me like that," he said with a low chuckle. "But overall...I mean, I know how much she missed him. God, I don't know what I'd do if I lost Poppy."

Rufus's wife, a shifter, had to be close to seventy-five years old, but she maintained her youth because she hadn't left the realm since she was in her twenties. If the settlement were destroyed and she were forced out of Faerie, all of those missing years would fall upon her at once, rendering her an old woman in the blink of an eye, if not killing her from the sudden strain on her body. Surely Poppy and Rufus understood as well as anyone what was at stake if Irem declared the settlement a blight to be eradicated.

"We're going to protect her," I promised Rufus. "We'll protect them all."

He lifted his beer again and drank to that.

SEPTEMBER 4: TOULA PAVLI

To no one's great delight, I'd made a habit of convening the full Council twice a month for general status updates, usually on the first and third Mondays. One meeting was set for the early morning, the other for the late afternoon, a concession to the many time zones represented. The first meeting of September was a breakfast seating for my Continental colleagues and the Giza magi, a late lunch for the Mongolian crew, nearly teatime for the Australians, and just painful for the delegations that shuffled in from Montana and Brazil, but I tried to have caffeine hot and ready long before we sat down to business.

I had little on my agenda for the meeting. We were two weeks into the school year without a major casualty among the newly armed youngest class, which I counted as a win. As the teaching magi offered brief reports, I leaned back in my chair and listened with a cup of fine Assam—one of the junior Arc 4 magi, Indali Datta, had a cousin who owned a tea plantation, and she was never shy to express her disdain when the only brew on offer was PG Tips.

When the local magi finished, I moved east and turned to the Arc 3 contingent from Switzerland, giving our New World members a little more time to wake up and put their thoughts in order. "You're not snowed in yet, I trust?" I asked the installation head, Gunther Wolff.

His bushy white eyebrows rose as he sipped his coffee. "Alas, my skis remain beneath the bed," he replied as his delegation tittered. "The roads are clear, the Alps beautiful as always, and affairs proceed as usual."

"Good to hear—"

"But I did see this curious story," he said before I could move on, then pulled a printout from his folder and slid it down the table to me. "Perhaps it's nothing, but tell me what you think."

I scanned the illegible text—a short article in a Scandinavian language, I surmised, but I couldn't be more precise than that. "Want to translate this for me, Gunther?"

"I will defer to my colleague," he replied.

Ingaborg Säfström, our only Swedish magus, was Gunther's second in command. I offered her the paper, but she shook her head. "It was I who found the story," she said. "Curious tale. A young girl disappeared between school and home, was missing for several days, then returned bruised but otherwise unharmed. Her parents said she claimed to have been taken by elves. One of them returned her, repaired the family car, and vanished into a hole ripped in the air." Ingaborg paused, then said, "The girl reported that the good elf's name was Toula."

"Goddamn it," I muttered, rubbing my temples, "I *told* them not to say anything—"

"I'm sorry," a voice from the other end of the table interrupted, "but *who* took this kid?"

Glancing up, I found Kathleen Fuchs staring at me, waiting for an answer. As I silently cursed Arc 1 and all its magi, I tried to give the Council the truth without inciting panic. "One of Eleanor's sisters murdered her a little over three weeks ago. Irem. She's fully fae, so there's been some friction, but Ros has put her foot down—"

"Wait, *wait*," said Kathleen, her perfectly coiffed gray-blonde bob quivering as she shook her head. "The queen is dead? And we're just now hearing this *why*?"

"Because I didn't want to unnecessarily worry anyone until the dust settles—"

"We have a right to know! If there's a full-blooded faerie at the helm now, that's a massive security issue, and if I heard Ingaborg correctly, someone snatched a changeling."

I held up a hand for quiet as the table rumbled. "One of Irem's boyfriends grabbed the kid to curry favor. Once the guys found out—"

"Oh, yes," Kathleen snapped, "'the guys.' Didn't stop her, did they?"

One perk of the grand magus gig was that it gave me ample practice at controlling my temper. "Their hands were tied," I explained. "Long story short, the pact that established the Three was poorly designed for situations like this. But if I may finish"—Kathleen and I glared at each other across the table—"they told me immediately, I went over to retrieve the girl, and when Irem started to give me a hard time, Ros threw her into the wall and said there would be no more changelings. Irem's got a thick skull, but I think the message is sinking in."

When I fell silent, the other magi turned to Kathleen as if watching a tennis volley.

"You *think* it's sinking in?" she retorted. "That's no guarantee. If they're going to snatch people, then we need to strike now and show them we won't be cowed."

At that, the Arc 1 magi—well, all but Iris Johansson, who had more sense than the rest of her installation's leadership combined—began to mutter in the affirmative.

"Are you suggesting that we *attack* Faerie?" I asked, incredulous that the notion had so much as crossed her mind. "If we were to mount an invasion, we'd end up with all three courts against us, and that would be suicide."

"Then what do you propose?" said Kathleen. "Wagging your finger and hoping for the best?"

"Val and Coileán have it in hand. They were just as horrified as I was, and there's no love lost between them and Irem. They have our back, and now that Ros has asserted herself—"

"So you're saying that your grand plan is to bank on more faeries to defend us? Really?"

A larger swath of the table began to murmur, and I waited until the volume fell. "I'm saying that we have allies," I replied. "Allies who are stronger than we are. Who've come to our defense—remember that faerie army that showed up when Nath invaded? We need to sit back and wait to see whether Irem will pose a genuine threat before we start talking about going to war."

"And you'll forgive me, Grand Magus," said Kathleen, staring daggers at me over her glasses, "but I don't trust your judgment, especially not where your *guys* are concerned. Are we not strong enough to defend ourselves? Would you have us become a vassal state to one of the courts? Your *brother's*, perhaps?"

I bristled, but before I could respond, Indali came to my defense. "Don't sit there and accuse her of treason unless you have proof," she said, leaning over her neighbor to look Kathleen in the eye. "The grand magus has done nothing to harm us."

Kathleen laughed and shook her head. "What further proof do I need? She blatantly consorts with them—she's *one* of them! And I know you had only just made magus when Nath invaded, but—"

"Are you still blaming her for Nath?" said Antonio Paz, the Argentinian installation head of Arc 6. He and I had never been the dearest of friends, but we'd developed a mutual respect over the years. "Nath was waiting for an excuse, and you know it."

"But Toula gave her one, did she not?" countered Kathleen.

"To save that girl—"

"One of *Nath's* people."

"Actually," I interjected, "Hope's half human, and since her mother was basically a changeling in Conota, I think it's rather hypocritical of you to call for war over a kid who made it home after a few days but turn a blind eye to the Lozanos."

"And you know, it's worked out in our favor," said

Arnold from my left. "Our relations with that realm have never been stronger."

"Right," said Kathleen, "because we have so much to do with the *Gray Lands*. Of course it was worth all of the lives Nath's invasion cost us to get on good terms with them. Silly me."

Arnold grunted at her sarcasm. "They're an ally now, too. Hope knows what we risked and lost to protect her...and since no one has greater influence on Arik than she does..." He paused as Kathleen's brow furrowed. "Arikol. Their king. Hope's husband. Remember? I know that the silo is taxing, dear," he added, "but do try to keep up."

"In other words," said Bert, "if Irem *did* try something catastrophically stupid in this realm, we would have help with a phone call. And then there's the Minor Arcanum—maybe we're not quite on the same page, but some of them don't loathe us. We've got inroads with the Fringe, connections to the Company...we're in a stronger position than we've held in decades, and much of that is due to Toula."

By then, I could pick out the battle line as it wound around the conference room. Most of Arc 2 would back me, as usual. Arc 4 and Arc 6 could be swayed, as could at least a decent chunk of Arc 5. But Arc 3's senior magi seemed troubled, and they kept an eye on Kathleen, who dominated her end of the room. If those two installations joined forces, then Arc 7 would back them—their head, Connor Norleigh, seldom had an original thought, and he was no great fan of mine.

"Funny," said Kathleen, propping her chin on her fist, "I preferred when the Arcanum was a force to be feared instead of just another player on the board. When everyone knew that we didn't have to be nice to get what we wanted."

"And when, exactly, was that?" Bert snapped.

She ignored him as she gathered steam. "No one

respects us now because they know we're toothless. The Grand Mongrel isn't going to upset her big brother—heck, she won't even stand up to the Minor Arcanum."

I bit my tongue at the slur. The room was hot enough without throwing fuel on the fire.

Looking to her supporters as the noise around her grew, Kathleen said, "Lady Fotoula stole the chain she wears twenty-five years ago, and look how far we've fallen during her reign. It's time for her to go. We need a *real* wizard at the helm."

The room erupted like a dam bursting, and I finally had to resort to pulling a gavel from the ether and banging it on the table to restore order. "Kathleen, you've said your piece. Gunther, was there anything else you wanted to report, or should we continue with the ad hominems?"

"I call for a no-confidence vote," she interrupted.

Scanning the faces around the table, I ran the numbers. By our rules, a simple majority could sanction a vote if the grand magus objected, and from what I was seeing, I'd probably be overruled if I tried to stop it. But ousting a sitting grand magus required three-fifths of the Council. I didn't think Kathleen had the numbers that morning, but with tempers running as high as they were, I didn't want the meeting devolving into a brawl.

"I'll agree to a vote," I said, "but let's give it a week and reconvene. Let everyone cool off first."

"I second that," said Nour Tazi, the head of Arc 5. A soft-spoken woman, Nour seldom engaged in debate, preferring to sit back and listen to all sides rather than make a snap judgment. "Unseating a grand magus is a serious matter, and I would like time to consider the issue with due care."

"Third," said Antonio. "And I want a good night's sleep. My colleagues from the silo should do likewise," he added, shooting Kathleen a hard look.

Seeing that she wouldn't have immediate satisfaction, Kathleen grumbled her agreement to the plan. "One week," she said, holding my stare.

"If everyone else could send pertinent news to my aides," I told the table, "I'll see that it's disseminated. I don't think anyone's in the mood to finish this meeting as planned, so with that, I'll see you all next Monday."

As the installation groups began opening gates home, I retreated to my office, but I'd barely had time to pour myself a glass of water before Maria gave a perfunctory rap and let herself in, followed by Bert and Arnold. "What the *hell*?" Maria began, her cheeks flushed with anger. "She can't treat you like that—"

"Close the door, hon."

Maria slammed it shut and locked it, and I engaged my office's soundproofing wards before I sank onto the couch. "She has every right to call for a vote," I told my fuming grandniece. "This isn't a monarchy, remember."

"But on what grounds?"

I shrugged. "Concealing information from the Council? Improperly fraternizing? I mean, I did strong-arm my way into office, I'm not going to deny that."

"We didn't have a better candidate," Arnold offered.

"Yeah, but showing up with Val with a bit of a stunt. Can't say I'm sorry, but..." I drank and tried to calm the tremor in my hand. "This may be it for me, folks. Even if Irem makes a tearful, heartfelt apology this week"—Bert snorted his disbelief—"I think Arc 1 may finally have enough ammo to get what they want."

"Why didn't you tell us?" asked Arnold, taking a seat beside me. "You know the Council would have backed a rescue mission."

"Sure, followed by *this*. Trying to stave off the inevitable, I guess. Should have known not to trust Johanna's family to keep quiet. I mean, hell, that kid went through the next-best thing to an alien abduction." I lifted my glass and sighed. "Aliens might have been kinder."

"You're not just walking away, are you?" Maria demanded. "We can win this. They need more than a simple majority."

"Understood, but we need a plan in place in case they have the numbers." Looking at each of them in turn, I murmured, "If the vote goes against me, promise that you'll stay on the Council and keep fighting to maintain the status quo. Whoever gets the chain next is going to need help and a *quick* education, especially if Irem keeps screwing around. I trust you three," I said. "Forget me— the Arcanum needs you."

And though they tried to downplay the severity of the situation, I secured that promise from each of them before they left me to brood alone.

What followed was one of the longest weeks of my life.

Showing up at the potentially friendly magi's offices for an unscheduled little chat would have been considered unseemly, so all I could do was clear my calendar and make myself available in case anyone wished to meet with me. Of the few who did, I felt confident that I'd have their support, but that faction wouldn't be enough on its own. Still, I spent most of my days in my office, arriving early and leaving late, hoping that more of the magi would seek me out and trying not to think about the quiet meetings going on down the hall.

At night, I made no pretense of returning to my flat, instead opting for my rooms at Coileán's. He played the role of dutiful boyfriend well as he tried to calm me, insisting that the Council would see reason once they thought about all we'd accomplished during my tenure. "You're not a failure," he soothed one night, holding me in bed at two in the morning. "Moon and stars, woman, look at what you've done! What you've *built*." He rubbed my back as I tried to calm my breathing, fighting the anxiety that wouldn't let me sleep. "You righted that ship, took down the Conclave, held back Nath...and you squared off against one of us to free a mundane changeling." He paused, then added, "In case I haven't been clear enough yet, dearest, *please* don't do that again."

"Ros handled it," I mumbled against his shoulder.

"Great, let *her* set things right. I don't want to lose you." Planting a quick kiss at the base of my neck, he said, "If the Council can't see your worth, then they don't deserve you."

"I just don't want everything to fall apart if they kick me out."

"They're not stupid enough to kick you out," he said with far more confidence than I felt. "Arnold will go to bat for you, wait and see."

Sure, Arnold would make my case, but where Coileán saw a former grand magus who'd thrown himself into a Fringer-smuggling ring to fight Mulligan, too many of the magi saw an old rogue whose own allegiance to the Arcanum was dangerously close to suspect. But I let myself to be reassured anyway, as believing that fairytale was the only thing allowing me to sleep at night.

Too soon, yet after an interminable wait, Monday arrived.

"Whatever happens, you're going to be fine," Arnold murmured, pulling me away from the press in the corridor outside the main meeting room. "I'll let you know as soon as we have the vote." He squeezed my hand and offered a tense smile, then retreated behind the soundproof door.

For the first time in twenty-five years, I wasn't welcome among the Council. I remembered the last time I'd stood in that hall, waiting with Val to see whether they'd accept me as their leader. I'd been nervous then, but I'd also been prepared for rejection—after all, why would the Council want a witch-blooded Pavli anywhere near them?

I thought of the girl I'd once been. The Arcanum's least favorite foster child, bound for crimes I never committed, my father imprisoned with blood on his hands, my mother such a terrible secret that it took me thirty-five years to learn the truth. The families who'd tolerated my presence for two or three years as a favor to the Council before handing me off to be someone else's problem. The abuse from the kids around me who'd known that no one would come to my aid—all of them in their mid-eighties now, many of them respectable grandparents, *none* of them on the Council.

I thought of the eighteen-year-old girl, not even an adult by the Arcanum's measure, who'd packed her belongings into garbage bags and headed east in a lousy van to find a life for herself. Of the young woman who'd killed a faerie queen and returned unbound and empowered beyond her wildest dreams, working with the grand magus himself. Who'd gone on the run again with a squad of assassins behind her. Whose death count surely surpassed her father's by now.

I thought of the woman who'd fought Ellie into unconsciousness to save her court, who'd stormed the silo that had raised her to free the Fringe, who'd made the long, terrible case against Mulligan and his Council.

Who'd returned to the Arcanum to demand the seat at the head of the table.

And now?

Now I was two and a half decades older, and maybe a little wiser, but I'd proven myself. As an administrator, a diplomat, a warrior, a *wizard*—I had no reason to apologize. Every decision I had made had ultimately furthered the Arcanum's interests, guiding it from being an unsteady, untrustworthy danger back toward a respected partner in the magical community. And if I just so happened to be in love with one of the Three, that didn't make me any less competent as grand magus.

The last time I'd waited in the hall, I'd been inexperienced but hopeful. This time, I wore the red robe and heavy chain of office to remind the Council that I had what it took. No, I wasn't perfect, and I'd been no one's first choice, but I'd done well by the Arcanum. And I meant what I'd promised all those years before: once a wizard appeared who was qualified to replace me, I'd step aside. I didn't intend to rule forever, but damn it, hadn't I earned the right to a dignified retirement?

I was leaning against the wall, staring at the rug and listening to my heart pound in my ears, when the door cracked open again and Arnold emerged. Glancing up as I caught the motion out of the corner of my eye, I tried to read his expression, but Arnold's wrinkled face was a studied blank.

"And?" I forced myself to ask.

He crossed the hall and clasped my hands. "It was so close."

Hope leapt within me for an instant before he whispered, "I'm sorry, Toula."

I willed time to stop, to hang there in space between breaths, to leave me with my defeat without forcing me to face it. But not even Ros could stop time indefinitely, and as my lungs filled again, I forced on a mask of stoicism. "Then I will respect the wishes of the Council," I told Arnold.

As he released me, I lifted off my chain—not *mine*, the grand magus's, the chain that he and Bert had worn before me—and handed it to him. "You'll be needing this back," I said with artificial calm. "So, what are we doing about my successor?"

He grimaced as he took the chain. "Discussions have commenced."

"Do I not get a voice in this?" I asked, frowning.

Arnold hesitated, then said, "That was voted on as well. You'll retain a seat on the Council, but it was decided that you should not participate in the selection process."

I clenched my jaw before the mask could slip. "Understood. Then I suppose I'll pack in case the next grand magus wants my space."

The meeting room door opened and closed again

behind me as I made my way to my office, but I didn't stop to watch Arnold return to the debate. Instead, I locked my door, turned on every privacy ward I'd built over the years, and sank into my desk chair.

I thought of the girl who'd left the only home she'd ever known because the people in charge had executed her father without letting her say goodbye, then made it clear that she was no longer welcome.

And finally, alone amid the trappings of my career, I allowed myself to cry.

SEPTEMBER 14: BERT WOLD

In retrospect, I was a *terrible* choice for grand magus. Put aside the matter of my youth, inexperience, and undeserved self-assurance that I alone could steer the ship of state—I detested meetings. Give me a quiet library and a stack of books in a language I could barely read, and I was happy as a clam. Make me sit in a room with several dozen other people who shared a burning desire to make their thoughts known in excruciating detail, however, and I longed for the sweet release of a mild coma.

To her credit, Toula had kept the full Council meetings to a minimum and managed them well, usually getting us out within an hour. But Toula had been sacked, and now, bereft of a moderator, the Council's debates extended long into the evening as otherwise reasonable magi insulted each other across the table.

Going into day four, I wished they'd sacked me, too. I had half a mind to tender my resignation and be done with the mad circus, but I'd promised Toula that I'd stay—and anyway, *someone* had to occasionally shout down the smug bastards from the silo.

The problem the Council faced, just as it had twenty-five years before following my inglorious exit, was the lack of a clear successor. Toula, Arnold, and I had done our best to avoid this nasty scenario, but with our hand forced, I put aside my reservations about some of the candidates we'd discussed and threw their names out for consideration. The position was open to anyone in the Arcanum with the right combination of power and backing, and as one of the only two people in the room who'd worn the blasted chain, I intended to make my preferences known.

My first choice, based on our trio's observations, was Amita Bhattacharya. Much as I hated to do it to the girl, I knew she had a magus's talent and a brilliant mind, and I suspected that she'd be willing to take advice from Arnold and me while she found her footing. Arnold seconded her as a candidate, and once the two of us presented our case, Arc 4 took over to sing the praises of its promising young scholar. There had never been an Indian grand magus, and as the last to come out of Arc 4's territory had been Maksim Petrov shortly before the Russian Revolution, its magi jumped on the notion of elevating Amita. But her candidacy failed: she wasn't well known outside of Arc 4, and when Indali called her to broach the topic without sufficiently easing into it, Amita balked, thanked us for our consideration, and firmly declined the honor. I couldn't blame her.

My second choice was Kibwe Jumbe, the would-be doctor out of Arc 5, but I knew that one was dead in the water as soon as we provided his stats. Bright and talented though he was, Kibwe was but sixteen, and no one wanted the unprecedented situation in which we'd have to set up a sort of regency for an underage grand magus.

In all honesty, I wasn't thrilled by either Amita or Kibwe because of their youth. The two youngest grand magi in centuries had been Helen Carver and me, and our tenures were disastrous. We needed a senior magus to step in, someone who could mediate between the aggrieved magi who saw Toula's presence as tyranny and those who respected what she'd done in office. But there was no such person on the Council. Arnold, who'd twice served, was too old and sick of it all to shoulder that burden again, and while I was almost prepared to invoke the Ivanovich Rule as Toula had done and challenge the other magi to a fight for the chain to end the squabbling, I knew I'd never have the necessary Council backing to accomplish much.

I could have put forth Maria, but none of us saw the point in wasting breath. On paper, Magus Corelli was a contender: a product of Arc 2's school, the prodigy who'd bested a Council aide in individual combat as a ten-year-old child, a respected teacher, a solid scholar, and the only magus willing to be saddled with oversight of the Away Team. But she was also Toula's distant grandniece, raised by Valerius himself, and the work that Ros has performed on her to save her life had rendered her more or less fae. Of all the Council, Maria was the lone magus who couldn't cast a single spell, though she more than made up for it with her talent for enchantment. Never mind the fact that she'd undergone augmentation only because Francine Leighton and Eva Stanhope had tried to murder her, leaving her body a charred husk pinned to the floor with an iron spike through the chest. Never mind that she'd almost been killed in the line of duty by trying to uncover the Conclave's spy. She was completely out of the running for Toula's vacated chair.

Which left…well, a lot of nothing. And as Arnold's and my suggestions were uniformly shot down, I'd begun to fear that we were being shut out as the new regime dawned. Unfortunately, by the second day of debate, I knew who the face of that regime would be. Though I hated to even think it, my gut insisted that our next grand magus would be Leander Kirby.

I could see the writing on the wall. The Arc 1 delegation continued to name him a contender and sing his praises: young, sure, but an excellent talent, a charismatic fellow, the sort of energetic leader we needed. He was from a good, solidly Arcanum family, they insisted—an old family, the sort that understood the importance of tradition. My protestation that a significant chunk of Leander's extended family had joined the bloody *Conclave* fell on deaf ears. Like so many old-blooded wizards who couldn't stomach the notion of Grand Magus Pavli or accept that their new-blooded neighbors were just as deserving of advancement within the Arcanum, they'd fled in the dead of night for a remote corner of Alaska. For years, I'd served as Toula's quiet go-between to the Conclave, watching the situation worsen until Francine Leighton and Eva Stanhope went after Maria…and then Toula had stepped in and destroyed their compound in a matter of moments. The former Conclave members were on long-term probation—all but Eva and Francine, who'd earned themselves a life sentence in the castle's secure cells for their trouble. But if that was what Arc 1 considered a good family, then I had a fair inkling that I wouldn't care for Leander's politics.

Maybe I'd be mistaken, I mused on Wednesday while the loud half of the Council ignored Arnold's warnings about putting inexperienced twenty-somethings in charge—and though Arnold held me up as exhibit A, I didn't take offense. He was absolutely correct. I'd been a little shit when I assumed power, indoctrinated by my Mulligan-sympathizing parents and the magi who'd tutored me. Back then, to me, talent made right, witches and faeries were to be removed from the realm, and good old Grand Magus Mulligan had been so misunderstood. It had taken an uprising from his supporters, a faerie attack, and the near loss of magic as we knew it to show me the error of my ways, plus years to really mull over all the rubbish I'd been spoon-fed, but I'd come round in time. Maybe Leander would be a better student than I had been. Maybe he already understood the danger of believing that old-blooded wizards were automatically the finest creatures in existence.

But the way that Arc 1 was blathering on about him, I rather doubted it.

Still, I tried to dissuade the Council from dancing to Arc 1's tune. "Take it from someone who became grand magus far too young," I told the table. "A boy his age has no business leading the Arcanum. Helen Carver would say the same thing, I guarantee it. If you don't believe me, I'll call her right now," I offered, holding up my mobile as proof.

"That's three former grand magi telling you that Leander would be a mistake," said Arnold as I glanced around the room. "The next grand magus should be someone in here—someone who knows where we've been, where we're headed, and who the other players are. Someone who can keep the peace."

"Or," Kathleen interjected, "we could have someone to be proud of, for a change."

With his cheerleaders swaying more and more magi to their side—that, or wearing them down to the point of conceding just to end the torture of our long arguments— I wasn't surprised when Leander won the vote before lunch on Thursday morning. That time, it was Kathleen who stepped into the hall to share the good news with the candidate, and we dutifully clapped when she escorted him into the meeting room. To be fair, he was a handsome young man, blond and blue-eyed, and he wore the chain like he'd been born for it. But as the Arc 1 magi shook his hand and clapped him on the back, I traded looks with Maria and Arnold and prayed to any listening deity that I was mistaken about him.

SEPTEMBER 18: TOULA PAVLI

I would have invited Maria into my office, but it was barely large enough for a desk and chair, and I certainly had no guest furniture to offer her.

With the good offices having been snagged by the senior magi and even the longest-serving Council aides, Leander's only real choice in the executive wing was my spacious suite unless he wanted to trample some toes. I'd vacated by then, moving my more precious books and mementos to safekeeping in my apartment at Coileán's place, which proved to be a wise move. While I could have made some of the aides downsize, I wasn't in the mood to uproot even more people during the transition, and so I snagged an unused aide cubicle at the end of the hall, planning to keep my space minimal until the dust settled. It wasn't the worst working environment I'd ever had, but its close confines made having visitors an awkward proposition.

"Ready?" Maria muttered from the doorway.

No. No, I was absolutely not ready to be summoned by that fucking *child*, but one of us needed to be the adult—and since Maria seemed primed to disembowel him, that task fell to me.

Not that I didn't want to murder the little shit, too, but time had taught me a bit of patience and restraint. I'd outlasted Mulligan, and I would survive the Kirby years…or months, I hoped, given our track record with young grand magi.

Friday, Leander's first full day in office, had been

unexpectedly terrible. I'd assumed he'd do little in his first week or so on the job—pick an office, move his things over from Montana, plan his ceremony, meet the rest of the Council, adjust to the time change, et cetera. I'd hoped he'd be smart enough to chat with Arnold, Bert, and me over the weekend, seeing as we could offer him far more information about his new gig than just the location of the bathrooms and the Council kitchenette. Having had my lonely pity party and a few days in Faerie to clear my head, I'd resolved to be gracious. After all, Leander hadn't been the one to kick me out of my position, and it was in the best interest of the Arcanum for me to help him get off to a good start. To that end, I'd assembled a binder for him of pertinent documents: maps of the castle, contact lists for the other installations, minutes of recent meetings, a breakdown of the magi's supervisory assignments, brief biographical sketches of the heads of the other magical factions, and even suggestions for dining out in Glastonbury.

But all of my planning went out the window when Leander scheduled his first full Council meeting for Friday afternoon. Much of the Council was less than thrilled, considering they'd already spent the week behind closed doors, but we dutifully trooped in and found our spots, me in a chair a few feet down from my former seat, safely in the middle of the Inner Council. Leander's boyish charm was on full display as he made his opening remarks, standing there in a dark green robe and his chain of office like a child playing dress-up, but I reminded myself to give him a chance as the Arc 1 contingent guffawed at his casual jokes. He was new, he was trying, and he had to be scared to death to be facing down that table. I remembered my own first meeting at the head—how, even at twice his age, I'd worried that I wouldn't have what it took to command the Council's respect, that I'd be a failure before I so much as opened my mouth. Still, Leander carried himself with a confident air, which I thought boded well. Whatever nerves he was feeling, at least he could play the part.

And then he got down to business.

"I want my first official act as grand magus to be something meaningful," he told us, folding his hands atop the table. "So I'm going to right an injustice." With a glance at the secretary, who was monitoring the transcription spell, Leander announced, "Today, I issue full pardons to Eva Stanhope and Francine Leighton, and I reinstate them to the Council. They will rejoin us soon."

The room erupted—cheers from Arc 1 and their friends, shouts of disbelief from the other half of the table. In the tumult, Maria jumped to her feet, magnified her voice, wheeled on Leander, and demanded, "Is this a *joke*?"

The Council—most of whom had been members when Eva and Francine were removed—quieted as she glowered at Leander, waiting for an answer.

He cocked his head and considered her. "No, I'm absolutely serious. And you are…"

"Maria Corelli," she said through clenched teeth. "And since you seem to have forgot, let me remind you that Francine fled to the Conclave, Eva worked with her from inside to compromise our security, they tried to *kill* me, and they tried to frame *him* for the crime," she concluded, pointing to Bert. "Two lying, murderous traitors. Why would you release them, much less reinstate them? That's a slap in the face to all of us here who've done our best to uphold our oaths to the Arcanum."

The murmuring crescendoed again, and many of the magi whom I'd counted among my supporters nodded along with Maria's assessment.

But Leander remained unruffled. "The Conclave, as I recall, was born as a reaction to a larger problem within the Arcanum," he said, holding her stare for a moment before turning his eyes to me. "Besides, they were in danger from a Gray Lands gate they couldn't close. All kinds of monsters slipped through to attack them. Good wizards died. *Children* grew up in danger. Magus Leighton and Magus Stanhope were trying to save lives."

"No one needed to live in danger," Maria countered. "They were welcome back here—"

"Oh, yeah, *such* a welcome," he retorted. "How long have the Conclave members been on probation? Three years, now? That ends today, too," he added, giving his supporters a brief smile before returning his gaze to Maria. "If you have some grudge against those magi, it's time to let it go. They've been punished enough for trying to do the right thing."

"*They tried to kill me!*" she shouted.

Leander shrugged. "Obviously, you didn't die."

Though she was fuming, Maria waited for the tittering to fade before she spoke again. "I was defibrillated six times," she said, her fists clenched at her sides. "Over ninety percent of my body was burnt, much of that third-degree burns or worse. And not to be unduly graphic, but they *impaled* me on a barbed spike and almost destroyed one of my lungs. The fire they used was so hot that the spike partially melted to my back. I still have nightmares, and my therapist says I may relive that trauma for the rest of my life. So don't sit there and tell me to let bygones be bygones."

Cutting my eyes around the table, I saw grimaces, scowls…and even a few expressions from the better of the Arc 1 crowd that might have been embarrassment, though the magi said nothing.

Maria's protest fell on deaf ears. By dinnertime, Francine and Eva were free.

I called Maria late Friday evening to check on her, only to learn that she was sleeping over at Kitty's flat. "Couple glasses of wine and bed?" I asked.

"No," she said, her voice low and strained. "Beth's so freaked by her mother's release, she's vomited twice already. I'm here to help hold her hair back and keep Artur from stabbing someone."

"Good of you."

Maria snorted. "Much as I hate to admit it, the last thing we need right now is corpses."

By the time Maria came to get me Monday morning, I knew through my back channels that Beth was skipping school. In the chaos of Friday night, with Kitty trying to reassure her little sister that their mother couldn't hurt them, Marcus had slipped into another room to quietly relay the developments to his father. Val, who'd seen firsthand what Eva was capable of, had responded with an offer of sanctuary—Beth could stay at his place until things calmed in Glastonbury, and Eva wouldn't be stupid enough to barge in and demand her return. When Val relayed this to me over the weekend, however, I pointed out that Faerie was already in the Council's bad books, and no one was going to snatch Beth from her bed in the middle of the night. He insisted that the offer stood—in truth, I didn't trust my brother not to strike Eva dead if given the slightest opening—but Kitty had agreed with me that the safest course of action was for Beth to lie low in her room for a bit. Given how poorly the kid had slept over the weekend, she'd earned herself a sick day.

Much as I would have liked a sick day of my own, that was out the cards. The Council was meeting, Maria and I had been summoned for a private talk beforehand, and…well, everyone knew I was far too fae to fake a cold.

No, I wasn't ready for my friendly chat with my replacement, but I had to be mature about this.

Maria squeezed my hand as I met her at the door. "Game faces," she whispered in Fae.

I plastered on the most saccharine smile I could muster, and she stifled her laughter as two of Leander's new aides passed.

We headed down the hall to my old office. Leander's office now, of course—I'd seen my furniture hauled out and a pair of burgundy leather couches brought in on Friday afternoon. I'd *also* taken the time to dismantle every protective measure I'd built in there. Sure, my work on that front had been mostly spellcraft, but I doubted he could have powered those wards had he tried. And yes, perhaps it was petty of me, but I'd restored the tops of the arched windows with their fantastic view of the distant town, removing the stained-glass flowers I'd installed on my first day. If he knew of them and wanted them back, then he could damn well ask me.

Knocking on that door was just another humbling reminder of my reduced standing on the Council, and I had to suspect a power play when Leander didn't immediately admit us. Waiting in the hall like an idiot, I watched the aides wander back and forth from the kitchenette, refilling mugs for magi too busy to bother making their own tea. Few of them looked my way, and the ones who did offered brief, tense smiles before ducking their heads and scurrying off on their errands.

Finally, the door clicked open, though Leander hadn't bothered to rise from his desk. "Come in," he said, barely glancing up from his computer. "Close the door behind you."

We did as he bid, and I made a quick inspection of the place. My deep blue accent wall was gone, as was the plaster—Leander had exposed the stone everywhere but the ceiling. The couches weren't horrible, but the color clashed with the rug he'd spread beneath them, which leaned toward the orange-red end of the spectrum. Whereas I had kept a pair of nice chairs in front of my desk for visitors with quick business, Leander had opted to leave the space between the door and his new desk—a monolithic chunk in an unfortunate maple stain— unbroken by anything so welcoming as a seat. He'd hung thick curtains over all the windows in yet another shade of red, and I wondered briefly if he might be colorblind.

I traded glances with Maria, then stood before Leander's desk like a misbehaving schoolgirl and resisted the urge to speak. Silence was a powerful tool—any interrogator worth his salt knows to sit back, let the silence stretch, and watch the nervous subject race to fill the uncomfortable void—and if Leander was going to be rude, then I wasn't about to play his game.

But Maria was young, and she broke first. "Did you want to discuss something, Grand Magus?" she asked as he peered at his screen. "If this is a bad time, we can come back."

"No. Stay there, I'm almost finished."

It didn't take a mind reader to sense her irritation, but she bit her tongue and folded her arms over her dark green robe. Against hazel eyes and chestnut hair like hers, the color suited her nicely, and I was about to tell her as much when Leander finally gave us his attention. "I brought you here to ask for your resignation," he said with a faint, satisfied smile. "There's no place for your kind on the Council…nor in the Arcanum."

As Maria began to sputter, I jumped in. "I've been leading this organization for most of your life, Leander," I said, digging my fingernails into my palms as a release while I held my voice low and steady. "Name one thing I've done in all that time to hurt the Arcanum for Faerie's benefit."

"The Gray Lander," he replied, smirking like a chess master on the verge of checkmate.

"I take it you mean Hope Lozano. If you're going to use her against me, you should at least bother to learn her name. Oh, and it's 'Lady Imaranta' these days unless she tells you otherwise, so be aware."

His brow knit.

"She's the queen consort," I explained. "But I digress. First of all, protecting Hope didn't do Faerie a damn bit of good—they lost people defending us. Now, let's see, three years ago…you would have been about twenty-six then, right?" I asked. "Maria did her part in the defense, and she wasn't yet twenty-five. Did you bother to come help us, or did you hide out in the silo?"

"Not that you have any right to criticize me," he said as his cheeks colored, "but Magus Fuchs asked that I help keep order in her absence."

"Of course she did. But since you weren't here," I continued as he glared, "let me fill you in on a few truths that Kathleen might not have mentioned. Nath didn't go to war to get Hope back—Hope was just a convenient rallying point. I never got a chance to ask her, but I think Nath assumed that Faerie would stay out of the conflict if she had a valid reason to start shooting. But since Hope's mother was kidnapped as a teenager to be a *concubine* and Hope was about to be given away in the same system, I didn't mind taking the risk. Sexual slavery has never sat well with me, you know?"

Leander started to speak, but I steamrolled over him. "Anyway, Nath's invasion was a matter of *when*, not *if*. Badger held on here as long as she could, but with her in Faerie, there was nothing stopping Nath from making the attempt. The biggest surprise to me in all of this business is that Nath waited twelve years."

"In fairness to Nath," Maria interjected, "she asked Kitty for confirmation that summer that Badger was gone."

"Yeah, but I suspect she knew that already—"

"Who the hell is *Badger*?" Leander cut in.

I rolled my eyes at Maria before turning back to him. "Badger Parsons is Arnold Lowe's cousin," I explained. "One heck of a wizard. Absolute *legend* in the Fringe. If she'd wanted to be grand magus, Arnold would have stepped aside. And during the Mulligan years, when the Council couldn't be bothered to protect this realm, she forced Nath to swear not to invade as long as she was here to defend her claim. Like I said, legend." Glancing at Maria, I added, "I know the curriculum here has changed since you were a student, but the upper-level magical history class does cover Badger, doesn't it?"

She nodded. "These days, yes."

"Mm. Guess no one at Arc 1 bothered to mention any of this to you, huh?" I said to Leander.

His eyes narrowed as his flush deepened. "You couldn't know that Nath was going to attack us as soon as this Badger person was gone—"

I laughed in his face. "Of course I could, kid. I'm not an idiot. From everything I've seen and heard, full-blooded tennuwaya and cynaeli think a lot like full-blooded faeries. They can be patient when they have to be, but when they want something, they're tenacious, and Nath had expansion on the brain. Her brother seems to be a different story, now, but..." I paused and considered Leander, who was looking at me like I was trying to explain advanced calculus. "Nath's brother would be Arikol, the current king. The guy who married Hope. Ring a bell?" When his expression didn't immediately clear, I sighed. "Tell me you know *something* about Conotan politics."

His face scrunched up at the term. "Conotan?"

Wishing there'd been a written comprehensive exam before Leander took the job, I said, "The realm we call the Gray Lands is known as Conota to the two primary species there. Conota is also the name of that realm's consciousness, and he's apparently something of an ass, but that's not important. He's the father of all of the realm's monarchs. Nath was tennuwaya on her mother's side; Arik is actually human on his, but he was raised cynaeli, and he looks it. Those aren't the only two peoples in that realm, but Arik's the only leader with whom we have any sort of relationship."

"He knows about your elevation," Maria offered. "And about Eleanor's death and Irem's foolishness. A good portion of the Away Team helped save his life and get him on the throne, and he and Hope stay in touch."

"*What?*" Leander snapped.

"See, that's the problem," I said, shaking my head. "You don't even know how much you don't know—about the Arcanum, about our history, about our allies. Maria and I have been intimately involved in the major conflicts of the last few years, and now you want to kick us out? All we've done is protect the Arcanum. That woman almost *died* to protect the Arcanum," I added, pointing to Maria. "If you force us off the Council, you'll be making a terrible mistake."

He sat up a little straighter and held my stare. "Is that a threat? If I say you're gone, is big brother going to swoop in and prove my point?"

"No," I shot back, "because Val respects me more than that. But don't think for a minute that he wouldn't if I asked for his help." I didn't tell him my other thought—that Val would burn this place to the ground if someone hurt Maria. Instead, I said, "You're feeling like a tough guy today because enough of the Council still thinks you're wonderful. But if you start trying to play strongman with Val and Coileán, you'll get your ass handed to you. Those two have shoes older than you, and they don't take shit lightly."

"Neither one is thrilled about what's happened to Aunt Toula thus far," said Maria. "Are you just *trying* to make matters worse?"

"They'll show me the respect I'm due, if they know what's good for them," said Leander. "And I seem to recall that they respected Grand Magus Mulligan."

I fought the impulse to throw him into the wall. "That wasn't respect. Coileán and Ellie held their fire to save Mulligan's hostages. Had he not kidnapped—and *tortured*—hundreds of innocent people, Faerie would have wiped the floor with him on the day of his coup. And you," I said, planting my palms on his desk, "would do well to refresh your memory as to what happened when Faerie *did* attack the silo. Maybe you were sick on that day of class. Do I need to tell you how quickly the whole damn Council surrendered?"

His eyes opened wide with mock incredulity. "Am I

mistaken, or are you *defending* an attack on the Arcanum by a hostile power?"

Leaning over him, I said, "I was with them, and you damn well know it, little boy. I'm *proud* of what we did. That Arcanum was an evil, corrupted thing. Now, I understand that you weren't even a twinkle in your daddy's eye when shit went down, but we recorded the trial. It would behoove you to watch it. Understand what sort of atrocities Mulligan committed, and then you may come talk to me about hostile powers." Straightening, I said, "We've come a long way since then. Mended quite a few fences within the community. Made *peace*. Mulligan couldn't do that by force. Hell," I said with an exasperated laugh, "even Simon Magus couldn't do that."

"That's exactly what the Magus did!" Leander protested.

"In *this* realm, partially. He realized the error of his ways as soon as he tried to invade Faerie."

Ask him sometime, I started to say, but managed to stop myself before it could slip out.

"Look," I told Leander, "you don't have to like me. You don't have to agree with every decision I've ever made. But I'm asking you now, for the good of the Arcanum, to listen to experience. I've been at this for a long time, and I can vouch for Maria—she's been a great magus. Let us help you, at least until you know all the players on the board. I guarantee that your Arc 1 friends don't know half as much as they think they do about how this organization is run."

We stared at each other across the desk in silence for a long moment.

Finally, Leander held out his hand. "For the good of the Arcanum, surrender your chains."

"*Leander*—"

"Unless you want to put the matter to another vote today. Do you think this one will go any better for you? Or for the so-called magus who can't even *cast*?"

Unfortunately, all it took to remove a reluctant magus was a simple majority. As I fumed, desperately looking for the words that would sway him, I heard Maria in my mind: *We're not going to win this here. Not today.*

She slipped her chain of office over her head and placed it in his palm. "Good luck," she said simply. "You're going to need it."

He snorted and looked at me expectantly, but all I could do was shrug. "I never actually received a magus chain, just as you won't. You're wearing my only official jewelry. Hope you can accept my resignation without another necklace." Stepping back from the desk, I said, "We'll be out of our offices by the end of the day."

Leander whispered a word, and the door behind us opened to reveal a pair of security guards. "You have one hour to pack and vacate."

I looked from the guards to the smug child behind the desk. "This is completely unnecessary! At least let us pack in a civilized manner."

"Your time is running."

Even as he smirked at me, I held my head high. "Keep the peace, if you know what's good for you," I said, then turned and headed for my waiting escort.

One guard accompanied Maria back to her office, while the other followed me to my cubicle. As we passed the kitchenette, he leaned toward me and whispered, "I'm really sorry about this, Grand Magus."

Surprised, I took a closer look at him—one of our many security officers, no one I knew particularly well. "Thank you," I murmured.

He waited until we reached my space—almost empty, thank goodness—then said, "I was on the gate closure teams when Nath invaded. Got shot pretty badly outside of Toronto. Your brother kept me alive." Cutting his eyes toward Leander's office, he quietly added, "It's not right."

I shoved all of my belongings into a cardboard box I'd pulled from the ether, then sealed it and tried to smile.

"Don't worry, I won't give you any trouble. Let's go help Maria, okay? She's got more to pack than I do."

"Can I carry that for you, at least?" he asked as I toted the box toward the door.

"No need," I replied, giving the cubicle a last check before I left it behind. "Not the first time I've packed my things and said goodbye to the Arcanum."

SEPTEMBER 20: MARCUS

Bert sat awkwardly on one side of the Team's conference room table on Wednesday morning with his fingers wrapped around his chipped purple tea mug. I suppose he'd expected a frosty reception—Bert had been the Team's supervisory magus before Maria, and from what I'd heard of those days, he'd been a reluctant participant in the best of times—but looking around the room, I saw no animosity. Bert hadn't asked to have his old assignment back, and he certainly hadn't been the one to boot Maria from the Council.

Once he heard the news, Ted had postponed our traditional Monday meeting that week, which suited me well. I'd been slated to give a presentation about a potential cache of medieval manuscripts hidden in an Austrian cave, but with Beth's severe anxiety, my wife's better-hidden but more generalized anxiety, Artur's growing desire to knock heads together, and Eadwig's vacillation between raving against the new regime and tending to Beth, I'd managed to accomplish little in the way of preparation over the weekend. At least Quinn had seemed relatively serene—Leander had yet to turn his attention to the Archives, for which she and her colleagues were grateful. Even those archivists who liked the idea of a new grand magus didn't want bureaucrats interrupting their work.

Then Monday's bad news had hit, and while Beth hid in her bedroom with movies, Maria made camp in our den, drinking wine and trying to talk Pater down over the phone. Toula had abandoned the castle for a time, taking the last of her office supplies straight to Coileán's, and so Maria had a long afternoon of convincing Pater that she was still safe in Glastonbury. Near dinnertime, she had wearily handed me her phone, and my father had dispensed with pleasantries when I came on the line: "If that fool tries to harm Maria, kill him."

"Understood, but that would *probably* start a war," I'd reminded him.

"I don't care. Make it painful," he'd replied, and cut the connection.

Needless to say, my scheduled presentation wasn't my finest work, but I suspected that Daphne, who'd been supervising me on the project, could answer any difficult questions. Brilliant, twice my age—well, my physical age—and far more experienced, Daphne taught by allowing her pupils to walk to the edge of the cliff, then yanking them back and explaining why taking that next step would be a poor choice. I was fortunate that she tolerated my flailing.

The full Team had assembled that morning, with the exception of Eadwig, our member in name only. Still, we had to pull up an extra chair, as Maria had joined us. She sat beside Bert in a long T-shirt and leggings, so different than the robes in which I usually saw her during the day, with her hair pulled back in a sloppy bun. She'd finally left our flat for her own after dinner the night before, but the shadows beneath her eyes suggested that she'd watched the clock until dawn.

Few people touched the platter of doughnuts that Ted had stolen from the dining hall, unusual for a Team meeting…but then again, as Lakshmi had muttered while doctoring her tea, we were living in interesting times.

As Antony turned on the projector, Ted called the meeting to order and stood. "All right, people, thanks for your flexibility this week," he began. "Bert…I know it's been a while, but it's nice to have you back. We'll try to go easy on you, eh?"

Bert smiled wanly and lifted his mug in salute.

"And Maria," Ted continued, nodding to her, "thanks for coming. I don't care if you've got a chain—you've been one of us, you will *remain* one of us, and you're welcome here in any capacity. The Team is a family," he said, casting his gaze around the table, "and we protect our own. You got that, Corelli?"

She flashed a lopsided smile. "Thanks, boss."

"Oh, it is I who thank *you*," he replied with a wicked grin. "Seeing as someone isn't going to be tied to the classroom this term for the first time in years, I hope you're excited for fieldwork. A talent like yours shouldn't be squandered."

"Ooh," Daphne interrupted, raising a finger. "Dibs."

"You know, I *do* have seniority," Frank softly rumbled from down the table.

"And you two can duke this out later," said Ted. "Okay, Marcus, hit it before they come to blows, will you?"

With that, Antony dimmed the lights and loaded my presentation. I could have run it myself, but with my technological skills still lagging, Antony tried to take some of the pressure off me by handling the software. The Team's resident tech guru might have made a lousy wizard, but everyone leaned on him just the same.

"Right," I said as a map of the Austrian Alps appeared on the wall screen. "Let's begin by giving credit where it's due. Daphne found the first reference to a potential hidden book cache on the site of a former monastery. We know the inhabitants used at least one cave on the property to store wine and other necessities"—I paused as the room chuckled—"and we have documented proof of at least thirteen wizards in residence there over a ten-year period in the early fourteenth century. Contemporaneous records now in the Archives mention that several badly damaged manuscripts were sent away from an Arcanum stronghold outside of Vienna for repair, and we know that the magus in residence there had a cousin in the monastery. The evidence isn't solid, but since there's no further mention of those books, it's possible that they remain—"

A sharp knocking at the conference room door interrupted my presentation. Before Ted could invite the guest inside, the door opened to reveal Leander and a young aide—one of Maria's, I thought, as I tried to place her. Perhaps only twenty, the girl clutched a clipboard and seemed to hunch behind Leander, looking as if she'd rather be anywhere than the subbasement. When I listened, I felt her unshielded discomfort, embarrassment, and guilt rolling from her like a wave.

"Grand Magus," said Ted, going back to his feet and tugging his hibiscus-patterned shirt straight as Antony brought the lights back up. "What a surprise! It's not often we get company down here, but you're just in time. Have a seat, and we'll bring you up to date on our schedule for the rest of the year. Can I get you a cup of coffee?"

Ted, I knew, was as upset as anyone by what had happened to Toula and Maria, but he poured his heart into the welcoming act that morning.

"Thanks, but I'm not here for show and tell," said Leander, and snapped his fingers at the aide. She offered him the clipboard and scurried back into her hiding place, but I saw her lock eyes with Maria and mouth *Sorry*.

Leander clicked his pen open, nestled the clipboard into the crook of his arm, and offered the room a smile that died long before it reached his eyes. "Since I'm new to Arc 2, I'm conducting a survey of the residents. Let's see…" He scanned his notes. "Theodore Girard?"

"Ted," he replied, nodding when Leander looked his way. "And, uh, close on the surname, but it's French. The G sounds more like a J."

The grand magus made no effort to amend his pronunciation or apologize. "New-blooded, I see."

It wasn't a question, and Ted stiffened. "Yeah, more or

less. The Girards are an old family, but my dad's mom was second-generation, and my mom's parents were both new-blooded. Why?"

"Mm. There's never been a Girard who amounted to much of anything, huh?"

"I don't know about that—I think we've done pretty well for ourselves," Ted replied. "If you mean magi, then no, but my sister's grandkids are bright little things, and—"

"Yes, thank you, that's fine," he said, already looking over his notes again. "Which of you is Lakshmi...uh..."

"Gupta," Lakshmi replied, going to her feet in a swirl of fuchsia sari and dyed black hair.

He frowned at his papers. "That's not what this says..."

"If I'm listed by my husband's name, that's incorrect," she said, and folded her arms. "But do try to pronounce it. That's always good for a laugh."

The love of Lakshmi's life was a bald, reedy Englishman with the unfortunate surname of Featherstonhaugh. "Like 'fan-shaw,'" Lakshmi had explained the first time I stumbled across it. "Don't ask me how that works. English is *bizarre*."

But Leander didn't take the bait. "Old-blooded?"

"Yes," she said testily, "though I don't see why that matters."

"Says here you're only on an ash wand. Not the greatest specimen of the family, are you?"

At that, Lakshmi drew herself up to her full—albeit short—height and glared at Leander. "As I suspect the disappointed young ladies in your life may have told you, boy, it's not the wand that counts—it's what you do with it. Now, is there some purpose to this charade, or did you just come downstairs to be an ass to your elders?"

He jerked as if she'd slapped him in the face. "How dare you!"

"Oh, you have no idea what I *dare*—"

"Easy, now," Bob murmured, pulling her back toward her seat. When Lakshmi glared at him for the interruption, he said, "Not worth it, dear." Turning to the fuming grand magus, he offered, "Bob Norge, new-blooded through my father. My mother's family's well established around here."

Though Leander looked sullen, he let himself be distracted. "Your mother couldn't marry any better, then? Was she weak like you?"

"Last time I checked," replied Bob, arching a white eyebrow, "an ash wand was nothing to lose sleep about. And yes, Mam used an ash all her life. What about yours?"

"None of your concern," said Leander, "though I have to say, it's probably for the best that you've never had children. Weak wizards are such pathetic things."

"You know," said Bob in a remarkably conversational tone, "truth be told, I've never wanted children. My husband, now, would have made a wonderful father. Another ash wielder, if you're taking notes."

Before Leander could respond, Daphne stood and folded her arms. "Let's get this over with. Daphne Hopkins. Old-blooded. Maple wand. Have you got a problem with that?"

"Only that it seems you've wasted your talent with this band of riffraff," said Leander. "You turned down a job offer as an aide."

"Didn't want it, did I?" she retorted. "Didn't see the point of spending my life fetching tea for old men like a glorified intern. Suppose it was an old woman in your case, eh?"

"If you'd been smart enough to take the job, then maybe you'd have a career that amounted to something by now," he snapped. "Of course, given where you came from, I guess even this is a big step up."

"What the hell is *that* supposed to mean? I was born in this damn castle! At least we have windows...oh, wait," she said as he frowned and reread his notes, "bad intel? What, you thought I came from a shack on the beach?"

she asked, putting on the thick accent she employed whenever she quoted her Jamaican cousins. "If you must insult me, at least do so properly, you racist bastard."

"Whatever," he muttered. "My assessment stands: you're still the one of us in a dead-end job."

"At least I'm not surrounded by backstabbing animals," she spat. "These are some of the finest colleagues I could've asked for, and they've always supported my research. You could learn something."

Leander rolled his eyes. "How sweet. Next…Antony Copeland? Where are you?"

Antony got to his feet as Daphne sat. "Hi. Old-blooded. Can we get back to work now, please?"

But Leander wasn't finished with him. Looking him up and down, he wrinkled his nose and said, "Aren't you a witch?"

To his credit, Antony tensed but held his composure. "Wizard, actually."

"Says here you've never tested above an oak wand," he replied, tapping his pen against the clipboard.

"I won't deny my wand, but I would think my work speaks for itself."

"Antony has been with us from the beginning," Ted interjected. "I've worked with that man for twenty-five years, and he's been a major asset to us all."

"So you say," Leander replied, "but it seems to me like his talents would be better served with…what's it called, the Fringe?"

Those, as Kitty would have put it, were fighting words to any wizard, but Antony barely flinched. "If you're trying to make me feel bad about my talent, you're too late to the game. Russell Mulligan beat the crap out of me over this, like, thirty-five years ago. Hell, *Bert* was better at that than you are."

"And once again, I apologize," Bert mumbled across the table.

"Accepted. Now," said Antony, turning back to

Leander, "you've made your point. Congratulations, you've got the fanciest wand in the room. I would think that shiny little chain would be enough to soothe anyone's ego, but hey, kid, you do you. So unless you'd actually like to learn something about what we do down here, maybe you should mosey on back to the executive wing."

Leander smirked and chuckled to himself as he checked his notes. "Oh, no, we're not finished yet. Hmm…" His expression shifted toward feigned bemusement. "It seems my records are incomplete for a few of you. Which of you is Malcolm Stowe?"

Mal didn't bother standing. "What do you want to know?" he asked, and calmly sipped his tea.

"Well, for starters, let's talk about your family. Old- or new-blooded?"

I cut my eyes to Mal, though that was all I could do. Getting inside his thoughts was impossible without his permission. But Mal glanced my way, caught my stare, and barely dipped his chin, and I felt his barrier fall.

He knows already, I thought.

Though Mal couldn't employ telepathy on his own, I could see the thought at the forefront of his mind: *Oh, yeah. He's just forcing confessions.*

Plan?

Roll with it.

Setting his mug aside, Mal leaned back in his chair and linked his hands behind his head. "Neither. My mom's a lupine shifter, my dad's half fae."

"Then what the hell are *you*," Leander replied with a look of distaste, "and more importantly, how did you get into a secure installation?"

Before Mal could answer, Ted once again jumped in on defense. "Mal is Mal," he told the grand magus, "and he's been a dedicated member of the Team for fifteen years. Fine young man. He's saved our bacon in the field more times than I like to count."

"See, if you were decent wizards," Leander replied,

"you wouldn't need a pet dog." As Mal bristled, Leander continued his assault. "Why are you here? Is it because the Company wouldn't take you, or is it because the courts don't have any use for a flea-bitten half-breed?"

Mal held his gaze for a long, uncomfortable moment, then said, "You're really a piece of work, aren't you, bub?"

"Well? I'm waiting."

"And I've got nothing to hide. I'm Fringe, born and raised in the settlement. If you doubt me, then you're welcome to call Lonnie and check my bona fides. She'll vouch for me." Leander frowned, confused, and Mal laughed in his face. "Dr. Yolanda Ford, you ignorant asswipe," he explained. "The Fringe coordinator in this realm. Anyone on the Council should know her…*oh*, that's right," he said, milking his mock epiphany, "you were never a magus, were you? You were just getting coffee for Fuchs until a few days ago—"

I saw the bolt form in Leander's hand an instant before he flung it, and I threw a shield in front of Mal. As the bolt fizzled out on the thin carpet, I rose and glowered at the would-be grand magus. True, he was the taller of us, but he seemed surprised that the bolt hadn't struck true, and I exploited his momentary uncertainty. "You don't want a war with Faerie," I said. "Mal's protected. Try that again, and there will be consequences."

Though Leander still seemed unsteady, he tried to continue his obnoxious game. "And who might *you* be?" he asked, clicking his pen.

"You know damn well who I am, and you're wasting our time. But for your records, augmented quarter," I said, pointing to myself, then indicated Kitty, Artur, and Maria in turn. "Augmented witch-blood, another augmented quarter, *another* augmented witch-blood, and…" Reaching Frank, I paused, unsure of exactly what Leander's notes contained.

Frank, however, cleared his throat and slid into the opening. "Yet another augmented quarter," he told

Leander. I barely had time to register his unexpected answer before I heard Frank in my mind: *Surprise. Ted and Antony know. My dad's one of Titania's grandsons.*

Seriously? I asked, fighting to keep my expression neutral.

I found out at the end of July, and Ros did a little arts and crafts on me. Yeah, just like that, he added as I mentally winced. *Sorry, I would have said something sooner, but I'm still adjusting, and it's weird being in control of my own body, and—*

"You?" Leander barked at Frank, interrupting our silent conversation. "*You're* quarter-fae?"

Frank shrugged. "It was news to me, but, uh…" He held out his hand, and a small white fireball manifested in his palm. "I mean, I'm not working with much talent, here, but there's a little."

Leander squinted at him in disbelief. "My notes say you're a dragon."

"Half, as it turns out," said Frank, and smiled at him with far too many teeth. "Would you like a demonstration?"

"Look," Ted interrupted yet again, "Grand Magus, whatever you're getting at, the Away Team has been a mixed group since its inception. I've looked for people with interesting skillsets all along. Antony and Frank joined up first, Mal's been with us a long time, and…" He paused to consider the other four of us. "Kitty only learned she was witch-blooded three years back, Marcus and Artur are unique cases, and until two days ago, Maria was our magus. Our diversity has been our strength."

Unsurprisingly, Leander wasn't swayed. "I count exactly five wizards around this table," he said, pointing to Ted, Daphne, Lakshmi, Bert, and Bob. "Plus one witch, a pair of faeries, two mongrels, and whatever the hell you two are," he said, flicking his hand toward Mal and Frank. "Sitting here at the heart of the Arcanum without a care in the world. This is *completely* unacceptable." He glanced at the clipboard once more. "Who's Eadwig?"

"*Eadwig*," said Bob, pronouncing it properly. "Not *wig*, *wee*. Never read much Old English, have you?"

"Who cares about that?" Leander snapped. "And who is he?"

"A wizard," said Artur. "Most talented, and working from home. Fair warning—he'll be cross if you bother him with this bullshit. Doesn't appreciate interruptions."

He glared down the table at her, but Artur didn't so much as twitch. "I'm sorry, which of us is grand magus, again? I'll interrupt anyone I damn well like."

"You're no more the grand magus than I am." She watched impassively as Leander puffed with indignation. "The grand magus is a leader. You're a petulant child dismissing your best advisors and insulting the people you should be supporting. Give yourself a crown and call yourself a king—it would be just as empty a gesture."

As his face crimsoned beneath the fluorescents, Leander scowled at Artur and demanded, "Do you know who I am? What I can do to you?"

"I know exactly who you are," said Artur, drumming her fingers on the tabletop. "But you don't know who *I* am, and that puts you at a grave disadvantage." She smiled as he sputtered. "It's adorable, really, the way you think you're intimidating. Like a boy playing with his father's armor who fancies himself a warrior."

He jabbed his pen toward her as she continued to smile. "There's no place within this installation for abominations like you. *Any* of you," he said, pointing to anyone at the table who couldn't claim beyond all doubt to be a wizard. "I want you packed and gone by nightfall—and now, if you know what's good for you, you'll take me to this Eadwig."

Something tells me this isn't going to end well, I thought to the rest of the table, then stood again and shrugged. "Sure, we can take you," I told the furious grand magus. "It's your funeral."

SEPTEMBER 20: EADWIG

To my great surprise, I'd discovered that my best resource in my quest to remove Quinn's curse was not a treatise, nor a tome, nor even Simon's extensive study and work. Rather, it was her grandfather, the untalented son of wizards who'd been cast out without any memory of his family and made a life for himself as a cardiologist. Though he'd eventually remembered his childhood as Philip Mulligan, the man had found happiness as John Dellucci and answered exclusively to that name—Doctor, if one were feeling formal, or John, but never the name bestowed by the parents who hadn't wanted him.

Knowing what I did of his brother's bloody coup, I couldn't blame him for disassociating himself from his Arcanum roots. John was a kindly old man, nearly ninety-six but still sharp, and he'd sworn to do no harm. The destruction his brother had wrought left him aghast, a feeling with which I'd grown all too familiar. Now, having moved to Glastonbury from Chicago and come partly out of retirement, he would have been content dividing his time between the castle infirmary and his bridge club, but when I'd approached him for help, he'd cleared his schedule. John was Arcanum enough to know something of the evils that I—that *Simon*—had committed, but since I seemed to be his granddaughter's best hope, he put aside whatever distaste he felt and agreed to assist me.

Breaking a spell or enchantment—almost any magical construction, really—is accomplished in one of three ways. First, there may be a "lock" of sorts built in, which will open under the proper conditions. In stories, this might be true love's kiss; in practice, the presence of the right person or object usually suffices without dragging sentiment into the equation. The other two methods are simpler: either overload the spell with magic sufficient to break apart the channels holding it together, or else remove enough magic from the area that the spell collapses. Tossing an afflicted person into Conota would do wonders—and oddly enough, as constructions on living persons are destroyed on crossing into Faerie, one could toss the victim in either direction. In other words, I had options for getting the curse off of Quinn. The problem was the state in which that would leave her.

Take someone healthy who's been under a stasis bind for a period of years and wake him, and assuming he's been largely unconscious all the while, he'll be unharmed—the "Sleeping Beauty" effect, as one treatise described it. But if that person is critically injured before going into stasis and there's no healing spell added to the matrix, then once the bind is broken, he'll be just as badly hurt he was before. Artur had been such a case, forced into stasis on the brink of death, but she'd been strong enough to keep breathing for a few moments until she could be brought to Faerie and surrendered to the realm's painful ministrations. And then there was Quinn, who wasn't at the edge of death—she'd already crossed that threshold. Medically speaking, per her grandfather, she was a conscious corpse. I could break her curse in any fashion I chose, but doing so would leave her beyond all hope of healing.

Obviously, I needed a different approach. Rather than break the enchantment and try to fix her, I needed to repair and restart her body, *then* remove the bind. Simple enough, I'd thought about a month into my research. How difficult could it be to make her body work on its own?

Incredibly difficult, as it turned out. I had no idea how many moving pieces a human body contains, much less how delicate the balances are that sustain life. Just constructing the necessary scaffolding to control them all would take a herculean effort, and I feared that I wasn't strong enough to manage it on my own.

At least Quinn was a gracious test subject. In early August, I'd finally managed to make her blood move in its veins, but only because I was forcing it along with a spell. Restarting her heart was another matter entirely, and much as I tried, I couldn't simply will it to work.

"The problem is that you're treating it like it has an on-off switch," John had told me as I'd laid bare my problems. "A heartbeat is the name we give to a series of contractions and pressure changes triggered by a wave of electric impulses. It's delicately synchronized, and a full cycle takes less than a second. Quinnie's heart isn't beating because all of that electrical activity has ceased."

I'd started to suggest a potential fix, but he'd cut me off: "And you can't just zap her with a lightning bolt."

That having been my best suggestion, I'd instead fallen back on John's idea: continue to study anatomy and physiology with him until I understood the pathways that had fallen dormant in Quinn's body. The experience was incredibly humbling. Armed with Simon's knowledge and experience, I could build complex wards and pull off spells that would give even a well-trained wizard pause, but I knew nothing of John's field of expertise—and as I'd grown up believing that illness was caused by the workings of evil spirits, he'd been forced to begin with the basics. But John was knowledgeable and patient, the sort of tutor I'd never had in my prior mundane or magical studies, and if he was disgusted by the darkness inside me, he put his feelings aside for Quinn's sake.

Still, anatomy was only half the puzzle. Once I understood the body's workings, I would need to figure out how to set everything in motion once again—and if I wasn't successful on the first attempt, the patient would die.

No pressure.

I'd accomplished little work in the previous week. Toula's unexpected dismissal had been distressing, but then had come the news of Beth's mother's release, which had sent Beth into a panic. Much as I hated to delay my work, I wasn't about to allow Beth to rock in a corner alone all weekend. She'd skipped school the following Monday, but with Toula's and Maria's removal from the Council, whatever therapeutic relaxation she'd envisioned had failed to materialize. Beth had slept in Tuesday and was spending Wednesday in her room, but with the Team planning to meet for much of the morning, I eschewed my subbasement office and took over the kitchen table, where I would at least find sunlight.

Had I been asked, I wouldn't have been able to guess at the time, so deeply was I concentrating on my modeling. To restart the heart, I would need to trigger the production of action potential in the sinoatrial node, which meant restarting the depolarization cycle, which in turn meant regulating the electrolyte balance in Quinn's body—a challenge for another day. Assuming perfect conditions, I could build a series of channels to act as an external pacemaker until the natural rhythm was reestablished, plus another to move blood in and out while the contractions stabilized...

My fingers twitched of their own accord, building in midair a model of the system I might employ on Quinn, as my lips silently mouthed a concentration mantra I'd never learned. All of this—the planning, the construction, the skill necessary to convert my ideas into a working product—was Simon's doing.

I might not have liked Simon, but I needed him. Ordinarily, I strove to keep him compartmentalized in a corner of my brain, hidden far from my conscious thoughts. I didn't want him bleeding over into *me*, and if I could keep him caged, then I could pretend he wasn't lurking within me. But Eadwig was a novice at magic, and Simon was a master. I couldn't sufficiently focus and manipulate my power to accomplish what needed to be done for Quinn, and so I released my grip ever so slightly, stepping back and allowing Simon to come to the fore. With him guiding me, I could practically intuit what I needed to do. It wasn't a terrible system for a young wizard learning his craft, aside from the uncomfortable moments in which my hold slackened enough that Simon's memories blossomed from the recesses of my mind.

I'd almost worked out the electrical rhythm when I heard the door unlatch. Sighing, I began to prepare myself to make small talk—my flatmates meant well, though they seemed to have an uncanny knack for interrupting me with friendly banalities—but when I turned around, I found a small crowd hurrying inside: the entire Team, judging by a quick headcount, plus Leander and an anxious brunette who slunk in at the back of the pack. A Council aide—she was dressed too formally to be anything less—which meant that Leander's presence wasn't a social call. Confused by the interruption, I reached out and grabbed the first mind I could feel, Marcus's. *What's happened?*

He's throwing us out of the castle. Interrogated us, then ordered anyone less than full wizard out. Had questions about you. We've told him nothing, he hastily added. *Are—*

Quinn is asleep upstairs, I replied, divining the direction of his enquiry, *and Beth is watching a movie.* I flicked a finger toward Beth's closed bedroom door and murmured a word, locking her in. Assumedly, she had her headphones on, but in case she heard a commotion, I didn't want her barging in on a surprise confrontation with Leander.

"*You,*" the upstart barked, marching across the flat toward me. "Who are you?"

"I'm Ed," I told him.

"Full name?"

Simon began to grumble, but I tried to be civil.

"Eadwig, son of Oswald."

His eyebrows rose. "Old- or new-blooded? What's your wand?"

I pointedly cut my eyes to the unfinished construction hovering over the table, its channels faintly glowing in the magical spectrum, then looked back at him. "You're wasting my time."

At that, Leander puffed up like a strutting rooster. "Do you know who I am, kid?"

"You're the know-nothing child pretending that he's qualified to replace Toula," I said as Simon's temper—*my* temper—started to boil, "and your mistreatment of the Team is both pointless and puerile. Now, since I have far better things to do than watch you put on airs, do us both a favor and see yourself out."

Though I could sense the warnings from my flatmates, by then, my frustration with the past week's affairs was bubbling over. I'd grown to respect Toula, I liked Maria, and the Team had taken me in when I had no one and nothing. For that boy, that impertinent *fool*, to cast them out of the castle, then demand answers of me—*me!*—as if I were an inept servant...

I recognized Simon's voice thundering in my mind, but by then, I was too angry to care. Eadwig was seventeen and still unsure of himself, but Simon had no such reservations.

Angered by my response, Leander reached behind him, but before his fingers could even brush against his wand, I flung him off his feet and tossed him to the ceiling. He yelped in surprise and struggled against my spell, but I easily held him aloft, casting wandless and with little more than a thought. A few whispers wrapped constricting bands around Leander's chest and limbs, squeezing him until he could do no more than wriggle and cry out in pain.

As he fought in vain for his freedom, I rose from my chair and strolled into the den, the better to watch him squirm. By then, the Team and the frightened aide had retreated toward the kitchen, giving me ample room to work. I considered Leander for a moment, his face red and blotchy, his hair mussed, his feet kicking as if he could find purchase against the ceiling, and I might have spared a pitying thought for him had Simon not held the reins firmly in hand.

I'd killed far better men than that mewling boy.

"You asked about my wand," I said, keeping my tone conversational. "I don't have one. Don't need one, as I'm sure even you have noticed. I had one once for show, ceremonial moments and such, but these days, I don't see the point."

"Put me down!" he yelled. "You're going to break my fucking ribs—"

"You're not fit to be a magus, much less lead this organization. People's lives and fortunes are in your hands—this isn't some *game*."

I squeezed a little harder and smiled to myself as he screamed.

"The Arcanum was meant to bring peace and security to our people," I continued. "You are poised to squander all of that. What do you mean, throwing Toula out? What sort of idiot are you?"

Adding a new pressure band to a particularly sensitive location of Leander's anatomy was, perhaps, low of me, but Simon was furious, and it was so satisfying when the boy screeched.

"Look at what she accomplished!" I said over his pleas for mercy. "How many relationships she built. The *stability* achieved over her tenure. My God, you fool, until a month ago, there was no looming threat to the Arcanum, and do you know what a precious occurrence that is? Why would you cast Toula aside?"

He squeaked something that might have been, "Changeling."

I folded my arms and watched the tears roll down his face. "Yes, Faerie may be on fire right now, but if given time, they will sort themselves out. The Arcanum needs to hold the line and support the kings against Irem until she stands down. But what do you do instead? Toss aside the woman who's weathered multiple crises? Try to purge this organization of anyone with the slightest connection to Faerie *or* Conota? You truly want to rid yourself of the people who understand your supposed allies?" I shook my head, thinking of my lessons with John. "The sad fact is that you're either too stupid to know how ignorant you are of the way the systems work together or too proud to ask for guidance. Personally, I have neither the time nor the desire to educate a fool."

I stared at Leander a moment longer, wrestling with my anger.

Kill him, Simon whispered. *He's a threat. Remove him.*

He wasn't wrong. I could solve the problem of Leander by simply executing him—strong though he might have been, we weren't evenly matched, and I could crush his skull with a bit of concentration. But...

No. That was Simon, not me. As little as I thought of Leander, I had no true cause to kill him...and, I recalled, the Team was watching, holding their breath while I tortured him.

Though Simon disapproved, I released my grip.

With nothing holding him up, Leander plummeted toward the unforgiving floor without bothering to break his fall. He landed on the rug, which slightly cushioned the blow, but when he raised his head and moaned, his nose was bent and bleeding.

I kicked him over while he was still taking stock of his injuries, then planted my foot atop his stomach and watched him as he trembled beneath me. "I'm occupied with matters far more important than your little games, boy, so it's time for you to leave this flat."

As I stepped off of him, Leander scrambled to his feet, almost tripping over his robe in the process, and held one hand over his bloody face as he backpedaled toward the door. But the distance between us, however small, seemed to embolden him, and he made a last stand in the entryway. "I demand to know who the hell you are!" he said, his attempted dominance made almost comical by the vocal distortion of his broken nose.

I waved the door open, then flung Leander into the corridor. His head slammed into the wall, and as I joined him outside the flat, I tossed him down the staircase and halfway to the landing. "I am the one you call Simon Magus," I yelled down to him as he groaned, "and if you've learned anything here today, you will *never* raise your voice to me again."

Leander might not have made it out of the tower without his aide, who darted past me to help pull him to his feet. Seeing the clipboard she'd dropped, I read over the top page—notes about the Team, none of them complimentary—and reduced the whole thing to dust. Returning to the flat, I found the Team still packed in near the kitchen, and I closed the door with a sigh. "Well, that was amusing."

"Did you think that one through?" Kitty asked.

I shrugged. "Leander either thinks I've spoken the truth or believes me a madman, but he *knows* I'm stronger than he is. Maybe he'll back down and leave us all alone. And if he does believe me," I continued, motioning the rug straight, "and Simon's name still has any clout, then no one will be thrown out of the castle." Glancing up from my tidying, I told the others, "You've sheltered me for the last year. This is the least I can do."

"And it's appreciated," said Ted, "but blowing your cover…"

Before I could answer him, a pounding and a muffled shout reminded me that Beth was still locked in her room. I hastily released her but winced as she stormed out and grabbed me by the shoulders. "What the heck was *that?*" she said. "What were you thinking? Did he just beat up Leander?" she asked Kitty, who nodded. "Damn it, Ed," she said, giving me a brisk shake, "why would you put a target on your back?"

Pulling free of her grip, I smiled grimly as Beth continued to scowl. "I can't hide forever. And if it's necessary that I go public, then I may as well make Simon useful."

SEPTEMBER 20: BERT WOLD

Once Leander left the Team's suite, I'd hurried to the executive wing to inform Arnold of our new grand magus's doings. Fortunately, our conversation was brief, and I was back in my office when Leander limped onto the floor.

I stepped into the corridor to intercept him, but my planned speech about the virtue of slow change died unspoken. "Bloody hell," I said as his aide helped him away from the staircase. "What happened?"

Bloody was an apt descriptor. Leander's bright blue robe bore dark purple and black splotches in the front, presumably the result of the blood drying on the lower half of his face. He'd have looked like an extra in a bad vampire movie who'd been gorging himself if one ignored his apparent amateur rhinoplasty.

But much as I reasoned that Leander deserved his injuries, I'd made a promise to Toula, which meant that I had to at least try to seem sympathetic to the idiot's plight.

"Come in, this way," I said, taking Leander from the overburdened aide and hustling him into my office.

A few of the other magi, alerted by the commotion, poked their heads in the doorway and gasped at Leander's state. "What on earth happened to *you*?" asked Anna Popova—and if I wasn't mistaken, she was endeavoring to hide a smirk. Anna had made no secret of her allegiance to Toula, but as she was solidly old-blooded, Leander would be hard-pressed to remove her from the Council.

The boy said nothing as he slumped in one of my guest

chairs and held his hands over his battered face.

"Here, now," I murmured, and whispered a wet flannel from the ether. "Let's clean you up, eh?"

Silent and flushed, Leander endured my ministrations as the other magi stood by, watching while I wiped the blood from his face and crafted a healing spell. While his teeth were intact—fortunate, as I was no expert at dentistry—his nose was twisted and swelling, and I hoped I could repair the damage without giving him sinus problems. I added what numbing measures I could to the matrix, thinking of how much more efficient a healing construction could be in the hands of a competent faerie. Of course, after Leander's stunts of the last week, I doubted he'd be able to find one willing to work on him if he'd dropped to his knees and groveled.

Once the spell was cast and working, I removed the blood from Leander's clothing, then sat back and considered our sullen leader. "What happened?" I asked. "Did you fall? Those stairs are unforgiving, and in a castle this old, you've got to watch for depressions in the stone."

He ran a hand though his hair in agitation, wincing as he reached the back of his skull. "You should have been there," he muttered.

"Where, sir?" I forced myself to say.

"That apartment! There's a violent lunatic in there!"

The other magi traded concerned glances, but I played dumb. "A lunatic? Who?"

He huffed and crossed his arms over his restored robe. "Some kid living with the Away Team's faerie freaks thinks he's Simon Magus. He *attacked* me."

My colleagues tittered, but I quickly thought through the ramifications of Leander's statement. If Eadwig had outed himself...well, there was no point in denying it, was there?

"Actually," I said as the bloodied flannel disappeared, "that *is* Simon Magus. *Simon*, rather," I amended, pronouncing it more in the French style.

Anna looked at me as if I'd announced there was a gang of rabid leprechauns running amok in the main courtyard. "What are you talking about, Bert?"

"That's Simon," I said, shrugging as the others frowned. "Faked his death, as it so happens. He wanted to track down a grail—"

"Wait...*the* Grail?" one of the junior magi pressed.

"There isn't just one," I replied testily, reminding myself that not every magus shared a deep love for the Archives. "He spent years searching for the so-called Antwerp Grail, the one rumored to make the drinker immortal. Found out when he was being tortured in Faerie that it does accomplish that, but only by putting one into what amounts to a vampiric state. When he returned to this realm, he decided that destroying it would be a step in the right direction, karmically speaking, but he was too old and weak, so he put together a complex set of spells that would basically rewind him. Give him some of his strength back. He didn't want the Arcanum to know, so he moved to a monastery in Ireland and claimed to swear off magic."

The other magi's jaws began to droop.

"Anyway, he only intended to sleep for about fifty years. Let one of his grandsons—the witch, what's his name—in on the plan and told the boy how to wake him at the right time, then faked his death and let the spell work. But the grandson died young and obviously never passed on Simon's secret. Long story short, the monastery became a car park, some archaeologists discovered the tomb last year, and a couple of Minor Arcanum wizards happened to be doing their catering and called the Fringe for help. Fringe called the Team, and they found a teenage boy entombed in there. He's been living with them ever since...and if you don't believe me," I added, sensing some understandable incredulity among my colleagues, "talk to Arnold. Toula ran the kid's aural signature, and he's the common link among every wizard she has on file with a claim to the Magus. Has all of Simon's memories, his ability…he just has his youth back. Brilliant fellow. *He's* the one who showed us the missing three-quarters of his diary—that wasn't just a fluke find in the Archives."

Anna stared at me for a brief moment, then said, "If this is a joke—"

"It's not. Oh, and he prefers Eadwig to Simon. It's his birthname."

She clapped one hand over her mouth and murmured something decidedly Russian and almost certainly profane. "Why were we not *told?*"

"Because he's seventeen and conflicted and doesn't particularly care for his former self," I replied. "Doesn't want to have anything to do with leadership. And he's been rather busy for the last year—"

"*Who* is he living with?" asked Michael Fellows, who'd been hard of hearing even during my grand magus days.

"Kitty Connolly and Beth Stanhope," I said. "You know, Eva's daughters."

My conscious omission might have slipped past most of the Inner Council, but Anna was sharp. "Did I mishear a rumor, or is Kitty witch-blooded?"

That got the others' attention. "Hang on, now," said another junior magus, "was Magus Stanhope, ehm…attacked?"

"It's my understanding that the acts resulting in Kitty's conception were consensual," I said as delicately as I could, and glanced at Leander in time to see the flicker of disgust cross his face. "Though neither party was fully informed about the other. But Kitty has been a fantastic asset to the Team since her internship. You know she took a first at Oxford? Actually studied archaeology—"

"That may be," Anna interrupted, "but I *do* know she's involved with…"

She hesitated, and a look of understanding passed between us.

"With a man," she finished. "Maria mentioned a half sister as well, someone other than Eva's younger daughter.

An odd flat, that one. And you're telling us that *Simon Magus* has been living with them?"

"He's just some nutty kid!" Leander protested, swiveling in his seat to look at the gobsmacked magi. "You can't really believe he's the Magus. He broke my damn nose!"

But Anna, who'd taught for far too long to pay heed to the whinging of young people, ignored him. "I'm calling an emergency meeting of the full Council for this afternoon," she told me. "We need to judge this Eadwig for ourselves."

I'd never seen the boy look so old.

In the past months, when I'd had occasion to cross paths with Eadwig, he'd struck me as a youth of his apparent age. Physically, he was still gawky and awkward in the way of boys caught in the grip of puberty, shaving only because the dark fuzz that grew in on his cheeks and chin was too patchy to constitute a proper beard. The illusion of ordinary adolescence had slipped a little whenever we'd discussed anything concerning magic, but even then, I'd found his cover plausible. I'd been a child prodigy, too, and it wasn't entirely beyond reason that he could pull off spells impossible for most senior wizards.

But that afternoon, Eadwig finally dropped the mask. His blue eyes seemed burdened with years, his steps heavier and surer than those of a boy. Whoever Eadwig might usually have been, it was Simon walking beside me through the castle that day—quiet, contemplative, perhaps still somewhat angry, but resigned.

"The full Council's come," I told him as we climbed to the executive wing. "Don't be alarmed by the packed room."

"Not my first turn in front of a crowd," he murmured.

"Be that as it may, I'm sure it's been a time," I replied, thinking of my initial foray to the head of the Council table as an ignoramus of twenty-three. I'd spent half an hour in the toilet, sick with nerves, prior to that meeting. "Anyway, you won't be alone in there. I'll be on hand, and Arnold, of course. Leander will be present, naturally, but Anna Popova is running this meeting. Inner Council, Russian, old-blooded. A no-nonsense sort of woman."

"How did she vote?"

"She had confidence in Toula."

He grunted. "Then I suppose she's not a complete fool."

We reached our floor and headed down the hall, but as we neared the meeting room, I said, "Eadwig?"

When he stopped and looked at me queryingly, I saw the old soul behind the young face, the boy bowed by the weight of the man's remarkable, terrible life.

"You're not alone," I repeated. "If you need a break, just tell us. All right?"

"I will be fine," he replied, then took a deep breath, let it out slowly, and nodded to the closed door.

Mentally sending up a prayer to any merciful god in range, I ushered him into the room. The place was more than merely packed—no seat at the table but mine was empty, and curious aides lined the walls, some clutching mugs of tea and coffee against the hour in their proper time zones. The crowd stilled as we entered, and I tried to envision what they were seeing: a short, lean young man, his black hair marred by a white forelock, pale from long days spent underground with his reading. If they'd expected a warrior magus in a rich robe, chain glinting and wand sparking, they were surely disappointed.

Before Anna could call the meeting to order, Eadwig asked the table, "Which of you is Saito Rei?" One of the younger Arc 4 magi raised her hand, and he dipped his head. "Magus Saito. Magus Lowe, of course," he said, nodding to Arnold in turn. "And...Leander," he said with distaste, glancing at the back of the grand magus's head.

Leander hadn't so much as turned around when we

entered, and I was almost surprised to find Kathleen's golden boy sulking until I recalled the extent of his facial reconstruction. Taking a few steps away from Eadwig around the table, I saw that even with my healing spell at work, the grand magus's eyes had begun to blacken.

"There may be more of you," Eadwig continued, "but the three I named claim descent from Simon Magus, yes?"

Though Leander continued to ignore him, Arnold and Rei nodded.

Eadwig's spell came whispering forth like a soft sigh, summoning the aural signatures of the three magi, spheres composed from brilliant green lattices. One of his eyes barely twitched, and the trio of spheres began splitting in half, over and over, dividing each person's lattice into its progenitors'. After a few moments and dozens of splits, the three lattices that remained floating above the table were identical, and Eadwig flattened them and moved them together to show their perfect overlap—a common ancestor, or at least ancestors who had been full siblings or double first cousins.

With the matching lattices on display, Eadwig whispered again and brought forth his own, then flattened it and moved it into position atop the others. The assembled gasped or traded murmured commentary, and he folded his arms and waited until the noise subsided. "Let's look at my parents," he said, then snapped his fingers. All four lattices split again, but this time, they turned dark blue, the sign of a mundane human.

"I'm new-blooded," he said, looking around the table. "A freak in my family. Nine children altogether, and I was the only wizard among them. For what it's worth," he said, glancing at Arnold and Rei, "you are, in fact, my distant grandchildren. Congratulations, I suppose," he muttered.

No one seemed eager to break the silence that followed, but Anna finally stepped up. "What Bert told us is true, then?"

"Yes," he said simply, and shrugged. "Magus Popova, I

assume."

"The same."

"Then if you're satisfied that I am who I say I am, I'll take my leave. I have work to do, and this boy's *bullshit* has wasted enough of my time," he said, glaring at Leander.

As Eadwig turned to go, Anna called, "Magus, wait!"

He paused and closed his eyes for the space of a long breath, then opened them again and wheeled back toward the table. "Yes?"

A brief, almost giddy laugh escaped her. "You've returned," she murmured. "This is where you belong—*here*, the first among us."

Glancing at the other magi, I was surprised to find some of Leander's supporters nodding along as she spoke. Even Kathleen was staring at Eadwig with a look of awe.

"Why should we take orders from *him*," Anna continued, gesturing toward slumping Leander, "when the Magus himself is standing right there? If anyone can lead the Arcanum, it is—"

"Not me," Eadwig interrupted, cutting her speech short. "You don't want me."

She looked at the awestruck magi around the table and the wide-eyed aides ringing the room. "I am…pretty sure we do, sir."

"You don't," he insisted. "I built the Arcanum with blood. What you need is someone like Toula Pavli—someone who can maintain a peace without using it as an excuse for a half century of war. Besides," he said, folding his arms, "this is not my world. I'm still trying to understand it, and a year is hardly sufficient for mastery. But if you would listen to me—if you would heed my counsel—you would invite Toula back. Reinstate her. You need wisdom at the head of the table, not a boy throwing punches just to see how hard he can hit. If it would help, I'd ask her on your behalf."

"Exactly—*wisdom*," said Anna. "No one here has seen what you have, Magus! We need you."

"You flatter me, and thank you," he replied, "but no. Even if I wanted it, I couldn't take that chain."

"Why not?" asked Gunther, who'd finally managed to pick his jaw up off the floor. "You would have our support. Aides, tutors, whatever you require."

Eadwig sighed, his shoulders tightening. "I'm oath bound."

"To *whom*?" he demanded.

"The Minor Arcanum. Rather than execute me for mass murder—another reason you don't want me," he added—"they made me swear never to lead the Arcanum again."

Kathleen's face scrunched. "Huh? What mass murder?"

I cleared my throat, and Eadwig glanced my way. "The official account of the Great War puts its end in 1062 with the Asia conquest," I told him.

"Then they've missed the final chapters," he said with a weariness wholly at odds with his youth. "Which of you can travel in dreams?"

"Sleepwalking," Arnold offered. "And no one here. It's not taught." Most of my colleagues seemed perplexed by the term, and he explained, "The Minors still know how, but it's an uncommon skill among them, too. My cousin Badger has the knack, but no one would ever teach me. They don't like the idea of us poking around in the dream space."

"What *is* it?" Kathleen pressed.

"I suppose it's a bit like astral projection," said Arnold. "Fall into the right sort of trance, and you can apparently see things, travel great distances, talk to people—"

"Anyone with magical talent, no matter how slight, glows in there," Eadwig interrupted. "Easy to seek out other wizards, and since language is no barrier within that place…you see the benefit, yes?"

But Kathleen only scowled. "You're telling us the *Minors* know how to do some sort of strange magic that we don't?"

"It was a New World discovery," Arnold replied, unfazed by her displeasure. "And you know how much Europeans love to adopt new practices from people they consider just slightly better than savages," he added with all due sarcasm.

"That," said Eadwig, "and I slaughtered many of them."

The few hissed whispers around the room stilled.

"About seventy-five percent of the wizard population of the Americas and Oceania," Arnold murmured. "Or so Grivam told Badger."

"He's probably not wrong." A flash of something like nausea crossed Eadwig's face, and I wondered if the boy was preparing to wrestle back control. "Most wizards can't cast in the dream space," he explained to the silent table. "But I am a freak of nature in many respects...as is Badger," he said, cutting his eyes to Arnold.

"She got your hair and the sleepwalking."

"Poor thing. At least she's done some good with it." Addressing the table once more, he said, "Two years after the last Asian holdouts fell, I discovered the far lands in my sleep and gave their people an ultimatum: submit to the rule of the Arcanum or die. They laughed. What was I going to do from across the wide sea? A few days later, I returned and struck down everyone I could find over that long, bloody night. They died helpless in their sleep."

Pulling a glass of what smelled suspiciously like whisky from the ether, he knocked it back, shuddered, and destroyed the evidence. "That wasn't even the true end of the war. I'd conquered the mortal realm, but there was always the threat of Faerie to consider, so I decided I'd sneak in, sleepwalk, and murder the Three before they knew I was there. Turns out you *can't* sleepwalk in Faerie, Grivam warned them I was coming, and Oberon and Titania tortured me for almost five years before sending me home. And *that*, children, is how the Great War ended," he muttered. "So fucking *glorious*."

It was a good fifteen seconds before Gunther broke the silence. "But when did you swear an oath to the Minors?"

"Last year. Bert, do they know of the grail?"

"He gave some of us the short version," Anna answered for me, "and I informed the rest. What of it?"

"Your former head archivist, Jude Duffy...did Toula mention what became of him?"

"Vaguely," she replied. "Got mixed up in something he shouldn't have and committed suicide, she said. Did you have something to do with it?"

"I tried to stop him, but..." He sighed and absently rubbed his neck. "Even before my full memory was restored, I knew things I shouldn't. Showed Toula how to reveal the hidden pages in my diary. Jude realized who I was before I knew it myself. And when I told him that the grail he'd been seeking for years conferred immortality at a terrible cost, all he heard was 'immortality.' He took Frank's sick baby as a hostage and said we could have her back when we delivered the grail. Grivam had it, but he refused to give it to me unless I surrendered to the Minor Arcanum...so I did."

Kathleen's eyes narrowed. "Who's Frank?"

"Dragon," Leander muttered.

"Sort of," said Eadwig. "He said the technical term was 'draconid lesser fae,' but..." He paused to peer at the bemused magi. "Frank White. He's huge, pale, Away Team. Have none of you noticed him?"

"You mean the big albino guy?" one of our younger aides piped up.

"Precisely. He was under a transformation bind for years—did *none* of you notice? It was right there in his aura. More than that, he's massive and eats little more than meat, and he's been here for twenty-five years. Truly, no one guessed?"

"Toula kept that one close to the vest," said Arnold. "For his protection."

"Wait, *wait*, stop," Kathleen demanded, waving her

hands for attention. "You swore to those losers that you'd never lead us again to save some damn lizard?"

Eadwig let the silence stretch between them as he held Kathleen's stare, and after a moment, she blinked first and looked away.

"Yes," he said, "I did. And the Minor Arcanum showed me mercy, you realize. I hadn't expected to leave their meeting alive, but my victims weighed in, and they decided that there was enough of me now who hadn't been Simon to spare my life. So yes, I made my vow and claimed the grail from Grivam, and the child lived. There's an ocean of blood on my hands—it was the least I could do."

Nour delicately coughed. "An honorable choice, Magus, but you could break your oath. There are ways, even with strong bonds…" She let the thought hang, arching a brow.

"True," he replied, "but it's safer for all of us if I keep my word. I know far too well what evil I'm capable of. But hear my counsel," he continued, sweeping his gaze around the table. "I built this organization. I led it for most of my life…my previous life," he amended. "And I tell you in all sincerity that *he* is a disaster waiting to happen." His finger jutted toward Leander. "Perhaps he's talented—I can't say, he couldn't fight me. Perhaps he has potential. But not now. He's alienating the powers that should be our allies. Do the wise thing and choose someone else before he burns the Arcanum to the ground. If you won't accept Toula, then I would suggest Arnold."

At that, Kathleen, her brief moment of shock long past, began to laugh. "You're kidding. *Arnold?*"

"Why not? He's intelligent, reasonably talented, on good terms with the other powers, and he's done it twice before. He's a decent man."

But Kathleen just snorted her derision. "Might as well nominate Bert if you want a proven loser in the job."

Leander's supporters, emboldened by her example, laughed along. I stood there and took it—I couldn't exactly defend my time in office—but Arnold cut them short.

"I appreciate the vote of confidence," he said to Eadwig and our half of the table over the others' chuckling, "but I've taken the helm twice already, and I'm too old to do it a third time. That said, you're right—we need someone better qualified than the current candidate," he continued, not dignifying Leander with his name. "We should ask Toula to return."

This launched a dozen heated arguments as magi squabbled with their neighbors. After a minute or two, with no sign of decorum being restored, I was almost relieved to hear a sound like a thunderclap ring out around the room until I realized its source was Leander. The boy stood and glowered at the Council, black eyes and puffy face on full display, and the debates quickly fizzled. "*I* am your grand magus," he said, seething with indignation. "Your chosen, duly elected grand magus. The chain is mine by right."

"Sure, we voted you in," said Iris, the one Arc 1 magus not in lockstep with her installation leader, "but that was before we knew the original grand magus was available. Come on, Leander, you're going to stand there and tell us you're better qualified than Simon Magus himself?" Propping her head on her fist, she smirked at his fury— but as Iris had been a magus longer than Leander had been alive, she had little to fear. "Kid, I know Kathleen's been inflating that pretty head of yours for years, but I think you need to take a long look in the mirror before you start claiming to be the better choice. Those shiners of yours suggest otherwise…especially as there doesn't appear to be a scratch on *him*."

For a brief, hopeful moment, I thought we might have found the chink in Leander's armor. If Iris could talk to him like he was still an aide, then perhaps we could end his tenure before it truly began.

But Leander held his ground. "He is a danger and a

traitor who made an alliance with our enemies." Glancing over his shoulder at Eadwig, he said, "You're to be gone from this installation by nightfall, unless you'd prefer to take up residence in the cells. I banish—"

That was as far as Leander got before he was flung off his feet and thrown toward a wall. As the aides in the strike zone screamed and dove for cover, Leander smashed against the stone and struggled to free himself. Looking at Eadwig, I saw the fire in his eyes, but he refrained from doing more to Leander than humiliating him.

"I am no traitor," he told the hushed Council as Leander squirmed like a pinned beetle. "I built the Arcanum to bring peace and security to our people, and if you don't tether your dog"—he flicked one hand toward Leander—"he will destroy it." He calmly watched as Leander continued to kick and strain against his invisible bonds, then said, "I'm not going anywhere. My work is here."

"And what work would that be?" Anna asked.

Eadwig turned to the table, noticed Kathleen begin to stand, and flung her back into her chair with a whisper. "Some of you seem inordinately fond of the Mulligan family. One of them drank from the grail to stop Jude, and now she's cursed. I've been searching for a cure for the last year. So I will remain in my current quarters," he continued, his stare daring the Council to argue, "as will my hosts. *All* of them. All of the Away Team, in fact. Their assistance has been vital to this project."

That caught me off guard. We'd respected Dr. Dellucci's wishes and kept the truth of his bloodline quiet…but then I saw the interest in the faces of several Conclave sympathizers. Eadwig was playing his trump card.

"What sort of curse? And *what* Mulligan?" asked Conner Norleigh, the head of Arc 7. "Pavli wiped them out, unless you're talking about the daughter lines here…"

"She pruned one branch," Eadwig explained. "The

usurper had an older brother. You would call him a 'dud.' When he showed no talent, he was abandoned as a child, and his family stole his memory. Then Faerie was closed, the spell broke, and…" He shrugged. "Still untalented, but one of his granddaughters is a competent wizard. She sacrificed herself to save Frank's child and retrieve the grail from Jude, and now she's trapped in a sort of living death. So," he continued, glaring at the Arc 1 contingent, "in brief, the family lives on, but its scion is in danger. The *least* the Arcanum can do is give me time and space to work toward breaking her curse. And if I can tolerate faeries in my flat, then surely you can ignore their presence in this castle while they work with me."

Leander fell to the rug with a thud and a cry of pain, and Eadwig rolled his eyes as the grand magus moaned. "I'll thank you kindly to stay out of my way," he concluded, then turned on his heel and marched from the room.

Arnold nodded at me, and I hurried after him. By the time I caught up with Eadwig, he was descending the spiral staircase at a jog, and he turned imploring eyes on me. "Toilet?"

I pulled him down the hallway at the next landing, opened the door to the men's room, and locked it behind us as he ran for a cubicle. A few seconds later, I heard the unmistakable sounds of retching and opted to give him his space.

When Eadwig emerged, his face had paled, and I called forth a cup of mouthwash. "Swish and spit," I said, nudging him toward the sink. "Are you all right?"

He rinsed and tossed the cup into the rubbish bin, then clutched the counter and closed his eyes. "No, Bert, I am not."

"Still queasy?"

Eadwig said nothing for a moment, but his face worked in the silence. Finally, he murmured, "It's too easy to be him. Like sliding my feet into well-worn boots. Feels natural." Grimacing, he swallowed hard. "I hate him, but if that's what it takes to keep us safe…"

"Masterful performance up there," I replied. "You could have fooled me. I think more than a few magi may need new trousers."

"Not enough." He opened his eyes and stared at his reflection, a face simultaneously young and weary with age. "Quinn gave us a temporary reprieve, but Leander won't tolerate my presence for long."

"He won't have a choice," I protested. "You're still the Magus—"

"I'm compromised, and his acolytes know it." Turning to me, he wiped the sweat from his clammy brow and sighed. "We need an exit plan."

SEPTEMBER 21: BETH STANHOPE

Under ordinary circumstances, I wouldn't have minded being called out of class. I'd slept poorly for a week, my roommates—my family—were packing and making preparations to abandon the castle, and since I'd won combat at the Games, my classmates were gunning for me in practical casting. The reprieve was appreciated until the teaching aide who'd appeared with the message explained that the grand magus wanted to see me—*now*.

I didn't want to be anywhere near the executive wing. Ed had been a mess all night after the stunt he'd pulled, but at least he could take a swing at Leander and make the twerp bleed. I wasn't half the wizard Ed was, however, and my combat victory didn't make me the equal of a guy more than ten years my senior and wielding a pine wand. And *oh*, I wanted so badly to make Leander hurt—for trying to kick my family out of the castle, for freeing Eva, for putting Ed in a position where he spent the night sitting on the rug beside my bed, holding his knees and rocking in the darkness.

But I couldn't, and I knew it. I couldn't beat him, but I'd have to face him alone, all the same. And so, as my guts knotted and I hurried through the castle toward my unexpected appointment, I talked to my father.

"Hey, Dad," I murmured when I found myself in a long, empty corridor between towers. "If you're here, if you can hear me...I'm scared. Not just about this. Everyone's getting ready to move out, and they're going to Afallon. They were going to go to Faerie, but Quinn can't cross, and I don't know what would happen to Aurie, so Artur's invited everyone to her place. But I'll be here by myself. Kitty told me I can't just commute—we don't want to accidentally let on where they've gone. And the dorms won't be so bad, don't worry about that, but…" I paused as a young woman slipped out of one of the offices and jogged toward the nearest staircase, then resumed once no one was around to think I was talking to myself. "Things were *good* here, but all of a sudden, everything's up in the air, and I don't want to lose another home. Everyone says they're going—like, the whole Team is abandoning ship, and I think even Dr. Dellucci is coming along—but Kitty says I need to stay here and go to school." I reached behind me and adjusted the wand tucked under my shirt, my last resort in case things went south. "I mean, she's not *wrong*. School's important and all. But I don't want to be alone here."

I had no way of knowing whether Dad heard a word I said. He'd died when I wasn't quite four months old, and the few times I could remember laying eyes on him had been courtesy of Hope. But he'd told me then that he hung around—not just for my sister, the one he'd raised, but for me, too. Even if I couldn't be sure that he was listening, the possibility gave me comfort.

"If you're here," I whispered at the bottom of the staircase leading to the magi's offices, "stay with me, okay? Please, Dad?"

Wiping my sweaty palms on my pants, I headed up. A pair of aides passed me coming down, but no one stopped to question me, no matter how much I silently begged them to give me a reason to stall. Fresh out of excuses, I stopped for a moment at the landing, catching my breath and checking my wand one more time, then headed for the place where Grand Magus Pavli's office had been.

Almost as soon as I knocked, the door opened, and there he was, sporting a black robe with fine silver detailing along the cuffs and hem. His face was still discolored, though, and I didn't have to look hard to see the healing spell at work around his head. The schadenfreude gave me a momentary thrill until I recalled that Marcus was about to move out, and since he'd been patching me up for years, I was in for some painful nights ahead. Healing through spellcraft was fine and dandy, but my brother-in-law's version was *highly* effective.

Surely, I mused, they'd let me sneak out to Afallon the next time I broke a bone in class.

"Elizabeth," said Leander, flashing a dimpled smile that might have made me weak in the knees had I not seen the man behind it. "Thanks for coming. I hope you're not missing anything important."

"Sparring, sir," I said, and forced a smile in reply. "Magus Popova understands."

"I should hope so. Come in."

There being no visitor's chair in front of his desk, I cut my eyes to the right, toward the place where Grand Magus Pavli had kept some comfortable seating. But when I saw who was waiting on one of Leander's new burgundy couches, I froze where I stood while Leander locked the door behind me.

I hadn't seen her in more than three years, not since the grand magus had hauled me down to the secure cells with Kitty for my one and only visit. I'd sent her letters for a few months during my miserable year with the Audleys, but she'd never answered me. And then Magus Corelli— well, Maria—had shown me the truth about her. She'd never loved me. She'd *lied* to me, teaching me to hate the sister who'd kept trying to be a part of my life—the sister who'd given me a home even after I did everything but spit in her face.

Her hair was still a honey-blonde bob, though I suspected at least some of that was artificial. It framed her thin face as she turned to consider me. I held my ground, meeting her stare with my own. I'd always thought we had the same coloration until I met Dad and realized, to my relief, that I had his brown eyes, not hers. The look she gave me was calculating, appraising—perhaps understandable, as I'd grown and filled out since we'd last met. I sure as hell hadn't sent her photos.

"Surprise!" said Leander, and guided me toward her. "Go on, don't be shy."

I sat stiffly on the couch opposite her, while Leander, who perhaps had anticipated a warmer reunion, looked back and forth between us for a moment before taking a seat to her right.

Her rouged lips moved into a semblance of a smile, though her eyes remained cold as ever. "Hello, Beth."

"Eva."

Finding himself out of his depth, Leander hesitated, as if giving the Hallmark moment one last chance to materialize, then coughed for attention. "So, uh…Beth," he said, sounding less like a game show host presenting me with a new car, "since your mother's been freed from her unjust incarceration—"

"Three years and change for treason and attempted murder?" I interjected. "Excuse me, *Grand Magus*, but that hardly seems fair."

Eva's face remained a mask, while Leander regarded me like a snake in his bed—possibly venomous, possibly not, but definitely not part of the plan. "That's your mother you're talking about—"

"Yeah, one big, happy family, right here," I muttered.

"Don't worry, it's been a while," said Eva, giving Leander's knee a pat. "And she's been stuck with those degenerates all this time—"

"Those *degenerates*," I snapped, glaring at her, "actually give a damn about me, which is more than I can say for you."

An internal voice suspiciously like Artur's cautioned me to be careful. How many times had she knocked me off my feet when my anger got the best of me in practice? *Anger feels good*, she'd told me. *In the moment, it feels like your friend. But it clouds your judgment, makes you hasty, and will get you killed if you can't master it.*

I took a deep breath, fought down the shout fighting to escape me, and focused on Leander. "I'm sorry, sir, you don't need our family drama. I have nothing to say to her, so may I go back to class now, please?"

Whatever touching moment Leander had envisioned, he certainly hadn't prepared for this contingency. "Uh...no. I brought you here because I'm returning you to your mother's custody. You'll be going home to Arc 1."

Careful, my internalized Artur warned.

"Sir," I said through gritted teeth, "that woman neither loves me nor wants me around. She's made that perfectly clear...and I'm sure the last thing she wants while readjusting to her Council duties is an angry teenager in the house," I added with a pointed smile. "I want to stay here—school at Arc 2 is way better than doing night classes in the silo. If you're kicking my sister out, then emancipate me," I suggested. "I'm seventeen—I can stay in the dorms and keep out of trouble. But I want *nothing* to do with Eva."

While Leander blinked in surprise, Eva oozed into the breach. "Sweetheart, I know this time apart has been difficult for you," she said, leaning toward me across the coffee table. "That awful woman sending you here, to *Katherine,* away from your home, your mother—"

"Can it," I said. "*Dad* has been a better parent to me than you ever were. At least he cares about me."

Her maternal act began to falter, and I caught a glimpse of the steel beneath. "And how would you know anything about what Orson ever thought or felt?"

"Because I'm on *really* friendly terms with the king of Conota and his wife, and she's the most powerful medium in any realm. Cynaeli talk to the dead all the time...or didn't you know, Magus?" I asked with a smirk. "Doesn't matter. I've met Dad, and it's nice to have a parent who's interested in my health and happiness."

Eva forced her face back into position and tried again. "Beth, honey—"

"Did you read any of my letters? A single one of them? I mean, you know, once I found out that you'd kept all of Kitty's letters away from me, I read her copies. She took the time to write to me every month, and I feel awful now that I never got a chance to respond to her. So…did you get my mail?"

Annoyance flickered in her eyes. "I was going through hell, sweetie—"

I laughed in her face. "*You* were going through hell? You made your choices! I didn't do anything wrong, and my life fell apart, and you couldn't send me one fucking *word*? Oh, that's right, I wasn't useful, was I? I was thirteen and wanted my mother, but I guess that wasn't your problem."

Turning to Leander, who seemed less comfortable by the second, I said, "Excuse my French, Grand Magus, but whatever she's told you is probably bullshit. My sister has been wonderful to me. My grades have never been better, my casting has improved exponentially, and Kitty even got me into therapy. She's been more of a parent to me—not a guardian, a *parent*—than Eva ever has. I've had experiences I never would have imagined when I was back in Montana. And really," I continued, "everybody in Kitty's apartment has been great to me. Hell, even Lord Val asks about me, and he doesn't owe me a darn thing. And what do I get from her?" I said, pointing to Eva. "Thirteen years of not being quite up to her standards, and then silence. I don't need her. I don't *want* her," I insisted. "So if you would kindly emancipate me, I'll get out of your hair."

Smile gone, Leander struggled briefly, then tapped his fingertips together in agitation as he thought. "I hear you, Beth, and I appreciate that you want to continue in your current classes," he said, "but think of how terrible it would look for me to strip a magus of her parental rights. You understand, don't you?"

"And what about my rights, sir? I've already been uprooted once because of her. Why should I be punished again?"

"I understand your frustration," he replied, holding my gaze, "but I'm returning you to your mother's custody."

"And you will be returning to school in Montana," Eva interjected. "*Tomorrow.*"

"Mm…Monday?" Leander suggested. "At least give her a few days to adjust to the time difference."

"Tomorrow would be best," said Eva. "She's missed enough school already this year. We can register you today, sweetheart," she told me with ice in her eyes.

Careful, girl.

Resisting the urge to grab my wand, I stood and stared down at Leander. "She can register without me. If I'm going home, I need to pack my things. Kitty can make the arrangements to get me back there tonight."

Relief swept across his face. "Thank you for your understanding. I think that's a very sensible plan," he said before Eva could interrupt. "You're dismissed from class for the rest of the day."

"May I go, sir?"

"You may."

As I neared the door, Leander said, "Things will be much better soon, Beth. We're fixing the problems within the Arcanum."

I turned, looked pointedly at Eva, then cut my eyes back to him. "You've got a long way to go, Grand Magus," I replied, and let myself out.

It took every ounce of my self-control not to slam the door behind me and sprint for the stairs. I didn't start running until I was out of the tower, and I made it home in record time.

My sister, who'd been packing the kitchen, poked her head around the corner and frowned. "Beth? You okay, honey?" she asked, her Tennessee drawl undimmed by her years in England.

I caught my breath as the others emerged from their rooms at the commotion—all but Quinn, of course, who'd packed the night before and was sleeping the day away. "Leander's making me go back to the silo with Eva," I announced. "As soon as I'm packed."

"*What?* He can't do that!" she cried. "Well...I mean, technically, he can, but couldn't he let you stay in the dorms? Don't you get a say in this?"

"I tried that, but apparently, it would look bad if I didn't go with Mommy Dearest," I said as my throat began to close. Spotting Artur as she came through the den, I crossed the room, tried to will away the tears that threatened to spill over, and begged, "Let me come, too. Please, don't make me go with her—"

Artur gripped my shoulders to silence me. "Dry your eyes, little sister," she murmured as I sniffled. "Where I have a home, you have a home. Understood?"

Relieved, I threw my arms around her, and she patted my back. "I'll help you pack," she said. "We leave at nightfall."

And while I didn't know if Dad was there, I imagined he'd approve.

SEPTEMBER 22: MARCUS

As the stars came out after our first full day on Afallon, all I wanted to do was fall into bed and lose consciousness. Kitty, however, was on her cynaeli-made phone with Hope, filling her in on the Arcanum debacle. Since I was poised to drop, she'd taken her call to one of the small offices Artur had built when she'd designed the lodge for the Team, ostensibly so that I could fall asleep in peace. But I knew that I wouldn't sleep until Kitty came to bed. When one of us was in the field, sleeping alone was seldom an issue for me, but when my wife and I were under the same roof, I craved the warmth of her body beside mine, the depression in the mattress, the bouquet of the various concoctions she applied to her hair. In short, I wasn't getting any rest until Hope was well and truly informed, and so I lay in bed with my mobile, playing cards against the computer in my palm.

It was, at least, a respite from Pater's frequent calls for updates. Were we out of Glastonbury yet? Settled on the island? Were the wards strong enough? Was Toula with us?

The last was easy to answer. My aunt had arrived from Faerie shortly after we did, thanks to a call from Maria. She claimed that she'd come to check the wards that the island's previous owner—one did not speak the name of Kitty and Artur's biological father around them if one were wise—had erected. In truth, Toula felt terribly guilty about the whole situation, as several families had now uprooted themselves and fled the Arcanum. It was, she remarked, a very Conclave play, and the irony was lost on no one.

Judging by the pictures I'd seen, our accommodations were far nicer than the Conclave's Alaskan compound had been. Afallon wasn't large, a grassy island between England and Wales that would have merited little notice but for the fact that it appeared on no map. Protected by Myrddin's intricate wards, both camouflaging and deterring, it had been a land unto itself for fifteen hundred years, his hideout from the world until his daughters crashed back into his life. At his death, neither had wanted anything of his, but Artur had agreed to claim the place at Kitty's insistence. Though it was a far cry from the territory she'd formerly ruled, the once and future king finally had a place of her own again…but since she was still living with us, she'd opted to use it as the Team's offsite retreat. Artur had wiped away her predecessor's stone tower, replacing it with a beautiful lodge like something from a resort advertisement—which, given her unfamiliarity with modern construction, was entirely likely. Kitty had seen to the interior, leaving us with twelve bedrooms, plus conference rooms, offices, a game room, a small theater, and a *highly* respectable wine cellar to enjoy. Protected both by the wards and by the island's steep cliffs, Afallon had been the perfect secret getaway for the last two years.

It had never been quite so full, however.

Naturally, Artur claimed the expansive master suite, but she'd sectioned off a third of the room and put in a bed for Maria. Kitty and I shared a room, while Beth bunked with Allie Copeland, who was only two years younger. Allie's parents slept down the hall between Bob and Sylvester's room and Lakshmi and Rodney's. The Featherstonhaugh sons and daughter-in-law had also come—Lakshmi wasn't about to leave her granddaughter unprotected—and the younger son, Philip, shared a room with Mal. Frank and Aurie took a smaller bedroom, while Daphne generously volunteered to bunk with Ted. The

Delluccis had to be split—Quinn set up a cot in the windowless wine cellar for her own protection, but Dr. Dellucci offered to share space with Eadwig. Then again, as Eadwig and his haul of pilfered books had taken over one of the offices, I doubted that his bed would be used.

The biggest surprises on Artur's guest roster had been Dr. Powell and her wife, who, informed by Maria of the plan, had slipped out of the castle with boxes and bags full of medical supplies. "I fought Mulligan when I was a kid," Dr. Powell had explained as they arranged their bounty in a storage room. "I'm not rolling over for a little shit like Leander. Once the Arcanum has its head on straight, I'll gladly return, but until then, he can patch himself up."

With the accommodations on hand filled, we'd offered to create a bedroom for Toula, but she'd opted instead for a couch in the spacious den. "Too much to do to bother sleeping," she'd told me, but I suspected she was too worried to make a bed worthwhile.

We shared her concern. Despite the holiday feel of the island, we were on the run. Those wizards who'd come with us had made their feelings clear, and Leander didn't strike me as the sort of man quick to forgive and welcome back. Some of us had opted to take walks around the island that day, enjoying the autumn wind and the eternally fruiting trees. Sylvester had been compulsively baking for hours, though given his skill in the kitchen, no one minded. Aurie had sneaked into the theater to watch movies with the older girls, and while the selections on offer were perhaps inappropriate for a child her age, Frank didn't stop her. After all, we had far more immediate problems.

If the Arcanum was about to self-destruct, whether by falling into a new Mulligan-style regime or as a consequence of Council infighting, we wanted to be out of the blast radius. Faerie was our safest option by far, and Pater had made it abundantly clear that the Team would be offered protection. Irem's plans to attack the Fringe settlement seemed to have stalled, and Toula reported that security along the wall had never been better since Nico joined up, but if the Team were concerned for their safety in town, Pater invited them to stay with him as his guests. As they'd put up with me for four years, he was more than willing to return to favor.

Having lost my latest hand of Hearts, I was poised to send him a message and reassure him that we hadn't been discovered yet when Kitty let herself into the room. "That was quick," I said, putting the phone away. "Is she all right?"

"Fine. Apparently, Toula's been keeping them apprised," she replied, and flopped onto our bed. "They're offering us sanctuary. Everyone here is welcome."

"Kind of them."

"They know it's the last-ditch option, but Arik wanted to make sure that we understand it's available. He's concerned, and Hope said they still owe the Team a massive debt. If things get dicey with Irem again and Leander figures out where we're hiding…"

"Something to think about in the morning," I replied, patting the space beside me. "Come on, you're exhausted. You barely slept last night."

Kitty sighed, then rolled over and crawled into place. "Lot on my mind."

"It's not all yours to carry, dearest," I said, and kissed her. "Probably for the best that you haven't tried to join Sylvester. He seems territorial with the oven."

"Honestly, my stomach's too knotted to even think about food." She pulled the blankets to her chin and waited while I waved the lamp dark. "Maybe this will blow over, yeah? Leander will piss off the wrong magus, they'll hold another no-confidence vote, and they'll settle for someone boring. Maybe Bert."

I grimaced in the darkness. "Ooh. Do we really want another round of Grand Magus Wold?"

"Got to be better than he was the first time. He's mellowed since I was a kid, so I don't think he'd be terrible. Wouldn't free my fucking mother, at least," she muttered. "The *nerve* of that bitch. What, now that Beth is a decent caster, she wants her around? For what? Some sort of trophy?"

"She can't find us here," I soothed, brushing Kitty's pale hair from her face. My aunt had seen to that, crafting spells on everyone to block blood traces—and then she'd pulled Eadwig away from his work long enough for him to double-check her casting and add his own touches. For the time being, we were undiscoverable.

"I know," said Kitty, "but…it's just so damn infuriating. If she cared about Beth—which she obviously doesn't—she wouldn't rip her out of school and force her back to Montana. Stupid, maybe, but part of me still hoped she'd do the right thing by at least one of her daughters. She wouldn't have lost face—all she'd have to do is say that she doesn't want to upset Beth's education. Hell, she sent me to board in Glastonbury without losing any sleep over it, and I was ten!"

I began chuckling to myself, and Kitty muttered, "What?"

"Thinking about Leander. How it must feel to be outsmarted in front of his magi. If he knew Beth at all, he would have known she wouldn't go quietly. Letting her out of his sight…what a fool."

"She *does* have a history of running off when she doesn't like her accommodations," Kitty replied, and softly laughed. "Gotten better at it, I think."

"To be fair, she had help this time."

"And she didn't steal my cash. Baby sister's growing up." She paused. "Then again, baby sister, Allie, and Aurie are giving themselves nightmares with a horror movie marathon, so maybe she still needs me."

Kitty soon fell asleep, but I lay awake beside her, thinking about Hope and Arik's offer. Generous, certainly, but not our first choice—any faerie or talented mortal felt just as unsettled in that realm as those two did in Faerie, thanks to the lack of useable magic. We'd be at their mercy, though I knew they would treat us well. In any case, the kindness was appreciated, though it wasn't a real solution.

Neither was Faerie. Most of us could go with no trouble, but not all. Aurie hadn't left the mortal realm since the day she hatched, and I could only imagine how she would react to suddenly finding herself at full size and crippled. Putting a bind back on her would be little trouble, but then there was her family to consider. Once her father's siblings knew she was around, would they try to kill her? I *really* didn't want to think about a standoff against multiple dragons.

And then there was Quinn. If she left the realm, she was dead.

Despite Arc 1's fondness for her granduncle, we couldn't trust the Arcanum to take care of her. Both Delluccis had been annoyed on learning what Eadwig had told the Council; neither wished to be linked to their murderous relative, particularly Dr. Dellucci, who would have become one of his brother's hostages or victims had he been allowed to keep his memory and join the Fringe. Though Eadwig swore he hadn't named them, it wouldn't take a genius detective to deduce that the elderly fellow who'd appeared one day in the infirmary and was never seen with a wand might just be a missing Mulligan. Even if they claimed the family name, however, they feared that they might meet an untimely end if left in Leander's care, Dr. Dellucci as a dud and Quinn as a cursed abomination.

That meant the Delluccis were with us, come good or ill. We couldn't abandon them.

Eadwig, especially, refused to leave them behind. As soon as he'd dropped his bag of clothing in a guestroom, he'd retreated to an office with his computer and books, affixing a handwritten sign to the door asking for privacy.

That request didn't extend to Dr. Dellucci, who'd joined Eadwig for most of the day and returned to the office after dinner.

"He's paranoid," Dr. Dellucci had confessed over the meal. "Worried that we're running out of time." Turning to Dr. Powell, he'd asked, "What sort of a supply were you able to snag for Quinnie, Bee?"

She'd cut her eyes to the chest freezer and made a face. "About a week's worth. I can replicate from that for a while, but I don't like to feed her on any one homemade strain for more than a month."

"I don't mind making the occasional donation," Daisy had offered, giving her wife's hand a squeeze. "Good veins."

Many of the wizards at the table had volunteered as well. None of us with fae blood could help—a pity, as I'd rather have taken a turn instead of asking the more senior Team members to contribute—but between the available donors and Dr. Powell's replication spells, Quinn wasn't in immediate danger of starvation.

Unless something forced us to flee. If Quinn were left to fend for herself, she'd be faced with a terrible choice: find a source of human blood or die. Given what I'd seen of her over the last year, I had a feeling that she'd choose suicide, an outcome we hoped to avoid.

Reluctant to disturb Kitty with my restlessness, I slipped out of bed and headed for the kitchen. One of the bottles of wine we'd opened with dinner was left half empty on the counter, and I helped myself and peered out into the night. Someone had lit a fire in the pavilion pit, and I counted the figures seated around it. Frank was easy—his size gave him away—as was Ted, and the woman seated across from them, sipping from a tumbler, had to be Quinn with her breakfast. I thought of joining them until I heard my aunt murmuring down the hall, then took my drink into the den to investigate.

As I poked my head into the room, she ended a phone

call and leaned against her couch bed with a groan. "Pater again?" I asked.

"Arnold." She waited while I took one of the leather recliners, then said, "Shit's hit the fan in Glastonbury."

"The Council wants Simon back, I take it."

She laughed mirthlessly. "Uh, *no*. Whoever's managing Leander's PR is doing a fantastic job of spinning your impromptu departure. According to Leander, Beth's disappearance is yet another case of faeries kidnapping changelings."

"That's preposterous," I protested. "What, we're meant to have kidnapped Beth *and* the other half of the Team? The doctors? Eadwig? All of them?"

"The others are being swept under the rug for now. Per Arnold, Eva is playing the role of grieving mother like she's gunning for an Oscar, and Leander is trying to paint this as some sort of reprisal for my dismissal."

"Is it working?"

"If you're seriously asking me that, bud, you haven't spent enough time with the Arcanum." She cast her gaze to the high ceiling and sighed. "And that's not my biggest concern."

I sipped my wine, resisting the urge to knock it back in one gulp. "What's worrying you, then?"

Toula watched me with weary eyes. "Remember that little souvenir you boys brought home from Russia last month?"

"The silver sphere? There's nothing little about it—"

"Exactly. I put it into secure storage. The room's warded against gates, for obvious reasons, and only I had the access codes. I gave them to Arnold when I left the castle, asking him to get the sphere out of there before Leander stumbles onto it. Unfortunately, Arnold thinks he's under surveillance—he's probably right about that— and he didn't get a chance to safely investigate in the Archives until tonight. The codes have been changed." She ran a hand through her hair, then asked, "Is there any more wine?"

I rose from my chair with sleep suddenly the furthest matter from my mind. "Stay there. I'll bring the bottle."

SEPTEMBER 25: BERT WOLD

On Friday, when I showed up for work at the break of dawn and feigned ignorance as to why Leander might still be sitting at his desk in Thursday's robe with the shadows of a sleepless night adding to the bruising around his eyes, I assumed that Monday's full Council meeting would be worse than usual.

On Saturday morning, when I caught Eva weeping crocodile tears in the dining hall over her waffles, I began to dread the week to follow.

And then came Saturday night, which pushed the matter of the Team's flight with the Stanhope girl to the back burner.

Arc 5, the Giza installation, was a short, nondescript block of flats in a middling neighborhood, quiet and unremarkable—and warded to be forgotten as soon as mundane observers looked away. Behind its wards, it was a different matter: twenty stories tall and extending several levels underground, a luxurious complex with opulent touches sufficient to rival the architectural flights of fancy in Dubai. The waterfall in the courtyard was my favorite feature, the centerpiece of a verdant oasis, constantly recirculating from a lake deep enough to permit lazy boating. A cool breeze always blew through the facility, an especially welcome bit of spellcraft in the middle of the Egyptian summer, while another spell kept the Saharan dust outside. Had I been stationed there, I doubted I'd have found much reason to leave the complex once I'd seen the monuments, but those residents of a more social bent often ventured out, taking in football matches and hitting the clubs in Cairo.

Around seven on Saturday night, Nour sent an emergency message to the Council: a young family had been returning from dinner in the city when a gate had opened in the middle of the pavement near Arc 5. The man who'd come through was unknown to them—and far too redheaded to be a local—but he'd thrown the parents halfway down the block with a wave of his hand, snatched their nine-year-old son, Ahmed, and sealed the rift behind him before they could do more than scream.

Another changeling taken would have been bad enough, but now the bastards had snatched one of our own.

On receipt of the message from Giza, I'd done the only sensible thing: I made tracks for my favorite pub on the far side of Glastonbury, found a booth away from the stag party in the front of the building, and rang Toula.

By Monday morning, I knew that shadow negotiations were underway—she'd kept me apprised of the generalities. Rather than face off against Irem for a second time, Toula had alerted her brother and...well, like it or not, her boyfriend, and the two kings had gone to the queen to demand the child's return. This was serious, they'd stressed—one of her people had taken a wizard child, and the Arcanum was *furious*.

But Irem had laughed, seeing no great threat from us. She had no idea who had taken the boy or where they might be, nor was she inclined to intervene. If a child had gone missing, *she* certainly hadn't been involved.

I'd pressed Toula when she delivered the bad news. What about Ros? Surely she knew where Ahmed was being hidden.

And she would have, had the boy been in the realm. Though Ros was nearly omniscient in Faerie, her power drastically weakened at the border, and she could no more look out into the mortal realm and spot the kid than I could. Worse still, Irem spoke the truth: she didn't know who was behind the snatching or where the boy might be within our realm, meaning that Ros couldn't mine her thoughts for an answer. While she was angry and frustrated, Ros could do little to assist us, though she did give Irem a nagging migraine and swore it would continue until Ahmed was home.

The weekend ended with no sign of him, however, and Arnold and I traded glances as we took our places at the Council table. Adding fuel to the Council's ordinary sparks, few in the room had slept much in the last two days, and I could well envision the conflagration if the wrong magus was provoked.

Despite the general weariness in the room, Leander carried himself with a straight back and squared shoulders. His face had healed, and as he sat and smoothed his crimson robe, he looked at us with steel in his gaze.

"Thank you for coming," he began, nodding to the magi from the unfriendliest time zones. "I'll keep this brief." Once our eyes were fixed upon him, he rose in a rustle of fabric and said, "Faerie's actions toward us are intolerable. First Magus Stanhope's daughter from within Arc 2 itself"—he gestured toward Eva, who dabbed at a nonexistent tear—"and now a child from Arc 5. Which installation will be next? How many of our people will we lose to those monsters?" He waited until the angry rumbling subsided, then slammed his palms onto the table. "I say not one more. This ends now. And so, for the safety of this realm, I hereby declare war on Faerie."

The room exploded. Leander's allies applauded and cheered his decision, while those of us with sense shouted in horror at the idiocy. But as the initial shock wore off and Leander basked in the chaos, Arnold pushed himself from his chair and amplified his voice over the commotion. "Are you *mad*?" he demanded.

The boy jerked as if he'd been struck. "*Excuse* me?"

"You heard me. This is bloody madness."

His pale eyes narrowed. "You have no problem with child abduction, Arnold?"

"Of course I do," the old magus snapped. "I also have a problem with launching a senseless war that we can't win. We *can't*," he stressed as Leander's people grumbled. "Especially not if we try to take the fight to Faerie. Look, I'm a relatively talented wizard, yes?"

Even his detractors were forced to concur on that point.

"Right. Well trained, well practiced, and I've been at this for a long time. Longer than many of you in here have walked this world." Pausing to let that sink in, he leaned toward the table and lowered his voice. "I am a child next to the kings. It's not merely a matter of age—though if you want to look at it from that angle, Coileán is *ten times* older than me. Valerius…" He grimaced as his calculations. "At least twenty-five times, I'd wager. They grow stronger as they get older, you know, just as we do. And the Three have an extra layer of power from the realm itself. Now, which of you brave boys and girls wants to fight a faerie older than the fucking Colosseum?"

Arnold's words acted as a bucket of ice water on the fire Leander had lit, and he pressed his advantage while the magi considered them. "Listen to me. I've been fortunate to spend time with Simon over the last year. He's frank about his mistakes, all the mess that never made it into the history we were taught. You heard what he said here last week—he went to Faerie, planning to kill the Three. The two of them still there made him beg for death," he said slowly, enunciating every syllable. "They *mutilated* him for sport and tortured him until they tired of the game. The strongest of us couldn't fight his way free. Simon's more talented than I am—I'll be the first to admit it. He's certainly stronger than you," he added, pointing to Leander. "Remember, too, it's not just strength," he continued, taking time to lock eyes with each of the Arc 1 magi. "Faeries specialize in magic that goes *boom*. They don't bother with fiddly, detailed constructions—they just make craters."

When no one contested that and even Leander's cheering squad were looking squeamish, Arnold folded his arms and shrugged. "You know, I lived with a half faerie for eleven years during the Mulligan era. Nice fellow, he's about a decade my senior. When I met him, he was *completely* untrained, and I was a junior magus, so I had the upper hand for a time. A *brief* time," he said, focusing on the Arc 3 group. "Then he learned what he could do. I'm still the far more technical of us, but if Seamus wanted to throw me into the wall and put his mind to it, I'd have a devil of a time defending myself. And that's against a man who hasn't yet seen his centennial. In their terms, he's *very* young."

"Now, look," Leander interrupted, "just because you—"

"I'm not finished," said Arnold, wheeling on him, and Leander shut up. "What happened in Giza on Saturday is appalling, full stop. We should use every available resource to recover the child. But right now, our best resources are our allies. The kings—*and* Toula," he said, glaring at Kathleen—"are doing everything they can. They've been negotiating with Irem all weekend, and I'll tell you plainly that no one is happy about this. Unfortunately, for the moment, we've got a rogue queen on our hands. Once she understands that she needs to bring her court to heel, things will settle again, but it will take time to reach that point, and not a little diplomacy. Meanwhile, we need to trust our allies and be patient, and I'm confident that we'll find the lad alive."

Finally, his spell fizzled. "Wait and see?" Kathleen protested. "That's your grand plan? You want Nour to go home and tell Ahmed's parents that we're banking on faeries to do the right thing?"

"And what about my daughter?" Eva interjected, turning on the waterworks. "Snatched from her bed—"

Arnold lifted a hand to stop her. "*Bollocks*, Eva. Beth's clever, she's fond of her sister, and she has a track record of not staying in places she doesn't want to be."

"Where is she, then?"

"I don't know," he lied, "but something tells me she went of her own accord. Certainly wouldn't be the first time a teenager ran away from a bad situation, eh?"

But Kathleen joined in on Eva's act. "Being with her *mother* is a bad situation? What the hell is wrong with you, Arnold?"

He remained unflustered. "I've overseen the school here ever since Toula revamped it, and I've seen many children come through our program. None of them had a parent as callous, uncaring, and generally horrid as Kitty Connolly did." Focusing his quiet anger on Eva, he said, "I saw everything that happened to that child. You never lifted a finger when she was beaten, and you never once brought her home. That girl was effectively orphaned at ten, and all she wanted was a kind word from her mother. A little praise."

"She's an abomination," Eva muttered.

"She was a child! *Your* child. And any of you in here buying Eva's act would do well to understand that Valerius raised her firstborn after Kitty's father died. Eva couldn't be bothered. So yes, Kathleen," he said, glancing at our red-faced colleague, "I think there are far better places Beth could be than with her *loving* mother."

"The mongrel brat should never have been allowed here!" Francine cut in, jumping to her coconspirator's aid. "Eva was protecting her younger daughter!"

"Believe me," said Arnold with a snort, "Beth's been more trouble than Kitty ever was. Girl's headstrong, but she's really blossomed living with her sister. And if you gave a damn for anyone other than yourself," he said, turning back to Eva, "you'd have at least asked what Beth wanted to do. I mean, this is two children you've abandoned, now. Toula kept an eye on your correspondence from the cells, and you never sent either girl so much as a note. But that's not important right now," he continued, addressing the table. "Beth is wherever she wants to be, and I'm confident that she's safe. Ahmed is another matter, but we'll find him with patience and cooperation, not by saber-rattling."

But Leander, who had listened quietly for the last moments, filled the silence as soon as Arnold paused for breath: "You lived with a faerie?"

I looked at Arnold, whose jaw had clenched at the enquiry. "I did," he admitted. "Before you were born, lad. We saved Fringers from being murdered by the regime. Me, my cousin Badger, Seamus, Amy Levey—probably the finest crafter alive, and I'm sure a few of you are using her wands," he said, focusing on the Inner Council aides sitting along the wall—"and a boy out of the Gray Lands, if you want to be thorough. Plus extensive assistance from the Minor Arcanum. So yes, I lived with a faerie," he told Leander. "A lord, actually. We did good work together. Saved lives."

Leander's mouth ticked into a slight smirk. "You betrayed your oath to the Arcanum."

"I *upheld* my oath," said Arnold, bristling. "James Mulligan seized power in a bloody coup—he was never rightly the grand magus. I left because I couldn't stand by and watch him kill innocents, and everyone in here who's old enough to remember those days know what I did and why. I can't help that you weren't around to see it for yourself."

"But...you *did* disobey your grand magus," said Leander. "Worked against him, you say." As Arnold sputtered, Leander went for the throat. "It sounds to me like your sympathies are divided. You can't be counted on to support the Council or the Arcanum—and correct me if I'm wrong, since I wasn't there, but didn't you join in when those faeries stormed Arc 1? You were there with Toula, weren't you?"

"You didn't see his victims," said Arnold. "Some of them have never recovered, and the ones who have are in therapy. Mulligan was a monster."

Leander ignored him. "You know, I don't recall authorizing any discussions with the kings about Ahmed. Guess you did that on your own initiative, huh?"

In fact, *I* had started that ball rolling, but Arnold protected me. "I want him found alive and safe as much as anyone does," he said, glancing at Nour. "Why not muster every resource?"

"Because those *resources* are enemy powers," said Leander, his smirk widening. "Doesn't sound like the act of a magus to me. Sounds a lot like treason."

The outcry was immediate and forceful—not merely from Toula's supporters, but also from a few of the older magi who had voted for her dismissal. Even Iris shouted her disapproval from the heart of the Arc 1 cohort. Just as quickly, however, Leander's faithful rallied to his defense and bellowed their condemnation of the traitor in their midst. But as the two sides yelled at each other, Arnold, his voice still amplified, shouted, "*Enough!* Peace!"

"Shut your mouth, dog," Francine snapped. "You were never a true grand magus, just the Carver girl's puppet. We've heard enough from—"

Her chair tipped backward at his whisper, dumping the murderous creature onto the rug with an undignified shriek. As she struggled to untangle her robes and rise, he faced the table, his back slightly stooped with age but his blue eyes bright as ever behind his glasses. "I freely admit that I count certain faeries among my friends," he said. "I have a healthy respect for many more of them. Been across the border too many times to count. I've broken bread with them, I've cooperated with them, and I've always been treated well. That doesn't mean I've forgot my oath to the Arcanum. It means I'm man enough—I'm *magus* enough—to reach out and forge a bond with an ally. To make us both stronger in the joining."

He paused as Francine righted her chair and plopped down, scarlet-cheeked and disheveled from her fall. "I've known Val and Coileán for a long time. I've seen what they can do…and I saw what they did for us three years ago when Nath brought an army, the two of them and Eleanor. They brought armies of their own, they fought with us, they *bled* with us, and their people *died* with ours to protect this realm. They asked nothing in return, and they took nothing from us. Now, that boy never saw combat," he continued, nodding toward Leander. "When the Arcanum needed its best, he hid behind Kathleen's skirts."

Leander, purpling, slammed his fist against the table. "Shut up, you—"

"*I will say my piece.*"

The look on his face was enough to make even the cocksure grand magus bite his tongue.

"I respected Eleanor," he resumed. "Unfortunately, her sister is rather different, and quite a bit more like their father than is good for anyone. But remember that the kings are half-blooded, just as Toula is. I've seen the humanity in all of them," he said, focusing on the most senior magi. "They're not monsters, and they're trying to find that child. We need to bide our time and wait for the situation with Irem to sort itself. Given what I've seen, what I *know*, I have every confidence that it will."

With that, he pointed to Eva and Francine. "Now, I don't know what they've been telling you, lad," he said to Leander. "Or maybe it's your friends from the silo filling your head with nonsense. But I'm here to inform you that anyone in this room with a grain of sense knows that a full-scale assault on Faerie is nothing less than suicide. I would be betraying my oath if I didn't give the grand magus good counsel now, before it's too late. And I am *certainly* no traitor for telling you this before a boy who has no business playing at war sends people to their death."

The grand magi, old and young, held each other's stare as the table waited for a sign.

"Are you finished?" asked Leander.

"I am."

"Good. Surrender your chain."

The protestation came as quickly as before, but Arnold lifted a hand for quiet. "Appreciated," he said, "but I won't put the Council to the trouble of a vote to eject me." With that, he lifted his chain of office over his neck, considered it for a long moment, then tossed it onto the table and walked out without another word.

As soon as the meeting ended, I hurried to Arnold's office, hoping for a plan. Instead, I found the shelves bare, the desk empty, and the man I'd grown to consider a mentor and friend packing the last of his effects into a cardboard box. He'd removed his robe, exchanging it for jeans and a light jumper, and he flashed a grim smile as I closed the door behind me. "Has security come for me?" he asked.

"Not yet. Arnold—"

"Shh." He waved at the walls and muttered a focusing mantra, and the privacy wards engaged. "We knew this was coming, Bert. Sooner than I'd hoped, but that's life, I suppose. It's up to you, now. Be the eyes and ears."

"Leander doesn't trust me," I replied.

"If he's wise, he'll trust no one. Now, see here," he said, and beckoned me closer.

Looking into the box, I found a jumbled collection of blood vials. "Did you—"

"Straight from the Archives Sunday night," he said proudly. "Toula says they're blocking blood traces, but one can't be too careful...and if I'm able to tweak that little shit's nose on the way out, so much the better. They're all in here—the two of us, the Team and their spouses, Bee and Daisy, all of them. And between you and me, the fact that no one on the Council has started a blood trace yet is rather telling, is it not?" He grinned as he sealed the box. "The ones who can aren't volunteering their services, leaving poor Leander with a fat lot of magi who think themselves far more impressive than they are."

"I like your style, but let's hope the blocking spell holds," I said. "With Eva on hand here, Kitty and Beth are sitting ducks."

"Ah," said Arnold, "you're forgetting the bit about how damn difficult it is to find your way to Afallon uninvited. The Team took every reference photo with them and wiped their backups before leaving." With that, he tucked the box beneath one arm and gripped my shoulder with his free hand. "Be careful, lad. There's nothing in my flat worth having, so if they toss the place, don't lose any sleep. Keep your mouth shut and your eyes open. Stay in touch, and, ehm…disable the wards in here on your way out, won't you?"

I nodded and tried to smile. "Bon voyage."

As soon as Arnold released me, he opened a gate into the courtyard and slipped away. I watched from his window as he sealed the rift, nodded to a few passersby, and headed out of the castle. Once he'd reached the edge of the wards beyond our walls, he pulled a mobile from his pocket and held it to his ear. An instant later, a small gate opened about a meter from him, and I thought I caught a glimpse of the sea before he hurried through and closed it.

Arnold was gone, and I was alone.

With a heavy heart, I turned off his wards, gave the oddly empty room a last glance, and headed back to my office to read before anyone noticed Arnold's disappearance. But I couldn't seem to focus on the words, and soon I found myself staring at the page I'd been trying to read for ten minutes, seeing nothing.

SEPTEMBER 26: VALERIUS

Faeries are primed for anger. It runs deep and explodes into view with the weakest provocation, and depending on the slight and the parties involved, the results are more or less destructive. With practice, focus, and perhaps a touch of meditation, one can learn to control the rage, holding it at a manageable simmer instead of unleashing the boiling torrent. This skill becomes particularly important as one ages and one's power commensurately grows, *vital* if one is a king. Thus, under ordinary circumstances, I could keep calm even if prodded toward anger, a strong façade against the fury within.

Appearances, of course, are often deceiving. I tried not to reveal the depth of my rage—ruling by instilling well-deserved fear is one thing, by terror another matter entirely—but I could afford to show Coileán the darkness behind the mask.

"I just don't see why we can't kill him," I said as we walked up the long road toward the Arcanum's hidden castle. "It would solve at least a few problems."

"And make just as many," Coileán retorted.

He'd picked the gate location, a modest copse halfway between the town and the installation. The low, leaden sky threatened rain, but the autumn afternoon was otherwise inoffensive, breezy and pleasantly chill. He claimed that he'd selected a spot far from the castle so that anyone manning the gate wouldn't feel threatened by our sudden appearance, but I suspected that he needed the walk as badly as I did.

"I see your position, and it's valid," I replied, kicking a pebble into the dying grass, "but that whoreson made my little sister cry." I glanced his way and found Coileán concentrating on the horizon. "A limb. We take a limb. Maybe his left arm—he's probably not using it."

"Tempting, but not productive."

I clenched my fists and scowled at a tree, already stripped halfway bare of its yellow leaves. "How are you so calm about this?"

"Calm?" He turned to me and arched an eyebrow. "No. But I keep reminding myself that adding more dead wizards to my kill tally isn't going to be helpful in the long run."

He had a point, damn him.

Even if we were confident of victory, we didn't want a war with the Arcanum. We'd gain nothing in defending Faerie, both sides would suffer losses, and Leander, assuming he'd lead from the rear, would be left with a chance to lick his wounds and use the incident as another grievance against us to be filed away and brought forth as was convenient. Plus, with the Irem situation as unsettled as it stood, I couldn't be certain that some of her court wouldn't reinforce the Arcanum line for the sport of it— that is, assuming their queen chose not to turn a two-sided conflict into a three-way bloodbath.

With the Arcanum on edge, the Arc 5 child still missing, Beth incommunicado, and Leander eager for blood and glory, someone needed to diffuse the situation. Someone had to be the mediating adult in the room. And so, with Toula's blessing, Coileán and I had resolved to go to Glastonbury and ask for a meeting with the warmongering child in the hopes that treating him as an equal would calm him sufficiently to see reason.

It was the right and proper thing, the *wise* thing, to do. Still, I would have rather fed him his own entrails for what he'd done to Toula and Maria—and now Arnold, who'd joined the party on Afallon and was maintaining contact with Bert.

As we neared the castle, I studied its wards, which glowed in the magical spectrum like a net thrown over a half dome. They seemed far brighter than usual, and I had a good idea of what that portended for our impromptu peace talk.

Coileán, blind to magic, paused and took a deep sniff. "Is it just me, or are all the wards active?"

"It's not you."

"Moon and stars," he muttered under his breath, and pushed on down the lane.

The castle was almost invisible behind its camouflaging ward, which disguised the site as a wooded patch behind a metal fence. If I squinted, I could see the truth through the spellcraft bubble—and bright as the wards were, I found myself squinting more frequently as we approached. We passed through the outer ward that hid the place, which had a mild repellant effect on mundanes but did nothing to us, then paused at the barrier ward and considered our options. Punching through was possible, if messy—the ward had been designed to withstand attack, but if Coileán and I combined our efforts, we could breach it. The more diplomatic idea was to wait and ask for entry, and though it wounded my pride, I joined Coileán by the main ceremonial gate and waited to be acknowledged. With the security post outside the door unattended, I wasn't sure how one gained entry in a polite fashion.

A moment later, one of the Arcanum's black-garbed security personnel appeared at a window above the gate. "Ehm...hello, there," he called down, regarding us like a mouse confronted by a pair of hungry cats. "No closer, if you please."

Coileán lifted his empty hands and rotated them back and forth—a pointless gesture, all things considered, but apparently reassuring to the lone wizard. "We've come to see the grand magus. Will he meet us?"

The wizard hesitated. "No, I, ehm...no. No one in or

out," he replied. "Sorry."

"Would you ask him?" said Coileán with remarkable patience.

He pulled a phone from his pocket and stepped away from the window. Coileán rolled his eyes at me and muttered, "Think he needs new pants?"

"Possibly," I replied in kind.

When the wizard returned, the reception was no better. "Grand Magus Kirby will not receive you," he said, then quickly added, "Please don't shoot the messenger. Really, I've got kids—"

"No one's shooting anyone," Coileán soothed, then considered the castle for a long moment and sighed. "Well, since he won't talk to us, if you see him, tell him that we're doing everything we can to find your missing child. No luck yet, but we're on it. He's not in Faerie, and no one in Conota has seen him. Have you tried a blood trace?"

He glanced around himself as if expecting eavesdroppers, then leaned out the window and said, "They're still setting it up. I don't understand what's taking so long. Grand Magus Pavli always…well," he mumbled, averting his eyes when I caught his stare. "She, ehm…she's good."

"That she is," I said as the wizard retreated into his room. "*She* could set up a blood trace. I've seen her do it."

The guard hesitated, then said, "Listen, I don't know what to tell you. The grand magus might be willing to talk once the boy's found, but I can't guarantee anything."

He had the decency to sound apologetic, which I counted in his favor.

"Don't worry about it," Coileán told him with a nod. "We'll be on our way. If Leander decides that he has anything he'd like to say to our faces, my number should be in my file in the Archives. I haven't changed it in decades."

I did the honors, opening a gate home behind the safety of the camouflaging ward. We stepped through into

Coileán's office, and as soon as the gate had sealed, he groaned and headed for his well-appointed bar. "What are you drinking?" he asked.

"I don't care," I replied, joining him, "but you should make it strong."

The call came from Bert to the island not quite two hours later.

Young Ahmed had appeared in Cairo, alive and unscathed but for a few scrapes and bruises. He'd borrowed a shopkeeper's phone and called his parents, who had raced to retrieve him with several of Arc 5's senior guards. Once safely home, he'd been taken straight to the installation head, who'd questioned him and reported her findings to the Inner Council.

Ahmed didn't know where he'd been taken other than to say there were pine trees like the ones he'd seen in books. The faerie who'd kidnapped him had kept him chained within a house and seemed to take pleasure in watching the boy's weak attempts at escape. He'd been fed and allowed a mattress on the floor, he'd been given Fae, and he'd only been beaten once. But that morning, another faerie had spoiled his captor's fun, turning up shortly after breakfast with a warning: the realm was furious, and if he ever wanted to set foot in Faerie again, he needed to send the boy home. And so he did, dropping Ahmed relatively close to the place from which he'd been taken before vanishing by gate.

"That's wonderful news," I said, standing close to Coileán's phone so that we could both speak to Toula. "Did Bert give any indication as to Leander's state of mind?"

"Yeah," she muttered. "This changes nothing, guys."

"But the kid's home!" Coileán protested. "Is this about Beth? What's the problem?"

"Beth is just a convenient symbol," she replied wearily.

"You need to watch your borders."

"What," he scoffed, "against *Leander*?"

"No. Against Leander, plus Eadwig's giant Siberian ball of explosive fun."

Coileán and I traded looks, and he frowned at the phone. "You think it's that strong?"

"I don't know," said Toula. "I barely got a chance to study it. But…"

"But?" I prompted.

"Keep your guard up. Love you," she said, and cut the connection.

SEPTEMBER 27: BETH STANHOPE

I should have been thoroughly enjoying myself, sitting out on Artur's pavilion by the fire pit while the stars and the protective wards glowed overhead. I had an afghan against the wind, a cup of tea, and company who didn't talk to me like I was ten—better than average on all counts. But these were no ordinary times, and I was sitting outside with Kitty, Artur, and Quinn at eleven-thirty that night because my sleep of late had been nothing more than a conduit for nightmares.

"What if I went back?" I murmured, holding my mug for the warmth.

My sister almost jumped out of her chair. "*Hell*, no! Over my dead body!"

"He's using me like Nath used Hope," I countered. "If I take that away from him, then—"

"You're a prop," Artur interrupted. "Should you return, he won't give you an opportunity to explain yourself. The story will change: you were returned because Faerie's afraid of the might of the Arcanum, and now is the time to strike."

Kitty nodded. "He'll silence you. Stasis at least, mark my words. Not like Mom would do anything to protect you, right?" She slid forward in her seat until she could stretch and grip my wrist. "You're smarter than that. Assuming the worst, I don't want to come back in a decade and find you in a stasis bind. We can call Grand Magus Carver if you need more persuasion."

"He's *using* me," I muttered. "I'm making everything

worse. If I could help…"

"You *are* helping." Quinn sipped at the last of her belated breakfast, ending in a noisy slurp, and set her tumbler at her feet. "You're giving everyone here one less thing to worry about, for starters."

"Right," said Artur. "And we're safe here for now. No one's dying on my watch tonight, which means you're not going anywhere."

"But I'm not doing anything," I protested.

"Sometimes, the best strategy is to bide your time," Artur replied. "Study your enemy, learn his strategy if you can, and resist the urge to rush to action. We won't overthrow the Council by ourselves," she added, twirling one finger to encompass the fire pit and the lodge, "and so we wait." Going to her feet, she cracked her back and winced. "I've barely slept in two days. You'll forgive me if I retire."

"Right behind you," said Kitty.

Quinn stood as well. "Think I'll go inside and do some reading. Beth, are you staying out here?"

"For a while," I replied, and gave them what I hoped was a convincing smile.

No one seemed to buy the act, but they left me to stew in peace.

When I heard the door close behind them, I curled up in my chair and tucked the afghan more tightly around me. "Hey, Dad," I whispered. "So, uh…guess you know everything's gone to hell right now." I paused, hoping for a response, but I heard nothing but the crackling of the fire and the distant rush of waves against the island's cliffs. "I'm scared," I confessed. "This wasn't supposed to happen. This was going to be a good year, you know? My internship was fun, and Ted said I could join the Team once I graduate, and…and things were working out. But now Faerie's messed up, the Arcanum's pushing for a freaking *war*, and…I mean, worst-case scenario, I'm sure Hope and Arik's place is great, but I don't want to have to hide in Conota. I don't want to hide, period."

I drained my mug and stared at the fire. "Things weren't supposed to change again. I really liked Glastonbury. And it's great that we're all here together, but I don't know how long we're going to be safe, and I don't know what to do. Think you could give me a sign?"

Though part of me knew it was stupid to hope, I strained to pick out any subtle change in my surroundings—a flicker of color in the flames, the chill of a cold hand against my cheek, a shadow out of the corner of my eye. So focused was I that when I heard a twig snap behind me, I yelped and leapt out of my chair to find the culprit.

Not Dad—Frank, who gave me an odd look as he took Artur's vacated chair to my left. "Sorry for startling you," he said. "Is this a private fire pit?"

"Nah. Just thinking," I replied, resituating myself as my thundering heartbeat slowed.

"Likewise. Wanted some air. I finally got Aurie to sleep, no thanks to you and Allie. Which of you highly responsible girls decided that letting the hatchling watch *The Shining* was a good idea, eh?"

"Sorry," I mumbled.

He sighed and stretched his legs toward the fire. "Well, could be worse. At least there are no topiary animals on this island." When I didn't respond, he looked at me more closely, his naked eyes crimson in the flickering light. "You're troubled. May I?"

I felt Frank's soft mental touch as he reached for my thoughts, but I didn't protest or try to stop the intrusion. Of all the mind readers I'd encountered, Frank was the one least likely to leave me with a headache.

Satisfied, he withdrew and looked away from me again. "I'm not going to tell you not to worry. That would be condescending, and you're old enough to handle the truth."

I snorted and pulled the afghan to my chin. "You're a

ray of sunshine, you know that?"

"I'm a realist. None of this is ideal, and there's no point in pretending that anything about this mess is okay. But you're tough," he told me. "Tougher than you know. Kitty sees that strength in you, and so does Artur. She wouldn't have worked with you all this time if she didn't think you could handle yourself."

"Oh, yeah. Let me just pop back to the castle, grab a sword, and see how long I last against Leander."

He chuckled. "Not tonight. And that's not the kind of strength I'm talking about, anyway. Whatever happens, I'm confident that you'll rise to it. You've made it this far," he added.

"I've had a lot of help," I admitted.

"Okay, yeah, you were dragged along kicking and screaming for a while, but you've found your feet. You're one of us now. You know, we should really make Away Team T-shirts one of these days."

Frank was trying, but my thoughts continued to circle like a whirlpool. He watched the fire for a moment, then said, "Tell me. Say it aloud. You'll feel better."

I sighed and curled more tightly into myself beneath the afghan. "This is my fault."

"And why would that be?"

"If I hadn't run away—"

"Then that missing kid from Arc 5 would have sufficed. You're not Helen of Troy, and nations aren't clashing over you. Your departure makes for a convenient bit of propaganda, I suppose, but if Leander stops threatening war and actually engages, that won't be your fault, Beth." When I made no reply, he said, "You still carry that guilt for your mother. As if you had *anything* to do with her crimes."

"I don't—"

"You can't lie to me—I've looked," he added with a reproachful stare. "The fact that we're here and Eva is free is in no way your fault. Try to accept that and stop taking on guilt you have no business shouldering."

Looking away from him, I mumbled, "She's my mother."

"Yeah? And?" He waited until I met his eyes again, then said, "Family can be wonderful and awful. Believe me, I know what it feels like to be rejected by someone who's supposed to love you. My mother was bad enough when she told me to leave—my siblings wanted to kill my kid." He reached across his wide wooden armrest, and I took his hand. "We'll make it through this together, yes? Keep your chin up."

"I'll try."

"*Good*, because people are depending on you."

At that, I laughed aloud. "Wait, sorry, *who* is depending on me? Nobody here is that desperate."

Frank's smile was a curious thing, never quite right, but once you'd seen it a few dozen times, it started to make sense, even with its imperfections. "Where is Ed?" he asked.

"Ed?" I puzzled at the non sequitur. "Where he's been ever since we got here. That office he kind of commandeered."

"You saw him there?"

"Yeah, right after Dr. Dellucci went to bed. Ed got too focused and forgot to eat tonight—*again*—so I made him a sandwich and told him not to drool on his notebooks, but what do you bet we'll find him doing just that in the morning?"

Leaning toward me, Frank replied, "He depends on you, kid. For much more than the occasional midnight sandwich." After a brief pause to consider my reaction, he said, "You *have* noticed, haven't you? Please tell me this isn't a complete shock."

I felt my face begin to flush. "Um…I mean…I guess?"

"Well, now," said Frank, lowering his voice to a soft rumble, "if the most powerful wizard the Arcanum has ever known is looking to you for support, then I guarantee you're no weakling."

"I'm just me. I'm not a great talent, I'm not as strong as Kitty, I can't fight like Artur, and now Leander's using me…"

He waited until my voice faded, then said, "Let me tell you a secret. Magic isn't everything. It's nice, sure, but the universe isn't built around it. And I know for a fact that magic has *nothing* to do with what that guy sees in you. It's amazing how he lights up whenever you're in the room, and that's been happening for the last year." With that, Frank rose and stretched. "Do us a favor, eh?"

"What?" I asked, craning my neck to take him in.

"Don't go back to Glastonbury. He'll freak out if you do, and it would be nice to have him focused on our present troubles."

"He doesn't leave his office," I said as Frank started to go. "I bet he wouldn't even notice."

"You say that, but find me the next time Ed has a nightmare," he replied. "And speaking of which, I'd better get inside before Aurie wakes up and notices I'm gone. Try to pick some kid-friendly movies tomorrow, won't you?" he said, and disappeared into the shadows as he stalked across the lawn.

I leaned back in my chair for a time, watching the smoke curl toward the grape-laden trellis, then sighed and pushed myself to my feet before I could fall asleep by the fire. "Goodnight, Dad," I whispered, and blew a kiss toward the waves. "Help me be brave."

SEPTEMBER 29: BERT WOLD

My utter lack of a social life did occasionally come in handy. As the few people I regarded as anything close to friends had left the castle, I had no reason *not* to be in my office at odd, sad hours, like eight o'clock on a Friday night. In the past, when my colleagues had asked why I didn't take my work home with me, I'd explained that all I had waiting in the flat was a more comfortable couch—good for napping but poor for productivity. Since Arnold's departure four days before, however, my reason to work late had shifted. The tiny, unobtrusive spells I'd cast all around the executive wing of late—the wizard's equivalent of bugging the place—were best monitored from nearby instead of in my residence several towers away. My long-established pattern of being first in every morning and last out every night gave no one cause for suspicion and offered ample cover for my espionage, and with my own office tightly warded, I could sit at my desk and listen in on conversations in conference rooms and offices... including Leander's.

One truth I'd learned through hard experience is that a grand magus must be able to protect himself against eavesdroppers. Toula could ward her space masterfully, and I'd picked up a few pointers from her over the years. With a gesture at the wall, my office could be rendered soundproof in an instant. Another spell alerted me to any changes in the wards made in my absence, though I still conducted a full sweep every few days. My diligence had paid off: I'd lost count of the number of bugs I'd discovered and destroyed over my career, though the volume had decreased to a trickle in recent years. Most of the serious spies within the Council must have accepted that it would be simpler for a mundane to help himself to the Crown Jewels than for a wizard to steal information from me.

I'd even covered my electronic tracks. By default, magi's documents automatically backed up to Arcview. The software was serviceable for us but terribly outdated, and as few wizards ever bothered to learn coding, the program was a sieve in terms of security. Our luddite tendencies had an upside, however: since no one really understood programming, few within the Arcanum would ever bother to try to hack Arcview. Really, our greatest threats to the system were Ted Girard, who'd maintained our internal technology from the Mulligan years through my short tenure, and Lord Aiden, who would have had a delightful time at MIT had he not run off to Faerie with his brother. Ted was too busy with the legitimate side of Archives research to go snooping, and as for Aiden…well, I had to admit that his breaches had been in the service of the greater good, even if one had occurred on my watch. Still, I took no chances, disabling my computer's automatic backup service in favor of saving everything to an external hard drive. It was a risky move—given the amount of active magic in the castle, even protected electronics had an unusually high failure rate—but I'd long ago decided that I'd rather lose a few pages of notes than allow my files to be compromised.

Considering the ease with which I'd bugged his office, I doubted that Leander had taken any such precautions. True, my work was subtle—unless one knew what one was looking for, it blended into the background magic—but I'd have expected at least *one* of the bugs around his suite to fail in the days since I'd planted them. So far, though, it seemed like Leander had not a care in the world for security. Either he couldn't fathom the notion of anyone being so underhanded as to eavesdrop or he couldn't spare the time to check for intrusions…or, more likely, even if he suspected, he didn't know how to sweep and was too arrogant to ask anyone to check for him.

Though I'd stayed late to read, I hadn't truly expected any company in the executive wing, and so the soft alert ping from my own wards startled me out of my work. I hastily put the book aside and triggered my network of bugs. A visualization of their placements appeared beneath my desk, and I bent to see who might be in for a meeting. The five I'd scattered around Leander's office glowed green, and I slipped my homemade earpiece in to listen.

"I don't understand what's taking so long. I'm not asking for miracles, here," he groused. From the shifting volume, I surmised that he was pacing his office, moving in and out of range of a pair of bugs. "How hard is to run one fucking blood trace?"

"These things take time," a woman's voice replied, and I gritted my teeth. Francine Leighton. What the devil was she doing with the idiot boy?

"They've been missing for eight days!" Leander continued. A dull thump suggested he'd hit a convenient piece of furniture. "*Eight!* How do I have a Council that can't run a blood trace in a week?"

"It's not the trace that's the problem, sir," said another woman—Eva Stanhope, I realized, and swore. "There's a technique that can block traces. Grand Magus Mulligan had the knack—it's a diary spell," she explained. "And since our little Simon disappeared with the rest of the trash, it's probably a safe bet that they're all shielded. Either that, or they're out of the realm."

"There *is* a workaround," Francine offered, "but it's slow. I've been catching up on the newly discovered parts of the diary. If they're in this realm, we should have them soon."

"I want the girl," Leander snapped. "I don't give a damn about the rest of them."

"Don't worry about Beth," Eva soothed. "She's far more useful missing."

It gave my heart hope to hear how taken aback he sounded when next he spoke. "Uh...that *is* your daughter..."

"She chose her side," Eva snapped. "Trust me, I'm not losing sleep."

"Well, the fact that I can't lay hands on her still makes me look weak, and the delay's not helping." He heaved a sigh. "How long does it take with this workaround, anyway?"

"At least five days, I'd think," said Francine, "but while you put some magi on that, we've got a better idea."

"Magical bloodhounds? Going to put her face on a billboard?"

"Think beyond the girl," she replied, her voice smooth as oil. "Eva and I have got a power play in mind. Pull this off, and Faerie will wish they'd never crossed you."

"Shit," I muttered, and grabbed a notepad from my desk drawer.

"I'm listening," said Leander, sounding decidedly less peeved than he'd been moments before.

The furniture creaked—a couch, perhaps, someone shifting her weight. "As Eva said, sir, we've been studying the hidden portions of the diary. *Fascinating* material, particularly when you read it in conjunction with Pavli's notes about the '13 closure."

The boy snorted. "Pavli..."

"Don't scoff. She's a dangerous mongrel, certainly, but she's clever. She studied the combined spell and enchantment that sealed off Faerie—she actually had the tracers in front of her."

"More than studied," Eva added. "She helped break it."

"That, too. She's been adding to her notes about the closure for years, refining her theories on the thaumaturgy...and she left them in the Archives, accessible to anyone with magus credentials."

I could practically hear Francine's smirk.

"A lifetime's work, still in progress, but already cited by several theoretical wizards. Whatever else she may be, she's a technical caster par excellence," said Francine. "Give the mongrel her due. It's never wise to completely discount your enemies."

"And now we've got Simon's musings as well," said Eva. "All sorts of notes about spells he never attempted. Even in the known portion of the diary, he'd worked out a spell to rip Faerie's consciousness right out of the realm. If anything happened to her, Faerie would be destroyed," she explained with far too much relish. "Russell Mulligan pulled that one off."

"With massive faerie support," Francine pointed out. "The spell needs too much power for any one wizard to channel."

"Right, and that's the problem—all of these delightful ideas include a power source."

"Got some faeries hanging around, then?" Leander asked.

The women chuckled. "No need," said Francine. "I know you've been awfully busy, sir, but have you yet had an opportunity to look in the restricted storage?"

A worm began to writhe in my stomach.

"Not yet," he admitted. "Something interesting?"

"*Oh*, yes," Francine replied. "We had IT give us access to the Away Team's files. They've kept a log of every trip, every find."

"We were hoping for notes from Simon," Eva confessed, "but we found something much better. They just recovered a *giant* ball of stored magic in Siberia. According to Simon, it was made by the same crafter who made the balls that kept Arc 1 running during the closure, but it's exponentially larger. They say Pavli hid it in her storage room in the Archives for further study, so you're the only person with the codes right now. They were changed after she left the castle."

"Are you *kidding* me?" said Leander. The boy sounded like he'd won the lotto. "Like, how powerful is this thing?"

"Can't be sure until we study it," said Eva, "but based on what the Team's notes suggest…"

"Unlike anything we've ever seen," Francine finished. "Which brings us to our idea for you. Why not seal off Faerie and the Gray Lands once and for all?"

"Huh?"

"Seal them. Like the '13 closure, but make it unbreakable."

"Look, Francine and I have had several years to do nothing but think," Eva cut in. "We'd talked about the theory, but now that we've seen the full diary…it's doable. It's *really* possible."

"But…don't we need Faerie open if we want magic?" Leander asked. "I mean, that's kind of important…"

"Simon found another solution," said Francine. "A way to make the barrier between the realms semipermeable. We won't have any more inter-realm gates to worry about, but magic will still be able to flow out. Think of it: you could be the grand magus who stops the faerie menace forever. Not even Simon could do that."

"The greatest grand magus of all time," Eva purred. "Leander Kirby, the man who cast the monsters out forever. Who made this realm safe for his people."

I stared at my scribbled-over notepad, flabbergasted. What the hell were the two of them going on about? I'd read the full diary, and while it contained ideas about how to destroy Faerie, there was nothing in it suggesting anything like the plan they were proposing. The notion went against everything we knew of magic: it flowed out of Faerie, just like dark magic flowed from Conota, but only as long as the skin between the realms could be breached. I had no memory of the '13 closure—I'd been born a year later—but I knew from my studies that the mortal realm had run out of magic in less than a fortnight. Surely Leander was sufficiently well read to see the impossibility of their suggestion…

"I'll get you into that storage room," he told the women. "See what we've got on our hands, then bring me your plans. If this is doable, then I think I owe it to the Arcanum to try."

I waited until Leander and his pet magi left for the evening, made certain that I'd hidden every trace of my surveillance activity, and slipped out of the castle. Around ten, telling the guard on the gate that I was going out for a drink, I created a gate into the alley behind my favorite pub, then hurried inside and nodded to the barman. Equipped with a pint of strong ale in short order, I glanced around the pub to ensure that I'd not been followed, then hid in a quiet back booth and rang Arnold. "Hi," I said to his groggy greeting. "I need Eadwig, *now.*"

I'd downed a third of the beer before he came on the line. "Bert? What's happened?"

"I'll keep this brief," I murmured, cupping my hand around my mouth to muffle the ambient pub noise. "Did you ever write anything about a way to close off Faerie but still allow magic to flow through?"

"No," he said immediately, perplexed. "Of course not. That's stupid. Why?"

"Because Francine and Eva just told Leander that they've been reading your notes and Toula's, and with the big ball to power whatever they plan to do, they think they can make the barrier semipermeable."

"That's impossible," he protested. "That's…*no.* Ridiculous. That contravenes everything we know about the interplay among the realms."

"I suppose Leander slept through that lesson," I replied, and took a swig. "Pass the word. I'll be in touch," I said, then rang off and tucked my mobile away.

The ale wasn't bad, I thought as I drained it. Maybe I'd have another.

SEPTEMBER 30: FRANK

The chirping of my phone pulled me from a sound sleep shortly after four in the morning, and I grabbed it and hurried out of the room before I could wake Aurie. "Hello?" I mumbled, not bothering with the identification screen.

"Hi!" came the reply in cheery Fae. "Did I wake you? Oh, damn it, are our times off-synch again?"

My brain fog lifted enough for comprehension to register. "Hi, Dad. Just a little. One minute…"

The place was dark but for the strip of light beneath the door of Ed's office—nothing unusual there—and the television in the big den, which Quinn kept on for noise while she played with her computer on the couch. Not wanting to bother her, I took the call outside.

"Sorry," I said, heading for the pavilion. "What's up?"

"Nothing much. I hadn't heard from you in a few weeks, and I was wondering if I could come over and see you two. I'll make breakfast," he offered.

"Not a good time, but that's much appreciated," I replied as I sank into a chair. "I'm sorry for the silence. Autumn's off to a miserable start."

"Anything I can do?"

"Not unless you want to assassinate the grand magus, and I don't think Coileán would approve."

"I thought you liked her! What's she done?"

I stared at the low-burning fire, wishing I'd had a few more hours of sleep. "You haven't heard the news? Toula was unseated. This kid who's, like, two years younger than me is running the show now. He's kicked us all out of the castle, he's threatening war on Faerie because Irem's crew keep snatching people...you know, the usual."

"*Frank!*" My father sounded horrified. "Are you safe? Where are you?"

"We're fine, we're hanging out at Artur's holiday home off the coast," I reassured him. "It's well warded."

"And it's still in that realm, which means the Arcanum can find you. Why didn't you tell me?" he asked. "You and Aurie should come stay here, where it's safer."

I chuckled and rubbed my neck. "Faerie's got its own problems right now, yeah? Irem?"

"I'm nowhere near the southern border, I don't receive regular company, and her miscreants have no reason to bother me. Please come. I'd be thrilled to have you."

"And I truly appreciate that, Dad, but Aurie can't just go. She's bound, remember? It'll break as soon as she crosses, and Toula's got more important things to worry about here than fixing my kid."

"You can work a transformation bind with enchantment," he pointed out. "I'll put her back together."

"She hasn't been unbound since the night she hatched, and she's had enough upheaval over the last weeks without adding *that* to the mix, you know? I don't want to add one more shock to her system."

"I hear you, I do," said Dad, whose tone suggested that he was not at all convinced of the logic of my position, "but I'm worried. May I come over?"

"Hold on." I rose and headed back to the lodge, looking for someone far more talented than I was. The sound of rattling in the refrigerator didn't disappoint, and I caught Marcus digging through the soft drinks at the back of the shelf. "Hey," I said, holding the phone to my shoulder, "mind making a gate?"

He pulled a Coke free and gave me an odd look. "Going somewhere?"

"My dad's concerned," I explained, and pointed to the

phone. "Do the honors?"

I called to mind a reference image of his study and shared it with Marcus, who yawned and waved the gate open. Poking my head through the hole, I called, "Dad? Are you in here?"

"Frank!" He jogged into view from behind the gate, then hung up and joined me. Giving the kitchen a brief inspection in the light of the stovetop lamp, he said, "Well, now, this isn't half bad. Where are—"

He turned at the hiss of carbonation as Marcus uncapped his drink, then gasped and took a step back in alarm. "*Oh*, my lord…uh…wait…*who*—"

"It's all right, Owain, he told us about you," said Marcus, and nodded toward the coffeemaker. "Help yourself. Grounds are in the pantry."

My father waited until Marcus had shuffled back to his bedroom, then quietly asked, "Is that…who I think it is?"

"Yeah. Marcus takes after his old man," I replied, filling the coffee carafe. If I was going to be up well before dawn, I thought, I might as well make the best of it.

"Especially in the dark. I could have sworn that was Lord Valerius," he muttered, then noticed the coffee before I could load it into the machine and *tsk*ed. "Oh, no, that smells wrong. Here, son, allow me."

News spread that I had a visitor, and by the time I finished giving my father the tour, Toula and Artur were marching across the lawn to join us, fireballs in hand. "It's all right," I said as they neared, "he's not hurting anything—"

"*Good*," Artur snapped. "You're Owain?"

"I am," he began, turning to see them, then ended the thought as a nod.

I couldn't blame him. Artur had come kitted out for battle, leather armor, drawn sword, and all, and war danced in her blue eyes. "If you intend treachery," she said, her voice almost a growl, "you will not leave this place alive."

"If I intended treachery," he replied, showing her his empty hands, "don't you think Frank would have picked up on it by now?"

Artur glanced at me in query, and I made a quick perusal of Dad's thoughts. "He's honestly concerned," I reported. "Impressed by the wards around the island. A little scared of you." Cutting my eyes to Dad, I thought, *That would be Artur.*

She traded looks with Toula, then grunted and sheathed the glittering blade. "If you say so. What's your business?" she asked him.

Dad seemed to relax a degree once the sword was no longer aimed at him. "Frank just informed me of what's happened to you," he said. "This is a beautiful place, and it appears to be decently protected," he allowed, pointing to the sky. Blind as I was to magic, I saw only stars and scattered clouds, but he'd been marveling over the craftsmanship of the wards before the welcoming committee arrived. "Still, you'd be safer from the Arcanum if you left this realm. Allow me to host you. All of you," he proposed. "With the number of Fringers in Faerie, surely Lady Roslyn wouldn't mind a few wizards as well. Plenty of room, no neighbors in easy walking distance, and no way for this new grand magus to find you without crossing. What do you say?"

"A generous offer, but let's take this inside," Toula suggested.

When we returned to the lodge, the den was packed with people in various states of dress, though the fashion leaned heavily toward bathrobes. "No reason to panic," I announced as Artur latched the door. "Everyone, this is Owain. Dad...everyone."

Despite the early hour, Ted was already sporting a silk shirt patterned with coconut palms, and he pushed his way to the front of the crowd with a grin on his face. "Oh, my goodness!" he said, turning his brilliant smile on my father. "*Finally!* Hi, I'm Ted."

Dad beamed back at him. "Lovely to meet you. I've heard so much about you…"

They didn't bother with a handshake, instead proceeding straight to one of Ted's trademark hugs, though my father didn't seem to mind. Soon, they were almost talking over each other:

"Frank speaks so highly of you—"

"Oh, I love that kid, he's great—"

"Thank you for looking out for him—"

"Are you kidding? He's family—"

"*Theodore*," Lakshmi interrupted, clutching her thick peach robe closed.

Duly chastised, Ted cleared his throat and released his grip on Dad. "Sorry, sorry. So, uh, what brings you to Afallon?"

I watched the Team while Dad repeated his offer. A few seemed to perk at the idea—Mal especially, who had his childhood bedroom in the settlement to fall back on—though some of the Featherstonhaugh clan looked decidedly apprehensive.

But it was Quinn who answered first. "You guys should go," she told the room. "I'll be safe here—it's not like I'm some great target."

"My home is open to the wizards here as well," said Dad. "There's no reason for you to stay alone."

"Cursed," she replied with a shrug. "I leave the realm, I drop dead. Deader, I guess. But the rest of you—"

"I'm not leaving until you're fixed," Ed interrupted. "And John—"

"Of course I'm not leaving you, Quinnie," said Dr. Dellucci.

Beth lifted a finger. "I'll stay and help. Someone's got to remind those two to eat," she explained.

"And if those two are here," said Kitty, pointing to her sister and Ed, "then you know the rest of the flat is going to stay."

"But *you* should go," Ted interjected before more

volunteers could reveal themselves, and pointed to me. "You and Aurie."

"I'm not walking out on the *Team*," I started to protest, but Ted shook his head.

"She's young, and she needs stability. Maybe some age-appropriate movies, eh? Go on, you two go with your dad."

I stooped to be closer to his eye level and lowered my voice. "Ted, I can't leave you in danger."

To my surprise, Ted's response was a rib-crushing hug. When he released me enough to let me breathe, he said, "Family looks out for each other, Frank. That includes you. And Owain's got a point," he continued, turning back to the crowd. "Madison, Antony, why don't you take Allie and go with them? Rohan, Kim, I don't know if Lakshmi will let you out of her sight, but the baby might be safer out of this realm. You know, if worst comes to worst. Bob, Sylvester, I love you guys, but we all know you're not bruisers—"

Ted's pitch was cut short when Aurie peeked around the corner, Blue in hand, and spotted the newcomer. "*Granddad!*" she shrieked, and raced into the room.

He caught her and hoisted her up as she threw her arms around his neck. "Well, hello to you, too, little lady," he murmured, patting the back of her nightshirt as she hugged him. "Why aren't you in bed?"

She raised her head and looked back at the full den. "No one else is."

"Point." Shifting her weight to his hip, he grimaced at the room in apology. "I didn't realize the time was this far off again. Can I at least make breakfast?"

I didn't think that anyone on the Team had been entirely horrified when I'd explained the peculiarities of my paternity, but whatever reservations they might have harbored about Dad had gone out the window by the time the last of his French toast was consumed. Though he still seemed more than a little cautious around Toula and Marcus, he'd relaxed once he took over the kitchen, and Sylvester had jumped in as a capable sous chef. The two of them had got on famously—Sylvester was a passionate amateur, and Dad wasn't set in his ways—and the general consensus by the end of the meal was that the spread was worth the early wakeup. Even Quinn had sniffed greedily at the food and sighed before retiring for the day.

Still, breakfast hadn't served to change any minds. The Team was staying on the island, though my elders insisted I should take Aurie to safety.

While the others spread out to enjoy their food comas, I took Aurie into our room for a talk. "We don't have to go," I told her. "I know it would make Granddad happy, but we don't have to. If you'd rather stay here, he'll understand."

"I want to go," she insisted. "I want to see it."

I took her little hands in mine and gave them a squeeze. "You know your bind will break, yes? Granddad thinks he can fix it, but you'll still be back in your real body for a little while. And that..." I paused, trying to reduce the sensation to words. "It doesn't hurt, and it might actually feel good, but it's *weird*. I know how to handle that body. You don't, and there's a *lot* more of it to consider."

"I'm not scared," she replied, which was mostly true. "And maybe I could meet my aunts and uncles, huh?"

Fortunately, locking down my thoughts was the work of an instant. "When you're older, hatchling."

She huffed her impatience. "What if I went ahead and got augmented now? Then we wouldn't have to worry about binds and stuff."

"Aurie—"

"I'm strong enough!"

"Aurora," I said, tightening my grip, "listen to me. It's the most painful thing I've ever done. More than that, I don't know if Ros can fully augment you. That's a question for her—"

"So call her."

"Sweetie—"

"Please, Dad?"

Before she could block me, I looked past her sad puppy eyes to the motivation behind her request. Aurie wasn't worried about going to Faerie—she was worried that I would leave her, that I might go somewhere she couldn't follow, that having to deal with her bind would make me run off without her. We weren't playing by the same rules anymore, and she fretted that she wouldn't be able to keep up.

I pulled her into my arms and held her close. "You know I will never leave you, hatchling. *Ever*," I murmured as I stroked her mussed hair. "Understood?"

"I still want to ask Ros," she mumbled against my shirt.

"And I'll call Sam, but I'm telling you that you don't need to worry about augmentation right now."

With Aurie still curled in my lap, I placed the call—if Dad was up and about, then surely Sam would be, too. He answered on the second ring. "Hey, bud. How's Fantasy Island?"

"Can't complain. Is Ros around?"

"Sure. Send me a reference photo, okay?"

I snapped a picture of our bedroom, and a few seconds after I sent it, a gate into Sam's kitchen blazed open. "Let me guess," said Ros, standing at the border with a smirk. "This has something to do with Owain's quick departure this morning."

"He wants us to come over," I replied. "Aurie wants to talk about augmentation."

She made a face. "*Ooh*. Already?" Peering through the gate at my daughter, she said, "Baby doll, whatever I do, it'll hurt like hell."

"See?" I told Aurie. "You can think about it when you're older—"

"Now, hang on," Ros interrupted. "It's her body."

"She's *one*!"

"She's not asking for a tattoo or a nipple piercing. And correct me if I'm wrong, but you would have preferred to be in control of your own form a long time ago. *Yeah?*"

I glared back at her. "Yeah," I admitted, "but—"

"But nothing. It's not going to hurt her any less if we wait until she's grown. Might actually be a little easier now, but I won't know for sure until I get her over here and poke around. And since Irem's not currently setting anything on fire, I have time."

For a child who was three-quarters reptile, Aurie had the puppy eyes down to a science. "*Please*, Dad?" she begged.

"If I can't do it with a high degree of confidence, then I won't try," Ros assured me. "But I need her here before I can make that call."

As I stewed, Sam poked his head over Ros's shoulder. "You're outnumbered, Frank. May as well make the surrender a graceful one."

"Do you *want* me to eat your face?" I retorted, but I knew the battle was lost. "Give us an hour to pack," I told Ros, "and I suppose we'd better do this at Dad's house again."

"See you shortly," she replied, and sealed the gate.

On schedule, having said our goodbyes and thrown our belongings into bags, Aurie and I stood in our room while Dad opened a gate back to his place. "Wait there," I told my daughter as I collected her things. "Do *not* cross until I tell you, okay?"

"Okay." She nervously danced from foot to foot in her little purple bathrobe as Dad and I carried the luggage over. I'd also donned a robe for the occasion, as I didn't feel like losing a pair of jeans without good cause. Waving to Ros as she manifested, I looked back at Afallon and told Aurie, "I'm going to step out of the way and shift. Back in a minute." I hesitated, then added, "Don't be scared, now."

"I'm not."

She *was* anxious, but it seemed more focused on the promised pain than anything else. Aurie had seen her baby books, which I'd taken with us when we fled Glastonbury. She knew what she was meant to look like, at least in an academic sense. Still, I worried about how she'd react when faced with the reality of her natural form.

I tossed my robe to my father, who turned his head to give me a moment's privacy, then took up a position on his wide lawn and let myself shift. The change was almost instantaneous, and I double-checked my limbs and claws before returning to the area of the gate. *Your turn*, I told Aurie, who stared at me with wide eyes. *This won't hurt, hatchling.*

"You're really *big*," she said.

You'll be much bigger, too. Listen carefully, I told her as I backed away. *When I say go, take a running leap at the gate. Don't get stuck halfway. You'll be taking some of the landing on your arms, so don't be surprised. And that robe is toast.*

Dad waved a copy into existence and held it up for Aurie's inspection. "Not a problem, dear."

Once I'd cleared a landing zone, I nodded. *Okay, Aurie. Whenever you're ready.*

She stepped backward until her legs hit my bed, then balled her fists, scowled at the gate, and sprinted. As soon as she passed into Faerie, her bind began to shatter, but she made it all the way over before it fell apart...

...and there she was. My little hatchling, my daughter, blue-green, about thirty meters long, and sliding toward me across the lawn like an airplane with damaged landing gear. I braced myself for impact, but she skidded to a halt before plowing into me, then promptly faceplanted in the grass.

You're all right, I soothed, hearing her distress. *Good job, that was perfect. Let's get you on your feet. Ah, wait*, I cautioned as her short, footless foreleg moved. *Favor your right side, that's my girl.*

After a false start, she found her footing, but she stared down at her incomplete left foreleg in alarm. *What happened to—*

The bottom half was never real, I reminded her. *That was the bind. We'll get a replacement worked out, don't worry. In the meantime, here.* I moved into position against her left side, giving her something to lean against. *Take it slowly. You're acclimating.*

She stretched her long neck up and down, adjusting to the sudden difference in vantage point, then turned her head to take a closer look at herself. *I like my scale color.*

You look like your mother, I replied as a band tightened painfully around my heart. *She was beautiful, too.*

With my help, Aurie took a few awkward, limping steps, trying to manage three feet where she had previously had two and should have had four. She tripped and sprawled, landing with a surprised squawk, which seemed to shock her more than the fall had. *Was that me?* she asked, looking up at me for reassurance.

Perfectly normal.

Weird. Wish I could talk.

And what are we doing right now, then?

Exasperation colored her thought. *You know what I mean.* Tucking her good foreleg beneath her, she tried to stand but lost her balance once again. *Why does it smell odd here?*

You're smelling concentrated magic, I explained, nudging her to her feet. *The dark magic here is so minimal that it barely registers. Can't breathe fire in Faerie, I'm afraid.*

What?

As a parent, that was the most relief I'd felt in weeks. *Dark magic fuels the fire. You may need an extra blanket—your core temperature will drop here. It's nothing horrible.*

She still seemed appalled at the loss of her breath weapon, and I tried to be sympathetic and hide my feelings on the matter. We'd only needed the fire extinguisher five times in her first year, but any day that passed without my daughter accidentally starting a blaze was a good one in my books.

Before long, Ros interrupted Aurie's ungainly walk around the grounds. "Hey, sweetie," she said, manifesting in our path. "Good news. I can do to you more or less what I did to your dad. Shouldn't interfere with my previous work on you. If you still want to do it now, we can—"

Aurie flopped down in the grass and nodded. *I'm ready.*

"No, you're not," she muttered, then looked at me and made a shooing motion. "Back up, Frank. Do *not* touch her until I'm finished, okay? I mean it."

Fear surged through me, and my mind flashed to those horrible days when all I could do was keep Aurie's egg warm and beg her to live. I couldn't let Ros hurt her, she *needed* me...

"Frank," Ros insisted, breaking me from my spiraling thoughts, and floated off the ground until we were at eye level. "I wouldn't do it if I weren't sure," she murmured. "I need you to trust me now, bud."

That's my world in your hands.

"I know. Let me make her stronger." She pointed to Owain, who was standing by with our baggage. "Go wait with him. This'll be over soon."

Aurie looked up at me and smiled—and seeing that particular expression on her true face for the first time, I realized just how unsettling it could be. *I'm fine*, she told me. *Tough. You'll see.*

Reluctant but resigned, I shifted again and felt my robe appear around me. "I love you, Aurie," I said. "And I'll be there when you wake. It won't hurt for long."

As I joined my father, he muttered, "I'll get a numbing enchantment on her as soon as this is finished. We learn from experience, eh?"

"Thank you."

He reached up and gripped my shoulder. "Be strong—"

His exhortation ended when Aurie roared in pain, but his fingers dug in as I tensed. Every instinct screamed at me to run to her, protect her, *save* her, and it took all of my willpower to stand my ground and wait. I closed my eyes, not wanting to watch her thrash, but that only made the roaring seem louder—that, plus her inescapable mental wail of fear and agony.

And then, as quickly as it had begun, the worst was over. Aurie's voice fell silent as she passed out, and with a brief gesture from Ros, she was back in her human form...though as I ran up to see what Ros had accomplished, I saw that something was different.

"I still can't fix her left arm or give her wings," Ros told me. "The prosthetic that Toula worked up in her bind won't be that difficult for Owain to replicate. Now, I'm not sure I'd trust a magic-made prosthetic for her at full size, not since it'd have to be a weight-bearing prosthetic, but she can have her hand and forearm back once she wakes."

As my father started cocooning Aurie in the construction that would minimize her discomfort, I pointed to her hair. "What about that?"

Ros grinned. "She was only ever blonde because of the bind. Come on, you know how it works. Georgie has black hair, yours is basically white, and Aurie..."

"Has blue hair. And eyebrows," I muttered, crouching for a closer look. "The fuzz elsewhere still seems light, but..."

"It's a natural reflection of her scale color. Come on, *Dad*."

I grunted and picked Aurie's limp body off the lawn while the numbing enchantment coalesced around her. "Will she be okay?"

"Just fine," she replied, patting my arm. "Let her sleep it off."

"Thank you, Ros."

"Of course. I'm here for you, bud," she said as she faded. *Always.*

Just as I had done, Aurie slept through the day, only beginning to stir near dinnertime. Thanks to my father's preemptive work, she had an easier return to consciousness, and I smiled as I heard her voice: *Dad?*

"I'm here," I said, stroking her head. "It's over. You did it, brave girl."

She sighed, then whimpered as she started to roll toward me. *Hurts.*

"You'll feel fine by morning, but I'll see what Granddad can do. Want to try to sit up?"

Slowly, I helped her ease upright in bed, at which point she was sufficiently aware to notice her missing left arm. "Why don't I have—"

"Granddad will make you a new one," I promised. "And he'll fix this, too," I added, scooping her out of bed and carrying her to the mirror. "Don't worry, your hair—"

She squealed in delight. "It's *blue*!"

"Scale color. Toula made you a blonde to begin with, but really, we can fix it—"

Aurie grabbed her hair with her remaining hand and frantically shook her head. "Don't you dare! I like it!"

My little girl was growing up, I mused, and headed for adolescence far too quickly. "We'll talk about it tomorrow, okay? Come on, let's eat."

Once again, Dad had prepared a marvelous spread—though unhelpfully, he oohed and ahhed over Aurie's new hair—and he strengthened the numbing and gave her another working hand while she ate. With her stomach full, Aurie's eyelids drooped, and I tucked her back into bed before she passed out once more.

"I'll show her the perks in the morning," I whispered as my father and I headed down the hall to his nearby study, where I could read and still listen for signs of distress. "Poor kid's exhausted."

"You weren't much better," he replied with a soft chuckle. "Come in, I'll start a fire."

As he pulled up a pair of well-stuffed chairs and waved life into the fireplace, I said, "Thanks again for taking us in, especially on such short notice."

Dad hugged me before I quite expected it. "This is your home, too," he said as I awkwardly patted his back. "And I'm sure as hell not losing you to a pack of damn wizards." Releasing me, he looked up and smiled. "You'll be perfectly safe here, son. Welcome home."

OCTOBER 2: BERT WOLD

Within the first month of Leander's tenure, I'd grown to loathe Mondays. The full Council meetings had seldom been fun during Toula's years, but the odds of their devolving into a shouting match—or of someone losing his chain—had been markedly lower.

And Leander was in a *foul* mood that morning. As the last of the under-slept Arc 1 magi took their seats, he stood and barked, "Would someone like to tell me why none of you, the elite of this fine institution, have been able to track down one stupid girl?"

I drank my tea and watched my colleagues grow suddenly interested in their papers and notepads.

"Most of you are worthless," he continued. "Pathetic. How did you get your positions, anyway, flattering the mongrel?" When no one jumped into *that* trap, he huffed and shook his head. "Well, I'm sure you'll be pleased to know that some of our real magi—Kathleen, Honor," he said, acknowledging them with a flick of his hand—"are even now working to break through whatever spell has been blocking our trace attempts. We'll have our little runaway before long, thanks to them…and to Eva, who so generously gave us a blood sample," he added. He paused, allowing the implications of that statement to register.

Gunther, who'd apparently had his coffee that morning, heard the cue and chimed in. "What about the samples in the Archives? Unusable?"

"Missing," said Leander, then waited as the murmurs rose and subsided. "Not all of them, but an interesting assortment. The vials for anyone affiliated with the Away Team are gone, as are those for the damn doctor—"

"Doctor?" one of the junior Arc 7 magi interrupted. "Is the doctor here missing, too?"

The idiot boy, who'd seemed to realize his mistake as soon as the word left his mouth, attempted to recover. "She and her partner have gone on vacation. Sounds like it was long overdue. Which raises the question as to why their samples would be missing. Arnold Lowe's is gone as well—I think we all know where *his* loyalties lie," he continued, faintly smiling at the muttered agreement from his supporters. "But there's one other missing vial that bothers me. Would you care to explain, Bert?"

As the eyes of the table turned to me, I calmly put my teacup aside and feigned ignorance. "Explain what, sir? I'm afraid you've lost me."

"I want you to explain to us all why your blood sample is missing from the Archives," said Leander, staring at me like he could pierce my mental block by ocular force alone.

"That's news to me," I replied, and shrugged. "Check the records—I haven't been anywhere near the blood storage area in…goodness, I'm sure it's been years. We had a missing child out of Arc 6 about five years ago, and I helped with that trace, but I have no reason to visit that part of the Archives."

"Oh, believe me," he replied with false conviviality, "I've already checked. You're right, you haven't been over there. But *Arnold* was logged there the night before I took his chain and he fled. Now, why would he leave with your blood sample, huh?"

I took a sip of tea, giving myself a moment to best arrange my thoughts. "First, if he did, I have no knowledge of it," I told Leander. "Second, as my parents are both alive and well, and I'm their only child, anyone who needed to find me could run a trace off of them. They live in a cottage closer to town, should you need them." The rest of the Arc 2 contingent nodded, and I continued.

"Finally, if Arnold did take my sample, he may have done so out of fear for my safety."

Leander's smile didn't reach his eyes. "What might you be afraid of? Has someone forgotten to turn in his library books?"

I endured the tittering until it died down. "We've both noticed the company you keep, sir," I said, and pointed to Eva and Francine. "They *did* try to frame me for murder once, not so long ago. Were you aware of that? Terrible thing to be falsely accused of a crime that serious."

Toula's supporters on the Council began to grumble their agreement, and I caught Leander's eyes cutting to the culprits. But before he could respond, Eva jumped in. "You were consorting with a known faerie," she told me. "That's treason on its own, Bert."

"Since *when*?" I retorted. "And for the record, the 'known faerie' in question was Maria. A *magus*. One of us."

"Fae," she countered.

"Witch-blooded, actually, and the polluting drop was so minor that it never affected her casting. Surely I don't need to remind you of her skill," I said to the table, and was gratified to see even some of Leander's less devoted allies nodding agreement. "A *precocious* caster, one of the finest wizards I've ever worked with. She had dozens of generations between herself and her last fully fae ancestor."

"You mean Mab?" Francine asked sweetly.

"Yeah…and seventy-odd generations between them. Take you own family tree back that far, and I dare say you'll find questionable relations."

"Not such a wizard anymore, is she, though?" said Eva. "Can't even cast, I hear."

"And that's your bloody fault!" I yelled as my patience wore thin. "If you two hadn't impaled the woman and set her on fucking *fire*, she'd have had no need to augment. Ros messed with her only because she was on the brink of death. You *know* that," I snapped, looking around the room at my colleagues…and to my relief, they had yet to turn on me. "You saw her scars. Not you," I added to Leander, "but perhaps that's why you released those monsters."

He began to puff up. "They were wrongfully convicted—"

"They tried to kill another magus," I said, lingering on every word. "Who did nothing to them beyond defend Eva's daughter against Francine's."

Eva stood, her face reddening. "That's not why—"

"That's *exactly* why! You never liked Maria because she stood up for Kitty! Let me tell you, Eva, that girl of yours is worth *ten* of you, and her sister's right behind her. Not that you give a damn. Now," I said, directing my attention back to the larger Council, "I don't believe I was the only one of us here when Maria recounted exactly how she came to have a spike through her chest and massive burns over most of her body. Surely I wasn't the only one paying attention."

Toula's side of the Council rumbled with a mixture of concurrence and complaints against the recently reinstated magi, and even a few of Leander's followers had the decency to look sheepish.

"Eva and Francine are vipers," I told Leander, "and I don't say that lightly. I wouldn't trust a word they tell you. And if you're man enough, you'll reach out to Maria and ask her to tell you *in detail* what happened when she tried to protect the Archives and the Arcanum against those two."

With that, I took up my teacup again and stared at our grand magus over the rim. I almost felt sorry for the boy as he deflated, and the meeting came to a quick, ignominious end.

"Let us give you the truth," said Eva.

"Like hell," I muttered, listening in from my office. I'd

retreated immediately following the meeting, and sure enough, the two of them had appeared at Leander's door not ten minutes thereafter.

"Corelli is so tightly bound to Faerie, it's not even funny," she continued. "Valerius raised her, Corelli sank her hooks into Kitty, and before I could stop it, Kitty had practically moved in over there, too. Pavli let it all happen and threatened me when I tried to save my daughter."

"This would be the mongrel daughter?" Leander asked. "The one you dumped here as soon as she was old enough?"

Interesting. Maybe the kid was beginning to question his advisors.

"Because that's what Kathleen told me," he continued. "You sent Kitty to live with her dad out in the country somewhere, and once he died, you turned around and shipped her off to Glastonbury."

"I had an infant to care for," Eva protested. "And besides, I knew the girl was a mongrel. I was hoping she'd leave of her own choice once she was exposed to real wizards. *She* is a backstabbing snake," she continued with increased vigor. "I'm sure she begged Pavli to execute us."

"Actually, no," he replied. "I looked over the trial records after your release. There's a note in there about Kitty asking Pavli to let you live."

A fact that Eva knew damn well, I thought. Toula had told me about that meeting: the poor girl, torn between filial duty to the woman who'd abandoned her and loyalty to her best friend, had still requested that her mother's life be spared.

"Still," said Francine, taking the lead while Eva sputtered, "the fact remains that Kitty is as much a traitor as anyone. I'm sure you've seen the file—she's more fae than anything now, not to mention she *married* the heir to a court. Corelli was certainly fae, and every one of our secrets was open to those monsters through her. We did the right thing," she insisted. "We tried to cut out the cancer before it could kill us all. It backfired, yes, but *you're* righting that wrong. You've cleaned house. There's probably not a mongrel left in any installation, and that's no small feat."

I heard him drum his fingers on his desk. "How much longer on the blood trace? Any update from Kathleen?"

"They left aides tending it during the meeting," said Eva, "but she thinks another forty-eight hours. If my daughters are still in this realm, we'll know then."

I made a few quick notes on my pad as their conversation wound down, hoping I'd given Leander food for thought. In the meantime, I had a job to do.

That night, as I hurried into my pub and shook the rain off my umbrella, I was disappointed but unsurprised to find one of the new aides sitting at the bar. The boy had recently come from Arc 1 as part of Leander's party, and it didn't take a genius to know what he was doing in a pub far from the trendier watering holes in Glastonbury.

Well, two could play at acting.

"Hello, hello," I said, taking the stool beside his.

The aide jumped at the sound of my greeting—an amateur spy, to be sure—but recovered enough to nod. "Uh…"

"Bert Wold," I said, shaking his hand. "Remember? From the office?"

"Horatio Fuchs," he replied.

"Oh! Any kin to Kathleen?" I asked as I flagged down the bartender. "The usual, please," I told him, "and put this fellow's drink on my tab."

"She's my aunt," Horatio mumbled as the bartender turned away to grab a glass.

"Wonderful. And how are you finding Glastonbury, then? Bit of a culture shock, I'm sure."

Though frustrated and flustered, he had no choice but to play along, and I wondered how long I could keep him tied up at the pub. Business was slow on a wet Monday night, and with little of interest on the screens mounted around the room, I thought I could make the evening an unpleasant outing for the lad.

His salvation came from an unexpected quarter. Halfway through my first pint, my mobile chimed, and I checked the readout. "Excuse me," I told Horatio, and took the call. "Mum? Everything all right?"

"It's the television again, Bertie," she said, as flustered as I'd ever heard her. "Something's wrong with the system, and I can't sort it, and your father's no help…"

I sighed to myself. My parents were useless with any technology of the last century, and the TV was a frequent source of trouble.

"Be over soon. Don't push any more buttons," I told her, then rang off and downed my drink. "Sorry about that. I've got to see about my parents before they take a hammer to their TV," I said to Horatio, who didn't seem entirely disappointed by the news. Meeting the bartender's eyes, I dropped a pair of notes on the counter, picked up my dripping umbrella, and slipped out into the night.

Ten minutes later, having switched the television's input and changed the language back to English from Mandarin, I borrowed my parents' guest toilet and sent a quick text to Arnold: *Trace is running. Get K&B out.*

His reply came before I'd finished washing my hands. *Are you safe?*

For now, I wrote. *Being followed.*

I considered my reflection in the mirror: middling stature, curly hair going to salt and pepper, the half-moon glasses of an old man, and a brown jumper. James Bond I was not.

"Game face, Bertram," I told myself, and plastered on a smile as I rejoined my grateful parents.

OCTOBER 3: FRANK

Morning found me in the formal garden behind my father's house, clutching my coffee and watching the sunrise. I heard the back door open, and a moment later, Dad slid onto the bench beside me. "Did you not sleep well?" he asked.

"Ros stopped by overnight," I explained. "Leander's got a better blood trace running, so Kitty and Beth evacuated a few hours ago."

"Are they hurt?"

"No. They're with Val. But everyone else is still on the island…" I sipped, letting the warmth mitigate against the unfamiliar cold within me. "I don't know how far back those blood samples go, but even if it's just a generation, no one out there is safe. Well, Artur, Mal, and Marcus," I allowed, "but anyone with an Arcanum bloodline is at risk of detection. Hell, if they've got the Mulligan parents on file, they could even track Dr. Dellucci. Though I guess Ed would give them trouble," I mused, and nodded my thanks as my mug refilled.

"I thought he has a rather impressive Arcanum pedigree," Dad replied.

"Oh, sure, he's at one end of quite a few family trees, but he's *deep*. All I've ever heard is that blood traces work vertically, and they grow more difficult with each generation between the target and the sample. Easiest to track someone with his own blood, a little more complicated with a parent's or child's, and so on. Ed's nearest great-grandchildren would have to be at least thirty generations removed, so good luck finding him."

"If it's taken them this long to run one trace," said Dad, patting my knee, "then surely your other friends are in no immediate danger. The Arcanum will be forced to start over with a fresh target, yes?"

"I assume so."

"Then there's no need to worry today." Producing his own cup of coffee, he watched the horizon lighten and sighed with contentment. "I have a proposition for you, Frank."

"Oh?"

"One of my cousins is throwing a party tonight. Nothing massive or too fancy, but it would be a chance for you to begin meeting people," he said, nudging me in the side. "Come with me. I don't often attend these things, but I think it'd be good for you."

The idea of spending the evening at a soiree wasn't high on my list, but I tried to be polite. "I don't know. Leaving Aurie alone..."

"Is there no one who could watch her for a few hours?" When I hesitated, he said, "You've been under a great deal of stress, son. It's no sin to take a little time for yourself. Besides, I'd very much like to introduce you."

Reluctant though I was, I didn't want to disappoint him, and so I agreed to run the matter by Aurie. To my surprise, she wasn't opposed to the idea...but then I realized why. In the time I'd been outside, Kitty had sent me a message informing me of their arrival, and Aurie eagerly suggested asking Beth to babysit. "If she agrees," I warned my daughter, "there will be no slasher movies, understood?"

To that, Aurie flashed her most disarming smile.

After dinner, and with a fair bit of trepidation, Dad used my memories to open a gate to Val's. "We're not supposed to be here, you understand," he said, hesitating at the edge of the hole. "The king forbids it. Trying to stop inter-court fights, you see."

"I'm pretty sure he'll get over it," I replied, and strode through, holding Aurie's hand. Val's mountain villa was surrounded by a wide meadow, and I knew my child well enough to preemptively stop her from running off to explore.

A pair of guards waited at the nearest door to the complex, and I raised my free hand in greeting. "We're expected," I said as Dad jogged up behind me. "Would you tell Kiet that Frank's here?"

A moment later, another gate opened to disgorge Val's captain, a dark-haired man with disturbingly old eyes. "Frank," he said with a curt nod. "You're well?"

"For now," I replied, and gestured to Dad. "My father, Owain, and this is—"

But Kiet beat me to it. "You must be Aurora," he said, stooping to smile at her. "My, that is, uh…*striking* hair."

She beamed. "It's not even dye!"

"Really?" He cut his eyes to mine, and I heard him in my thoughts: *I've had five girls of my own. They're delights at this age.*

She's one, you realize.

This age, relatively speaking, he amended, and straightened. "They're waiting for you inside. Come, I'll bring you to them."

As we passed through the villa, I noticed guards stationed in courtyards along our path—none brandishing weapons, but a presence nonetheless. "Captain?" I asked.

He glanced over his shoulder at us. "Hmm?"

"Have I caused offense?"

"Not at all," he replied, and I detected the bemusement in his mind. "My lord considers you a friend. Why do you ask?"

"Is this place always so well guarded? I was exhausted the last time I was here, but I think I would have remembered."

He laughed to himself, though there was nothing reassuring in it. "You *have* heard of the new queen, yes?"

"She's made threats against your lord?"

"Not yet. Not in so many words. But we're taking precautions, especially now that Kitty's come." He looked back again with a brief, grim smile. "I don't suppose I need to explain."

"No." It was no secret that Val loved Maria like his own child, and Kitty was a close second, especially since she'd made things official with Marcus. He'd almost lost Maria once, and I doubted he was taking any chances this time around. "Thank him for me, if you'd be so kind. I don't mean to complicate the security situation—"

"It's no trouble. I'm sure the girls could use a distraction."

We found Kitty and Beth in a dining room, playing cards across the table while the remnants of their dessert sat pushed to the side. Aurie squealed and wriggled free of my grasp when she saw them, and the two promptly began gushing over the hatchling's new hairdo.

Something told me I wasn't going to convince her to go blonde again any time soon, but that was the least of our worries.

As Beth coaxed Aurie to the table to explain the rules of Go Fish, Kitty joined Kiet, Dad, and me at the door. "We'll take it from here," she said, giving me a friendly punch in the arm. "You boys go have fun."

I'm not sure "fun" is quite the word, I told her privately, then added, "I won't be out late. If you could give us a few hours…"

"Take your time," she insisted. "*Someone* should be having a nice evening. And once Aurie loses interest here," she continued, jerking her head toward the table, "I've got nothing but Disney movies lined up. Princesses, bedtime, no nightmares."

"What's the one with—"

"*Sleeping Beauty*, and it's off the list," she quietly assured me. "No dead dragons tonight." Turning to my dad, she grinned and said, "Make him have a good time, won't you? He needs a night out."

The modest party I'd been expecting was nothing like the extravaganza to which my father's gate brought us. In Faerie, no one who lived beyond the Fringe settlement bothered to build a dwelling that might have passed for reasonable. Outside the grand mansion, the trees practically dripped with colored lights, like fireworks frozen at the point of explosion. Up-tempo music drifted out the open front door, though I couldn't name the tune or point to any band. Guests drifted across the gardens in their confectionary-like apparel, laughing, talking, and drinking. One group appeared to have commandeered part of the lawn as a croquet court, though no one seemed sober enough to hit straight, and the hoops kept moving.

"This is small?" I asked Dad.

"Reasonably so," he replied, and led the way toward the house.

We passed by a pair of faeries guarding the door, who waved us through once they recognized Dad. "Bouncers?" I murmured.

"Essentially," he said as we passed through the foyer, which wouldn't have been out of place in a palace. "They're lower-ranking members of the court trying to curry favor with the host. If the night gets too exciting, they'll step in to help break up any fights." Apparently sensing my unease, he patted my back and murmured, "You have nothing to worry about. You're of the blood— you outrank at least half the people here. Keep your head up, son."

Having never been to a social function outside of an Arc 2 event or a Team get-together—and one cynaeli royal wedding, though that hardly counted—I fell back on what I knew and made for the safety of the wall. The nearest drinks table was a pitiful bar, several unlabeled bottles of wine and a few beers, so I poured myself a polite amount of red and made do. I couldn't stand the stuff, but the prop was important. Duly equipped, I stood back and watched as my father made small talk, greeting most guests with politeness and a few with actual warmth. He seemed adept at the task, one I had yet to master, and I tried to pay attention to his body language as he conversed.

I wished I'd worn my glasses. It was far easier to observe in peace when no one could determine quite where one was looking. But Dad had suggested that I leave them at home for the night. "It'll be dark, anyway," he'd said, "and you have no need to hide behind them." While I appreciated the sentiment, I missed the familiar weight on my face, a security blanket of partial anonymity.

Perhaps half an hour into the evening, with the wine warming in my hand, I glanced away from a pair of men undressing each other in their haste to escape upstairs in time to catch a blond man approaching my father. "I'm surprised to see *you* here," he said, regarding Dad quizzically.

My father smiled. "Engam," he said, reaching out to grasp the man's arm. "Thank you for the invitation. This is truly a lovely event."

"For what it is," he replied, snatching a beer from the table and downing a long swig. "You missed my last party."

"I was, unfortunately, booked," said Dad, which I trusted to be an outright falsehood. "I brought a guest with me tonight—I hope you don't mind."

Engam waved dismissively. "Where is she? Or, uh…is it he these days?"

"Neither," he said with a little chuckle, then beckoned for me to join them. "Let me introduce my son, Frank."

I could feel the pride radiating from him like a warm hearth as I left the security of the wall, and for an instant, I allowed myself to believe that this would go well. But before I could even open my mouth, our host laughed aloud and almost dropped his beer. "When did *you* ever sire a brat? And who's the mother, some mortal you picked up in a shipyard?" he asked Dad, then gave me a brief inspection.

The fact that he had to crane his neck to do so gave me only minimal comfort.

"Who's your mother, boy?" he asked me. "What the hell is wrong with you, anyway?"

"Nothing is wrong with him," said Dad, bristling.

"Looks like a giant freak to me," said Engam. "What is he, albino? You couldn't bother glamouring that?"

My temper flared with his assessment, and I fought to keep it in check. Artur, Marcus, and Kitty had warned me that this might happen, that augmentation came with a generous uptick in hotheadedness, and I struggled to keep my cool before I let slip something unwise.

"To answer your question," I said stiffly to Engam, "my mother was born and raised in Faerie. I'm quarter-blooded."

Close enough, I decided.

He rolled his eyes and turned to my father with a look of exasperation. "You brought one of *those* to my house? Really, Owain?"

By then, Dad's temper was mounting, and a flush crept up his neck as he stared Engam down. "That is my son, cousin," he said through clenched teeth. "Have a care how you—"

I squeezed his shoulder to stop him from making a scene. "It's fine, Dad. Go talk to your friends. I'm going to keep drinking in the corner."

"Frank—"

"*Go.*"

Perhaps finally seeing the contours of the looming fight, he slunk off to cool down, and I considered Engam as he smirked. "I'm not here to cause a scene," I murmured. "My father asked me to accompany him, and I did. If that's somehow insulting to you, then maybe you should be clearer about plus-ones on your invitations."

"I thought it obvious that lesser bloods have no right to walk among their betters as if they were equals," he replied. "You must be stupid as well as untalented." With a snort for good measure, he added, "Go back to the settlement where you belong, freak."

My blood boiled, but I clenched my fists until the pain distracted me from the impulse to rip his stomach open. "My father's having a nice time," I said, nodding to him as he spoke with a small group across the room. "Please don't ruin this for him. I'm doing no—"

Before I could finish the thought, a blast of force threw me several meters into a wall. My wine flew from my hand across the white marble floor, and the plaster cracked with the impact of my substantial bulk at high velocity. I sagged to my knees, gasping...and as I looked up, I saw Engam advancing on me, almost smiling, with a yellow fireball in his hand.

The combination of pain and fear proved too strong for my willpower, and I *snapped*.

I didn't fully shift—I had enough presence of mind to know that I didn't want to bring the building down on the rest of the partygoers—but I could feel the changes rippling through me, riding the wave of my rage. My useless fingernails sharpened into talons as my teeth reconfigured themselves into a mouth full of knives. I barely noticed when my horns manifested, but the back of my shirt shredded as my claw-tipped wings burst forth.

Engam stopped in his tracks, fireball forgotten, a yapping Chihuahua who'd suddenly realized that the shape in the shadows was a wolf.

I stepped in before he could recover his wits. Grabbing him by the throat, I hoisted him off the floor until he was looking down at me, scrabbling at my arm and kicking for his freedom. I wasn't fully choking him, though I squeezed just enough to remind him that this fate was well within the cards.

"You said you were a quarter-blood!" he squawked as the guests around us either shielded or ran for cover.

I almost didn't recognize my own voice, which had descended past its usual bass to a distinctly inhuman growl. "You made assumptions about the other three quarters," I told him, then tossed him into a table of delicate canapés. "*Idiot.*"

"Frank!" my father cried, running up to intervene. "What's going on? Are you—"

"Stay here," I said, then stormed out of the house. The frightened guests parted along my pathway to the exit, and I punched one of the doors off its hinges—and knocked a bouncer into the bushes—as I made my egress.

Air. I needed *air*.

Somewhere behind me, I heard Dad calling for me to stop, but I ignored him. My wings spread, and with a leap, I was up and on my way to the sea.

About an hour later, my fury spent and my underused flight muscles throbbing, I crouched on a cliff by the ocean and stared at the lonely night. No one seemed to have followed me, and though Ros certainly knew where I was, she left me in peace.

I was grateful for the solitude. I didn't want to face her. I didn't want to face my father.

"*Fuck,*" I muttered to Faerie's transient stars.

The one thing—the *one thing*—he'd asked of me, I'd ruined. Okay, yes, maybe he'd been unwise to think I would pass unnoticed at the party—strange giants seldom go unremarked—and maybe he hadn't realized what a faux pas it was to bring me. He'd admitted that he wasn't the most social of his kind—maybe he honestly thought the night would be fun. He would see his kin and his friends, and he'd introduce a son he could be proud of.

I should have left before Engam turned physical. A

quiet exit—that would have saved my father's evening, at least. Saved his reputation. But he'd been fool enough to claim me, and now they all knew that he'd sired a monstrosity.

That's what I was, wasn't it? A little of one thing, a little of another, a combination amounting to nothing. I belonged nowhere. My mother and siblings had driven me out of the barn, Leander had driven me from the Arcanum...how had I been so *delusional* as to think I'd find a place among the fae? A future? A *family*?

If my father never wanted to see me again, I'd understand. I'd ruined everything. His reputation, my future, my *daughter's* safety...

Aurie. I needed to pick her up, but I couldn't bring myself to slink back to Val's just yet.

I thought then of the Fringe settlement, Faerie's community of the unwanted. True, they were mostly lesser bloods and witches, but there were outliers among them— mundanes like Ros's grandfather, a few witch-bloods, even a lone kadalin. Maybe I could find refuge there, though judging by the looks of shock and fear I'd witnessed on the faces of Engam's guests, I doubted that the residents of the settlement would want me around.

The wind was growing colder, my muscles were stiffening, and I couldn't very well sit on a rock and brood all night. I needed a plan, a playbook, someone to take my hand and point me in the right direction and explain what I was meant to be doing with my life.

But I'd settle for a drink.

The settlement wasn't difficult to pick out from above. I'd flown over it hundreds of times, and its tidy grid of lit streets made for an easy target in the dark. Landing outside the walls, I concentrated until I'd shifted back into my humanish form, then took a deep breath and winced. Between my impact with the wall and my time in the air, my muscles would be screaming by morning.

Calling forth a tiny fireball, I examined myself. No visible blood—always a good sign—though when I reached behind me, I could feel the tattered remnants of my shirt. Nothing to be done there—even if I had sufficient talent, I'd yet to learn how to channel it properly. Still, the night wasn't getting any younger, and I certainly wasn't getting any prettier, so I extinguished the fire and headed for the main gate.

The settlement was surrounded by a pile of bricks that might constitute a formidable wall if one were piq and wingless, or perhaps a toddler. It was no more than a meter high, a symbolic barrier rather than a defensible barricade, but from what I understood of the place, the fae knew to respect the border, *if* they were allowed in at all. Deciding not to ruffle any additional feathers, I walked up to the proper entry point, a gate with a quartet of guards standing by. They stiffened as they noticed me, and I kept my hands visible, trying not to seem like a threat.

"Hi," I said once I was within hailing range. "I'm not armed."

"No closer," said a dark-haired man. The white orbs floating near the gate glinted off of his metal breastplate, which was only partially obscured by a zip-up hoodie. "What's your name?"

"Frank," I replied. "Frank White. I, uh—"

"Whoa, *whoa*, stand down," said the brunette on the other side of the gate. She, too, wore armor, but of the black, Kevlar variety—a younger faerie, I supposed, or maybe a true Fringer. Slipping through the opening, she approached me and cocked her head. "Away Team Frank?"

"Uh…yes…"

Her youthful face split in a wide grin. "Oh, goodness, *hi*! It's okay, he's legit," she said to the other guards, who relaxed their stances. "Hi," she repeated, offering her hand. "Poppy Kane. I'm Mal's mom."

I knew little of her but the basics: she'd been trained by the Dark Company, her son had a *healthy* respect for her anger, and she could shift into a wolf large enough to stand with all four paws on the ground and look the average man in the eye. Shifters weren't immortal, but Poppy had been in Faerie for decades, safe from time's ravages.

"Pleasure," I said as I shook her hand.

"Mal said you and your little one had come over," Poppy continued. "Told us to be on the lookout. What brings you here?" She paused then and peered around me. "I didn't see a gate. You didn't come on foot, did you?"

"Flew, actually," I mumbled. "I'm sorry to ask, but is there anywhere in town that a guy might get a drink?"

"Sure." She looked at my face more closely in the shadows, and her voice softened. "You okay, hon? Is something wrong?"

"Just had a rough night."

"Mm. Well, The Tavern's seldom packed on a Tuesday, so they can hook you up. Come with me."

As she fell in behind me, I heard her hiss. "How rough *was* your night?"

"The wings had to go somewhere," I explained.

"I suppose. Hey, Mattie," she said, beckoning to another brown-haired guard, "come here and fix this, would you?" The man slid off the wall and ambled over, and Poppy huffed and tapped her foot. "Sometime this year, if you please."

"Patience, little sister," he replied, heading behind me. "Let's see the…oh. *My.*"

"This is Away Team Frank," she said as he repaired my shirt. "Frank, this is Matthew, one of Mal's uncles—"

"And an amateur tailor tonight," he quipped, and patted my shoulder as he finished the job. "There, much better. Thanks for not wearing tartan—that would have been a beast to align in the dark. And nice to meet you," he added, rejoining his sister-in-law. "Mal's told us a few field stories."

"Yeah, and he's probably not giving me the best of the bunch," said Poppy. "Listen, Frank, I just want to thank you for taking such good care of my boy."

The night was veering in an unexpected direction, and I tried not to blink stupidly at her. "Uh…of course, Mal's great…"

"He thinks the world of you," she said, then stepped closer and lowered her voice. "Mom moment, here. Do you want to go sit down somewhere and talk? I'm a shifter—no one's getting in here," she added, tapping two fingers against her forehead. "Except Ros, but she can keep her mouth shut. Do you need an ear?"

I needed *something*, but at that moment, I had no desire to wreck yet another person's opinion of me. "Thank you, but I'm fine," I fibbed. "Maybe just a drink."

"Sure thing. Mattie, you're in charge," she said, and motioned for me to follow her into town. "This way, hon. I'll take you."

A short walk inside the walls brought us to an idling trolley, and Poppy hopped aboard. "Perfect timing," she said as I climbed the short step. "This is the end of the line."

The car had no driver, nor was it connected to any rails or wires. "How does this, uh…"

"One of my husband's brothers designed the trolley system," she replied, taking a seat. "Honestly, it's hard to remember which sometimes—he's got eleven of them. Probably Robbie. Anyway, there are no cars here, so the trolleys run all over town. We're heading for the business district, so you may as well take a load off."

The trolley passed down a wide, lamp-lined avenue of single-family homes—decently large and of various styles, though nothing overly ostentatious. I could make out green lawns, tidy gardens, mature trees, and the occasional picket fence as we sped by. The trolled stopped when it encountered a group of children playing late-night basketball in the street, and Poppy leaned out of the vehicle to call, "You've got school in the morning! Go to bed!" As the kids split to the pavement on either side, she resumed her seat and shook her head. "I teach phys ed at the school here," she explained. "Mark my words, one of them is going to complain about a sprained ankle tomorrow because he's too tired for gym."

"You teach on top of guard duty?" I asked.

"Guard duty is new. Hopefully temporary. You've heard Irem's thoughts about this place, right?"

I had, though something within me counseled against expressing my fears concerning the outcome of a fight between a mob of faeries and a shifter, no matter how impressive her lupine form.

Soon, the neighborhood gave way to manicured fields—sports facilities, I thought—and then to a sort of downtown. Having never seen the settlement from a ground-level perspective, I tried to match the buildings around me with my aerial map, only succeeding when the trolley approached the park at the town's heart. The vehicle slowed to a stop by a covered bench, and once we disembarked, it rolled onward into the night.

Poppy led me toward the west, behind the first row of neat brick storefronts and two streets more, then stopped before a two-story complex monopolizing a whole block. Much of the space was occupied by a stone building, while the rest was a fenced-off green area set with picnic tables and strung with lights. A few people relaxed outdoors with pint glasses and plates of fried food, laughing and talking.

"The Tavern," said Poppy. "Inside or out, the offerings are the same. Rooms upstairs in case you need to sleep something off."

"I hope to avoid that," I told her, and accepted her hand again. "Thank you."

"Sure. Hey, if you're going to be around for a while, come to dinner. That might even lure Mal home for a night," she added, then smiled and took her leave.

I pushed open one of the double doors and preemptively ducked, a reflex forged by long experience, but the ceiling was high enough to eliminate my risk of accidental concussion. The front room was dimly let, ringed by wooden booths and dotted with candle-topped tables. I couldn't tell whether the flickering lamps on the walls were oil or the product of enchantment, but they gave enough light to reveal the long, polished bar against one wall, a heavy piece of mahogany and brass. Behind it, a mirror stretched along the length of the back bar, split into segments by shelving for bottles and glassware. The only bartender on duty was a brown-haired man of middling height—I would have called him young, but one could never be certain in Faerie—who looked up from his book and nodded as I slid onto a stool.

"Evening," he said, turning the book over to save his page. Such an action would have constituted a war crime in the Archives, but then again, the book in question appeared to be a paperback detective novel instead of a priceless eight-hundred-year-old manuscript. "How's it going?"

His accent sounded vaguely British, though unskilled as I was at the game, I couldn't pinpoint a region beyond "south of Scotland." Then again, Mal and Yolanda had said that the Fringe had a sort of creole all its own, so I drew no conclusions about my new companion.

"Been a long night," I replied. "I don't have any cash on me, but—"

"No one here does," he said with a grin. "You must be new. What are you drinking?"

"Any chance of a Bloody Mary?"

One of his eyebrows rose. "I make mine strong."

"All the better. And don't worry about the garnish," I added as he pulled a glass from the back bar. "I'm not one for gherkins on a stick."

"Same. I'm all for eating at the pub, but keep your drinks and your grub in different containers."

The concoction he delivered was pale red—heavy on the vodka, I surmised—and unadorned, and I sighed as the first peppery sip hit. "Quality."

"Thanks." He slid a bowl of mixed nuts within reach and leaned on the bar as I drank. "What are you called, stranger?"

"Frank."

He wasn't locking down his thoughts, and so I felt his burst of mingled recognition and pleasure. "Away Team?"

"The same."

"I should have guessed. There's quite a bit of you, man." Smiling, he said, "Adam Stowe. I'm Mal's uncle—well, one of them."

"How many of you *are* there in this town?" I asked. "I just met Poppy and Matthew…"

"Depending on the weather and who's sneaked off to sea, most of the family. Mum and Dad have their own place, but the dozen of us boys, baby sister, Poppy, and Hal…everyone else but the little fellow is here, and you seem to be keeping him out of trouble, so thanks for that."

"I haven't done anything special," I replied, and drank deeply.

Adam waited until I returned the glass to the bar, then moved closer and lowered his voice. "Maybe Poppy doesn't know everything you lot get into, but I've heard a few stories. Switzerland? You, Mal, a glacial crevasse?"

"That was years ago—"

"He said you caught him when the snow broke and hauled him out with one hand. For that alone, if we accepted payment here, you'd be drinking free tonight. Speaking of which, were you only planning to drink, or are you feeling peckish as well?"

"You put those out," I said, gesturing to the bowl of nuts.

"Yeah, but if half of what I remember from Mal is true, you don't eat them. Wait there."

He slipped out of the room via a swinging door, then

returned a few minutes later with a plate of pigs in a blanket. "I also do nachos," he said, "but I've been told that my wings are atrocious, so I hope that's not a disappointment."

In truth, I was too upset to have much of an appetite, but I appreciated the gesture, and the food was good. I nudged the plate toward Adam as he returned to his post behind the bar, and he helped himself.

"Mal called home two days ago and said you and your little girl had come over. His parents are urging him to do likewise...but then again," he said, making a face, "what's more fun, living in your parents' house or hanging out on a private island?"

"It *is* a pretty nice island."

I continued to nurse my drink, and Adam took up his book. But as I reached the dregs, I felt the weight of his eyes and looked up to find him watching me. "Is something wrong?" I asked.

"Look," said Adam, abandoning the book again, "I'm no shrink, but I've been a barman for a *very* long time. What's on your mind, lad?"

"Trust me," I replied, "you have better things to do."

He snorted. "Like what? There's an open-mic night going on in the big room next door, and the stand-up comedy on offer is atrocious. I'm not leaving this side of the building until we shut down for the evening, and I already know who offed the old lady," he added, closing his novel, "so you may as well try me."

While I considered his offer, he whipped up a replacement Bloody Mary and switched out my glasses, then poured himself a beer. "I've heard it all," he murmured. "Had a woman confess to poisoning her husband after her third shot of whisky. *All* manner of infidelity. A few questionable activities with livestock. So whatever's bothering you, odds are good that you'll not shock me."

I hesitated a moment longer, letting the fresh drink

wash over my tongue, then muttered, "I threw my father's cousin into a buffet table at his own party tonight."

"Is that all? That's par for the course around here. Where two or three faeries are gathered together," he said with false solemnity, "at least one of them will end the night with bruises." Adam waited, but when I didn't speak, he said, "Mal mentioned you'd had some news about your family. Which court?"

"Coileán's. My father is one of Titania's grandsons."

He whistled. "Half-blooded, I trust."

"Yeah."

"So," he said, resting his elbows on the bar, "what's it like to be a lord, then?"

"I wouldn't know," I replied, and sought comfort in my cocktail again.

"Mm. This cousin—full-blooded fae?"

I shrugged. "You'd have to ask him, but I think it's probable."

"Fair. Well, remember that full-blooded faeries are assholes." Adam grinned as my head jerked up. "What? It's true, and I can say it. We've all got it to an extent, but the purest of the race tend to be insufferable. I assume there was some impetus for you tossing him around. Did he insult you?"

"Something like that," I mumbled.

"Not unusual, I fear, especially when tempers run high. If he's terribly upset, he'll go to the king, and you can explain yourself."

Adam watched me with one eye while he drank his beer. "There's more to this," he finally said. "What's really bothering you, Frank?"

I sensed nothing but concern and curiosity from Adam—he meant what he said. Explaining myself in mere syllables, however, was beyond my skill at that moment.

He rocked back in surprise when I hit him with a stream of pure telepathy, sights and sounds and impressions and meaning and feeling wrapped around each other and delivered in a multisensory burst of information, but he stood his ground and kept his mind open. Once I finished, he drained his glass and poured a refill, then slowly sipped it while he tried to parse what I'd shown him.

The pigs were almost gone when he said, "Let's start with your mum. I think I missed a few details."

Slowly, with painstaking questioning, Adam pulled the words from me. Mom's quasi-abandonment. The clutchmates who'd never had the patience to understand me. Twenty-five years of odd looks and whispers from wizards who thought they were being sneaky. Ione—just Ione, always Ione. Winning her, losing her, the guilt I carried for the sons who'd died and the daughter born disabled. My inability to give Aurie the life she deserved with her cousins all around her. The terror I still felt every time I thought she'd stopped breathing in her sleep. Leander. Losing my home, then abandoning the Team to protect my girl.

And Dad. The shock, the fear, the pain, the hope that I'd measure up. The crushing realization that I never would.

"I so wanted to believe that I could belong here," I concluded, avoiding my reflection in the bar mirror. "That this was what I'd been missing all along. *Such* a fool. Stupid Runt," I muttered. "I don't fit in here—I never will. The way the other guests looked at me tonight, that…that's everything I needed to know. But damn it," I said, looking back at Adam, "is it too much to ask to belong *somewhere*?"

He thought for a moment as he absently picked peanuts from the bowl, then folded his hands on the bar and met my gaze. "Remember that people aren't puzzle pieces," he said. "No one is ever quite a perfect fit. Even if it's close, there will always be a little extra space, or a bit that's still sticking out and can't be forced in. Take me, if you want an example," he continued, and laughed as my eyebrows rose. "Let's see, where to begin? Half fae don't fit in this realm because we are, by comparison to our full-blooded peers, reasonable killjoys. Of course, I've only been here for the last forty-five years or so because my parents said to hell with court life and fled to the mortal realm. We never fit in there, either. Even with glamour, we had to keep moving so no one would realize the truth about us, and it's difficult to make friends when you're often a stranger. That, and imagine trying to play with other children when you must avoid iron at all costs. Or when you make the bare minimum of appearances at church and find an excuse not to take Communion whenever the silver chalice comes out. Or, you know, church in general," he said, shaking his head. "I was a youth when good old King Henry made his own. For a while, there, attending the wrong service was an easy way to wind up dead."

I waited as he sipped his beer and attacked the nut bowl again.

"But let's get more personal, eh? I was my parents' third boy. The eldest, Ned, was seventy when I appeared. The rest of used to say that Ned ranked us by how well we could wield a sword. He's fought in at least five wars, and he used to work as a banker in London. He's the *responsible* one," Adam added, rolling his eyes. "Robbie was acceptable—that's the brother between us, Robbie. Not a great fighter, but he worked his way to master mason. An architect's eye, an engineer's attention to detail, and an interior designer's flair, that's our Robbie. And then I came along. The gadabout who wasted his time telling stories in taverns until he decided to take a turn behind the bar. I ran a speakeasy in New York during Prohibition," he added with a little grin. "Ned was *appalled*, and our parents didn't care for the idea—unnecessary risk, see? But even in a family with as many career paths as ours, soldiers, lawyers, teachers, a chef—even Peter, who spent about four centuries just fucking *wandering* to see what was out there— I'm the irresponsible one. The immature one. Sure, I ran a string of successful bars, and I've been brewing my own wares for ages, but I'm the one whose doings wouldn't make the family Christmas letter, if my parents did such a thing."

"I'm sorry," I said, and glanced around the room. "This place is nice."

"Thanks, but it's not even mine. Slim Matherson's the boss here—I'm just the second. He's a Fringer, you see," Adam explained, lowering his voice. "Great guy—I'm not at all complaining about Slim. But the people here in town want to feel safe. They want a bar run by one of their own. And even though I've been here for years, even though I built the brewery..." He shrugged. "People are polite to my face, but they don't invite me to dinner. Same for the rest of the family. We built this town, we protect it, we keep it provisioned, we teach their children, but we'll never fully fit in here. Well, Vivi gets a pass," he amended, "but she's a bloody coordinator. And she's got almost no talent. The only way Vivi could hurt you is with a hook to the jaw. The rest of us?" He held out his hand, and a red, basketball-sized flame bloomed to life in his palm. "A friendly monster is still a monster at the end of the day."

He drained his glass and filled it a third time while I considered that.

"It's not just me, not just my family," he continued after he'd slaked his thirst. "The kings don't fit because they're half-blooded sticks in the mud. Irem would fit except for the fact that the rules have shifted since her father ran the court, so now she's the odd one out. Toula seemed to do well at the grand magus gig, but she wasn't even a wizard—*that* was never going to last. Or look here in the settlement. You know Badger and Seamus?"

"We've met," I replied.

"All right. So you've got a coordinator who, as it turns out, is a scarily talented wizard, married to a lord from what was, until Irem took the throne, everyone's least favorite court. Those two spent the Mulligan years evacuating Fringers. They're heroes, no question. But if you get the chance, watch the way that everyone else here acts around them. I won't say they cross the street when they see those two coming—it's more subtle than that—but it's there. Not to mention the general disfavor for mixed couples," he added. "They didn't get together until after children were no longer a possibility, but no one in the Fringe likes the idea of producing witch-bloods."

"And yet, Amy Levey," I countered. "She's been making wands for the Arcanum for years."

Adam laughed. "Oh, *Amy*. Anyone with the slightest casting ability appreciates having her around for what she can craft, but she's a double witch-blood. And that's before you factor in Kip. Apparently, a good portion of the Fringe believes that witch-bloods should be celibate at all costs. I don't know which they think is worse, that she's in a loving marriage or that her partner's a Gray Lander. Those two were with Seamus and Badger during the Mulligan days, did more than their share for the Fringe, right, but if you only knew half the shit I've overheard…" He whistled. "And let's not forget my nephew. We don't even know how to classify the boy—he's unique. I don't think the Company wants him, but the average Fringer isn't too keen on having a guy around who can shift *and* do a bit of enchantment."

"Well," I muttered, "at least he's not alone in that respect anymore."

"No?"

I showed him my modest hand flame, and he smiled. "That's a beginning," he said. "May I offer you some advice that has nothing to do with magic?"

"Please."

"Find your clan. The people who celebrate you for what you are instead of criticizing you for what you're not. You're never going to fit in anywhere perfectly, but you'll find the places where the fit's close enough. And if Mal's reports from work are any indication, you're off to a solid start with the Team."

"That's because Ted assembled a group of misfits," I explained, reaching for my drink.

"So you're a bunch of puzzle pieces that don't slot in anywhere else. Have you ever thought that the lot of you fit *together*? You're a finished puzzle unto yourselves, if you'll forgive the metaphor."

As I considered that, Ted flashed into my mind's eye, standing at the conference table during our last meeting in the subbasement.

The Team is a family, and we protect our own.

"Maybe I've been blind," I said, swirling the last of my drink around the bottom of its glass.

"You're young," said Adam. "And another thing: go talk to your mum."

I grimaced and finished my drink.

"I didn't say it would be fun, but you two need to clear the air. Does she know about your dad?"

"Not to my knowledge, no."

"Well, if she knew you were wired a bit differently, then maybe she'd understand why you're so upset. It's worth a try. You do love her," he insisted. "You wouldn't hurt so badly if you didn't. Tell her what you've told me tonight— all of it, not just the polite bits. You might be surprised, and if nothing else, I think you'd feel better saying your piece."

It wasn't a terrible idea, but I was in no frame of mind to confront my mother that night. Besides, there was the matter of relieving my babysitters…and I'd have to take Aurie somewhere to sleep. I couldn't bring her back to Dad's place, not after the scene I'd caused, but where? I could ask Ros to send us to Afallon, I mused, or maybe there was a place we could camp…

"Poppy mentioned rooms upstairs," I said to Adam. "Would it be possible to borrow one? I need to pick up my daughter, and I'd rather not sleep in the park—"

Before he could answer, the front door slammed open,

and I turned on my stool in time to see my father run in. "*There* you are," he said, relief washing over his face. "I've been looking for you everywhere, but Lady Roslyn wouldn't tell me where you'd gone, and..." He faltered as he caught his breath. "I'm sorry, Frank. I'm so very sorry about tonight. I shouldn't have put you in that position—"

"Stop," I interrupted, raising my hands. "I'm the one who owes you an apology. My behavior tonight was—"

"Perfectly reasonable. Moon and stars, Engam threw you into a wall! How badly are you hurting?" he asked, drawing closer.

"After two Bloody Marys, not badly. But really, I'm sorry, I didn't mean to embarrass you like that—"

"I'm not *embarrassed*," he protested. "That bastard attacked you, and you defended yourself."

"I shouldn't have shifted like—"

"You are my *son*, Frank," he said, gripping my shoulders. "I don't give a damn what you look like, and I care even less for any opinion Engam's empty-headed friends might offer on the subject."

To my utter surprise, Dad hugged me.

To my own surprise, I hugged him back.

When we separated, he took the stool beside mine and turned to Adam. "Any chance of a beer?"

Adam poured another glass of the brew he'd been drinking and slid it across the bar. "And I assume that I will *not* be telling your uncle about your presence here tonight."

"Under the circumstances, I don't think he'd mind. Cheers," he said, and downed half.

"He approved this, did he?" Adam asked with a knowing smirk.

"Not in so many words, no," said Dad, "but I spoke with him just before I went in search of Frank, and he didn't say the settlement was off-limits, so..."

"You called Coileán?" I asked. "If Ros wasn't going to tell you where I was, then he certainly wouldn't."

"Oh, no, he attended the party," Dad explained. "Arrived not five minutes after you left. Engam was still tidying himself, but the hole in the wall was there, and I quickly told him how it came to be. By the time Engam returned from his room with fresh clothing, Coileán was *furious*. Glowing. Shouted at him so loudly, I'm surprised Engam still has eardrums. I won't give you a verbatim recitation, but the gist was that no one is to lay a finger on you, and the next person who tries will enjoy the hospitality of the king's cells."

"You're kidding."

"Not in the slightest. So then Coileán stormed off, and Engam returned to his room, probably for fresh trousers, and I went looking for you." He drank deeply again, then put the glass aside. "This is nice," he said to Adam. "What is it?"

"Last of my summer ale."

"Really?" He took a sip, pausing to assess the flavor more properly, then nodded. "Well done. Do you bottle that?"

"I could send you with a growler."

"A what?"

Adam pulled an amber-colored glass jug from beneath the bar, and Dad's eyes widened in comprehension. "Good man," he said appreciatively. "Frank, if you're ready, shouldn't we retrieve Aurie and go home?"

"We should," I replied, sliding off my stool, "but, uh…well, that's exactly what I need to do. Go home. To the mortal realm, I mean."

His brow furrowed. "Whatever for? You're safe here—"

"But the Team isn't safe, and they've been my home for most of my life. My family when I didn't really have one. I can't walk away from them now, when everything's falling apart. I mean, shit, they're camping at Artur's and hoping the Arcanum doesn't find them, and I can't just kick back here like nothing's wrong."

Dad finished his beer, then offered me a curt nod. "I understand. And if you're set on this course, then I'm coming with you."

"What—"

"I'm not a great bruiser, but I'm experienced, and I'm sure I pack a better punch than those wizard friends of yours do," he said before I could tell him no. "If you're jumping into that mess again, then let me help. If you'll have me, I mean."

My eyes began to blur, but I swallowed down the sudden tightness in my throat. "I appreciate that," I replied, "but could I convince you to keep Aurie instead? She'll be safe with you here."

"What about *your* safety?"

"Toula, Ed, Arnold, Marcus, and Artur are back there. If they can't manage a defense, I'll be shocked. And I'd sleep much better knowing Aurie had someone watching out for her here."

Dad stood and collected his takeaway beer. "If that's what you want, then I'll guard her with my life."

"Thank you," I said, then nodded to Adam. "And you. Sorry for being a downer."

He brushed it off with a grunt. "I told you, lad, I've heard worse. Be safe out there. Remind Mal to call his mum, eh?"

"Will do," I promised.

As I rolled my shoulders, wincing at my stiff muscles, Dad opened a gate to the meadow outside of Val's. "Come on, son," he said, giving me a nudge toward the rip in reality. "Let's put the little one to bed."

OCTOBER 4: BERT WOLD

"You said the trace would work!"

I cringed as the volume spiked on my bugs. Leander might have seemed charming to his friends and followers, but when he was peeved, he showed no restraint.

"It *did* work," Eva replied, a testy edge in her voice. "Perfectly. I double-checked at Kathleen's request."

"Then where are your daughters?"

"Either dead or out of the realm." She sounded far too unbothered by these options. "So now you get to spin it, sir. You could claim that Faerie's kidnapped Beth, or you could argue that they're harboring a fugitive."

"Fugitive?" he echoed.

"You ordered her back to Montana. She lied to your face. Maybe she hasn't *specifically* broken any laws, but they have no right to assist her in evading you."

"Damn right they don't," he muttered. "They've made a fool out of me for the last time, I swear it…"

"We thought you'd feel that way," said Francine after a pause. "So we brought you this."

I heard a rustling of paper, then Leander's voice. "What is it?"

"Eva and I have had a chance to study the sphere in your restricted storage. Our plan is feasible. Say the word, Grand Magus, and we'll seal off Faerie forever."

Holding my breath, I listened to the silent transmission, imagining Leander reading the cover sheet. How detailed was that document? Surely he'd send them away to read it at his leisure…

"You really believe you can do this?" Leander asked. "Seal off Faerie *and* the Gray Lands, but keep magic flowing here?"

"Without a doubt," said Eva. "The diary confirms it. Give us the green light, and you go down in history."

"Don't be a fool," I whispered from the safety of my office.

"How long do you need to set this in motion?" he asked them.

"Three days should do it," said Francine. "You'll have freed this realm by Sunday."

"Then let's not waste any more time on the runaway. Whatever resources you need, you'll have."

Though I was desperate to barge into Leander's office and confront the three of them then and there, I forced myself to wait until I heard Eva and Francine take their leave. I peeked out my door, making sure they'd gone, then marched down the corridor, rapped twice on Leander's door, and let myself in without an invitation.

Startled by the intrusion, he looked up from a thick sheaf of printer paper—the plans, I assumed—and frowned. "Bert? Is something on fire?"

"Not yet, but you're about to douse this realm in kerosene and strike a match," I said, crossing the room to his desk. Looming above him to the best of my limited ability, I slapped my hand onto the papers and said, "They're lying to you."

"Who?"

"Francine and Eva. About *that*," I added, giving the stack a good thump.

His expression darkened. "Were you *eavesdropping*?"

"Nothing of the sort," I fibbed. "You began shouting as I stepped out to wash my mug. I was concerned, and I overheard what they have in mind. Hear me, Leander," I said, not bothering with the pretense of respect. "Whatever they have planned is dangerous."

"You don't know that—"

"I know what happened in the '13 closure! If Faerie's sealed off, we lose magic. End of discussion. If those two are telling you otherwise, they're either delusional or lying through their teeth."

He huffed in the manner of put-upon youth confronted by their cautious elders. "The '13 closure's been studied. We've had almost fifty years to work out the kinks, and Francine and Eva think they've done it. No need to be jealous," he added with the ghost of a smirk.

I closed my eyes and pinched my nose, as the sight of his stupid face was bringing on a migraine. "Have you read Simon's diary in its entirety?"

"No," he admitted after a moment's hesitation.

"Well, I have. And I've even had occasion to discuss it with the man."

"The kid, you mean?"

"He's bloody brilliant," I snapped, "and if you hadn't run him out of the castle, you might have had your own sit-down. But that's not important right now. What I'm getting at is that I've studied the diary, and there is *nothing* in those pages that would result in severing the realms while keeping magic. It's not possible."

Leander regarded me incredulously. "*Or* it's possible, and you just aren't as smart as you think you are. This makes perfect sense—*hey!*"

I snatched the papers from beneath his hand and glanced over the top page of the plan. "Right. I'm counting one major thaumaturgical flaw in their work in the second paragraph and five references to the diary, none of them with actual citations. Speaking as someone who knows the diary, I don't remember anything about what they're supposedly referencing here. This is nonsense," I said, dropping the stack back onto his desk. "But as we know that Faerie *can* be sealed off, it's dangerous nonsense."

He propped his chin on his fist and stared at me. "Prove it."

"Gladly," I retorted, folding my arms. "Assume that I'm correct and the rubbish they're feeding you is just that. There is no possible semipermeable barrier between the realms, but there *is* a way to make an impermeable barrier. That's what the Arcanum faced in the '13 closure. Arc 1 had its backup power supply, but the wards here were reliant on the raw magic built in and came within forty-eight hours of catastrophic failure. This place was almost revealed to the mundane world, and that was after only a few days without magic. What if your two friends accidentally create a true barrier? Do you want to be the grand magus who deprived us of magic for a week? A month? A year? Longer? *Forever?*"

As my voice rose, the boy glared at me. "Faerie is a threat to every man, woman, and child in this realm. One we've tolerated for far too long. The way you're talking, if I didn't know any better, I might question your loyalties—"

"Bollocks," I spat, which shut him up. "I know what they're capable of—I was held captive by faeries, for God's sake!"

His head tilted in query, as if he were a confused dog.

"The end of my spectacular tenure with that chain," I said, pointing to his jewelry. "Rogue faeries and Russell fucking Mulligan. Those lunatics were prepared to kill Faerie herself to get what they wanted..." I sighed as the signs of his confusion deepened. "Ros Bolin's predecessor. Surely you were taught about Faerie's consciousness?"

"I know about that," he muttered defensively.

"Good. Then you know that if she is killed, that realm dies, and we all lose magic. Russell was willing to risk that to become grand magus. Don't lecture me about what treason sounds like."

I gestured and whispered a word of focus, and one of the chairs from the small conference room adjoining Leander's office rolled through the door and behind me. Taking a seat, I leaned back and crossed my legs. "There is no one in the Arcanum, much less this castle, who better understands what you're going through than I do. I *was* you, Leander," I said, and held up a hand to cut him off before he could argue with me. "I was a young man elevated to the highest office in this organization because I was talented and had the proper pedigree. And as I sit here with you tonight, I can tell you that I didn't know shit back then. Oh, I *thought* I knew everything—I had grand plans for the Arcanum. I was going to either send whatever witches we produced to Faerie or mind-wipe them and make them someone else's problem, did you know that? Absorb the Minor Arcanum by whatever means necessary. Generally puff up my chest and strut around like I had all the answers."

Shaking my head at my younger self's idiocy, I said, "I get it, kid. You're young, you've been given incredible authority without the proper training to handle it well, you feel the eyes of your elders on you, judging you, and you're desperate to earn their respect. Every setback feels like a disaster because your ledger is still so blank, and you're terrified that someone will wake up one morning, realize this has all been a terrible misunderstanding, and demand your chain. I had those nightmares, too," I told him. "The insecurity is awful, but that sick feeling you've got—that's a warning sign. You may put on the best of façades, but *you* know that you're treading deep, dark water. I felt that—I still feel it sometimes, in all honesty. Anyone who's not an utter fool second-guesses himself. Listen," I continued, unfolding myself and leaning toward his desk, "when I was in your shoes, I was too proud to take advice—"

"I'm taking advice!" he protested.

"Not *good* advice. You listen to the people who flatter you and tell you you're this brilliant, messianic leader, here to wipe away the stain of your tainted predecessor," I said with mock gravitas. "I did the same damn thing. They told me much of what they're telling you, only it was about

Arnold. At least I had sense enough to listen to some of what he said. You either ignore or remove anyone who suggests that your plans aren't wonderful, and that's such a *stupid* mistake. Not everyone who pushes back wants to see you fall!"

Leander's face, quick to flush, glowed scarlet in the lamplight. "You're on Pavli's side! You've never liked me!"

"I'm on the *Arcanum's* side," I countered. "Which now means supporting you and helping you make wise decisions. Do I like and respect Toula? Absolutely, and I'm not going to lie and say otherwise. But even if you stepped aside tomorrow, I doubt the Council would ask her back. You're the grand magus, my thoughts on your selection are irrelevant, and my job now is to assist you in doing the best thing for all of us. That doesn't mean blind agreement."

His scowl took at least five years off his face. "Francine and Eva said—"

"Exactly what you want to hear. You want to take major action, something with flash. Something that will cement your legacy and prevent anyone from questioning your fitness for office ever again." I cocked an eyebrow, waiting for him to deny it, but Leander kept his silence. "Well, that's exactly what they're dangling in front of you. I'm sure it sounds lovely, coming from those two snakes, but you're jumping at a proposal that hasn't been vetted by the full Council—magi with decades of experience in practical and theoretical thaumaturgy. That joke of a proposal they've given you wouldn't withstand scrutiny, I guarantee it." Softening my voice, I said, "A wise man would step back, offer the proposal to the Council, and see what problems we can find."

"They're sure they can make this work," he argued. "And they wouldn't lie to me—I'm the one who freed them, remember? They owe me their loyalty."

"Those two are loyal only to themselves. You're useful to them, Leander. That's all. And if you knew half of what

Eva allowed to happen to her elder daughter, you wouldn't leave Beth anywhere near her." When he didn't immediately object, I said, "Come on, has Eva shown the slightest genuine concern for Beth?"

He offered me no response, which was answer enough.

"More importantly," I continued, "I don't know what game they're playing, but they *cannot* deliver on this promise to you. If Simon were here, he'd tell you that attacking Faerie was one of the most idiotic things he ever did. Hubris cost him everything."

"Try to get your facts right," said Leander. "I'm not *attacking* Faerie. We're just going to wall it off."

"Which isn't possible if you want to keep magic flowing!" Taking a deep breath, I tried to stop myself from shouting at the boy. "Let's say I'm right, they try to make the barrier semipermeable, and we instead end up severed from Faerie. How the hell are they meant to do the same with Conota? Have you ever closed a gate into that realm?"

"No…"

"It's bloody hard! You're fighting against an outflow of dark magic, and the patches we make at the weak points between the realms degrade over time. So let's say that we're cut off from Faerie. That leaves us wide open to Conota and anything that comes out of that realm…and defenseless. You want to fight a troll without magic? A fucking dragon? Believe me, the wild ones aren't anything like Frank." I stood again and leaned over the desk. "Are you so desperate to prove yourself that you're willing to risk the future of magic and this realm? Because if that's the case, you need to step back and think about the oath you swore."

I straightened but kept my gaze fixed on his uncertain eyes. "You're *young*, Leander. You have time to prove that the Council was right to select you—and you do that not with war, not with mad attempts at grand gestures, but with diplomacy. Take your time, listen to those of us who've been in the game, and whatever you do, don't trust promises from Eva and Francine. If that's the best they can offer you," I said, pointing to the proposal, "then they're taking you for a fool. You're better than that."

I waited then, hoping that something had hit home for Leander. He could block his thoughts—I knew damn well not to even attempt to pry—but I saw the unease in his expression as he regarded me.

"Thank you for your counsel, Bert," he finally said. "I need to get some work done."

"Of course," I replied, and waved my chair back into the other room. "Should you ever want to talk, my door is always open to you. I know how heavy that chain can be and what loneliness the office entails."

"Appreciate it."

I nodded and left him, praying I'd done some good. Hurrying back to my desk, I triggered the bugs again and listened in.

He was already on the phone, and he'd left it on speaker mode. "There's a problem with the theory in the second paragraph of your proposal," I heard him say. "Do you want to look that over?"

"Just a moment," came Eva's voice. "Let me pull that up…"

A minute later, as I twitched in my chair, she returned to the line. "Yes, sir, I see what you're saying. *Ooh*, that's embarrassing. I hate typos."

To my surprise, he sounded relieved. "That's all it is?"

"Absolutely. I'll send you the corrected copy momentarily. Wow, that was clumsy of me—thanks for catching it," she added with a little laugh. "I'd hate for this proposal to go the Archives with a flaw like that. And it *will* go to the Archives. We're about to make history, Grand Magus."

"Sunday?"

"Plan for Saturday. We'll call you as soon as we're ready to go. We'll need your skill to pull this off, obviously."

"Good. I'll see you then," he replied, and rung off.

I silenced the bugs in disgust and packed my computer into my satchel. If Leander was going to risk our world, then I was bloody well going to spoil his surprise.

Eschewing the long walk back to my flat, I made myself a gate, then double-checked the privacy wards on the place and the doors before pulling out my mobile and ringing Arnold.

"Everything all right?" he asked in greeting.

"No, and let's keep this brief. I'm at home."

"What's going on?"

"Short version," I said, perching on the arm of my couch, "Eva and Francine are about to try something that could end magic here as we know it."

I heard nothing but silence for a few seconds, and then Arnold said, "Might you flesh that out a bit?"

So I did, murmuring to him every detail I could remember. When I came up for air, he said, "Be outside the wards at three in the morning, down by the road. I'll meet you."

I might have been one of the Arcanum's least effective grand magi, but I was wizard enough to get around without dealing with the inconvenience of guarded doors.

At five minutes to three, I opened a gate just inside the barrier ward and slipped through in the predawn chill, my satchel over my chest and a duffel in hand. A quick construction temporarily disabled the alarm on the system, and then, forcing power into a concentrated spot in the active ward like a laser, I cut open a hole large enough for me to duck through. I resealed it from the outside, removed all trace of my handiwork, and hurried through the camouflaging ward toward the deserted road.

Precisely on time, a gate flashed open, and I released the breath I hadn't realized I was holding. Casting one last look at the castle, I slipped through the rift, expecting to land on Afallon.

But I was nowhere near the island. Rather, I found myself surrounded by the stone walls of Coileán's candlelit office, which grew darker as the gate sealed behind me. Turning, I saw a fire laid and crackling…and there, sitting on the couches before it, were both kings, Toula, Arnold, and Eadwig.

"Change of plans?" I asked.

"You can't go to Afallon," Toula explained. "Your parents would provide an easy trace—"

"And I bet they're just in *love* with the new regime," said Ros as her glowing form manifested. "What's up, Bertie?"

"Nothing good," I replied, dropping my duffel bag. "Do you want the quick version first?"

"Oh, I already got it," she said with a grin. "There are no secrets from me here, you know that. But skip the synopsis and get to the meat." Turning to the others, she folded her arms and said, "You're going to want to hear this."

OCTOBER 5: EADWIG

In some respects, I pitied the guards on the castle gate that morning. They weren't magus-level casters, merely average wizards who'd shown aptitude for bolts and shields under pressure. The few with whom I'd had occasion to speak had been pleasant, or at least professionally courteous.

They hadn't asked for *this*. Judging by the looks on their faces, not a few of them were engaging in silent, frantic reconsideration of their career choices.

I doubted they were concerned about me. I'd come unarmed, and unless Leander had shown my picture around after my departure, the six men watching us from the window above the gate had no idea who I might be. *Coileán*, however, was a different matter, and the fact that he was producing a brilliant white corona suggested imminent violence.

Honestly, being that close to him set me on edge, and we were on the same damn side. Wanda probably would have deemed my discomfort a reaction to past trauma, but I thought of it as nothing more than common sense.

"Here's what's going to happen," Coileán told the guards after one of them squeaked out a demand for our business there. "You're going to disarm the barrier ward, open the gate, let us through, and take us to Leander, *now*. If you don't like that plan, then I'll blast through your ward, through your gate, and through any of you brave gentlemen who stand in our way, and then I'll find Leander. Of course, if we go that route, I might be cross by the time I reach him…"

The bright glow of the ward dimmed and fizzled, and the door beside the ceremonial gate opened remotely.

"Good call," he said, grinning up at the guards, and marched through.

We'd decided to come alone. Toula had opted out, claiming that the look of an ousted grand magus returning with muscle wasn't going to improve the situation, while Val had agreed to stay behind so as not to overly intimidate the boy. The goal was a show of strength sufficient to grab his attention, not a show of force warranting escalation from the Arcanum. As I watched five of the guards file out of the gate tower—the man who'd won the right to remain at his post must have been muttering prayers of thanksgiving—I sized them up.

Easy, whispered Simon in the back of my thoughts. *They're undertrained boys. You've nothing to fear.*

The part of me that was seventeen disagreed with his assessment but deferred to Simon's experience. This was his moment, anyway.

The guards' apparent leader, who seemed all of thirty-five and exceedingly outclassed, cleared his throat. "We, ehm, will ask the Grand Magus if he—"

His thought ended in a strangled squeal as I opened a gate onto the executive wing. "That wasn't a request," I said. "You may accompany us, if you like, or we'll see ourselves in."

Though I suspect they'd have preferred the other alternative, two took the lead ahead of us, while the other three brought up the rear. As they fell into formation, I glanced back at them and murmured, "If we were here to kill Leander, don't you think we'd have brought a larger force?"

They didn't say anything, but the pointed glances they shot my glowing companion told me enough.

The executive wing was nearly silent, the offices empty, but the burble of voices behind the conference room's doors guided us to the target. As we neared, Coileán asked the guards on point, "Would you like to announce us?"

Their leader, who was without question not being adequately compensated for his job, knocked thrice and cracked open one of the doors. "Ehm…sorry to interrupt, sir," he began, his voice breaking like mine had only a year before. "You have…visitors."

"Tell them I'm busy," said Leander. "Or hadn't you noticed the Council?"

A few titters rose within the room, and as the guard slumped, Coileán patted his shoulder. "It's all right, that's good enough," he whispered, then brushed past him into the room.

The laughter stopped immediately, and I smiled at the sudden hush as I joined Coileán. Leander turned in his chair, saw us, and froze for a few seconds before putting on a brave face. "So glad you could join us," he said, projecting confidence, though I caught the twitching in the corner of his eye. "I was wondering, have you seen Bert Wold lately? Can't seem to find him anywhere. Or Beth Stanhope? Would you like to tell her poor mother where she's hiding?" he asked, gesturing to Eva. "Seems to me like Faerie's picked up a bad habit of taking people who don't belong to them."

"I assure you," said Coileán, "that I'm holding no one against his or her will, and neither is Val, so let's cut the crap, you idiot."

Leander's face flamed, but none of the magi leapt to his defense.

Pointing to the stack of paper on the table in front of Leander, Coileán asked, "Is that Eva and Francine's grand plan to sever the realms? Oh, I'm sorry," he said, looking around the table, "did I spoil the big announcement? Were you going to make a production out of this? My bad."

"Allow me," I muttered before he could further goad the boy, and Coileán yielded the floor with a nod. "Bert gave me the gist of this proposal," I began, focusing on Leander.

"You heard him!" he shouted, pointing at me while he searched the table for support. "Treason! That right there is *treason*! Bert's as dirty as—"

"Bert is trying to avert disaster," I snapped. "And since your precious plan is supposedly built on *my* work, do afford me the courtesy of a rebuttal."

Francine started to interrupt, but a woman in a dark headscarf spoke over her. "I count numerous references to the diary in the first pages," she said, flipping through her own sheaf of paper. "Who would know that book better than its author? Let him speak."

"*That* is not Simon Magus, Nour!" she protested. "That is—"

"Close enough for the present purposes," I said, and sent her chair flying into a tapestry with a casual flick of my fingers. The blow knocked the breath from her, and as she struggled to free herself, I warned her, "I can do this all day."

Leander watched with faint disgust as Francine fought me, then huffed, "Just say whatever it is that's so damn important and get out of my castle."

"*Your* castle?" said Coileán. "Wow, I never knew you got the place when you got the chain. Guess someone forgot to tell Toula...Bert...Arnold..."

Releasing Francine, I marched to the table, and the magi made room. "As I understand it, your plan is to seal Faerie off while maintaining a flow of magic into this realm. If those two claim there's support for this nonsense in my writings, they are either stupid or lying. What they're suggesting to you is impossible. Either the border can be breached or it cannot—there's no in-between stage. Now," I continued, trying to pick the most reasonable magi out of the ring, "that being said, there *is* a way to seal the border. I wasn't awake for the closure fifty years ago, but some of you surely were."

"I was at ground zero," Coileán offered. "You want to talk about terrifying, children? Welcome to a world in which magic is fading with every second and you have no idea how to bring it back. That's not a scenario I'd care to revisit."

Some of the eldest magi nodded along with him, and I pushed on. "Toula's notes of the event would be the best record of how it was accomplished—I never wrote about that. I did put down some theoretical musings as to how one might attack Faerie's consciousness," I admitted, "but I never acted on them, even on my worst day, because I understood how risky that was."

"Why *did* you have to write that?" Coileán muttered under his breath.

I turned from the table long enough to flash an annoyed glare his way. "You do understand the concept of a diary, yes? It was never meant for public consumption. I mean, for God's sake, had I known it would be venerated a thousand years later, I wouldn't have chronicled my sex life!"

Returning to the matter at hand—and feeling a flush creep into my face at the thought of Simon's less academic jottings—I said to the magi, "Had I found a way to safely attempt what your colleagues are promising, I'd have tried it. I was willing to murder the Three in their sleep—sealing Faerie would have been far preferable. But every theoretical avenue, every thaumaturgical hypothetical, led me to conclude that Faerie is either open or closed. If you attempt to seal it off, the closest you'll come to success is something like the closure fifty years back. You'll lose magic. You will *not* be able to seal Conota under these conditions because the magic necessary to power that spell will dry up in a matter of days. So there you'll be, every spell failing, every installation visible, and not a damn thing you can do to reverse it unless you build a lock into the spell like the one Toula wrote of. If you can't break it, you'll end magic in this realm and open yourselves to an invasion from Conota. That's all I came to tell you," I said, looking down at Leander. "Don't be a fool."

"Look, kid," Coileán interjected, "I realize we have our differences. Val and I agree wholeheartedly that what Irem's done is wrong, and we've told her as much. Ros, I think, finally got through to her about not taking changelings, but it may be a little while before she cracks down on her court. It's not in her nature to take orders. That said, I assure you that if there are any further kidnappings, you'll have our full support in getting your people back." When Leander's expression didn't change, he said, "Honestly, Irem is a pain in the ass, but we're working on it. We're not your enemy," he insisted. "Work with us, and we'll all come through this intact. But don't play with spells you barely understand in some misguided attempt to one-up us. You're not going to get what you want, and you might do far more harm than good."

Leander waited, and when Coileán gestured toward him, he said, "Is that all? Have you interrupted my meeting enough for one day?"

"I thought the warning of grave peril might warrant the interruption," Coileán countered.

The boy snickered. "'Grave peril,' he says. And I should believe you...why, exactly?"

"Because everything I'm saying to you is supported by that guy right there," he replied, pointing to me. "The best wizard in this room."

"You know what I think?" Leander replied, propping his chin on his fist as he turned to consider me. "I think you're just incapable of accepting that there are wizards smarter than you—pretending you're Simon Magus, of course. People who took the basics you left and built on them. I've read this proposal twice," he said, patting the stack of paper. "It's a work of *genius*. We're going to accomplish something you never dreamed could be possible. We'll still have magic, but those vermin will never trouble us again," he added, cutting his eyes toward Coileán. "Neither from Faerie nor from the Gray Lands. Nor you, I imagine, since you seem to have thrown your lot in with them. Now, if you simply cannot contemplate a way in which the plan works, then maybe you're not so smart after all."

As I looked around the table, trying to decide if enough of the Council would rise up to defy him—if any among them feared Leander's plans more than they feared their own dismissal—I heard Coileán's voice in my mind: *We could kill him.*

Wouldn't stop Francine and Eva, I thought.

We could kill them, too. Val would approve.

And prove ourselves the villains. If you have any hope for peace with the Arcanum, you can't simply walk in and execute magi.

Simon liked our odds of success—sure, we were vastly outnumbered, but he was confident that we could make the kills and still escape intact. I was less sure, and when I reached out to Coileán again, I sensed a similar calculus in the top of his thoughts. *Not the time*, I insisted.

He nodded, and we turned to leave.

"Not so fast," Leander snapped. "I don't recall dismissing you."

An invisible hand yanked him from his seat and threw him across the room, and he slumped to the rug, knocked cold from the blow.

"Does anyone else have any thoughts?" Coileán asked, cracking his knuckles.

No one uttered a peep.

"When he comes to, tell your little grand magus that if he gets cute with me again, the gloves will come off," said Coileán, and ushered me out of the room.

He opened a gate at the edge of the barrier ward, then punched through it with enough force to blacken the system for several meters in all directions. As the guards cried out in alarm, Coileán led us through and headed for the road. His corona dimmed, but I could see the frustration on his face as I walked beside him.

"You really don't think it can be done?" he murmured.

"No," I said firmly. "I gave it plenty of thought. So

whether they try to seal the realm off or attack Ros, the result will be the same."

"The mortal realm can kiss magic goodbye."

"Precisely. Which is why I leave you here. I've got work to do."

He frowned. "You don't want to come back and debrief Val with me?"

"No. In case those fools ruin magic, I need to fix Quinn while I still have time. If we lose magic…"

"She's dead," he finished. "Right. Uh…well, good luck, then. I'd help you if I could, but I don't think you want me meddling—"

The chirping of his mobile interrupted him, and he pulled it from his pocket. "Val? Hi, we're just leaving…"

I opened a gate back to Afallon but waited, troubled by the deepening frown on Coileán's face. When he put the mobile away, I asked, "Is everything all right?"

"Nope," he muttered. "Seems there's trouble at the settlement."

I groaned. "Irem?"

"Her people, at least. I've got to go." Sighing, he ripped open his own gate and departed without a backward glance.

OCTOBER 5: COILEÁN

While I'd aimed my gate at Val's office, Ros had better ideas.

I stepped through to find myself in a field, faced with Val, Kiet, Mina, and what appeared to be a mixed group of our two courts' guards. At first glance, I wondered why my people had come, but a quick glance at my niece reminded me of my place in this arrangement. Long before she became my captain, she'd been Val's second, and when *her* captain asked her to come with an army...

Well, at least I wasn't planning to go to war against Val.

"Where are we?" I asked, looking for a landmark. I spotted a crowd of people in the distance, along with the dome of an active barrier ward that I'd never seen before.

"A short walk from the settlement," said Val, pointing south. "We're between their territory and the piq forest."

"Thought it best to get a plan together before we attacked," Mina offered.

"*Are* we attacking?" I asked them. "Is this a skirmish, or what?"

Val's mouth tightened. "More than a skirmish. We've been in communication with Nico, and he estimates about four hundred of them amassing outside the wall. All full-blooded, from what he can see."

"Moon and stars," I muttered, rubbing my head. "We don't need this today."

"No luck with Leander?"

"Should have dropped that little shit out a window." Looking over my two dozen troops, I said, "This isn't going to be enough to stop four hundred faeries on a spree unless you and I step in. What's Nico's status?"

"He and the Stowe boys are coordinating the defense," Kiet offered. "They put together that barrier ward, but I can't vouch for its strength."

"And if the crowd outside gets restless, that thing's coming down," I said. "Right. *Shit.* Does anyone have a decent plan in mind?"

A burst of light out of the corner of my eye drew my attention to my left, where Ros had manifested in a fuchsia hoodie and dark leggings. "You're not killing Irem, so get that idea out of your minds," she warned. "Technically, she's within the rules."

"But the settlement!" Mina protested. "Even if she's not attacking it herself, she gave her people license to do so!"

"True," said Ros with a shrug. "And there is nothing in the old agreement prohibiting her from taking action against the settlement."

"Your *grandparents* live there, or have you forgotten?" I asked.

She gave me a look that would have sent a weaker faerie running. "Of course I haven't forgotten," she snapped. "I want her and her people stopped, okay? But I have to consider the rules. If she hasn't broken our agreement, then I can't take direct action against her."

"Migraine?" Val suggested.

"She's had one for the last week. I think she's acclimating, unfortunately. Now," she continued, eying Val and me, "even though I'm not getting involved, you two have my blessing to stop the assault on the settlement by any means necessary, *short of killing Irem.* And if you're smart, you won't kill her people. Don't give her reason to start a war, guys. You know she'd be all over that."

Val scowled in thought, but as I considered Ros's dark, worried eyes, an idea occurred to me. "You have access to all of Kura's memories, yes?"

She nodded. "Anything in particular you wanted to see? Siege tactics?"

"No, not that. Do you remember…or rather, have you seen her memories of when Ellie went a little mad?"

"*Oh*, yeah, but Irem's nowhere near the point of weakness that Ellie reached. If that's what you were hinting about…"

"After that. When Ellie slept it off a year, Kura empowered Rufus to run the court in her stead."

Ros glanced skyward as if watching an invisible screen. "Yeah, she did. He filled in nicely. Of course, considering that Dr. Stowe has now defected from that court…"

"Okay, what about the time that Oberon invaded and bound me? Kura empowered Aid to come to my rescue, right?"

"Yeah…" she allowed, suspicion shading her tone.

"So doesn't that mean there's precedent for the realm to empower a fourth person in time of trouble?"

As Ros wavered, Val pressed her. "Ellie respected the Fringe. You know she wouldn't want to see them attacked in their own homes. She and Coileán promised them protection here, and if we don't do something quickly, they will be hurt or killed."

"I know, I *know*," said Ros, "but in light of the rules—"

"You're the realm!" he cried. "Damn the rules. It's your game—change them!"

"But I can't just—"

"*Roslyn*."

Powerful though she was, Ros had spent too many years under Val's tutelage not to cringe at the edge in his voice. "Okay. I've got an idea. But you two are almost certainly going to need a bigger army," she said, and vanished.

"She's right," said Val, and turned to Kiet. "Put in a call to whoever's at the villa. We need guards and volunteers alike."

"What he said," I told Mina. "I'll defer to experience."

As the two of them stepped aside, a new gate opened, disgorging my little brother. "Hey, sorry," Aiden said to Val, "I got your message, but I was in the middle of a system update, and Joey and Georgie are still out at sea. It'll be at least a couple of hours before they get back here unless you need them now and want to work out a gate. Oh, hey, Coileán," he added with a weary wave. "Any luck with the Arcanum?"

"Nope," I replied. "And are we bringing in aerial reinforcements?" I asked Val.

"I thought it couldn't hurt," he explained. "Aiden, call your sister and Sam and see if they can't convince some of the dragons to stop by. Their presence may be sufficient to end this…"

His thought trailed off as the settlement's barrier ward flared with power.

"Interesting," I mused. "That can't be Badger's doing…"

Val and I seemed to reach the same conclusion simultaneously, and I grinned as I saw his expression shift. "Rufus," I said. "He's in there, isn't he?"

"The only person in the settlement experienced with the boost," Val concurred. "That should buy us time to gather our forces."

A muffled beeping from Aiden's pocket signaled an incoming call, and he pulled out his phone and tapped the screen without so much as a glance. "Sorry, it's not a good time…oh, uh, hi, Poppy."

I could hear a distorted squawk of agitation when he pulled the phone away from his ear, and he hit the speaker button.

"—and for *once*, it would be nice if someone gave us a little warning before hitting him! Now, what the hell is going on?"

"Poppy, it's Coileán," I said, taking the phone from Aiden. "Did Ros give Rufus a boost?"

"He's *glowing*, so yeah, I'd say so. I'd ask him, you

know, but he's a little preoccupied."

"Okay. It's for the settlement's defense," I explained. "We're putting together a force out here to fight back Irem's people—"

"Oh, good. I was wondering when you were going to lend a fucking hand."

"Never change, Poppy," I said, and hung up. Passing the phone back to my brother, I waited until Mina and Kiet rejoined our huddle, then said, "Rufus has the defense for the moment, but gather your people quickly."

"We need to keep this as non-lethal as possible," Val added. "Don't give Irem a reason to escalate this conflict."

The captains seemed to deflate at the directive. "Non-lethal is harder," Mina replied, grimacing.

"And I have every confidence in your abilities," he replied.

She sighed and fired off a halfhearted salute. "*Yes*, Captain," she muttered, and waved to her guards. "Let's move closer. The others will join us presently."

Val, Aiden, and I held back as Mina and Kiet shifted their people toward the settlement. "I'll go call Hel," Aiden offered, and slipped off in pursuit of dragons.

I looked at Val, who folded his arms and stared at the ward in the distance. "Going to be a long day," I murmured.

He nodded. "And one way or another, I fear there will be blood before this is over."

OCTOBER 5: EADWIG

"I'd feel so much better about this if we had actual equipment," said John, watching from the corridor with a sandwich as those with younger, stronger backs rearranged the den.

"Equipment would fry," Bee reminded him. "Come on, where's your spirit of adventure?"

"I think I lost that in an OR about twenty years ago." He considered the patient, who'd taken a chair as far from the shaded windows as she could hide. The sun wasn't quite down yet, but time was against us, and so Quinn had endured an early wakeup. As she sipped her breakfast, she caught her grandfather's eyes on her and gave him a little wave from her shadowy corner.

I forced myself to eat on the doctors' orders. Though I had no appetite, none of us could predict how long the procedure would take, especially if we experienced complications—and since the object of our work was Quinn, I could only imagine what we might find once we began. More than that, my stomach rebelled with the knowledge of what I would need to accomplish to give this process any chance of success.

Even Simon wasn't thrilled with the plan.

John, Bee, Daisy, Maria, Marcus, Artur, and I had talked it through that morning, running step by step until we were familiar with our ungainly choreography. It didn't help that only six of us could see magic—John was insensate to it, and though we'd be using a visualization spell to show the state of Quinn's systems, he would have no idea of the condition of the constructions working to reanimate them. Without his usual instruments, he'd be depending upon Bee's wife and unofficial nurse, Daisy, for cues.

The plan, in its simplest form, was as follows. Bee and Daisy, having pilfered bags and vials of supplies from the castle infirmary upon our departure, would start IV lines into Quinn with an electrolyte solution. Assuming her body didn't immediately reject it—we'd as yet had no opportunity to test that—I would then take over her respiration and circulation, building a spell to work her lungs and move blood through her body. I knew the general route from my studies with John, but controlling so many delicate movements in real time would take nearly all of my concentration. I would have to pump her heart myself at first, but with luck, the pressure would build. I would then manually trigger the first electrical impulses in her heart, and if my calculations were correct, I could maintain that rhythm until Quinn's own body could take over.

I hoped.

John's master plan had been to fit Quinn with a mechanical pacemaker, but there was no time left to create one. Bee certainly hadn't found a spare in the infirmary, and she had balked at his last-minute idea of creating a sensitive piece of electronic equipment with magic. "It would probably die a quick death," she'd explained, "and then so would Quinn."

Magic it was.

While we established breathing and blood circulation, the faeries on hand would act as standby support. They couldn't interfere with my work—they couldn't cast, while I certainly couldn't enchant—but if Quinn's other systems went into sudden collapse, they might be able to help her under Bee's or John's direction. Finally, once Quinn seemed sufficiently stable, I'd call upon one of the faeries to overload the enchantment on her, and we would see whether she could live on her own.

In the meantime, I tried to eat my sandwich and silently prayed that I wasn't about to kill her.

As the makeshift surgery took form, I abandoned my plate and joined Quinn on the other side of the room. "Hey," she said, and took a final slurp of blood. "You look nervous."

"You aren't?"

"I'm okay."

I suspected that wasn't entirely true. John, Bee, and I had awakened Quinn in her wine cellar shelter in the midafternoon to explain our predicament. If the Arcanum did something sufficiently stupid, then we risked being cut off from Faerie and magic. With every moment we spent in that state, our available supply would decrease, and we would soon reach the point that we'd lack sufficient magic to run the constructions necessary to save Quinn's life. Within days, she would be dead.

Instead, at Frank's suggestion and Marcus's pushing, we were making plans to evacuate from the mortal realm, just in case. Better to have everyone safe with magic available than leave people stranded with the results of the Arcanum's grand experiment. But if Quinn was to accompany us, we had to break her curse.

John wasn't happy with this reality for a variety of reasons—fear for his granddaughter's safety, a dislike of being rushed into questionable surgery, well-founded doubt about my physiological expertise—but he told Quinn that this was the best option available. "It's up to you, honey," he'd concluded, holding her hands as she sat on her cot, "but if you're willing to try, then we'll do our best."

She'd smiled then, though even in the near darkness of the room, I'd seen the flicker of fear in her gray eyes. "Don't think we have much of a choice."

"There's always a choice," he'd insisted.

"Then I choose to go down fighting."

As Quinn put her tumbler aside that evening, hopefully for the final time, I said, "Bee and John are leading this. With luck, they'll prevent me from doing anything too stupid."

She patted my knee. "Whatever happens, thanks for trying. I appreciate everything you've done over the last year."

"Unless I kill you," I muttered.

"Come on, man, I'm already dead," she countered, shrugging. "I'm a consciousness in a quasi-operational meat suit. If you can get the body working again, that'll be a bonus."

I searched her face, but the fear I'd seen appeared to have vanished. "You say that, but you're very young," I murmured.

She smiled. "I've seen more than most. Learned some crazy shit. Maybe done a little good, on balance. If this is the end of the road for me…like my grandma used to say, you're never guaranteed the sunrise. I get that now," she said more softly. "I mean, I sure would love to see one of those again, but I'm not going to haunt you forever if this doesn't go well."

"You're at peace," I marveled.

"Something like that," said Quinn. "Don't get me wrong, I'd probably be puking my guts out with nerves right now if my meat suit still performed that trick, but I'm okay. I am." She studied me in turn, then said, "You're afraid of death."

It wasn't a question, and I saw no reason to lie to her. "I'm afraid of what awaits me on the other side."

She chuckled gently. "Well, then, if I end up seeing it for myself tonight, I'll put in a good word for you."

"Thank you, but I hardly warrant commendation."

"Ed," she said with an incredulous lift of her brow, "you've spent most of the last year trying to fix me. You didn't owe me that, but you've done it anyway." She leaned back in her chair and linked her hands behind her head.

"You know, I never planned to be a damsel in distress, a creature of the night, or someone's research project, but…you've tried. So yeah, if there's a giant ledger waiting in the Great Beyond, I'll make sure you get credit."

"Sun's down," said Artur, interrupting us. "Shall we?"

Quinn stood and offered her a curt nod. "It's been real, folks. Let's get this party started."

The den's furniture had been moved to the walls, giving way to a padded table that put Quinn at roughly the height of my waist when she stretched out. As she made herself comfortable, she looked at John and grinned. "Are the pajamas okay? You're not going to make me wear a paper gown for this, are you?"

"You're just fine, Quinnie," he replied, though from the tension in his voice, I wasn't sure whether he was intending to reassure her or himself.

"But I do appreciate the T-shirt," said Bee, approaching the table with several lengths of clear tubing and a syringe. "Right, before I try to strike oil, let's see what we're working with."

Pulling her wand from the back of her trousers, she whispered the visualization spell into action. A bluish, translucent projection of Quinn appeared above her body, twitching with every move she made. Bee whispered again, and the image changed, first to reveal bones, then to her vascular network.

"As expected, no heartbeat," she announced, but frowned. "Blood volume appears low. Quinn, didn't you just eat?"

"It doesn't go into her veins," I pointed out. "Not directly, at least. The effect spreads throughout her body"—Quinn's face had taken on a slightly ruddy cast—"but the blood she consumes doesn't circulate. I don't know how the curse does that, and she never expels any waste product. It seems as if the enchantment simply consumes whatever she feeds it."

The doctor muttered something that might have been

"*Faeries*," then rotated Quinn's arm into position and began pressing around the bend. "I'm going to numb the area, dear," she told the patient, "as this may take a few attempts. Your veins seem deep, and that's not the least of the problems."

While John took up a position on the other side of the table, distracting Quinn while Bee repeatedly tried to find a vein, I considered the projection. "If her blood volume is low…" I murmured.

"We're about to give her fluids," said Daisy, showing me the mixing bowl of thawing IV bags. Having spent the last weeks in the freezer, they had been defrosting all afternoon in warm water. She pulled one free, read the label, then hung it from the metal pole Maria had made and dried it with a towel. "Saline first, right?" she asked Bee.

"If I can ever…okay, *yes*," she said, and sighed with relief as her needle struck its target. Quickly taping it in place, she adjusted the short bit of tubing to her liking, then brought another set of tubing to the IV bag and connected them. "Basin," she murmured.

Daisy held a soup bowl at the ready, and soon, a slow stream of droplets emerged from the end of the tube. Catching my bemusement, she explained, "Bleeding the line. You want to remove the air before you hook this to the patient."

"You've studied this?" I asked her.

"Hands-on training only," she replied, "and just for emergencies. My real training is as a speech pathologist, but when you're living with the castle's only doctor and the medics aren't available…"

"You're doing perfectly, love," Bee said, and screwed the line into Quinn's tube. She made an adjustment to a dial midway along the line, then watched the liquid drip from its bag. "Setting this at a decently high infusion rate. I think the vein can take it, but watch for me, please."

"On it," said Daisy. "How long?"

"This bag should take at least twenty-five minutes. We'll follow with a second one, then the electrolyte solution. Maria, get some blankets, will you?"

"I'm not cold," said Quinn.

"You're room temperature, this solution is still on the cool side, and I'd prefer to deal with as little hypothermia as we must tonight."

Soon, Quinn was buried in bedding—all but her arm, which Daisy continued to monitor. While John kept her company, Bee watched the projection. "Is it working?" I asked as she studied the ghostly veins.

Bee folded her arms and glanced down at the tubing. "Her body's not rejecting it, which gives me hope. I think I'll give her a couple bags of blood after the electrolytes, just to be certain, but so far, she's tolerating the saline."

"Will we still be able to work on her tonight?"

"I should think so, yes. And I need you to start now. I want her fluid circulating," she explained before I could question her. "No sense in having a buildup on one side of her body. Can you do it?"

I made the quick calculation. Two bags of saline, the electrolyte solution, and more bags of blood...I'd be tethered to Quinn for hours.

"Give me a moment to prepare," I said, and hurried to the kitchen. I gulped down a glass of water and took what I hoped was a calming breath, then returned to the den and flexed my fingers.

"All right, there?" asked Quinn.

"Perfectly fine," I lied, and began casting.

Though I'd planned and tweaked the spell I wove until I could almost do it in my sleep, I'd only attempted it once, using a rat I'd found dead in the stairwell by the Team's offices. The rat's body had been cooperative, but this was a much larger corpse, and she was watching me intently as the spell coalesced.

She twitched in alarm as my spell's glowing green tendrils descended in two hundred places and pierced her flesh. "Does that hurt?" I asked.

"No, just…creepy." She wiggled her arm and scowled. "Kind of hard to move."

"Please don't. This is difficult enough with you *not* fighting me."

"Sorry," she mumbled, and looked at John. "I'm a bad patient."

"You're not raving about body snatchers, so you're not the worst I've had," he replied with a weak smile. "There was this one poor man who did *horribly* under anesthesia…"

I didn't hear the end of the story. With the spell locked into place, I let my consciousness merge with it, running through the anchors as I mapped the vascular terrain. For months, I'd studied this part with John, and my lessons returned to me as I slipped through Quinn's blood vessels to her silent, cold heart. It wouldn't pump properly yet— Quinn needed considerable fluid first—but I kept my attention on it as I began to force the fresh saline through her underused veins. As it neared the heart, I recalled the series of events. Tricuspid and mitral valves open for inflow. Atrial systole forces blood into the ventricles. Valves close. Pulmonary and aortic valves open. Blood ejects toward the lungs or elsewhere into the body. Over and over, a dance completed in the space of a blink and repeated dozens of times a minute. I didn't need the heart to provide propulsion yet—I could manage that on my own—but without sufficient blood pressure to drive them, I manually set the valves in motion, timing them to mimic a slow heartbeat.

Part of me—inexperienced Eadwig, the boy who'd barely begun his formal studies in magic—panicked as more and more parts came under my control. But Simon whispered calm as he took over, holding together the complex spell and fine-tuning it with every second's fluctuation in the fluid volume and in the currents of background magic. Simon was inexperienced with this spell, but he knew how to control a large construction.

Eadwig barely needed to think. Simon had the matter in hand, and his practiced casting felt like second nature. And so I gave myself over to the moment, to processing the information I was receiving from Quinn's body and to reacting.

With my eyes closed and the room's light dim, I lost track of time until I felt something nudge my lips. A voice like thunder boomed across my mind: *Drink. You need it.*

The object bumping against my mouth was a straw, and I took it greedily, alerted in that moment of broken concentration to my own body's discomfort. I had a raging thirst, and as I sucked at the water on offer, I felt someone wipe a cloth across my face and neck.

You're flushed and sweating, the voice told me—Frank, I realized. *Bee's worried about you. Holding up?*

Fine, I managed.

No, you're not.

Fine, I insisted.

If you say so, kid, he replied with a dubious cast to his thought. *Last bag of blood is about five minutes from emptying.*

Already?

You've been at this for a while. Once the transfusion finishes, Bee says it'll be time to start the heart. Do you need a break?

No, I fibbed. *How's Quinn?*

Scared to death, but that's to be expected. Keep drinking.

As the last of the water hit my tongue, he added, *Backup is standing by. Just shout if you need help.*

It's in hand for now, I told him, then paused to take stock of Quinn. Her veins weren't exactly plump, but it was a start. I continued to move the transfused liquid along, directing it through the great and tiny channels alike in its unending circuit. Never had I been so intimately connected to another person—and considering Simon's long, sordid history, that was an accomplishment.

Finally, I heard Frank again: *It's time. Can you start it?*

Everything now came down to electricity. John had

spent long hours drilling me on the pathway and process: the sinoatrial node's depolarization and impulse, the brief, crucial delay at the atrioventricular node, the conduction through the bundle of His and the Purkinje fibers into the ventricular muscle. Sequenced properly, contractions would build pressure until the valves opened on their own. But terms repeated until they no longer sounded like gibberish and diagrams committed to memory—and one practice rat—were poor substitutes for the heart in my hands.

Still, I had to try.

I passed the tiniest of shocks into the atrial muscle and felt it contract. Another shock to the ventricles produced the same result. Again, I hit the atria, and the blood within them pressed out into the next chambers. Faintly, I thought I felt a corresponding electrical flutter elsewhere in the heart, but I couldn't be certain.

Keep trying, Frank told me. *They're transfusing more blood, then more electrolytes. John says the volume is too low.*

Is this hurting Quinn?

She says no, he replied after a brief pause. *Feels odd, and she's conscious of her heart twitching, since it hasn't beat in over a year. But she's not in real pain, and Bee's keeping her numb.*

Good, I thought, and focused on the task at hand.

Over and over, I sent tiny shocks into the muscle, tracking the conduction until the contractions were timed properly. As the transfusions continued and the chambers filled more fully, I felt the pressure increase against the valves. If I could just make the sinoatrial node depolarize on its own...

John says the rhythm is good, Frank thought, interrupting me again. *Is her heart beating alone?*

No.

A pause. *They want to know if you want help with respiration.*

Yes.

After what seemed like seconds but must have been longer—my sense of time was horribly warped that night—Frank reported, *Maria's on the lungs. John's holding her hand as she figures this out, but she's got the lungs moving.*

Good.

The problem is working out what the gas composition in there might be, he continued. *Bee's trying to set up monitoring, but they're talking about gas exchange and blood oxygenation, and honestly, this isn't my field—*

Concentrating, I thought.

Sorry, sorry, he hastily replied, and slipped out of my mind.

As the minutes passed, I could feel Quinn growing warmer—perhaps Marcus's doing, I reasoned in the distant part of me not pumping blood through the patient. Circulation and respiration would be sufficient at first, wouldn't it? If her brain was oxygenated, then perhaps it could survive the shock of the curse breaking. We knew the brain was still functional—Bee had mapped it months ago and shown John and me that her electrical activity seemed close to normal. Quinn could walk and talk, after all. But for everything else, for the unconscious, autonomic movements necessary to life, were the connections still present? I couldn't run her heart, her stomach, and her kidneys indefinitely.

I felt the straw touch my lips again and drank instinctively. *Bee thinks Quinn is as stable as she's going to get with the curse in place*, Frank told me. *They're transfusing electrolytes again. Are you still controlling the heart?*

Unfortunately.

Ready to break the curse?

Give me a countdown.

Bracing myself for the moment that my handiwork became crucial instead of merely useful, I fought the roiling in my gut and focused on Quinn's heart, willing the impulse to arise from within her own cells.

Artur's ready, thought Frank. *Breaking in five...four...three...two...*

Don't you dare die on me, I whispered into Quinn's mind,

then winced as I felt the curse crumble with the surge of power Artur shot through it. Though she might not have been the most skilled of enchanters, the woman was *strong*...

No time to think of that. I heard an urgent beeping from above my head—Bee's monitoring spell, I assumed—but I forced the heart to beat, faster and faster. *Come on*, I willed the muscle as I shocked it over and over again, *respond, depolarize, show me a sign*...

In the space between seconds, the silent sinoatrial node fired.

I tracked the rapid cascade of electrical impulse and contraction, the burst of blood heading for the rising lungs for oxygen, the pulse returning to the body for its circuit...and I held my breath.

It fired again. A little sluggishly, but that was twice.

The third discharge came more quickly, then the fourth. By the tenth, her heart was beating at a steady clip, and Frank returned with an update. *We've got a pulse. Is she doing it?*

Yes, I thought, and withdrew.

When I saw the room around me again, every lamp was lit against the night beyond the glass, and a storm had begun to blow over the island. Rain sheeted against the windows, and I had no idea when it had begun.

Quinn lay still within her cocoon of blankets, her head rolled to the side and her mouth open. John stroked her hair but kept an eye on Bee's monitors above us. I couldn't decipher them, but from the look on Bee's face, we weren't finished yet.

Seeing my dazed expression, she snapped, "Frank, get him juice. Sugar. Ed, *sit*."

I flopped to the floor and waited until Frank returned with apple juice and a straw. Though I had no taste for the overly sweet stuff, it went down like fine wine that night, and I soon drained my glass.

"Pulse is steady," Bee told me as I started to focus. "A

little weak, but we can work with this. She's breathing on her own, too, so maybe her autonomic system's coming back online. And she's not brain-dead," she added, glancing at John. "Honestly, I think this is akin to rebooting."

"I've never seen anything like this," he countered.

"No offense intended, love, but I doubt you've seen much in the way of enchanted patients. Magic gets *strange*." Glancing my way again, she asked, "Can you stand?"

I let Daisy help me to my feet and clutched the table, my head spinning. "What do you need next?"

"Renal. Let's see what sort of functionality she has." Scowling up at the projection, she added, "I'm seeing some tissue damage. Bit of internal bleeding. If Quinn's not bruised to hell and back by morning, I'll be shocked."

"But you think she'll be with us in the morning?" John pressed.

"With any luck," Bee replied, pulling out her wand. "Guide Ed with the kidneys. I'm going to start repairs. Marcus, keep her warm—she's still hypothermic. Maria, go into the kitchen and get another bag of saline, and bring it to room temperature, if you will. And Daisy?"

"Smoothie?" her wife asked as lightning flashed outside the lodge.

"I love you," she said with a sigh of relief, and bent to her work.

Quinn's heart stopped three times before dawn—only for a few seconds, but long enough to sound the warning alarm and send me racing to shock her chest. She stopped breathing twice. Her internal damage was more extensive and severe than Bee had first thought, presumably a result of the curse that would have killed her in its breaking. While Bee and Maria worked to mend Quinn's torn tissues, I focused on her other systems, trying to restore them one by one. As the sun rose, I removed the unspeakably foul blockage from her bowels, and then Quinn spontaneously urinated. The blankets were soiled, but Bee and John called it a good sign.

When the cloud-dimmed sunlight fell upon Quinn and her skin didn't begin to smoke, I gave myself permission to hope that the worst was behind us.

Marcus was the last to work on Quinn, wrapping her in a more generalized healing enchantment to complement Maria and Bee's detailed reconstructive work. Finally, after the long night, there was nothing to do but wait, set a slow IV drip, and listen for alarms.

I crashed on the rug beside her, not bothering with the furniture. But I've never been much of a daylight sleeper, and I woke not an hour later, disoriented and bone-weary. A rustling above me reminded me of where I was, and I pushed myself to my feet. Though Quinn was still pale, her eyes had opened.

"Hey," she weakly rasped. "Did I miss it?"

"Miss what?" I asked.

"Sunrise. Did I miss it?"

"Nothing special today." Seeing no active alarms on the projection, I said, "How do you feel?"

"Awful," she admitted, "but since that *is* daylight I'm seeing…"

I smiled at the hopeful note in her voice. "The curse is broken. You seem to be functioning on your own, but don't rip that out yet," I cautioned, pointing to the IV line. "Bee says you need the fluids."

Quinn considered that, and as my hand neared hers, she grasped it and gave it a quick squeeze. "Any chance of breakfast? I'm *starving*."

The answer to that was a resounding *no*. Bee and John limited her to water throughout the day—or so Quinn told me when I checked on her. On the doctors' orders, I spent most of that day in my theretofore largely untouched bed with the window blackened. Quinn's vital signs continued to improve, however, and her injuries healed. Sylvester made her chicken soup for dinner, and when she kept that down after half an hour, the doctors considered the experiment a success.

That evening, I helped move Quinn to Beth's former bed. Having sent Allie to a cot in her parents' room, I watched as Bee tweaked the monitoring spell, and then I assured her I could take the first watch. "I'll relieve you around two," she promised me, and left so that Quinn could sleep.

"I'm here if you need anything," I told her, settling onto Allie's bed with a book and a small lamp. "Try to rest—it will speed your healing."

After a moment, she said, "Ed?"

"Mm?"

"Come here, will you?"

I rose and went to her bedside, and she wrapped her bruised hands around mine. "Thank you," she murmured. "I don't know how to repay you for the fact that I'm not currently a corpse."

"Just be better than Simon, and I'll be satisfied," I replied.

Quinn chuckled. "I'll see what I can do. Hey, has anyone called the folks in Faerie today?"

"Not that I know of. We've been catching up on sleep," I explained. "Long night all around. Speaking of which, Bee will kill me if I keep you awake, so…"

"Yeah, yeah," she said, and released me. "Well, make sure you tell Beth soon. She's going to be *so* proud of you."

And exhausted though I was, I couldn't help but smile.

OCTOBER 7: BETH STANHOPE

I hated feeling useless.

It wasn't a new feeling—my mother gave me ample opportunity to experience the joys of feeling like a powerless screwup during my years under her roof—but familiarity made it no less pleasant. That Kitty was stuck in the same miserable boat made the situation only a teensy bit better.

The annoying part was that I didn't have a good person to blame for my predicament unless I waved my arms at Arc 2. I wanted to be on Afallon with the Team and my weird little family, not hiding out in Faerie, but that would have led Leander right to their front door. Now Faerie was entering its third day of a standoff at the Fringe settlement. I'd offered to help—I had to be more talented than ninety percent of the people in town, I'd insisted to Val, pleading my case—but I'd received a polite, firm *no* on that count. No one was getting into the settlement, thanks to Mal's dad, who'd firmed up a decent barrier ward. Unfortunately, he hadn't built exceptions into the ward—given the fae distaste for wardwork, I honestly couldn't say whether he had the knowhow—and so, aside from Ros, the settlement was cut off even from helpful visitors. He couldn't afford to turn off the ward, either, considering the number of Irem's people massing outside the wall. Val and Coileán's combined forces had been harrying Irem's, distracting them from an all-out assault on the ward, but Irem had sent some of her guards the day before, and tensions were climbing. Apparently, the last thing anyone wanted was a young wizard to babysit on the field.

Kitty, too, had offered to help—at least she had the chops to take care of herself—but Val had grounded her as well, telling her to stay with me. As forced vacations went, hanging out at Val's massive home was pretty nice, and he and his staff had been nothing but kind. Still, I felt useless and trapped. I took to pacing the garden behind my room, and when I grumbled about not being allowed into combat, Kitty wondered aloud if she needed to have a long talk with Artur.

By Saturday morning—or what I thought was Saturday, given how the days had begun to run together—I found myself lying in bed, staring at the ceiling, wondering why I should bother getting up. I could eat a nice breakfast, sit in the lovely garden by the fountain, maybe convince my sister to take me to the beach, but what was the point? I was too anxious to enjoy myself, too frustrated to be fun company for anyone, so why not just stay in bed and glare at the mosaic?

As I imagined the ways in which I'd like to personally make Leander hurt, my phone trilled. A gift from Val, it never needed to be charged, always found a signal, and downloaded anything I liked without payment—standard fare for the fae set, though I couldn't work out how the darn thing even *operated*. I kept it close at hand in case of updates or warnings, and when I saw Ed on the ID, my heart raced. Faerie was then slightly ahead of the UK's time, so it couldn't be later than five in the morning on Afallon.

"Are you okay?" I asked as soon as the line opened.

"Fine," he replied, and yawned. "Sorry, I just woke. I've only had a few hours' sleep, but...eh."

I could almost see him shrug. "What's going on over there?"

"Curse is broken."

"*What?*" I demanded, sitting up in bed. "Is Quinn—"

"Recovering nicely. She's healing. Has an appetite, and

her body seems functional—"

"That's freaking *amazing*, Ed! Congratulations!"

"It was a team effort," he said, but he sounded pleased.

"Yeah, but you've been working your ass off to get to this point. That's...I mean, wow. How do you feel?"

Even his laughter sounded exhausted. "Not as good as I'll feel after a few days' rest, but I made it to my bed this time instead of passing out on the floor, so...progress?"

"*Eadwig.*"

"I'm fine," he assured me. "And if you see him, tell Coileán I'm on my way over to finally destroy that damn grail. It's only taken a thousand years, but—"

"You're coming here?" I interrupted, perking at the news.

"Oh, uh...yes! Yes, sorry, I'm a little scattered today..." He laughed again. "Frank discussed it with his father last night. Since Quinn can leave now, we're going to stay with Owain until the Arcanum either calms or destroys itself. I sincerely hope it's not the latter," he muttered, "but in case they manage to seal off Faerie, at least everyone will be together. That's Ted's plan, anyway." Lowering his voice, he added, "I'm not sure if Quinn and John approve of the idea. They have family in this realm, after all."

"But she *could* leave?" I pressed.

"Absolutely. There's nothing left on her but healing constructions. We'll wait until later in the day to make the crossing—Bee wants her to have as much time as possible to recuperate, since everything keeping her comfortable will break when she comes through."

I swung my legs off the mattress and stared at the patterns in the rug. "Is she in pain?"

"She will be, once the numbing spell falls off. The curse left her with internal damage when it broke, but she *is* healing well. Still, though, we can reassemble everything in Faerie—Marcus is remarkably good at healing work," he said with audible admiration.

"Who did you think has been putting me back together after Artur finishes with me?" I teased. "He takes after his dad. Natural."

"I…suppose I hadn't noticed," Ed replied. "Guess I've been preoccupied…"

The silence hung between us for an awkward moment.

"How are you?" I asked. "Really?"

"As I said, I'm under-slept—"

"No, *no*," I said, cutting him off. "You did it, Ed. All the late nights and the reading and the lessons with Dr. Dellucci…it worked. Quinn's fixed."

He hesitated before responding. "You don't sound convinced that this is a good thing."

"It's a great thing! But I also know this has been your reason to get out of bed for the last year. So before you start trying to find a *really* intense hobby…are you okay?"

His answer surprised me. "It hasn't been my only reason," he murmured.

The silence that time seemed different. More comfortable. A pregnant pause, not an uncertain void of sound.

I heard the words unspoken in that silence, and I smiled to myself as they echoed in my mind.

"Maybe, once the standoff at the settlement breaks, you could schedule an appointment with Wanda," I suggested.

"Mm. I *have* missed her biscuits. Now, about that standoff…"

I sighed. "Don't ask me for details. Val won't let me near it."

"*Good.*"

"Stop taking his side!" I huffed.

"All I want is for you to remain alive and whole. Is that such a terrible thing?"

"I feel useless."

"You are anything but useless, Beth. And we'll talk about it in person later tonight, yes? Once we're all safe from the idiots in Glastonbury. Oh, and Toula called Conota," he continued. "To inform them of the situation in the other realms. She said their king isn't overly concerned about the Arcanum, but he remains on standby."

"No surprise there," I said, flopping back onto the mattress. "His brother and a bunch of other refugees live in Kentucky."

"Where?"

"In the States. They've got a compound. Nice folks, by and large, but a lot of them turn blue or purple when the glamour comes off. If Leander were actually able to seal the barrier between the mortal realm and Conota…I mean, he can't really do that, can he? They're not in danger, right?"

Ed's pause that time was far too long to give me comfort.

"No," he replied. "Not without a massive, constant source of magic. I doubt one could even remove Conota's consciousness with magic as one can Faerie's. Dark magic is such a neutralizing force…no," he said again, more firmly, "it would take more magic than Leander could muster, and he'd need magic at that level indefinitely to keep the barrier firm. Conota can't be sealed as Faerie was."

"You don't sound altogether happy about that."

"It's the outcome I fear. If those fools try to seal both realms and only manage Faerie, then the mortal realm will be overrun by monstrosities free to hunt."

"But Leander won't be able to seal Faerie," I said, forcing confidence into my voice. "It only worked that once because of a crazy hybrid construction, you know? And since I don't think Leander has faeries hiding in the castle, ready to help him…"

I *really* didn't like Ed's hesitation that time.

After a few eternal seconds, he mumbled, "Simon… gave the matter much thought. He wrote his ideas in his damn diary. Untested, mostly—they were too dangerous to try—but…"

"*But?*"

"The right spell," he said reluctantly, "with enough wizards channeling sufficient power…it's possible. But it would take a concerted effort, and a construction that strong, made only of spellcraft, would drain all local magic. They would need more than the background magic could supply."

My stomach clenched. "That thing you guys brought back from Siberia."

"It might be enough," he murmured. "I'm not certain, but I don't want to take that risk."

"So why don't we just punch through the ward around Arc 2 and snatch the thing?" I demanded. "Invade the castle!"

"Don't think I haven't had a quiet conversation about that with Toula," he replied. "The castle's on alert. If we worked together with the kings and their forces, we could probably take it, but not without casualties. And Toula is understandably averse to another faerie invasion of an Arcanum installation. The repercussions from the last one have been following her for years." He paused, then asked, "How talented a wizard is your mother?"

"Decent, I guess," I said. "Pine wand, so she's got talent."

"And Francine?"

"I couldn't say, but I think she's a pine, too. Why?"

"Because there are certain musings in the diary that should never have been put to paper," said Ed. "When John's nephew and Coileán's daughter attacked Faerie, they did so by using theoretical techniques from the diary. Simon didn't have the power alone to test them—and he wasn't stupid enough to try—but he had ideas about ways to maximize power. If Leander assembles a team of competent magi to try some of those techniques…with the sphere supporting him…"

"You think they'll attack Ros?" I asked.

"Probably not—they need her here if they value Faerie's continued existence. No, I'm more concerned that they'll accidentally lock the border."

His words did little to reassure me, but I tried to hide it. "Well, just in case, get your stuff packed. I'll see you tonight, yeah?"

"Absolutely. Stay safe, Beth. I miss you," he replied, and hung up.

Sitting up again, I squinted at a sudden brightness near the door and realized that Ros had manifested. "Did you hear all of that?" I asked.

"Yep." She crossed her arms and sighed, and I noticed how tired she seemed. "Let's hope Leander and his buddies aren't as good as they think they are. I'd really rather not die just yet." Still, as she glanced my way, a faint smile curled her lips. "To answer your other question, smart people do stupid things, hon."

"Yeah, but did he have to write down all his worst ideas?" I muttered, and slid out of bed. "Better go tell Kitty. Sounds like there's going to be a party at Owain's tonight."

OCTOBER 7: ROS BOLIN

Why, I demanded of Kura, *did you set up the arrangement like this? What were you thinking?*

I wished I had access to Kura in her entirety, not just the portion of herself left behind in the realm's collective consciousness. In truth, I seldom sought to separate any of my predecessors from the group mind—I had their memories and their wisdom, and frankly, it was strange talking to a partial version of a person I'd once known as an independent entity. But I was exhausted and peeved, and Kura had been the architect of the treaty with the original Three.

Because it worked, she said. *Because I had no desire to make myself an omnipotent queen. Look at what happened to Tenola.*

Her point was valid. The second of the realm's vessels had been fully fae, and when she became a little too oppressive for her people's taste, they'd massed in the mortal realm and worked an enchantment strong enough to rip her free. In her rage, she'd offered the position to half-fae Inkil, one of the few who'd remained in the realm when the multitude left to rise against her. Tenola thought that when she joined the group mind in death, she could use Inkil to crush her enemies. Her successor, however, though mild mannered, was clever and far more politically savvy than Tenola had been.

But why couldn't you have come up with a better override provision? I grumbled.

Let this play out, Ros. They do not need your help.

Irem still hasn't gotten the message.

Irem will either reluctantly join the kings or die at a usurper's hand, Kura replied. *She cannot rule forever in chaos. Her father learned that lesson, and so will she—or another will take her place who can better manage the court.* Her voice seemed to soften. *You have given the settlement the tools it requires for its own defense, and the kings' forces continue their work beyond the walls. You are distracting yourself.*

The group mind concurred with that, and I couldn't deny the truth—I *was* distracting myself. I was vulnerable to outside attacks, as Tenola and Kura continued to warn me, and the Arcanum was poised to attempt...*something.* I could feel the shifting currents beyond the border, just as Kura had once felt Moyna and Russell Mulligan's experimentation. I hadn't sensed much of the type of stirring that had led to Kura's death, but the reports I'd heard from those who'd been privy to the new grand magus's doings—and, more importantly, the information I gleaned from them that they didn't share aloud—had me on edge. Politically, I understood why it would be a terrible idea to attack Arc 2 and simply kill the problem child and his friends, but on a personal level, I'd have felt *much* better with Leander, Eva, and Francine out of the picture.

So yes, I was distracting myself with the settlement siege, and with good reason. My grandparents were in there, after all, and plenty of folks I'd known as a kid. I'd gone to school in the settlement for several years—I knew the people: the little old man who ran the sweet shop where I'd sneaked off for snacks; the kind librarian who'd requisitioned all sorts of graphic novels for me; Father Paul, who oversaw the most ecumenical Catholic church in existence. Even if I'd only been on the margins, even if the average Fringer had looked at me as someone to be feared *before* I took on the realm's power, I still cared about the settlement and the lives within its walls. They were my people, too, and I'd be damned if I let Irem's goons kill them.

The trick was getting to Irem. The blinding migraine

I'd given her was losing efficacy over time, and she continued to defy me out of sheer stubbornness. But until she attacked Val or Coileán directly, I couldn't turn on her. Tossing her around in her own throne room had been a step too far, and the agreement that bound the Three to me had exacted its penalty. Magical compacts are powerful things, and for all of Val's prodding of me to change the terms, I couldn't do so unilaterally. I knew the pain Kura had endured for years by not giving Val his mother's court. Even my little transgression with Irem had left me sore for days, though I'd tried not to let on. Better for Irem to think I was biding my time than for her to understand that I was subject to my own set of restrictions.

Still, worried as I was about the Arcanum outside the realm and the siege within, I came running when a gate opened on Owain's front lawn and I heard Frank call for me. No matter whose he was, he had been my hatchling, and I knew his mind like my own.

"Hey, bud," I said, manifesting near the gate. On the other side, I could see the sun setting over Afallon. The light was dimming in Faerie, too, but I'd decided long ago that I hated the sort of seasonal day-length shifting that the UK endured. "What's up?"

"I'm sorry to bother you," he began, "but—"

"You're not bothering me. Is everyone ready to come over?"

"You know about—*oh*. Of course you know what Dad and I discussed," he mumbled, rubbing his neck. "We just wanted to be sure you were okay with everyone."

I glanced past him at the assembled crowd with their suitcases and backpacks. "No complaints here. But, uh"— I pointed toward Quinn, who was still wrapped with healing constructions—"is she safe for transport?"

"Stable," said a voice I knew well, and I smiled as Bee stepped out of the pack. "This will hurt, but Marcus and I can see to her on the other side."

"Glad you're coming," I told Bee. "I've missed you,

lady."

"Missed you, too," she said, her face crinkling. "The plan now is for us to camp with Owain, but Daisy and I would love to spend some time with you and Sam again...post-siege, naturally," she added. "How's it working out?"

I shrugged. "Stalemate for the moment. Stay with Owain, okay? You're far enough here from the skirmishing that I won't lose sleep."

Bee's eyebrow rose. "You *don't* sleep."

"Figure of speech," I started to protest, then saw her teasing grin and huffed. "Whatever. Do me a favor and don't get killed. That goes for all of you," I told the crowd. "Stay away from the settlement, don't let yourselves become targets—"

Marcus cleared his throat and lifted a finger.

"Okay, *fine*, if you are specifically told to pitch in, then do so. Otherwise, stick with Owain—and that means you, Frank."

"No problem there," he said as a door slammed open behind me. I turned at the sound of footsteps on the grass and saw Aurie sprinting toward her father as Owain waved from the stairs. "I'll be here with the hatchling until this is over," he continued. "That said, if you need to blow off steam, you know I'm good for a flight and—"

Whatever he said next was lost to me, drowned in a cacophonous noise like a hundred rumbles of thunder. My inner warning shouted at me to *do something*, but a voice like Kura's whispered that it was too late.

From all directions, from every gate, brilliant bolts flew at me, but when they pierced my temporary form, they stuck fast. I dematerialized to free myself, but to no avail—I was caught on a thousand burning fishhooks, blinded by a blast of pain I'd never known.

Somewhere far away, I heard screaming—Frank, Aurie, Bee.

And then I heard Eadwig's voice above the riot: "Oh,

God, no. *No!* You *fools!*"

I forced my vision to return in time to see the sky splinter and crack like an eggshell, and the vibration in the ground told me it wasn't far behind.

The Arcanum wasn't trying to seal Faerie off. They weren't trying to pull me out, either.

They were killing me.

As the part of me that was Ros panicked, the group mind took over, broadcasting a warning across the realm: *GET OUT. FAERIE IS COLLAPSING. RUN.*

A wave of calm washed over me as I heard those words. This was it—this was inevitable, unstoppable, I knew with the certainty of the group mind. Strong though I was, I was too injured to break free. Even if someone ran to Glastonbury and ended the spell, the damage was done. My task now—my only task, my final task—was to evacuate as many as I could.

I ripped open gates across the realm, directing them to Afallon and safety, and watched as frantic faeries grabbed their closest possessions and fled.

Val opened his own gates and shouted for his guards to flee, then made another gate back to the villa just in time to see Marcus wave Kitty and Beth through. He yelled for his staff to evacuate and began running through the villa, looking for stragglers.

Coileán pushed Aiden through the closest gate, but as Toula screamed at him to come on, he turned and headed for the settlement instead. The barrier ward fell just as he reached the wall, and he popped into the center of town by gate, then amplified his voice and repeated my warning.

My eyes lingered on the settlement. Some of the Fringers fled—the young adults, the ones with time on their side. I saw babies and children passed to younger relatives by parents and grandparents too old to safely leave, mothers and fathers weeping as their older children carried their youngest into the mortal realm.

I saw Badger pointing to a gate, begging Seamus to

leave her. Instead, he took her in his arms and held her as the ground beneath them trembled.

Kip ran into Amy's workshop as her wands and supplies fell from their shelves. They stared at the chaos around them with terror and despair, and then they clung to each other like children, safe for one last moment in their embrace.

The Stowes—bless the boys—did what they always did in time of crisis: they opened more gates and ushered out anyone willing to go before evacuating themselves. But not all went. My gaze caught Vivi in her office with Hal. "We might make it," he was telling her. "Seventy-two's not that old. The shock would hurt, but…"

"I go down with the ship," she murmured, and kissed him as the windows shattered.

Across town, her nephew ran through a gate into his parents' house and found them in the den, Poppy frantic and Rufus exhausted from his struggle with the ward. "You've got to go!" Mal cried. "Come on, it's safe over here!"

"*Go*," Poppy told her husband. "I'll be fine. Go be with Mal."

But Rufus turned to her with tears in his eyes and shook his head. "No."

"Rufus—"

"*No*." To his anxious son, he said, "We love you. Be strong."

"Dad!" Mal cried as Rufus flung him backward through the gate. "Mom! What are you doing?"

"We love you, baby. I'm so sorry," Poppy told him, and Rufus slammed the gate closed.

I saw Fringers fleeing toward the church, where old Father Paul stood before the altar in his black shirt and trousers, having been preparing for Saturday vigil when the world around him began to crumble. He beckoned them in, some his parishioners, some just frightened townsfolk—even Stuart, my old teacher, who'd probably never been to Mass a day in his life—and drew them toward him with open arms. "It's all right, now," he soothed, and clasped the hands nearest to him. "It's going to be fine. Let's pray."

My eyes found Coileán again inside The Tavern, begging Slim to go as Adam hurried the stragglers out the front door. "I'm ninety-three, man," Slim told him, and took a bottle of scotch from the shelf. "That's a death sentence, and you know it." He downed a deep swig straight from the bottle, then cocked it toward Coileán in salute. "Take care of yourself, old timer. Now get out of here before Toula drags you."

I opened gates beneath the waters of the western sea wherever I found merrow congregating, urging them out. I opened one near the piq hideaway and watched them stream to safety like multicolored fireflies.

Somewhere far away, across the mortal realm, I felt Conota's shock before that realm sealed off. His mind was gone like an extinguished candle, but I didn't have time to think of what could have happened to him.

My Sam was already safe on Afallon, but my parents weren't. *Go!* I begged them. *I can't hold this much longer!*

"It's okay, Joey," Mom told Dad, giving him a fierce hug in their kitchen. "You go. I'm not leaving my baby. Tell Aid I love him. Remember me like this—"

"I'm not going anywhere," he insisted, tightening his grip on Mom.

"Joey, please—"

"I lost you once," he murmured into her hair. "Never again."

"Joey—"

"I love you, Helen."

They kissed as a fissure opened in the yard just beyond the house, splitting the sheep pen in two. The oblivious sheep continued grazing as the dragons took to the sky, fleeing the barn as its ceiling collapsed.

I couldn't save the dragons. In moments, I'd be dead,

and magic with me. Conota was gone. They'd be trapped and unprotected in the mortal realm, left to hide and starve or be hunted. A quick death seemed the kinder option.

And then, to my horror, I saw Aurie reenter the realm.

She was sprinting, running as hard as she could for Owain's house, and I found the cause at the top of her thoughts: her toy dragon. Frantic in the way of young children, Aurie was running through an apocalypse to save her beloved Blue. Shifting would have done her no good—not three-legged and wingless—and so she pumped her little legs as hard as they would go and made a beeline for the front door across the trembling earth.

I heard Frank scream her name and watched as he started to cross, but before he could take more than two steps in the grass, a spell tightened like a lasso around him and yanked him back through the gate. He writhed, struggling to free himself, and snarled at his captor—Eadwig.

"You'll never make it," the boy told him, then ran after Aurie.

By then, Owain's lawn was fracturing into wobbling islands, some only a few inches apart, others separated by growing chasms. Aurie, who'd only crossed a third of the way, was stuck on one of the larger masses, but as she tried to pick out a path, a gate opened beside her. Eadwig hurried through and grabbed her before she could attempt a jump, then gave her a good shake and barked, "What's so important? Show me!"

Chest heaving, Aurie broadcast an image of the toy sitting atop her bed.

"I'll get it. Go to your father," he ordered, and pushed her through the gate without another word.

Aurie stumbled across, but the ground around her was solid…and only a few feet from an exit. Owain ducked through, scooped her up, and carried her to safety, and Frank, shaking off the last of Eadwig's spell, clutched her to his chest in his wordless terror.

But that still left the matter of Eadwig, who was navigating the shifting maze by gate. One took him to the relative stability of Owain's front steps, giving him a moment to focus and create a gate into Aurie's bedroom. As the house groaned in warning, he ran through the room and grabbed the toy dragon, but he didn't immediately retreat. Instead, Eadwig hurried into the adjoining bedroom, where Frank had left his most important possessions on returning to Afallon. Eadwig searched for only a few seconds before he located the shopping bag containing Aurie's baby books, and he yanked it off the floor.

The part of me still capable of thought wondered what he was doing, and then I looked beneath the surface of his mind.

Whatever else Simon had been, he was a father of twelve. He understood.

As part of the roof collapsed, he opened a fresh gate out of Faerie and stepped through to find Frank anxiously watching the gate through which he'd run. "Here," he said, handing Aurie her beloved toy, then showed Frank the bag of scrapbooks.

Frank's eyes widened. "You—"

"They were at the top of your thoughts as soon as Aurie arrived the first time," he said between heaving breaths. "No trouble." Looking up at Frank, he added, "Team's a family, right?"

And Frank, who'd put Aurie down only seconds before, lifted Eadwig off the ground as he hugged him.

I never observed Eadwig's reaction. With my pain worsening, I felt grass beneath my knees and realized I was back on Owain's lawn, once more in physical form and still very much in agony. I saw Sam on the other side of a gate, his face stricken as he watched me scream. There was Frank, my darling Frank, staring helplessly at me. I could sense his fear as his thoughts flew to his mother and siblings, but there was nothing I could do. I was burning, a star on the edge of going supernova, a breath away from explosion...

And then I saw Beth, her face screwed up in determination, her blonde hair flying behind her. Eadwig, his eyes wide in alarm, yelled for her to come back, warning her that the realm wasn't stable, but she ignored him and sprinted into Faerie as Owain and Sam restrained him. Another man stood at the edge of the gate, fighting to cross between the realms and screaming for Beth—a blond in overalls I recognized as her father, invisible and inaudible to all but me.

Go back, I whispered to Beth's mind, wondering what she could have possibly left that was worth risking her life. *I can't hold on.*

I felt her grab me around the chest with a surprisingly strong grip and drag me toward the gate. *What are you doing?* I demanded. *I can't leave the realm—*

"It's collapsing, right?" she said through clenched teeth, hauling me along like a sack of grain. "You want to die?"

Beth—

"Just try to hold it together, okay? A little longer..."

By then, I could pick out Kitty's and Artur's panicked voices as they neared the gate and saw what she was up to. Looking back as Beth tugged my dead weight out of the realm, I watched lightning rip across the broken sky and heard the frantic cries of birds. And then, with a feeling like simultaneously being impaled and being caressed by razors, Beth forced me through the gate.

The hole sealed as soon as my feet left the realm, and I collapsed, panting. The air smelled wrong, it was too dark, I couldn't hear anyone, couldn't see...

I was *panting*.

I looked down at my hands—my perfectly normal, fleshy, non-glowing hands—then patted myself. I was in a body, a real body, *my* body, and I ached all over. With mounting horror, I realized that I was seeing only what was directly before me—my omniscient view had been blinded, and the multitude in my head had fallen silent.

"Ros," said Sam, holding me as he knelt beside me in the grass. "Come on, say something, babe. *Please.* Are you okay? What just happened? How do we get you back in there? Tell me what to do…"

As I raised my head and met his worried eyes, my own began to blur. "It's gone," I whispered. "It's all gone. They're all gone."

"*What's* gone?"

"Faerie," I managed, and burst into tears.

OCTOBER 7: TOULA PAVLI

This wasn't the first time I'd invaded an Arcanum installation with an army at my back. I'd been younger during the first go-around, nervous but buoyed by righteous anger, and I'd had a large force around me. This time, I was too furious to be nervous, too pissed off to care what happened after the dust settled, and accompanied by a much more select group. Coileán and Val felt like crap with the loss of their boost of power from the realm, but they'd pulled themselves together, leaving Aiden behind on Afallon to comfort Ros, his hysterical, freshly orphaned niece. Arnold, Bert, and Maria joined us, as did Eadwig, bringing our grand magus total to four. If that wasn't enough to get answers from the Council, then I'd never deserved the damn chain in the first place.

I made the smallest gate possible and closed it as soon as the last limb was through, hating to waste even that much magic. Passing through the camouflage ward, I saw no one on the gate, and my merry band of magi made quick work of the barrier ward. We didn't just turn it off— we *shattered* it. Magic was draining away by the second, and every unnecessary construction needed to come down. A small blast of force was all I needed to open the door by the ceremonial gate, and as I marched through, I found a mass of wizards congregating in the courtyard. Some huddled in small knots beneath the lamps, while others ran back and forth across the open space as if seeking answers in the dark corners.

"*Hey!*" I yelled, amplifying my voice to be heard about the ruckus, and planted my hands on my hips as the crowd turned to us. "Where the fuck is Leander?"

To my surprise, the wizards looked relieved to see us, and a few jogged closer. "Grand Magus!" said the fastest of the bunch, a one-time Council aide who'd stepped aside to take a position in the library. "Thank heavens you're back! Something's happened, there was a boom, someone tried to open a gate to Faerie to find you but couldn't—"

I stopped him with a raised palm and shook my head. "You need to pack," I told the crowd. "*Now*. Gather whatever you can carry, anything you can't bear to part with. The installations need to be evacuated."

Most of them jumped at my order, and I turned off the amplification and looked to the confused librarian. "Faerie's gone," I murmured. "We've got a few days of magic left at the most. Pack your things and start thinking about your exit strategy."

His face blanched. "What do you mean, *gone*?"

"It no longer exists. Can't find Conota, either. Pack," I said again, and he darted away, looking sick.

"Want a gate?" asked Bert.

"Don't waste the magic. We'll walk," I muttered, and struck off for the Council's tower.

I wasn't expecting to see Iris Johansson standing outside the tower's emergency exit door—the magus seldom left Arc 1 without official cause, especially on the weekend—but there she was, puffing at what smelled like a joint.

"If you've come for his head, he's hiding in his office," she volunteered. "Can you fix this, Toula?"

"No." From deep within my psyche, Young Toula pressed to ask Iris for a turn with the weed. Old Toula, killjoy that she was, knew I needed to be focused and quashed the notion. "What happened?"

"Fuck," she muttered, then took a deep drag. "He

called us all in to help. Said Francine and Eva needed extra muscle. I told him the plan was a bad one after you two interrupted us on Thursday," she added, nodding to Eadwig and Coileán, "but I was voted down. They sounded so damn confident, and he was talking it up, and after what happened to…well." Her eyes cut toward Arnold and Bert. "I figured I could do more to temper him if I was still on the Council, you know?"

"You're not at fault, Iris," said Arnold. "You were outnumbered—"

"Could have stabbed him in his sleep," she said, and looked at us as if she were expecting to see shock and horror. If she was disappointed to find none, she kept it to herself. "Anyway, we went up to the roof of the tower, and this big metal ball was waiting—"

Eadwig groaned.

"—and they started casting. Nothing I knew, but they claimed it was a modification of a diary spell, and I haven't gotten around to reading the extended edition, so…" She shook her head. "We were just building stacks, you know, nothing complicated, and the next thing I knew, this *light*—it was part of the spell, but it was glowing so brightly, I'm sure it was visible in the mundane spectrum—it shot out of Leander's wand. The tower began to shake. And after a couple of minutes, it just *snapped* off like a switch, and he started cheering. Tried to open a gate to Faerie, just to be sure, but nothing gave. Everyone was celebrating the success until Gunther noticed that the local magic levels were still low."

She paused for another drag, wincing as the smoke hit her lungs.

"So I ran down to the Archives to pull a pair of detectors—magic and dark magic, you know?"

"Amy's?" I asked as a pang struck my chest.

We'd lost her. Ros had choked out names when asked, and the only survivor of the old Virginia crew was Arnold. My nephew was gone. Badger was gone. Amy and Kip had stayed as well—though with the way magic was failing, Kip's transformation bind wouldn't have lasted long in the mortal realm. I didn't want to think about the life he'd have faced here, trying to survive in hiding without magic. Poppy and Rufus were gone. Vivi and Hal. Joey and Helen. Slim, my first crafter. Most of the Fringe had stayed behind, either unable to escape or unwilling to start over in the mortal realm. While the frightened refugees milled around Afallon in the dark, we'd set up what gear the Team had in the lodge's den and reached out, trying to find survivors. From the looks of it, Yolanda Ford was the lone remaining Fringe coordinator, and I'd had to break it to her that her parents hadn't evacuated.

My calls to Hope and Arik wouldn't connect.

Beth, who had a phone number for one of the Conotan immigrants in Kentucky, called to deliver the bad news. None of them could reach the other realm, either, and the gate nearby had sealed itself. I didn't know how Leander had managed it, and even Eadwig was baffled, but as far as we could tell, Conota had been severed at the very least.

"Yeah, Amy's," said Iris. "We checked three times. Both levels consistently falling. So Leander puffed himself up and demanded an explanation, and those two bitches started *laughing*. Said we'd left them bound and rotting for years, so now it was our turn to enjoy life without magic. And before anyone could grab them, they opened a gate and ran. We were too shocked to stop them. Don't know where they went. Guess it doesn't matter now," she said, lifting the joint to her lips. "Just tell me this: is Eva's kid safe?"

"She's been safe all along," I replied.

"Figured as much. Damn them all," she muttered. "You want help upstairs? I mean, it looks like you've got a decent posse already..."

I gripped her shoulder, and when she turned her eyes to me, I saw the fear in them in the security light's glow. "Go home," I murmured. "Pack as quickly as you can. Tell the others."

"But where can we go?"

"I don't know yet, but the installations have to come down. Once the wards fail…"

She nodded, then created a gate back to Montana and took her leave. When I was sure it was sealed behind her, I flung open the door at the base of the tower and started the long march up to the executive wing with my backup right behind me.

Several flights of stairs later, I stepped out onto the landing and glared down the corridor at the clusters of nervous magi and aides. A few turned my way in alarm, but I caught flickers of relief on many of the faces—even those of the magi who'd voted me out.

"Is he in there?" I asked, cocking my head toward my former office.

They nodded and parted, making a path for my entourage and me. I hated the hopeful looks I saw in passing, knowing I could do little to improve the situation.

I tried Leander's door, found it locked, and hammered twice on the wood. "Leander! Open up, you little shit!" I called. "You can't hide in there forever!"

Silence.

"*Leander!*" I bellowed. "If you run, I swear to God—"

"Allow me," Val offered, and pulverized the door with one well-placed bolt.

"Thanks," I muttered, and stormed into the room as the dust and splinters settled.

Leander hadn't run after all. I found him hiding beneath his desk, curled into a ball and rocking. He whimpered when he saw me, and I dragged him out by the arm, digging my fingernails into his flesh for good measure. I slammed him into the wall and held him there with my forearm at his throat, fighting the all-too-fae urge to turn him into a pile of ash. "*What have you done?*" I demanded through gritted teeth.

His eyes darted about, but if he'd hoped to find

support somewhere over my shoulder, he was sorely disappointed. "I…I…"

"Spit it out."

"They told me it would work!" he protested, his voice on the edge of a whine, the cocky young magus no longer. "Eva and Francine! They said I'd be a hero, the…the greatest grand magus ever—"

"And I warned you that they weren't to be trusted," Bert quipped behind me.

"If they had that sort of power," I said, pressing my arm into Leander's Adam's apple, "why would they use it to glorify *you*? Think about it, pretty boy."

"I…I freed them…"

"You were a tool. A stupid, vain, foolish *tool*," I said, and released my hold. As he rubbed his throat, I added, "You really thought they could deliver? When *that* guy's telling you it's not possible?" I said, pointing to Eadwig. "Were you that desperate to show them you're better than me?"

He looked so much like a scared child that I almost pitied him, but my anger swelled again and drowned that feeling. "Anything to say for yourself, boy?"

"They…uh…" He cleared his throat and tried again. "They sealed off Faerie. Can you—"

"They didn't seal it," Coileán interrupted. "They *destroyed* it."

Leander's jaw sagged, and his face drained of color. "What do you mean?"

"Did I stutter? It's gone. And quite a few people who never did a damn thing to you are dead, so I truly hope you're happy."

I squeezed Coileán's wrist before he could murder Leander on the spot. "You did it on the roof?"

Leander nodded frantically.

"I'm going up to look at the signature," I said as he cringed against the wall. "See if there's anything that can be done. But unless Ros is mistaken—and I really doubt that—you and your little friends have destroyed magic for all of us. Forever. And in a few days, when the last of it runs out, no one's going to give two shits that you ever called yourself a wizard."

He didn't see my punch coming, and he grunted and doubled over with the blow to his stomach. As he crumpled to the floor, I said, "Maria, keep an eye on him. I'm going upstairs. Eadwig, Bert, with me."

Stepping into the hall, I found the magi standing around, waiting for answers. "Roof," I barked, and they followed.

A chill hung in the air that night, and the passing clouds blotted out most of the stars. I glanced toward the lights of Glastonbury, then turned my attention to the giant sphere. Pressing my palm against it, I felt how inert it seemed, and Eadwig verified my suspicions when he touched it in turn. "Empty," he murmured. "They must have drained it."

With the Council watching at a distance, I stood in the center of the flat tower roof and whispered to bring my mind into focus. The spell didn't coalesce easily—it seldom did, even with ample ambient magic—but in a moment, I was surrounded by a web of glowing green lines marking the etheric traces of the spell that had destroyed Faerie. Runes appeared in midair, a shorthand revealing the spell's construction, and I frowned as I studied the mess before me.

"Do you want help?"

I turned and found Coileán behind me. "I'll feed it if you need me to," he offered.

"I'm not thirty-five anymore," I said with a strained smile, "but thanks, Gramps."

While I tried to make sense of the tracers, Bert and Eadwig joined me, moving around and through the lines of spellcraft to piece together what had happened. I didn't understand everything Eadwig muttered as he inspected the work, but I assumed from the tone of his voice that most was profane. I kept my thoughts to myself, but I knew why he was so perturbed. This wasn't like the hybrid construction that my parents had created, which could be broken with a key. This was designed to last.

After a few minutes' study, Eadwig wheeled on the Council. "I can't believe you *did* this. How many of you have read my full diary?"

About half the magi raised their hands.

"And what did I say in there about attacking the soul of the realm?"

"That if Faerie dies, magic dies," Ingaborg quietly offered as Gunther nodded beside her.

"Precisely. So why did you attack her?"

The magi looked everywhere but at him.

"She's alive right now only because she was pulled out of Faerie at the last moment," he continued as the magi shrank back. "I watched it fall apart before the gates closed. Ros says she's lost all of the power she had as the realm—she can't feel Faerie anymore. It's gone."

"Is there anything you can do?" asked Antonio, who, fresh from Brazil, had dressed far too lightly for the British autumn. "Any of you?" he asked, even looking to Coileán for help.

Gunther cleared his throat. "Please, Grand Magus. How do we fix this?"

"We can't," I said simply, and broke my spell. As the green glow winked out, I told them, "Pack what you can. The installations must be destroyed before the wards fail. This is like the '13 closure all over again, only Coileán and I can't save you this time."

The magus shook his head. "Surely there is another way—"

"The other way was not tossing Toula aside in favor of a stupid child," Eadwig snapped. "But it's too late for that now. You chose him, you did nothing when he cast out the magi who would have tried to stop him," he said, waving one hand at Arnold, Bert, and me, "you didn't speak up when Francine and Eva filled his ears with lies, and now you've destroyed magic. I can't do a damn thing to fix this, and neither can anyone else here. Your best option is to help us evacuate the installations and scourge them from the earth."

I heard a noise like a strangled sob coming from the rear of the pack, then saw a woman running for the wall at the roof's edge. Before anyone could stop her, she slipped into a gap in the crenellation, pulled her legs over the stone, and tossed herself over the side.

Running after her as screams rose in the courtyard below, I peered down through the darkness and saw a broken form in the grass.

"Kathleen," Gunther murmured beside me. "Mein Gott…"

Shouts behind me made me turn in time to see a few other magi dashing for the wall, perhaps distraught at the notion of starting over without the magic we'd always known. I gripped Gunther's arm, but he broke free and stepped toward the gap Kathleen had used. "I am sorry, Grand Magus," he said, then closed his eyes and pushed himself headfirst over the side.

"*Enough*! I yelled, and several magi stopped in their tracks. "Kill yourselves on your own time. Pull yourselves together now and do your duty. We have a long night ahead of us, *all* of us. Now get back downstairs," I ordered, and the Council, shaken as they were, meekly obeyed.

Time was of the essence. Every moment that we left the wards running was a moment of wasted magic, and we needed everything we could get if we were to make the evacuation a success.

I called in every favor I was owed, then begged for help. By midnight, Aiden, Yolanda, and half a dozen of the more tech-savvy Minor Arcanum wizards had set up a forgery shop in the dining hall. We didn't have access to much of the Fringe's information—anything saved in Faerie instead of on Yolanda's machines was lost—but she knew her way around a fake ID as well as the next Fringer, and the Minor Arcanum was willing to lend their resources on humanitarian grounds. Outclassed, I did my part to keep the caffeine flowing and coordinate the mob.

Most of the Arcanum needed papers—birth certificates, government identification, passports, school transcripts, documentation of a mundane past. Many had never held a job outside the Arcanum's walls and had minimal savings. We brought them in from all corners of the world, used any convenient translator, and set them up with the forgery team to start their new lives. Children were easy, but each adult needed an identity built largely from scratch, and some were able to provide their necessary information only through tears.

"What am I to do?" I heard a retired Arc 3 guard ask Aiden. "I'm sixty-five, I've never lived out there…"

"You're not going to be destitute," Aiden assured him. "And I'm sixty-four. We're in the same boat."

"You—"

"I was in Russell Mulligan's year. Got to love those fae genes," he added, and winked. "Now, do you have a preferred bank?"

Somehow—and I doubted I'd have understood the mix of magic and computer manipulation that made it all possible, had they bothered to explain it to me—the forgers established accounts in a hundred different banks worldwide, giving each family about a million dollars with which to start over. That would at least buy them a place to live and put food on the table while they figured out how to make their way in the mundane world. A few of the Council aides set up shop several tables down from the forgers, and as each family received its necessary papers, they sent them and their few belongings to the city of their choice, dropping them near a hotel and wishing them luck.

Some asked to take their furniture, but there was no time to dawdle—the installations had to be destroyed as quickly as they could be emptied. If it couldn't be carried, it remained.

Arc 3 was the first to go, wiped off its mountain home as if it had never existed. Next came Arc 5, turned into a parking lot. Arc 4 was reduced to rubble, another Soviet-era complex fallen victim to the wear of time. Arc 7 was easy, the subterranean portion reduced to dirt, the topside layers obliterated, and the insulating geodesic dome vaporized. The cattle were set loose to fend for themselves. Arc 6, tucked deep in the Amazon, was also easy to destroy, and I doubted that anyone would notice the difference.

Which left Arc 1, the place I'd called home for so many miserable years.

As night fell in Montana on Sunday, I stood in the snow with my brother inside the trailer park that disguised the entrance to the old missile silo. "Are you ready?" he asked, his hand on my back.

"Yeah."

Working together, we transformed the silo into so much dirt and rock, then removed all trace of the trapdoor within the main trailer. I broke the illusion of the government installation down the road, a Mulligan-era mirage used to explain the influx of people in that rural town. People would panic—large military complexes don't tend to disappear overnight—but there was nothing I could do to fix that. I certainly wasn't going to waste magic erecting an empty building.

"Good riddance," I muttered to the quiet night, and returned to Glastonbury.

In the wee hours of Monday morning, Coileán found me as I took a break to pack my apartment. I'd been kicking myself ever since I dragged my bags from beneath the bed, as I'd left my most valuable possessions in Faerie for safekeeping. Most of my books and many of my favorite clothes were lost now, though I reminded myself that the books were about to be useless. What need did I have for magical tomes in a world devoid of magic?

As I struggled to condense my belongings into two overnight bags, he brought me a cup of strong coffee and coaxed me into the den. "You need this, Glinda," he told me, directing me toward my couch. "I'll wrestle with the bags."

"The zippers are steel," I warned him. "I'll deal with them in a minute. Join me."

He poured himself a cup and sat beside me, and I noted the weariness in his expression. "Do you want a nap?" I asked. "Take the bed—I'll be out of there in a few minutes."

"I'm fine." He blew the steam from his coffee and sipped, then screwed his eyes closed as the hot liquid went down. "Relatively speaking, I mean. I've got a refugee problem."

"How so?"

"There's a bunch of them on Afallon—some from my court, some from Val's, a few from Irem's, the Fringers. Ros directed them all there, and that was wise, but—"

"They can't stay," I finished, thinking of the powerful wards around the island. Within days, the UK would discover a rock it had overlooked for centuries. "What do you want to do about it? And Artur—has she given any thought to the island? It's hers, after all."

"She's planning to sink it, barring a miracle in the next few hours," he replied. "Understands the situation. It was always a poor substitute for her Afallon, I guess."

"And everyone out there? What do you see *us* doing, anyway? Buying a place in the suburbs with a picket fence?"

He snorted and almost managed a smile. "If that's what you want."

"Tempting, but I really can't see you pushing a lawnmower."

"I've mowed," he protested.

"Within the last century?"

Coileán made a face as he tallied the decades. "No…but listen, the Stowes have an idea."

"Oh?"

"Alaska."

"*Alaska?*" I echoed, laughing. "What on earth would—"

"They lived there for years, and if we find a place sufficiently out of the way, then we could build quickly and keep everyone together for safety. What about the old Conclave site? You remember how remote that location is."

"Yeah, and it's also freaking Alaska. Crazy winters, bears, weird survivalists…I mean, can you imagine Val dealing with blizzards?"

"He's tough," said Coileán.

"He grew up on the *Med*. One real winter, and he'll be out."

"Well, he's in for the moment," Coileán countered, "and Robbie's been drawing up plans. It wouldn't be anything massive, but we could throw together some houses in a compound."

"And live up there, in isolation, without magic?" I pressed. "What happens when the food runs low?"

"We've already looked at the maps and the site. Bert took us—"

"Oh, Bert's coming along?" I asked incredulously.

"No, he's staying in Glastonbury with his parents, but he remembers the way to the Conclave site. We've cleared it. There's an old hunting trail, fairly rutted but passable. The nearest house is a big cabin about two miles away, but it looks uninhabited. We could build there, stay together, and find a way to make it work."

I sipped my coffee and considered his proposal.

"You've put thought into this. How far from actual civilization are we talking?"

"Nearest real city is Fairbanks, and that's about seven hours, we're estimating...once you hit the paved road. But if we bought some decent trucks and vans, stocked up on supplies, made a long weekend of a grocery run once a month—"

"During the summer."

"Canned and dry goods. And if Aiden works it out to give us a million apiece, we could invest it and live off the interest. Ned and James Stowe have backgrounds in finance, did you know that?"

"When did either of them last work in the industry?"

He sucked his teeth. "East India Company era, maybe?"

"Well," I said with a sigh, "it's not like you have to be a fiscal genius to trade stocks online. I suppose we could make that work, but..."

"You hate the idea."

"I'm not in love with it, no," I replied, "but I don't have a better one."

Coileán stared into his mug. "Invent a time machine, go back a few weeks, and kill Leander in his sleep?"

"Forget Leander—I should have executed Eva and Francine when I had the chance. Nipped this in the bud." I glanced at Coileán, but I saw no reproach there. "I'm sorry. I thought I was doing the right thing by being a little merciful, and then going along with it when the Council voted me out..."

"You did, darling," he replied, taking my hand. "You were decent, and you tried."

"I should have tried harder."

"Toula, look at me." When I raised my eyes to his, he murmured, "It's not your job to save the world every time there's a crisis. You've done your best."

My throat tightened. "And now it's all fallen apart..."

"Hey. *Hey*," he said, putting his cup aside. He pried

mine from my hands, then wrapped me in a tight hug. "Do you know what Eadwig said?" he asked, rubbing my back.

"About what?"

"You. He said you were a damn fine grand magus, and he was appalled that they voted you out. Now, if Simon fucking Magus thinks you did well, then what more do you have to prove to the Arcanum? Grand Magus Pavli held this shitshow together for twenty-five years. They didn't deserve you, Toula. They never have."

As he loosened his hold and I sat back, Coileán said, "It has been an honor to know you, and I mean that from the bottom of my heart. If you want to settle somewhere warm and forget everything before this moment, and if you'll have me along, I'll go with you."

I laced my fingers through his and squeezed. "Of course I'll have you. And we should stick together. Us, Val, Aiden…the whole freaking court, I don't care. Let's see about Alaska."

He kissed me deeply, and as a few burning tears escaped my eyes, he murmured, "You're going to want a coat, Glinda. A real one."

Daylight had come to Glastonbury by the time the Alaskan excursion set off, but our destination was still quite dark…and absolutely frigid. I hugged myself and stamped my boots in the snow as I adjusted, then cut my eyes to my brother, who was stoically staring at the wilderness. The boys had done a nice job of clearing the site, leaving us with a bare patch of frozen ground the size of a small subdivision.

"Right," said Robbie Stowe, unrolling his plans atop a collapsible wooden table. He weighted the corners with camping lanterns and beckoned everyone closer. "I'll lay out the grid and make markings. Try not to go wild, here—low-key is our best bet. We don't want mansions in the middle of nothing. And whatever you do, for the love of all that's holy, *insulate*."

"Trust us on this," muttered his father, Martin. "Part of our house failed during the '13 closure—the bits we were holding together with magic. Even in March, we needed quality insulation."

His wife, Rohese, nodded vehemently beside him. Though generally a warm, maternal sort of person, she was understandably subdued, having just lost two children in Faerie. Her orphaned grandson, unable to sufficiently enchant to be of use, was back in Glastonbury with the rest of the Team, making final preparations for departure.

"Take the houses one at a time," Robbie continued. "*Don't rush*. Structural stability is key. You can worry about paint colors later—let's get foundations down. If you have questions, ask me. Lord Aiden, do you need assistance?"

Aiden, who carried his own plans and a laptop, shook his head. "Not at the moment, thanks. And really, it's just Aiden, okay?"

"Give me time," said Robbie, and nodded as Aiden went on his way. "Okay, let me lay this out. Light?"

I created a few orbs and flung them high into the air to show Robbie what he was doing. My soul ached as I felt how much lower the magic levels seemed already, and I turned to the others. "The name of the game is precision, folks. Try to be economical with your enchantment. This is going to be hard enough without draining the local supply."

That was an understatement. By midmorning Alaska time, we'd thrown together a tiny community behind a protective wooden fence, and I was exhausted from the effort. The houses were utilitarian, two-story structures with basements for storage, fireplaces, and double-paned windows. We would add touches like appliances and furniture once everyone moved in. Meanwhile, Aiden had dug wells, come up with a filtration and sewage system that drained waste into a deep cavern he'd hollowed out in the nearby mountain, and built a fantastic solar array outside the wall. He and Robbie were busily adding wiring and plumbing to the houses as the rest of us took a break.

It was a start, I mused. The forgers had set up our bank accounts and fake documents, and I planned to buy new phones on our first trip into Fairbanks, as the ones Coileán had created from the ether would soon cease to function. We'd need more to get us through the winter—which, judging by the snowy terrain, was already upon us—but this place on the edge of the wild might just be a home.

We were refugees now. All we had was each other.

A few hours later—barely after lunch in Alaska, but late at night in Glastonbury—I oversaw the final exodus from Arc 2.

Artur had sunk Afallon while we were away that day, and so the faeries planning to move to the frozen north had congregated in the dining room to wait. The Fringers who'd escaped Faerie had gone their own way—most had opted to either strike out for London or join a modest Minor Arcanum compound in California—but that still left us with a mixed bag. A few Arcanum members had opted to join us. Arnold had no place better to go, and Bee and Daisy had decided to give it a try, to my relief. Once magic truly failed, we'd need a doctor on hand. Another group of wizards was trekking north from Montana in the Arcanum's RV, hurrying before the spells that added extra room to the vehicle failed.

We'd offered a place for anyone on the Team who wanted it, but only some had taken us up. Lakshmi's family was set up in London—with so much of her extended family still in India, I understood why she wanted to be near a decent airport—and Daphne, too, had opted to remain in England near her parents and her brother's family. Bob and Sylvester, who were barely younger than me but felt their age, had decided to retire to the south of France. With many thanks and a few tears, Quinn and her grandfather had returned to Chicago, but that was no surprise. John was old and frail, a bad combination for the wilderness, and Quinn, who'd lost less than a year and a half on her Arcanum adventure, had real credentials and the skills to make her way in the mundane world.

But the rest of the Team—Ted, the Copeland family, Mal, Artur, Marcus and Kitty, Frank and Aurie, Beth, and Eadwig—were coming along. Frank was moving into a house with his father and daughter, while Beth would be living with her sister, Marcus, and Artur for at least another year or two. As for Eadwig, Robbie had put him in the house next door, leaving him within hailing distance of his former roommates.

Ros and Sam, naturally, were joining us. Having seen little of them since Saturday, I was struck by how haunted Ros seemed as she slouched at a table in the dining hall—how utterly *lost*. She spoke little, and though her grandmother's grandmother, Liza, kept bringing her food and urging her to eat something, she picked at whatever was placed before her. Sam stayed close, comforting her as best he could, but the one time I saw her break down at the castle was in an anteroom, clinging to Frank and sobbing her heart out.

The person I was sorriest to lose was Bert, who would remain in Glastonbury to look after his parents. It made sense—they were getting older, they had room for him, and he was their only child—but I'd grown fond of him over our time together, and I'd miss his company. He promised to stay in touch, but I knew that would be no substitute for the meetings I'd held not so long ago with him and Arnold in my office.

Had that only been *July*? The summer seemed like half a lifetime ago.

Robbie had built extra houses within our walls in case additional refugees turned up. Most of the faeries in our company were of the half-fae variety. The full-blooded ones had scattered when the realm collapsed, running off before we could equip them with money or credentials. Coileán and Val couldn't locate them now, nor had anyone seen any trace of Irem. Ros told us she'd escaped Faerie, but where she'd landed was a mystery.

If I ever had the chance, I decided, I'd kill her. I'd learned from my mistakes.

But despite my basest instincts, I'd chosen not to kill Leander, whose primary crimes were stupidity and arrogance. Instead, I'd had Aiden set him up with about fifty grand and returned him to the States. He was a twenty-nine-year-old wizard with no mundane skills, I reasoned—letting him figure out a path forward in the world he'd wrought would be a sort of justice.

Coileán ushered our group through a gate as I stayed back and took a last look at the castle. The place was eerie in its abandonment, darker than I'd ever seen it, and far too quiet. I concentrated, working against the dwindling magic, and sealed every door and window to make the towers airtight and waterproof. With that accomplished, I stepped out the front gate, closed it behind me, and readied myself for what I assumed would be the last great construction of my life.

As Coileán stood by in silent support, I focused on the castle, shrinking it to the size of a mansion, a backyard fort, a dollhouse, and then a miniature model able to fit in my palm. I plucked it from the ground, set it atop a wooden base I pulled from the ether, then wrapped it in the dome of a glittery snow globe. Spells on living beings would soon fail, but this was a static construction, a permanent reduction in size, and with any luck, Arc 2 would survive. It wasn't the castle I was worried about, but rather the Archives. Though its contents were useless to us now, I couldn't bear to erase our history. In case of a miracle, that repository would be ready and waiting.

Heartsick, I pulled trees from the nearby woods and planted them where the castle had been, doing what little I could to disguise the area. Adding a few bulldozer tracks to give the neighbors something to complain about, I broke the camouflage ward and revealed the site to the neighboring city for the first time in an age.

Let the mundanes make of it what they would, I decided, and spared a glance at the lights of Glastonbury before I took Coileán's hand and departed for our new life.

OCTOBER 12: BETH STANHOPE

After nearly three full days in our new Alaskan home, I still hadn't adjusted to the time difference. The daylight situation made matters worse—as far north as we were, day length was rapidly on the decline, and the cloud-covered sky provided an unsatisfactory break from the darkness. Snow had been falling off and on since we'd arrived, though the forecast promised a respite within the next week.

I could deal with precipitation. I'd lived in England, after all, where rain was to be expected. But as the snow fell outside my bedroom window, part of me began to wonder if it would eventually swallow our house, entombing us alive beneath the ice.

My thoughts went in odd directions in those last days of magic. I barely cast, trying to save the dwindling supply for someone who really needed it, but I couldn't help but try a tiny spell every morning, just to see how much we had left.

Not nearly enough. The colorful swirls of magic that I'd long taken for granted were dimming and disappearing.

Through my closed door, I could hear Kitty and Marcus in the kitchen downstairs. They'd been at work all afternoon on dinner, making a hearty vegetable soup and homemade bread. The two of them had driven a van in the Fairbanks convoy the day before, and they'd returned with as many cans and freezer packs as they could carry, as well as a pair of rifles and ammunition. I'd never known either of them to shoot, but the Stowes said that we all needed to learn. We could hunt for meat to keep down costs—and beyond that, no one wanted to face a hungry bear unarmed.

Hunting took a backseat to cooking, however, as many of the compound's new residents could barely boil water. Faeries who'd been able to pull food from the ether all of their lives were suddenly faced with the prospect of feeding themselves by non-magical means, and many of the wizards in town, long accustomed to eating in installation dining halls, were likewise unprepared. The kings' cooks had seen the need and taken pity on their neighbors, and a schedule of mealtimes had rapidly been circulated. That night's dinner came courtesy of Luce Stowe and Astrid, though Frank's dad was scheduled to pitch in for breakfast. Luce made it known that he would start teaching beginner's classes within a week, but the development of greater interest to some of the residents was that *Adam* Stowe had begun distillation in a shed erected outside the compound's wall.

As for me…well, I was alive. I had a roof and food and a folder of forged documents, and Aiden had given me a nice chunk of cash to squirrel away in a savings account, but my life as I knew it was over.

The Away Team's mission had come to an end. There would be no job for me. No graduation from Arc 2's school. No chance, however slight, of rising through the bureaucratic ranks. Within a few days, my wand would be less useful than a pencil.

I would never see my dad again—not in my lifetime, at least. Never chat with Hope and Arik. Never return to Faerie.

Never amount to anything.

A knock on the door shook me from my thoughts, and I looked away from the window as Artur poked her head into the room. "You don't want a lamp?" she asked.

I pointed to the streetlight outside and shrugged. "It's okay. What's up?"

She closed the door behind her and sat beside me on my new bed. "You're brooding."

"I'm not—"

"I know you, little sister," she murmured. "And no one here is thrilled tonight, but...I worry. Kitty worries, too. I don't like the thought of you sitting up here alone in the dark."

When I said nothing, she wrapped an arm around my shoulders, and I leaned against her. "Starting over is a miserable experience," she said. "This place will be far less pleasant than Glastonbury, I fear. But you have a family that loves you. A family that will protect you as far as we can, assuming you don't run into any more collapsing realms."

I held my silence for a moment longer, then quietly said, "Maybe I shouldn't have pulled Ros out. If I hadn't done anything, maybe she would have been able to save Faerie."

"Is that what you think?" asked Artur. "That this is somehow your fault?"

"Well...I mean..."

"Because that's absolutely *not* what Ros has been saying," she continued, tightening her grip on me. "She couldn't have stopped Faerie's destruction. You saved her life, Beth. You're not the villain in this." She paused, then asked, "Why did you do it?"

"She was hurting, and I didn't want her to die," I explained, staring out at the snow. "Tried to do something brave. Something useful, for once."

Artur's head tilted toward mine until they were touching. "I am prouder of you than you know, little sister," she whispered, then gave me a last squeeze and released me. Standing, she unkinked her back and said, "Why don't you check on the boy? He's probably forgot to eat again. Tell him there's stew."

As she headed for the door, she switched on my dresser lamp and flashed a small, lopsided smile. "And take a coat. Kitty's orders."

Sufficiently bundled, I tromped through the snow to the neighboring house, where Ed lived with his ghosts.

Personally, I thought it was a terrible idea to give him an empty house to himself. When his nightmares woke him, he'd be alone in there, and I feared what he might do if left unattended for too long. Plus, I knew darn well that Ed couldn't cook—he could reliably make coffee and tea and microwave leftovers, but that was all—and though we'd taught him how to use a washing machine and disinfect the bathroom, I wondered how often he'd remember to do his chores if not prodded. Ed had a one-track mind, difficult to derail.

And if that track headed into a tunnel...well, there was a reason that Robbie had slipped us a spare key to Ed's house.

I kicked a little drift out of the way of the front door and rang the bell. When no one came to investigate, I turned to knocking, with identical results. I saw no lights on in the house, and I didn't want to just barge in if he was out, but intuition told me to let myself inside.

"Ed?" I called to the dark foyer as I stamped the snow off my boots. "It's Beth! Are you here?"

The fire in the den had burned down to ash, but the central heat continued to blow. I stood still and listened until finally, over the white noise of the air system, I made out a faint thudding coming from the back of the house.

Following the sound, I passed through the untouched kitchen and down a short hallway. Many of the compound's houses had been built on identical floorplans, and from what I could tell, Ed's was similar to ours. The room at the end of the hall was presumably the master suite—Kitty and Marcus's bedroom in our house, which left a pair of slightly smaller rooms upstairs for Artur and me. Manners told me to knock, though intuition insisted that the flickering light I saw in the crack beneath the door portended nothing good.

"Ed?" I called through the door. "It's me. Are you in there?"

When I heard another thud, I said to hell with manners and tried the knob.

The room behind the door was indeed the master suite, but whereas my sister had set up their room with a big bed, nice furniture, and even a pair of potted trees, Ed's held a wooden desk and a chair. A pair of candles on the desk provided the only light in the space, but their glow was sufficient to show me the rest of the decoration. The walls were nearly covered with scribbled-over paper, the handwriting on which seemed to deteriorate as the pages progressed. I could make out the shapes of diagrams, a few red lines for emphasis, and wads of rejected writing crumpled on the floor.

And there sat the author, banging his head against the desk like he was trying to crack his skull open.

"*Ed!*" I cried, and hurriedly jerked his chair away from the impact zone.

The movement seemed to rouse him, and he blinked up at me, his eyes dazed and his forehead swelling. A trickle of blood slid from a cut down one side of his nose. "Beth?" he mumbled.

I shook him by the shoulders until his focus improved. "Snap out of it. Come on, Ed, you've got to come back…"

Finally, his eyes began to track me, and I saw something like awareness return. "What the hell?" I asked, cupping his face in my hands. "What are you doing?"

"I…I can't find an answer," he croaked, and I wondered how long it had been since he'd stopped for a drink. "I'm trying, but…but it won't come, and I…"

"It's okay, Ed," I murmured, and bent to hug him. "It's okay."

"I'm trying," he mumbled into my shoulder.

"I know."

"Simon has ideas, but nothing works, and magic is fading, it's *dying*, and I can't fix it, I can't do anything…"

"No one can," I soothed, pulling him from his chair. His arms tightened around me, and I stood in the near-darkness with him as he shook.

After a few long minutes, when the worst of his trembling had subsided, I said, "We've got dinner next door. Let's get you cleaned up, huh?"

"No, thank you, I can't," he replied, pulling away from me. "My work…"

"*Eadwig*. That wasn't a request."

He resisted only a moment longer before he allowed me to blow out the candles and coax him into the kitchen. I turned on the sink light, and as I dabbed at the blood on his face with a wet rag, he said, "Beth?"

"Mm?" I replied, working carefully around the fresh swelling.

"Talk to me, please. It's all too loud."

"You're safe," I told him, wiping at the tear tracks on his cheeks. "It's going to be okay. Not like it was, but…we'll survive," I said with more confidence than I felt. "You and me, and everyone else up here. We're going to get through this."

"Don't leave me," he whispered. "Everyone else I've loved has gone away. Please don't leave me."

I dried his face and hugged him again, holding on as I felt him struggle not to cry. "You're camping with us tonight," I told him. "And I'm not going anywhere."

OCTOBER 17: COILEÁN

Adjustment would take time, or so Rohese and Martin had warned us. For every endless summer day came an endless winter night. By late October, the sun wouldn't rise until after nine, leaving me with hours to sit alone by the kitchen window with a cup of coffee and watch the falling snow twinkle in the streetlights' glow.

As much as I itched to lace the drink with something stronger, I refrained. I could no longer produce whisky from thin air, Adam's first batch was years away from palatability, and the bottles we found in Fairbanks were expensive, just like everything else imported to the top of the world. Whisky was for those nights when the dreams were too much to bear. This, technically, was morning, and Toula shouldn't find me drunk before breakfast. She hadn't needed to remind me that I couldn't magically sober up anymore.

I couldn't do anything.

Strange didn't begin to describe how odd it was to find myself in a perfectly mundane house once again. My spacious office with its well-loved bar, my library full of treasures, my eternally blooming rose garden, my *palace*—gone. In a blink, I'd been reduced to a king of nothing, stripped of the strength that had given me power in the realm…and now, stripped of magic altogether.

It wasn't a bad little house, as such went. I'd certainly inhabited far worse, and the fact that Aiden and Robbie had cobbled together plumbing pushed this place quite a bit closer to the top of my list. The solar panels were functioning nicely, and we had ample fuel for the backup generators. The refrigerator hummed, the stovetop clock glowed blue in the shadows, the simple coffeemaker did its lone task reasonably well. And now, with the rush of escape and resettlement slowing, with the memorial for the dead behind us, I had time to sit back and think of the long years ahead, century upon century deprived of the magic that had theretofore made my existence so much simpler.

A golden flash outside the window caught my eye, and I glanced over in time to see Kuni, our one-time piq ambassador, zip past the streetlight. He'd taken to long predawn flights, pushing himself through laps around the compound, no matter how inclement the weather. I suspected his exercise was a product of survivor's guilt rather than restlessness, and Aiden concurred. Ros remembered some of the other piq evacuating, but she couldn't say how many or where they had gone, and none had followed us north. Aid had set up a room for Kuni in his house, as the piq had nowhere in particular to go, and Aiden appreciated his company. I knew my brother was quietly hurting—he'd lost his sister all over again, and now Joey, too—but he'd thrown himself into the work of setting up the compound, and if he wished to keep his thoughts to himself, I had no right to pry.

Nor could I. Without magic, the only ones of us with any sort of telepathic ability were Frank and Aurie. That was a gift inborn for them, just as shifting was for young Mal. Ros's meddling seemed to have worked, too, as Frank had managed a full shift only the day before. I was pleased to see that, as there was a certain comfort in having a dragon on standby, even if he could no longer breathe fire. *That* required dark magic, which had been declining as well.

We'd used every drop of magic that we could wring from the ether, but I'd noticed how faint the familiar scent of burned citronella had become. Aurie's fake arm had failed three days before, and from that point, nearly any enchantment came from Toula, Maria, or Kitty, who used wizardly precision to conserve our most precious resource. Even still, we knew it was only a matter of time before our supply was exhausted. When the ambient magic ran dry, the only source left in existence would be the crystallized magic in Artur's sword, a last-ditch backup in case of emergency.

"Hey, you," said Toula, interrupting my solitary moping. "Did you make enough for me?"

I started to rise. "Sit down, I'll—"

"I've got it," she insisted, waving me back into my chair, then shuffled into the kitchen to doctor her mug. "Been outside yet?"

"Snowing again."

"As predicted. We should really buy a weather radio the next time we're in town—couldn't hurt to have one around." She poured her breakfast—from experience, I knew she'd take little else at six in the morning—and joined me at the table. "Couldn't sleep?" she asked.

I shook my head. "Do you feel it?"

"Yeah."

Putting my mug aside, I held out my palm and waited for the blue fireball to appear, the flames that had so readily come at my command. The attempt was futile, and we both knew it. Anyone attuned to magical currents would have felt that the well had finally run dry.

"It's gone," I said, and reached for my coffee again. "We've lost everything."

"Not *everything*."

I cocked an eyebrow. "If you try to take Artur's sword, she'll protest."

"I'm not talking about magic," said Toula.

Studying her face in the streetlight's glow, I noticed that she seemed more at peace than she'd been since the evacuation—not resigned any longer, but truly...content? Was that it? Unable to slip into her thoughts, I couldn't be sure, but her smile had lost its shadow of desperation.

"We're alive," she said, taking my free hand. "We have a home and food and warmth, and we'll figure this out, now that we have time to stop and breathe. And...you know, we have each other."

I turned my hand in hers until our fingers interlocked.

"No more Arcanum," she continued. "No more courts to worry about. No one giving us a million reasons why we can't be together."

"I have nothing to offer you," I murmured. "Not even a bookstore."

"You're enough," she said simply. "Am I enough for you?"

I leaned closer to kiss her. "Moon and stars, woman, you know you are."

"Good." She kissed me in turn, then sat back and sipped her coffee. "The worst is over, Coileán, and we made it out together. You and I will find a way."

ACKNOWLEDGEMENTS

Here we are again, dear reader, after fourteen books together, and I suspect that you may be a *little* upset with me right now. Hold on...

Many thanks to the Novel Chicks, who haven't kicked me out yet. To Adam Domby, who found time to give me his much-appreciated feedback even with his own work, I'm sincerely grateful.

And yes, here's to you, Mom and Dad.

ABOUT THE AUTHOR

When not writing fiction, Ash Fitzsimmons is an appellate attorney and an unrepentant car singer.

Find her online:
www.ashfitzsimmons.com

www.ingramcontent.com/pod-product-compliance
Lightning Source LLC
Chambersburg PA
CBHW020925020726
47495CB00002B/349